Adventures in

SYMPHONIC MUSIC

Adventures in
SYMPHONIC
MUSIC

by
EDWARD DOWNES

DECORATIONS BY JOHN O'HARA COSGRAVE II

KENNIKAT PRESS
Port Washington, N. Y./London

ADVENTURES IN SYMPHONIC MUSIC

Manufactured by Taylor Publishing Company   Dallas, Texas

ESSAY AND GENERAL LITERATURE INDEX REPRINT SERIES

To
My Mother and Father

Contents

	Preface	ix
I	Music and the Dance	1
II	The Symphony Is Born	35
III	Music and Politics	55
IV	Concertos and Virtuosos	75
V	Music and Legend	103
VI	Nature in Music	125
VII	The Suffering Artist	147
VIII	Humor in Music	183
IX	Composers in Love	203
X	Symbolism in Music	227
XI	The Other Romanticism	253
XII	The New World	287
	Index	307

Preface

The best lesson I ever had in music appreciation was given me by Adolf Hitler. We could not yet hear the armies of liberation thundering across the world. Hitler thought himself triumphant, and in the blackness of Europe there seemed no common-sense, practical reason to doubt his triumph. Little Austria had been crushed. Now it was being digested, and I had come to Salzburg for an American newspaper to report on what remained of the once-famous Salzburg Festival.

Some of my anti-Nazi friends were dead, some had fled, others were cautious and desperate. The great artists, Toscanini, Bruno Walter, Lotte Lehmann, Max Reinhardt, were gone. The great performances were past. Amid all the show of festivity there was but one strangely inspired production: a tragedy, "Egmont," by Goethe, with the music which Beethoven wrote for it. Now "Egmont" was an apparently innocent last-minute substitute for Reinhardt's banned production of "Faust." But there are a thousand ways of telling an unwelcome conqueror what you think of him, and "Egmont" was one. For it describes the subjugation of the Netherlands by the Spanish Duke of Alva; it shows their agony, their sullen defiance, and it ends with a call to revolt.

Beethoven's overture begins with a mighty lamentation for freedom lost. There are lyric passages which may portray Egmont's beloved, Clärchen. There are agitated murmurings, the voice of an angry, rebellious people and at the last, tumultuous, joyous affirmation. But why joy, since "Egmont" is a tragedy? It is not until the end of the drama, when the orchestra sweeps again into that same exultant finale, that its meaning is made clear.

The play shows at first the easygoing, liberty-loving Netherlanders, a people like the Austrians themselves; then the terror that Alva brings with his army of occupation. Netherland liberties are abolished. Criticism of the new tyranny is made punishable by death. And Egmont, the champion of Netherland freedom, is thrown into prison.

As the plot approached its tragic climax, the Salzburg audience became quiet and tense. Each bitter word spoken from the stage accused not only Spanish tyrants, it lashed out at those beyond the footlights, at brown and black uniforms and traitors sitting there. The tyranny of the Duke of Alva had become the tyranny of Hitler. The Netherlands were Austria. The tension grew.

Egmont has been sentenced to death. The night before his execution, Clärchen appears to him in a dream as the Goddess of Freedom. She shows him that his death is the spark that will fire the Netherlands to regain their lost liberty. She proclaims him victor and crowns him with a wreath of laurel. Then a drum roll disperses the dream and daylight shows through the prison bars. Egmont feels for the laurel.

"The wreath has vanished. Fair vision, the light of day has taken you. Yes, they were here, united, the two sweetest joys of my heart. Divine Freedom borrowed the form of my love. . . . She came to me with bloodstained feet, the swaying folds of her garment stained with blood. It was my blood and the blood of many a noble man. No, it was not shed in vain. Stride forth, brave people! The Goddess of Victory leads you on. And like the sea bursting through your dikes, so must you burst and overwhelm

the ramparts of tyranny, and sweep it from the land it has
usurped. [Drums approach . . . the background is filled
with Alva's soldiers.] Yes, bring them together! Close your
ranks, I fear you not. . . . My enemies encompass me on
every side. Swords flash—friends, take heart! Behind you
are your parents, wives, children! . . . Guard your sacred heritage! And to save all you hold most dear, fall
joyfully, as I give you the example now!"

As Egmont, surrounded by soldiers, marches off to
his death, a "symphony of victory" sweeps up from the
orchestra to end the drama with the triumphant fanfares
which mark the finale of Beethoven's overture.

For a moment, the Salzburg audience seemed
stunned. Then there was polite, perfunctory applause.
Those who felt like cheering did not dare, and those who
dared were not in a mood to cheer. But none, I think, who
heard that performance will ever listen to Beethoven's
"Egmont" music with the same quiet pulse as before. For
the players in that drama and in that music were my
friends and your friends, and, in the last analysis, it was
we ourselves who walked the stage. That is what we mean
when we speak of a universal art.

All music tells a story. Sometimes the composer
chooses a theme we know like "Romeo and Juliet" or "Egmont," or the siege of Leningrad. Or he explains his plot
as Berlioz did for his Fantastic Symphony. Then we call
it program music.

Often the composer has a more or less connected
story in mind, but leaves our imagination free to fill in the
details. The black pessimism of the Pathetic Symphony
conceals a story Tchaikovsky would not reveal. Richard
Strauss refused to give a program to his tone poem, "Till
Eulenspiegel." For were he to put into words the thoughts
it suggested to him, "They would seldom suffice," he

wrote, "and might give rise to offense. Let me leave it therefore to my hearers to crack the hard nut the rogue has prepared for them."

And sometimes music tells a story which cannot be put into words, in which case it is often called pure or absolute music. But such words are misleading. They imply that music is an abstract play of tonal design, separate from life, insulated from the rest of the world. There is no such thing as pure music; it is always a crystallization of human emotions. And the fact that its story can be told only in music, does not mean it has none.

In the following pages, a large part of the standard symphonic repertory and certain less frequently heard works have been grouped into short programs of roughly related subjects. For the convenience of music lovers and students who have record collections, the discussions are limited to compositions available on discs; and with a few exceptions, each program lasts under one hour. Much of this material was originally delivered in the form of intermission commentaries for the Symphonic Hour of Station W67NY, key frequency modulation station of the Columbia Broadcasting System in New York City. Certain pages appeared in the music section of the Boston *Transcript*; others are quite new.

Obviously these works might have been discussed from many points of view. The headings under which they appear in this volume are intended simply as suggestions which are far from giving the one and only key to the music. For any great work of art tells a dozen stories. And each listener, if he is lucky, will continue to find new meanings in his favorite masterpieces as often as he can hear them. Not only is the language of music universal; its subject is as universal as human experience. All music tells a story. The story is about you. *De te fabula narratur.*

I. *Music and the Dance*

FROM THE LATEST SWING on the Hit Parade back to the primitive pounding of drums or rattles to which our earliest ancestors cavorted, probably on some forgotten plateau of Central Asia, our music is haunted by the rhythm of dancing feet. There are primitive tribes of Africa who, though they don't have much of anything we would think of as melody, practice a marvelously complicated and exciting art of dance music on drums. And like the giant in the Greek fable who renewed his strength by touching the earth, the greatest composers return again and again to draw strength from the elemental impulse of the dance, from its forms, its rhythms and its inexhaustible driving power. Beethoven, Bach, Brahms, Mozart, Sibelius, Tchaikovsky—all have paid homage to the newest and oldest music in the world.

1

It would take a doctor, an anthropologist or a psychiatrist to tell us why we all respond to rhythm. Perhaps it all goes back to so simple, biological a thing as the rhythmic beating of our hearts. Anyhow, dance music is one form of the art which almost every human being who has ever existed has known and enjoyed; for dancing is as old as the human race, and possibly a good deal older. And in spite of all the refined techniques and imagination of modern music, both the newest Broadway boogie-woogie and such a sophisticated symphonic piece as Stravinsky's "Sacre du Printemps" are nearer to the jungle drums than most of us believe.

Mozart: Minuet from Symphony in E flat major (K. 543)
Wagner: Dance of the Apprentices from "Die Meistersinger"
Johann Strauss: Waltz, "Wiener Blut"
Tchaikovsky: Third movement from Fifth Symphony
Richard Strauss: Dance of the Seven Veils from "Salome"
Ravel: "La Valse"
Stravinsky: Sacrificial Dance from "Le Sacre du Printemps"

From the courtly grace of our great-great-great-grandmothers and their gallant, periwigged beaux, there came a dance which echoes still through the masterpieces of Mozart, Haydn and Beethoven. For the minuet was not only the favorite dance of the glittering court of Versailles and of lesser society through the eighteenth century; it was a favorite means of expression to generations of great composers. And while your great-great-great-grandmother might have had a hard time dancing to the minuet movement of Mozart's E flat Symphony; if it had not been for her dance, the movement would not sound the way it does.

The minuet had a long and honorable career, both as a social diversion and in its symphonic transformations. But by the time Mozart wrote his E flat Symphony, it was threatened by another popular dance from the country outside Vienna. For hundreds of years Austrian peasants there had clogged about to a burly, triple-time dance called the ländler, which Richard Wagner later used for local color in the third act of "Die Meistersinger." The origins of the ländler itself may have been none too respectable, but by the middle of the eighteenth century it was decent enough to have penetrated into the great cities of Prague and Vienna, where it was transformed into the waltz.

At first this wild, new dance was viewed with alarm and indignation. In Prague it was forbidden by an Imperial Edict of March 18, 1785 as both "injurious to the health and very dangerous as to sin" (sowohl der Gesundheit schädlich als auch der Sünden halber sehr gefährlich). Even after the French Revolution a shocked traveler to Paris remarked that it was only after the war that "the waltz, tobacco smoking and other vulgar habits became common." Gradually the waltz climbed the social ladder into more and more conservative circles until finally in 1816 it was danced in public at Almack's by Tsar Alexander II. Which of course made it all right.

Meanwhile the peasant rhythms from which it came were passing through the hands of Mozart, Beethoven, and Schubert to culminate in the immortal waltzes of the Strausses, father and son. Though the dance itself was tamed, its music had become richer and more imaginative, and from Vienna it conquered the world. The most serious musicians paid homage to the genius of Strauss and the waltz found its way into symphonies, tone poems and operas.

Tchaikovsky, for example, used it to express the peculiar mixture of gaiety and melancholy he sought in the third movement of his Fifth Symphony; there the waltz replaced the customary scherzo, which in turn had replaced the minuet.

Richard Strauss (no relation to the Viennese Strauss family) used the waltz in the Dance of the Seven Veils from his opera, "Salome." This is the famous dance with which Salome wins the head of John the Baptist from her weak-willed stepfather, Herod. The melodies here are transformations of those with which Salome wooed John the Baptist earlier in the opera. But John, or Jochanaan, as Strauss calls him, scorned Salome and pronounced a curse upon her. Herod has promised Salome anything she may wish, even to half his kingdom, if she will dance for him, so she dances to revenge herself. The music starts as a languorous, oriental "danse du ventre," but as the climax approaches we realize that its whirling rhythms come from the Viennese waltz. Toward the end there is a moment when the rhythms pause and Salome hovers regretfully over Jochanaan's prison well, before throwing herself at Herod's feet to ask her ghoulish reward: the severed head of John the Baptist.

Ravel too has used the waltz with brilliant imaginativeness in his symphonic piece, "La Valse," suggesting a great ballroom scene in the time of Emperor Napoleon III of France. From the dull, thudding beat of the opening, to the grinding dissonances and berserk rhythms of the climax, we hear the waltz in a dozen different guises. There is even a suggestion of the golden hurdy-gurdy, which the emperor himself used to play for Eugénie and their friends at intimate parties when they dispensed with an orchestra. The score of "La Valse" bears this descriptive note: "Whirling crowds give glimpses, through rifts, of couples waltzing. The clouds scatter, little by little. One sees an immense hall, peopled with a whirling crowd. The scene is gradually illuminated. The light of the chandeliers bursts forth, fortissimo. An imperial court about 1855."

With the Sacrificial Dance from his "Sacre du Printemps" Stravinsky takes us back again to primitive times. We hear the climax of the spring rites of a pagan Russian tribe, at which a chosen member of the group dances herself to death as a sacrifice to the fertility of the earth. Here the distortions and dissonances of Ravel are carried one step further. The music is a curious combination of the utmost sophistication and savage, naked rhythm; perhaps the strongest evidence we have in modern music of the eternal return of the artist to the most elemental instincts of the human race.

BACH: Suite for Flute and Strings, B minor
MOZART: "Eine Kleine Nachtmusik"
RAVEL: "Le Tombeau de Couperin"

"He loved music, he was well acquainted with it, he understood it." That was Bach's happy opinion of the master for whom he composed his popular B minor Suite for flute and strings. Prince Leopold was an amiable, well-educated young man of twenty-four who had traveled, was fond of books and pictures and reigned at the little court of Anhalt-Cöthen, one of the many tiny principalities that made up Germany in Bach's day. And like a cultivated amateur, he not only listened to music, he played the violin, the viola da gamba, the harpsichord, and he sang in a cultivated bass voice.

Those were happy years at Cöthen, for young Prince Leopold appreciated Kapellmeister Bach and the music he wrote for his eighteen-piece orchestra. There was little religious music at court, but in the orchestral works which his prince preferred Bach showed he could be as worldly and joyful as the next man, and that he could not only move his listeners but entertain them as well. Here it was that he

composed the six magnificent concertos dedicated to the
Margrave of Brandenburg, his violin concertos, and his
four orchestral suites, including the one in B minor.

As a matter of fact Bach himself didn't call this work
a suite, he called it an overture, after the first movement
which is modeled on the French operatic overtures of the
day. With the exception of the final badinerie, all the
remaining movements are based on dance forms. And what
a rich musical heritage these dances represent!

First we have a rondeau which is descended from a
medieval dance song. Various couplets alternate with
a chorus refrain.

Next there comes a solemn sarabande, a dance which,
according to the musicologist, Curt Sachs, came originally
from Central America! Spanish colonists, he believes,
brought it back to Andalusia, where it was dignified and
refined into a step for Spanish grandees. Others say it may
have been brought to Europe by the Moors from the Near
East. Eventually the stately rhythm of the sarabande
found its way even into operatic arias (like Handel's
"Lascia ch'io pianga") and instrumental suites. In this
movement, incidentally, Bach combines it with the ancient
medieval device of the canon.

The sarabande is followed by two lively bourrées, the
second with a fetching part for the solo flute. The bourrée
is an old French folk dance which was usually accompanied by the bagpipes or a hurdy-gurdy. The fact that its
name comes from the word "bourrir" (to flap the wings)
may mean that it goes back to primitive dances, possibly
even of totem origin, in which the performers imitated the
movements of ritual beasts and birds.

The lovely polonaise, very different from the brilliant piano pieces of Chopin, is a dance which probably
originated at the court of Poland in 1574, and devised

from old Christmas carols. Bach follows it with a variation called a double, in which the flute plays brilliant counterpoint over the melody.

The eighth movement, a minuet, comes from the court of Versailles, where Lully established it as the representative dance of Louis XIV and the aristocracy of France. But before that it had been a folk dance of the Poitou.

The final and perhaps most popular movement of the B minor Suite is a frisky badinerie (literally: a playful, trifling piece) in which the solo flute again runs off with all the honors.

We have mentioned historical background in such detail here only to show how ancient and diversified are the roots of the suite. Bach of course was not thinking of "flapping his wings" or of medieval dance songs when he wrote for the Prince of Anhalt-Cöthen. But all of these things contributed to the richness and fascination of an art form which we tend to look upon somewhat patronizingly today as "a predecessor of the symphony."

Mozart's "Eine Kleine Nachtmusik," "a little serenade" as he modestly calls it, is a sort of suite too, though it has only four movements. Or you might call it a cross between a suite and a little symphony. It was composed in Vienna some sixty years after Bach wrote his B minor Suite, and it is fascinating to see how the style of music had changed within a lifetime.

Gone is the contrapuntal grandeur of Bach's day and the endless stream of melody. Mozart's melody might be compared to the links of a chain, rather than an endless stream. His music tends to take the form of a series of rounded phrases, each an entity in itself, balanced against what comes before and after. It is neither more nor less beautiful than Bach, it is simply a different style of speech.

The first movement of "Eine Kleine Nachtmusik" is a sonatina, a tiny sonata of crystalline purity of form. Beneath the melodious surface of the following romanze there is murmurous agitation, suggestions of a subdued passion, of a romantic feeling which didn't become the fashion until after Mozart's day. The third movement is a minuet and the last is a rondo (the Italian version of the rondeau). The skipping, sparkling refrain of this finale is the very essence of Mozartean charm, with its echoes of Viennese popular song and the naïve Papageno of Mozart's "Magic Flute."

But before Mozart and Bach, an older composer, Couperin the Great, had written suites "for the little chamber concerts which Louis XIV used to ask me to play almost every Sunday of the year." From his position in Versailles Couperin's influence reached out not only to Bach but even to the twentieth-century Frenchman, Maurice Ravel. One year before World War I, Ravel decided to acknowledge his debt in a revival of the eighteenth-century suite which he called "Le Tombeau de Couperin."

Ravel was deeply conscious of his French cultural heritage and he was shocked by the experience of the war in which he served as an ambulance driver. When the piano version of "Le Tombeau de Couperin" appeared in 1917 each of its six movements bore a dedication to a comrade who had fallen at the front. Finally in 1919 Ravel made his masterly orchestrations of the prelude and three dance movements: the forlane, menuet and rigaudon. Modern in technique, ancient in form, and profoundly gallic in its clarity and restraint, this version of "Le Tombeau de Couperin" has become a classic of our current symphonic repertory.

BEETHOVEN: Eleven Viennese Dances
Symphony #7, A major

It was Richard Wagner who called Beethoven's Seventh Symphony "the apotheosis of the dance." But Beethoven didn't enshrine the dance only in a symphony. He wrote real dance music too. These Viennese Dances: four waltzes, five minuets and two ländler, were actually intended for dancing. Now when we read that Beethoven wrote minuets and ländler, and Mozart wrote contradances and teutsche, the names of those dances sound so quaint that we hardly realize that that was the same as if Sibelius today were to write fox trots and tangos and Hindemith or Stravinsky were to compose rhumbas and waltzes—not just concert waltzes either—waltzes for our leading dance bands.

It is hard to know why there has come to be such a gulf between so-called serious and popular music, but it's probably neither a very healthy nor normal state of affairs. I forget what composer it was who said that there is only one music, whether it is found in a waltz, a symphony or a lullaby. But he uttered a profound truth that we have nearly forgotten today. Do you remember how scandalized some musicians were when Raymond Scott and Benny Goodman started "swinging" Tchaikovsky and Haydn on the dance floor? Well, when Mozart went to Prague and found that his great opera, "The Marriage of Figaro," had been turned into dance hits, and all the people, in his words, were "hopping around to their hearts' content" to the airs of "Figaro," *he* wasn't scandalized or even annoyed. He was delighted. And he spoke of it as "truly a great honor for me"! Of course, he couldn't sue the arrangers anyway, because there were no copyrights in those days. But the point is that he thought it was a wonderful thing, and took special relish in writing his friends about it. And it's just possible that Mozart was right, and the modern aesthetes who hold their noses when they hear a swing band doing Tchaikovsky are wrong.

As a matter of fact you could follow the same idea as far back as you like through the history of music, and watch how popular music and serious music have always been intertwined, how even drinking songs and love songs have been woven into the music of church ceremonial, and both probably been the better for it.

These particular dances of Beethoven were composed during the summer of 1819 in the Austrian village of Mödling. They have no opus number and for some time it was doubted whether they were really by Beethoven at all. The German scholar, Riemann, thought at first they might have been by Weber, but finally decided that they are authentic Beethoven.

It was some years earlier, in the summer of 1812, that Beethoven wrote his Seventh Symphony, while a bloody remaking of the map of Europe gripped the attention of all men, as our colossal struggle does today. It seems a miracle that Beethoven was able, in the midst of such public and private disaster, to mold masterpieces which were to outlast both the Napoleonic and several other empires. Vienna, Beethoven's home, had been taken by Napoleon, but in the following year, by the time the Seventh Symphony had its first performance, that empire was already crumbling. Beethoven himself conducted the première at a concert for the benefit of wounded Austrian and Bavarian soldiers.

This benefit was a fashionable occasion, and famous

virtuosos took part in the orchestra: Spohr; the great
Dragonetti, accompanied by a small pet dog which was
his inseparable companion, played one of the double
basses; and a nervous young man by the name of Meyerbeer played the bass drum. In later years, when Meyerbeer
had become a famous opera composer, Beethoven would
laugh and say: "Ha, ha! I was not at all satisfied with
him; he never struck on the beat. He was always too late,
and I was obliged to speak rudely to him. Ha, ha! I could
do nothing with him. He didn't have the courage to strike
on the beat."

Of all the many explainers and interpreters of the
Seventh Symphony, Wagner probably came the nearest
when he called it an apotheosis of the dance. For once the
long slow introduction has led into the persistent rhythmic
figure of the first movement, the pulse never stops.

The introduction itself is long and richly developed.
A theme of majestic simplicity strides boldly downward
through the orchestra. First it is unadorned, except for
an occasional punctuating chord of the full orchestra, then
it is heard against a great upward surge of the string
instruments. There is a magnificent development of this
material together with a more graceful, feminine second
theme before we come to the main part of the movement.
This is a vivacious six-eight movement based on a lightly
skipping figure which inspired Berlioz to call it a peasant
round, but it soon bursts beyond the bounds of any dance
that ever was seen on land or sea. It is a dance, at the very
least, of the planets. Its tremendous power never gets out
of hand, though some of Beethoven's contemporaries
thought it did. There is the famous passage toward the
end, for example, which made Weber exclaim that Beethoven was now "quite ripe for the madhouse." This is
the place where the cellos and double basses get hold of a

powerful phrase of five notes down in the depths of the orchestra and refuse to let go. They keep on repeating their obstinate figure while the orchestra above grows and swells to a magnificent climax.

Now that this tremendous impulse of rhythm has been started, it continues with irresistible drive through to the end of the symphony. One result is that the Seventh Symphony has no real slow movement. In place of it, there is the celebrated allegretto.

Even at the first performance of the symphony, this allegretto was encored, a thing that rarely happened to slow movements, and it soon became so universally known and loved that some conductors used to insert it into the less popular Eighth Symphony to help put it over! In spite of the marking, allegretto, there is nothing flippant about this movement, and we know that Beethoven hesitated whether to call it an allegretto or an andante. It begins with a soft sustained chord of the wind instruments, then there is the quiet, rhythmic chant of the lower strings— less a melody than a heartbeat that never seems to stop. Around it there weave the poignant voices of violas and cellos. Later there is a switch from the melancholy A minor to the sunnier major mode and new and more flowing melodies in another rhythm for clarinets and bassoons. But even here, if you listen carefully, the same old rhythmic pulse sounds softly at the bottom of the orchestra. Finally the material of the beginning returns in fugal form, leading into a great peroration of the rhythmic chant with the full brilliance of the orchestra. As the climax dies down, fragments of the theme are whispered from one part of the orchestra to the other and the movement ends with a touching little sigh of the violins.

The rough-and-tumble scherzo, with its explosive dynamic contrasts, breaks its relentless drive only in that great poetic hymn of praise that is called, technically, the trio.

In the boisterous finale we have the same energy and drive of the dance—only this orgy of rejoicing goes far beyond anything we have yet heard. Outwardly, the themes have the character almost of a reel or a jig. But this foursquare rhythm with its restless, whirling power sweeps on with a sort of bacchantic fury to climax after climax and a coda of a grandeur past description. "The Grand Symphony in A," Beethoven commented laconically, "—one of my very best."

BACH: Passacaglia and Fugue, C minor
BRAHMS: Symphony #4, E minor

Great music, like great men, often traces a vulgar ancestry and is the better for it. From the two Spanish words "pasar" (to walk) and "calle" (a street) comes the name of a common street dance of medieval Spain: passacaglia. The dance itself apparently rose from the primitive music-making of wandering minstrels: one would grind out endless repetitions of the same bass, while the other would improvise all sorts of more complicated tunes to go with it. A more elemental musical form can hardly be imagined and perhaps that very fact accounts for its amazing vitality.

In the sixteenth century it broke into polite society as a dance and also as a popular form of salon music for the lute. From there it invaded the church, opera house and concert halls of the seventeenth, eighteenth and nine-

teenth centuries. Purcell used it for one of the most poignant of all operatic ariàs: "Dido's Lament" in his "Dido
and Aeneas." Bach's C minor Passacaglia and Fugue is one
of the greatest works ever written for organ. And Brahms
used the passacaglia for the finale of his epic Fourth Symphony.

Bach gives his mighty ground bass theme to the pedal
notes of the organ and over it he weaves an increasingly
intricate web of contrapuntal melodies, garlands of scales
and graceful arpeggios. Occasionally the bass theme will
appear in the upper registers of the organ, but that is the
exception, not the rule. Finally after twenty of the most
ingenious variations, the theme builds to its grand climax
in an immense double fugue.

Music of such power and depth has naturally attracted many arrangers. There is no lack of orchestral ver-
sions of the C minor Passacaglia and Fugue, which is
probably heard more often at symphony concerts nowadays than it is on the organ.

It was undoubtedly his study of Bach which inspired
Brahms to use the passacaglia in a symphony. For he admired Bach even more, if possible, than Beethoven, and
we know he felt very small beside him. One evening when
he was dining with some friends, a particularly fine vin-
tage was praised as the Brahms among wines. "Take it
away," said Brahms, quick as a flash, "and bring us a
bottle of Bach!" (Bach is "brook" in German.)

In spite of all the fame and adoration that came to
Brahms during his lifetime, he seems to have been wor-
ried about his new Fourth Symphony. He wrote it during
the summer in a tiny town in the Austrian Alps—a town
by the name of Mürz Zuschlag which lay so high that it
had a very short summer and the fruit which grew in the
neighborhood could hardly ripen before winter set in

again. From Mürz Zuschlag he sent the first movement of the Fourth Symphony to one of his very dear friends, Elisabeth von Herzogenberg, asking her to look it over.

"Might I venture to send you a piece of a piece of mine," he wrote, "and would you have time to take a look at it and tell me what you think? The trouble is that on the whole, my pieces are nicer than myself and need less setting to rights! But the cherries never get ripe for eating in these parts, so don't be afraid to say if you don't like the taste. I'm not at all eager to write a bad Number Four."

When Elisabeth didn't answer as quickly as he had expected Brahms wrote a typical note to her husband, hiding his injured pride under rough humor. "My latest attack was evidently a complete failure—and a symphony too! But I do beg that your dear lady will not abuse her talent for writing pretty letters by inventing any belated fibs for my benefit."

As a matter of fact, the lady was full of enthusiasm for the new symphony and she tried to reassure Brahms in a long and eloquent letter. Before it was performed, Brahms took part in a four-hand piano presentation for some other friends. From their attitude, he was afraid they hadn't liked it and again he was depressed.

Probably his friends were more surprised than disappointed, for Brahms had dared to do a thing that has rarely been done with success in a symphony: he gave it a tragic finale. The essence of the traditional symphonic form is the clash of contrasting musical ideas. Perhaps what puzzled Brahms's friends was that the Fourth Symphony is a consistently tragic work throughout. And the struggle, which is so typical for the symphonic form, is completely lacking in the finale. By the time Brahms reaches the last movement, the struggle is all over, and the finale gives him an opportunity for a great expansion of pure emotion.

The first movement opens with a vast, undulating flow of melody in a melancholy strain, which is very different from the vigorous first themes of the classical symphony. The vigor comes later with fanfarelike themes which interrupt the mood with strident cries.

In place of the traditional adagio or andante, the Fourth Symphony has an allegretto, which starts with a severe melodic motto in the ancient Phrygian mode. Later this same melody glows with Brahmsian warmth.

The third movement is vigorous and rhythmical and the finale is a grandiose procession of variations, built on a ground theme that is announced in the first few measures. The question whether this movement is really a passacaglia or a chaconne (practically identical forms) is still being fought out among musicologists, but most listeners hearing it for the first time wouldn't notice the form at all. The important thing is the magnificent stride of the music, the richness of Brahms's thought and emotion.

Brahms's friends weren't the only ones who found the Fourth Symphony difficult to understand. In his home, Vienna, the public was even slower than in some other cities to appreciate it. But gradually it took hold.

At the last Vienna Philharmonic concert heard by Brahms, it caused a storm of enthusiasm. After the first movement the applause would not stop until he came to the front of the box where he was sitting and showed himself to the audience. He was a tragically different Brahms from the hearty, stocky figure they had known.

He had suffered a terrible blow the year before, when his dearest friend and greatest champion, Clara Schumann, died. He never recovered from that shock. And the chill he caught at her funeral aggravated a long-standing cancer of the liver which killed him.

This last time he heard his Fourth Symphony, the demonstrations were repeated after each movement. And at the end there was an extraordinary scene. The clapping, shouting house riveted its gaze on the figure standing in the balcony, and seemed unable to let him go. "Tears ran down his cheeks," one eyewitness tells us, "as he stood there, shrunken in form, with his face lined and white hair hanging lank. And through the audience there was a feeling as of a stifled sob, for each knew that they were saying farewell. Another outburst of applause and yet another; one more acknowledgment from the master; and Brahms and his Vienna had parted forever."

❧❦   ❧❦

LULLY: Minuet of the Happy Spirits from "Proserpine"
GLUCK-GEVAERT: Ballet Suite #2
WAGNER: Overture and Bacchanale from "Tannhäuser" (Paris version)
OFFENBACH-ROSENTHAL: "Gaîté Parisienne"

For nearly three centuries France was the home of the ballet. All of the ballet selections discussed here were written for Paris, most of them for the grand opera or Académie Nationale de Musique et de Danse, as it is called. Yet curiously enough they were all composed by foreigners. For it is a strange fact of history that many of the greatest French operas and operettas were the work of foreigners who were attracted to Paris because it was the cultural and artistic capital of the world. French opera itself was founded by an Italian, Lully, and his tradition influenced all French opera for over two hundred years. In fact, the ghost of Lully still haunted the Paris opera when Wagner came to give his French version of "Tannhäuser" there in the 1860's, and indirectly caused the failure of that work.

Lully began his career as a kitchen scullion in the palace of Mlle. de Montpensier. But he managed to attract attention to his excellent violin playing, and in an amazingly short time he got a job in the private orchestra of Louis XIV, the famous "Twenty-Four Violins of the King." Louis was only fourteen years old at the time. Lully was not much older and the young king took a great liking to him. Lully was energetic, ambitious, a shrewd observer of men and tastes and he rose rapidly at court. He obtained patents of nobility, became Music Master to the Royal Family and it was not long before the former kitchen scullion was dancing with the king himself in his own ballets. Louis XIV loved to take part in the court ballets and his nickname, "Le Roi Soleil," came from the role of the Sun King which he danced in the "Ballet de la Nuit."

But Lully wasn't content writing just ballet music. He collaborated with Molière, composing incidental music for his comedies, and when the opportunity came, he persuaded the king to give him the exclusive right to perform opera in France. He had watched carefully the various futile attempts to establish Italian opera in France, so he wrote his French operas in a very different style, with lots of ballet and chorus and music which suited the French language and temperament. They were a magnificent reflection of the glittering court, the pomp and formality which surrounded Louis XIV, and they became overwhelmingly popular.

It may seem a little odd to us that the Happy Spirits in Elysium should dance a minuet, but that was quite according to the courtly seventeenth-century ideas of the classical heaven, and that is what they did in Lully's opera, "Proserpine," which he produced in 1680. When you hear this charming, formal music, you must imagine the stately nods and aristocratic bows of these quaint cavaliers and ladies of the Elysian Fields as they danced to Lully's music—dressed, no doubt in hoop skirts, silken knee breeches, mountainous wigs and ostrich feathers.

But after a century had elapsed nearly everyone in France who knew or cared anything about music, longed for some forceful personality to reform the ancient, outmoded imitations of Lully that still ruled the roost of French opera. And sure enough, the new genius of French opera, when he arrived, turned out to be another foreigner: the Austrian Gluck.

The first opera he wrote for Paris, "Iphigenia in Aulis," ushered in a tremendous battle between the supporters of Gluck's dramatic reform and the defenders of the old tradition. But Gluck had the spirit of the times as well as extremely powerful personalities on his side. Marie Antoinette, whose music teacher he had been when she was a little princess in Vienna, put her influence behind him; so did Jean-Jacques Rousseau and many of the most famous philosophers and writers of the day. But the old Lully tradition of much ballet hung on. The reigning god of the ballet, the Italian star, Vestris, kept clamoring for more and more dance music in the opera, and he declared it was impossible to end the performance without a chaconne. Gluck remonstrated that it would be stylistically inappropriate and finally burst out in despair: "My God, sir, do you think the Greeks ever heard of a chaconne?"

"No?" answered Vestris with raised eyebrows. "Then

so much the worse for them!" In the end he got his cha-
conne and a very beautiful one too. The Gluck-Gevaert
Ballet Suite Number 2 contains an Air, Dance of the
Slaves, Tambourin and Chaconne from "Iphigenia in
Aulis" and the famous Gavotte from one of Gluck's later
operas, "Armide."

After Gluck's day, French opera was dominated by
Italians and Germans till Wagner came to Paris in 1860
to produce his "Tannhäuser."

"Tannhäuser," of course, wasn't originally written
for Paris. It had been produced fifteen years earlier in
Dresden where Wagner was first conductor of the opera
house. But when he came to put it on in Paris Wagner,
like everyone else, ran up against the ghost of Lully and
the tradition of lots of ballet.

He was willing to give in to tradition to a certain ex-
tent, because there was a place in "Tannhäuser" for a
ballet: the Bacchanale in the Venusberg, which opens the
opera. This scene already had a small ballet and now in
Paris he was more than willing to expand it, for he felt
able to do it better justice than he had fifteen years before.
In fact Wagner went further: he rewrote the entire Bacchanale and all of the following scene between Venus and
Tannhäuser (to a new French text) and he arranged the
overture, which had originally been a set piece by itself,
so that it merged without interruption into the Bacchanale
at the rise of the curtain.

But this wasn't enough, he was told. There had to be
a ballet in the second act, for the simple reason that the
members of the fashionable Parisian Jockey Club never
finished dinner before the second act of the opera. These
influential young men had a more than artistic interest in
the young ladies of the ballet—their president was said
to wander about backstage like a sultan surveying his

harem—and they insisted on having a ballet when they arrived, whether it fitted into the dramatic action or not.

In spite of the warnings of the opera directors and his well-meaning friends, Wagner refused to compromise. He rewrote the Overture and Bacchanale, which·was artistically justified, and as for the second act, they could take it or leave it. The result was one of the bitterest theatrical scandals of all time. "Tannhäuser," in spite of the fact that the majority of listeners wanted to give it a fair hearing, was hissed and booed, interrupted by laughter and whistling till at times the noise completely drowned out the music. The same thing happened at the second performance and the third, until Wagner in despair withdrew his score and said good-bye to Paris.

But in spite of that initial failure, it is the Paris version of "Tannhäuser" which is performed today in almost every opera house of the world outside of Germany. The first part of the music with its mixture of the Pilgrims' Chorus and Venusberg music is familiar to everyone who has heard a brass band concert. The second part, where it merges into the Bacchanale, is in Wagner's more complicated style of the period of "Tristan und Isolde." In fact the climax of this orgiastic music is built on a theme which might have been taken bodily from the Prelude to "Tristan." And it's interesting to remember, when we hear the welter of passion, the wild, chromatic harmonies and the blazing orchestral color of this music, that it might never have existed if it hadn't been for Jean-Baptiste Lully, writing court ballets two centuries ago to please his royal master, the Roi Soleil of Versailles.

When Wagner said good-bye to Paris he left behind him a triumphant compatriot. Jacques Offenbach was born in Cologne. But he had come to Paris when he was young and soon turned more Parisian than the French.

His music became the perfect reflection of Parisian high life during the last glamorous years of the Second Empire when French society was going to pieces behind its elegant façade, much as it did in the last years before Germany invaded France in 1940.

On the surface all was well, Paris seemed the political and artistic capital of the world, and even more the capital of the world of pleasure. It was the age of the cancan and Paris was dance mad. After one Offenbach operetta, or opéra bouffe, it became the age of Offenbach. With his wit and elegance, his satirical lightness of touch, and the sparkling irreverence of his melodies, he held up the mirror to Parisian life with its strange combination of vulgarity and aristocracy, of sharp wits and foolishness, of imperial splendor and backstairs intrigue.

Paris was thronged by rich pleasure seekers from Rio de Janeiro, New York and St. Petersburg, millionaires from Brazil, mysterious potentates from the Balkans, bewhiskered diplomats from Berlin, and respectable English country squires off on a toot. The life that they saw in Paris came to be more and more like an Offenbach opéra bouffe. Sometimes it was disguised as life on Mt. Olympus or at the fashionable watering places of ancient Greece where famous names of legend danced the galop and the cancan. Sometimes Offenbach showed it without disguise, as in "La Vie Parisienne."

Not until it was too late did people discover that the shaky throne of Emperor Napoleon III and all the gorgeous show of his imperial court could be swept away by a few German soldiers, as easily as the stagehands shifted scenery at the opéra bouffe. Paris could still laugh at itself, and as far as it goes, that is a lovable and civilized characteristic. The laughter was good while it lasted, and it is that laughter, that inimitable Parisian charm, which we

hear in the selections from Offenbach's operettas called
"Gaîté Parisienne."

※   ※

STRAVINSKY: "L'Oiseau de Feu"
"Petrouchka"

There was a time when Stravinsky was the bold, bad
boy of modern music. That time began when Stravinsky,
aged twenty-seven, wrote the glowing music of his ballet,
"L'Oiseau de Feu," and it reached its climax just before
World War I with his cataclysmic score, "Le Sacre du
Printemps." Today, of course, he is a revered master,
who has probably had more influence than any other living man on the music of the past few decades. Like his
painter friend, Picasso, Stravinsky has changed styles a
dozen times, with the rapidity and ease of a chameleon.
Like Picasso's pictures, everything Stravinsky does is accomplished with incredible technical virtuosity, a verve
and brilliance that have fascinated at least two generations of composers and made them follow his drastic
changes of mood with an enthusiasm and lack of discre-
tion that Stravinsky would probably be the first to con-
demn. Stravinsky has never been an imitator, but all his
life he has avidly absorbed influences from people about
him, from musicians, from painters, from writers, from
the ballet. Perhaps the greatest and most fruitful influence of them all was Sergei Diaghileff, the great impre-
sario of the Ballet Russe de Diaghileff.

Diaghileff was not a creator in the usual sense of the
word, but he had a genius for spotting genius in other
people, he knew how to bring the right talents together

and bring out the best that was in all of them. Stravinsky had been studying for about a year with the Russian composer, Rimsky-Korsakoff, when Diaghileff happened to hear a performance of one of Stravinsky's very earliest works, a "Scherzo Fantastique" for orchestra. He was so struck with Stravinsky's gifts that he asked him to orchestrate some Chopin numbers, and then, without more ado, he commissioned him to write a full-sized ballet of his own. This was "The Fire Bird." It was produced in 1910 at the Opera in Paris with a fabulous cast that included Karsavina as the Fire Bird, Fokine as the Tsarevitch Ivan; and Gabriel Pierné as conductor.

It had an immediate success and Stravinsky was transformed overnight from a promising young student into a leader of contemporary music. Diaghileff's flair had justified itself again—brilliantly. For though the voice of young Stravinsky speaks with a skill and a sensuous magic that are partly inherited from his teacher, Rimsky-Korsakoff, what he has to say is new.

The story of the ballet is taken from one of the many Russian legends about young Tsarevitch Ivan. As he is wandering through a forest at night he espies, in a glow of light, the Fire Bird, plucking golden fruit from a silver tree. The Fire Bird tries to hide from him. He seizes the fair creature, but is melted by her entreaties and lets her go again. Out of gratitude, she leaves him one of her shining plumes.

As day dawns, Ivan finds himself in the park of an ancient castle, and with the rise of the sun, twelve beautiful damsels and a thirteenth, more lovely than all the rest, come out of the castle to dance among the silver trees. By the sweetness and modesty of their demeanor, Ivan knows them at once to be princesses. Unable to keep to his hiding place, he comes out to talk to them. The maidens plead with him to leave at once, for he is in the enchanted realm of the terrible ogre, Kastcheï, who lures travelers there, to turn them to stone. But Ivan, having looked into the eyes of the thirteenth maiden, decides to stay.

When they leave him, Ivan, made bold by love, throws open the castle gates. A grotesque throng emerges: slaves, courtiers, freaks, two-headed monsters, the Kikimoras and the Bolibochki, the entourage of the ogre, and finally the horrible Kastcheï himself.

Kastcheï tries to turn Ivan to stone, but the shining plume of the Fire Bird protects him and soon the Fire Bird herself appears. First she throws a spell upon the ogre and the ugly denizens of the castle which throws them into a frenzied dance. When they are exhausted, she reveals to Ivan a casket containing Kastcheï's death. Ivan takes from it an egg which he dashes to the ground. The death unites itself with Kastcheï, and the dreadful wizard dies. The castle vanishes, the captive stone knights come to life, there is general merrymaking and Ivan receives the hand of the thirteenth princess.

The introduction to the ballet begins in the deep, dark stringed instruments, suggesting the night, a fairy-tale night, of course, and the ominous nearness of the ogre's castle. Suddenly there is a splash of color, and the Fire Bird wings her way through the orchestra. Through the shimmering strings, high, brilliant wood winds and a few notes of the piano gleam like the legendary plumes of the bird.

The break of day is soft and lyrical. One of the melodies anticipates the theme which is transformed with such glittering pomp in the finale. The fairy-tale dance of the princesses is sung by a mellow horn; there is a tender question in the clarinet and a plaintive answer from the oboe.

The delicate tone picture is interrupted by an ugly crash as Ivan opens the gates of the castle. The orchestra snarls and the wild dance of Kastcheï and his monsters courses through the instruments with cross rhythms and clashing harmonies that seem to forecast the "Sacre du Printemps."

The berceuse and finale are pure orchestral magic. The dreamy phrases of the bassoon at the beginning are like the once upon a time of a fairy tale. A whispering tremolo of the strings floats down through the orchestra. Now the horn takes up the theme. There is a rippling glissando of the harp and the strings chant it with a crowing fervor. Finally the whole orchestra is exulting in the song of deliverance and, with a mighty progression of brass chords against a shimmering pedal point in the strings, the fairy tale ends in a burst of fantastic brilliance.

In "The Fire Bird" Stravinsky was still a youthful romanticist, still influenced by the glow and tenderness of his master, Rimsky-Korsakoff's orchestra. In the ballet, "Petrouchka," Stravinsky stands on his own feet. In "Petrouchka" Stravinsky's orchestra, instead of glowing, has an almost blinding glare, a brittle glitter. And instead of romantic tenderness, there is tight-lipped, laconic agony. Instead of a Russian fairy tale, Stravinsky tells us a fairy tale of his own making, about his own time, and the suffering of the Russian people. The difference between "The Fire Bird" and "Petrouchka" is the difference between young genius and mature genius, a development that takes many years in most composers' lives. Stravinsky made the jump in a few months' time. After the success of "The Fire Bird" Diaghileff commissioned another ballet from his young protégé. And Stravinsky thought of the "Sacre du Printemps." But with the intuition of all great artists, he realized that that stupendous project must have time to mature in his mind. In his own words: "Before tackling the 'Sacre du Printemps' which would be a long and difficult task, I wanted to refresh myself by composing an orchestral piece in which the piano would play the most important part—a sort of konzertstück."

But the konzertstück led Stravinsky down a very different road from the one he had intended. While he was composing the music, he was obsessed with the picture of a puppet suddenly come to life, "exasperating the orchestra with diabolical cascades of arpeggios." And when he tried to think of a title for his new piece, there jumped into his mind what he calls, "the immortal and unhappy hero of every fair, in all countries"—Petrouchka.

When Diaghileff came to see how the "Sacre du Printemps" was getting along, instead of reproaching Stravinsky for this relaxation, he was delighted, and he persuaded Stravinsky to transform the little concert piece into the second part of a new ballet—the pathetic scene in Petrouchka's little prison, the puppet theatre.

"Petrouchka" was produced during Diaghileff's third Paris season, with the legendary male dancer, Nijinsky, as Petrouchka, Karsavina as the Ballerina, Fokine as ballet master and Pierre Monteux conducting. At the time it was freely admitted that "Petrouchka" was an allegory, Petrouchka himself representing the suffering, simple-minded peasant classes of Russia, and the tragedy of their existence under the shadow of despotism and injustice. It was even said that the old Wizard, master of the puppets, was a symbol of the Tsar himself, and the Blackamoor, a symbol of his brutal agents.

The scene is set in the Admiralty Square of old St. Petersburg, at Shrovetide, the last three days of Carnival, in 1830. The music opens with the bright bustle of a fair day. The curtains part and we see the surging crowds.

The thousand and one glittering distractions of the fair are reflected separately and all together in the chaotic rhythms and harmonies of the music: an organ grinder and a dancing girl; a group of revelers reeling across the scene; then the organ grinder begins to blow a trumpet, and across the stage a music box and another dancing girl add their part to the joyous din. The crowd grows thicker and more exuberant. Finally two drummers appear outside a little puppet theatre and the rattle of their drums hushes the crowd into an expectant silence.

The old Charlatan, the Magician, appears. The impression he makes upon the gullible populace sounds in the mysterious hocus-pocus mutterings and whirrings of the orchestra. Then he plays a foolish little tune on the flute, and the charm is complete. The puppet theatre curtain rises, and behold! three animated puppets: Petrouchka, the Blackamoor and the Ballerina. They do a wild Russian dance to music as garish, frantic and angular as themselves. Then the curtain falls, the drums rasp and there is a change of scene.

We see Petrouchka's bare little prisonlike room. There is a crash, a door opens and Petrouchka is kicked through it onto the floor. And now we see that, sawdust as he is, Petrouchka has a pathetic, rudimentary glimmering of a soul. He struggles hopelessly and paws the walls to escape. We hear his wild gropings in the fantastic, exasperating arpeggios of the piano and finally the trumpets, cornets and trombones scream out his rage and frustration. Then the door opens and in steps the tinselly little Ballerina. Petrouchka is in love with her, and the orchestra endows her with all the glamour of Petrouchka's imagination. But she will have none of him. He is too simple witted.

The third scene is the luxurious room of the Blackamoor. The Ballerina enters and finds the stupid, handsome Blackamoor very romantic. He makes love to her. The empty-headed banality of their music and their mutual enchantment made Petrouchka's tragedy all the more heart rending. Suddenly shrieks from the next room interrupt their dance, and Petrouchka appears, but he is chased away by the Blackamoor.

The scene returns to the festive crowd outside. At the very climax of their gaiety, there is a wild thrashing behind the curtains of the puppet theatre and out dashes Petrouchka pursued by the infuriated Blackamoor. He deals Petrouchka a vicious blow with his sword and with a final desperate shriek, the puppet dies. There is consternation and silence in the crowd. A policeman is sent for, but the Magician arrives and shows them that, after all, Petrouchka is only made of sawdust. The merrymakers disperse in the dusk, but as the old Wizard is dragging back the sawdust doll, Petrouchka's ghost appears above the theatre, menacing him with his own little flute tune.

The Charlatan drops the body in terror and disappears into the darkness. There are four soft pizzicato notes in the depths of the orchestra, and the tragedy is over.

❧❧   ❧❧

RAVEL: "Daphnis et Chloë" (Second Suite)
STRAVINSKY: "Le Sacre du Printemps"

Some of the paradox of classic Greek art comes back to life in Ravel's ballet masterpiece, "Daphnis and Chloë." For here is music which unites that traditional clarity and balance of form with the Dionysiac frenzy of emotion which was also typical of ancient Greece. Perhaps only a Frenchman could have achieved such a beautifully balanced paradox in music.

It was commissioned and first produced by Sergei Diaghileff's Russian Ballet at Paris in 1912. Nowadays it is seldom given as a ballet, but the Second Suite drawn from Ravel's score has long been popular in the concert hall. The background of this portion of the ballet, including Daybreak, the Pantomime and General Dance is as follows:

There is no sound at break of day save the murmur of rivulets fed by the dew, and the song of birds. Daphnis, asleep before the grotto of the nymphs, is awakened and he looks about in anguish for Chloë. At last she appears and the couple rush into each other's arms. She has been saved by the god Pan, in memory of the nymph Syrinx whom he loved. Daphnis and Chloë mime the wooing of Syrinx by Pan. He fashions a flute of reeds and Chloë dances in imitation of the melancholy tune. The dance grows more and more animated until she falls into his arms. They are joined by girls dressed as bacchantes and a group of young men, and the suite ends with the joyous tumult of the "danse générale."

With all its melodic imagination, brilliant orchestration, intoxicating color, sensuous harmonies and orgiastic rhythm, "Daphnis and Chloë" remains an essentially patrician score. Ravel was a spiritual aristocrat. Yet he knew the elemental drives and could express them in music. His is the supreme artistic achievement of appearing to give them full rein without once relaxing his potent instinct for form.

To Diaghileff we also owe Stravinsky's ballet, the "Sacre du Printemps," which caused a riot in the Théâtre des Champs-Elysées the following season.

Opinions of the "Sacre du Printemps" still vary. Some musicians consider it the greatest score Stravinsky has composed and others, after thirty years, still denounce this revival of primitive feelings in music as a collapse into decadence. But whatever you think of the "Sacre," there is no denying that it has overwhelming vitality, that Stravinsky goes his own way here with complete confidence in his own inspiration and complete disregard of any arbitrary standards of beauty or propriety in music.

You don't argue with the "Sacre du Printemps" any more than you argue with a ten-ton truck or an express train. And like a ten-ton truck, it has had a lot of influence on musical traffic in these last thirty·years. Many composers have tried to imitate it. Honegger even wrote a piece which he named after an express train: "Pacific 231." Others have reacted violently against it and started off in the opposite direction. One of the most violent of these, curiously enough, is Stravinsky himself. But that is another story.

If opinions on the "Sacre" seem violent to us today, they are nothing to the feelings on the evening of the première, which was one of the greatest theatrical scandals of this century.

The smart audience, the "tout Paris," had sensed revolution in the wind. Both radicals and conservatives came ready for a fight.

At the very beginning the strange wood-wind figures sent a wave of nervous titters through the house. But as the dissonant music and the fantastic, geometrical choreography on the stage developed, the opposition grew more belligerent. There were hisses and catcalls. A famous dowager of Parisian society stood up in her box, brandished her fan and shouted angrily: "This is the first time in sixty years anyone has dared to make a fool of me." The

angry remarks grew louder and louder and more unprint-
able, until the people who wanted to listen rose with even
angrier roars to defend their right to hear the music. In-
sults flew back and forth and blows soon followed. For
many years after the young French composer, Roland-
Manuel, preserved the torn collar of his shirt as a precious
relic of that battle.

Behind the scenes Nijinsky, who had arranged the
choreography and was dancing one of the leading parts
himself, became very pale when he heard the noise and
wanted to jump out onto the stage to start a counterriot
against the demonstrators, but Stravinsky held him back.

"It was war over art for the rest of the evening,"
writes the American author, Carl Van Vechten, "and the
orchestra played on unheard, except occasionally when a
slight lull occurred." The poor performers on the stage
kept on bravely dancing to music they had to imagine they
heard. One young man who was standing up behind Van
Vechten in order to see more, got so excited he began to
beat his fists rhythmically on the top of the writer's head.
"My emotion was so great," says Van Vechten, "that I
didn't feel the blows for some time. They were perfectly
synchronized with the music. When I did, I turned
around. His apology was sincere. We had both been carried beyond ourselves."

There was more peace at later performances—five in
all—that season in Paris, and from there Stravinsky's
music has conquered the concert halls of the world.

Today the "Sacre du Printemps" no longer enrages
or frightens audiences the way it used to. Since then we
have heard louder and stranger noises and got used to
them. Most of them have long since died away into silence,
but the volcanic power of the "Sacre" remains.

The story of the ballet, added after the music was

composed, describes the spring rites of an imaginary barbaric tribe of prehistoric Russia. Part I, entitled "The
Adoration of the Earth," includes an Introduction, Har-
bingers of Spring, Dance of the Youths and Maidens,
Dance of Abduction, Spring Rounds, Games of the Rival
Towns, The Procession of the Wise Men, The Kiss to the
Earth, and Dance of the Earth. There are strange, nostalgic melodies that evoke the slumbering strength of the
earth, waiting to burst forth at the call of spring. Like the
melodies of primitive peoples, they are short, strongly
rhythmic phrases, repeated again and again. There are
sharp, quarreling harmonies, trumpet calls that sound
like a mimic battle, but above everything the overwhelming power of rhythm.

In Part II, "The Sacrifice," one member of the tribe
is chosen to dance herself to death as the climax of
the spring rites. It begins with a mournful introduction
called Pagan Night. There are a Mystical Circle of the
Adolescents, Glorification of the Chosen One, Evocation
of the Ancestors, Ritual Performance of the Ancestors,
and finally the Sacrificial Dance of the Chosen One, in
which music is reduced to its barest, most primitive element: rhythm. Like the rhythm of many savage tribes, it
is complex, subtle, strong, and it rises to a climax of bru-
tally exciting power.

From the drums of prehistoric man, to the rounds of
the Middle Ages and the courtly dances that found their
way into eighteenth- and nineteenth-century symphonies,
through modern jazz, to Stravinsky's "Sacre du Printemps," the circle is complete.

II.   *The Symphony Is Born*

A SYMPHONY IS ALL THINGS to all men. It may have almost any purpose from polite entertainment to the profoundest conflict of emotional and musical forces, from exalted prophecy of the brotherhood of man to description of the baby's bath. Its orchestra may include twenty or a hundred and twenty instruments, with or without voices; it may be in one to five movements and it may last anywhere from ten minutes to an hour and a half—and still be called a symphony.

A Mozart symphony bears very little relation to a symphony of Brahms, and Haydn would certainly marvel to be called father of the form in which Sibelius has written his greatest masterpieces. Happily the idea of a symphony cannot be tied down. The standard or classical symphonic form as it appears in textbooks is only an abstraction, an attempt to write a formula which will fit at least a few years out of two centuries' ceaseless development.

In the following pages we shall see some of the changes which took place within what we loosely call the classical symphony, from the operatic overture out of which it grew, to the First Symphony of Beethoven.

J. C. BACH: Sinfonia (Overture to "Lucio Silla")
MOZART: Paris Symphony (K. 297)
Haffner Symphony (K. 385)

When you listen to this enchanting little symphony it's hard to believe that it was written by the son of Johann Sebastian Bach, the composer of the St. Matthew Passion and the great organ fugues. It's hard because the symphony sounds as if it might have been written by Mozart. But the reason isn't far to seek.

When Sebastian Bach died, the great tradition of German religious music died with him. His youngest son, Christian Bach, quickly turned his back on everything his father had stood for in music and took the first opportunity to go to Italy, the home of opera—that Italian opera, which his father had never taken seriously and had rather looked down upon. But young Christian, who soon became known as the "Milan Bach" and later as the "London Bach," felt the trend of the times—the trend that led away from his father's music, and he was not sorry to follow it. He was eager for a brilliant international career, and he knew that only in Italy could he learn how to compose in the latest style, with that simplicity, elegance and brilliance which were dazzling all the musical capitals of the world.

He was drawn to Italy by the same thing that made Mozart's father bring his infant prodigy son there a few years later. After all, hadn't Handel gone to Italy too and used his success there to build the reputation that finally started him on his astonishing career in London?

So off went Bach to Milan. He started there as organist at the cathedral. But soon he was composing popular arias, and then whole operas which carried his name through Italy and across the Alps, even as far as Germany and England. Finally he did follow Handel to London, where he became Handel's successor as Music Master to the Queen, and quickly launched a series of extremely fashionable and successful symphony concerts.

One of Bach's symphonies which is still occasionally heard today, is the Overture (or sinfonia) to his opera "Lucio Silla." For the first symphonies were simply operatic overtures. They were in three movements, according to the style set in Italy; and it was only later, when the symphony became an independent form, that composers added a fourth movement—the minuet.

In the opera house these sinfonie avanti l'opera were usually drowned in the chatter of the audience, but in the concert hall they made a furore. In fact they were in such demand that composers began to write symphonies that weren't overtures at all, just for concert performance.

Bach was so successful and became so famous in this brilliant new style of composition that when Leopold Mozart brought his tiny son to show him off in the British capital, he took great care to be introduced to Bach. Mozart was still at the age when people took him on their knees and petted him. But Bach knew genius when he saw it. So instead of playing "Ride a cockhorse to Banbury cross" with the little fellow, he took him on his lap at the harpsichord and they played duets and improvised together as perfect equals.

Mozart loved Bach and he loved his music, so it's

easy to see why Bach's symphony sounds like Mozart. Only instead of saying that Christian Bach sounds like Mozart, we ought really to say that much of Mozart sounds like Christian Bach.

It was fourteen years before Bach and Mozart met again, this time in Paris. Bach, nearing the end of his brilliant career, was overjoyed to meet his young friend again. But for Mozart it was a tragic and disappointing visit. The one ray of light, aside from his meeting with Bach, was the success of his Paris Symphony, as it is now called. Mozart was frantic to get out of Salzburg and the petty provincial atmosphere of the city where he was born. He longed for the sort of position he should have had in one of the great European music centers. But he was not destined to find it in Paris. He had neither the talent for bootlicking, nor the ruthless, aggressive tactics that made the fortune of dozens of inferior talents in the French capital. Besides, the Parisians were much too excited by the current battle between the Gluckists and Piccinnists to pay much attention to an easygoing provincial Austrian, who had once been an enchanting infant prodigy, but was now merely a young genius.

Mozart, for his part, thought even less of the Parisians than they did of him. "I don't know whether they'll like the symphony or not," he wrote home, "and to tell the truth, I don't much care. The few intelligent Frenchmen who are there will like it. I'll guarantee that. As for the stupid ones, I can't see that it's any great misfortune not to please them. Still, I have hopes that even the asses may find something in it to delight them."

The orchestra of the Concerts Spirituels which had commissioned the symphony doesn't seem to have been much good either, according to Mozart's standards. It was overworked and the rehearsals went so badly that Mozart was scared to think what the performance would be like and decided to stay home. But toward evening he couldn't resist the temptation to hear it and he went, having first made up his mind that if it was too bad, he would go up to the orchestra, take the concertmaster's violin away from him and conduct the rest of the symphony himself. For in those days, it was the first violinist who conducted.

"Right in the middle of the first allegro," wrote Mozart, "there was a place I knew they would surely like. All the listeners were electrified and there was tremendous applause. And since I knew what an effect it would make, when I was writing it, I repeated the passage toward the end, and they began applauding all over again.

"They liked the andante too, and the final allegro even more. Since I had heard that all the final allegros here begin just like the first one, with all the instruments at once and usually in unison, I began with only two violins, playing very softly for just eight measures and a loud forte immediately afterwards. Just as I had expected, when they heard the soft beginning, the audience went: 'Sh-h-h-h . . .' Then came the forte. For them to hear the forte and clap their hands was practically the same thing. So after the symphony, out of pure joy I went right to the Palais Royal, had a nice ice, said the rosary I had promised and went home."

Mozart's Haffner Symphony was written four years later. It is called the Haffner Symphony because it was originally written as part of the wedding festivities for one of the daughters of Burgomaster Haffner of Mozart's home town, Salzburg. Mozart was twenty-six and had just gained a foothold in Vienna with his first big success, "The Abduction from the Seraglio," when his father wrote him from Salzburg, asking for a serenade for the coming festivities. "Serenade" was a very general sort of term for a series of pieces for small orchestra: music that might be played as after-dinner entertainment, or even as dinner music. Or it might be played as background music for a party or other festivity.

Mozart was so busy with other matters that he had to write the serenade in the time he could steal from his sleep, and yet he wrote it in the incredibly short space of two weeks! Even this wasn't fast enough for his father who kept writing to demand the next installment of the score. But fast as he composed, Mozart refused to do slapdash work, and he wrote that he had no intention of "just smearing down any old notes" to fill up the paper.

Six months later he asked his father to return the serenade. He needed a new symphony for a concert he was about to give, and by the simple process of discarding two of the six movements of the serenade, he intended to transform it into a symphony. That gives us some idea of how vague the difference was in those days between a small chamber ensemble and a full symphony orchestra.

When it arrived Mozart wrote back to his father: "The new Haffner Symphony was a great surprise to me. I had completely forgotten what it was like. I'm sure it will make a fine effect."

"Fine effect" is a modest description of this little masterpiece. Mozart's respect for the family of the burgomaster shows at once in the pomp of the opening theme, and the ceremoniousness of the entire first movement. The easygoing, Viennese, marchlike theme of the second movement is interspersed with whispers and laughter. Notice that in this symphony Mozart follows the model of his countrymen, and uses a fourth movement, a minuet, before the finale. The finale itself which Mozart said must go "just as fast as possible" is light footed and witty, with echoes of Mozart's comic-opera success, "The Abduction from the Seraglio."

There is both humor and pathos in this music; and how much richer it is than what he had written for Paris! A masterpiece in its own right, but a prophecy too, of the greater Mozart that was to come.

≫≮   ≫≮

MOZART: Linz Symphony (K. 425)
HAYDN: Symphony #88 (B. & H.), G major

Like so many others of Mozart's works, the Linz Symphony was written for a special occasion and at breakneck speed. Mozart had taken his bride Konstanze to stay a while with his father and sister in Salzburg. He had hoped old Leopold might be reconciled to the marriage when he had an opportunity to become acquainted with Konstanze. But that hope never quite materialized and both Mozart and his young wife were deeply disappointed when they started back to Vienna three months later.

On the way, they passed through Linz. In Linz there lived a Count Thun, the father-in-law of a distinguished pupil of Mozart's in Vienna. He asked the young couple to his palace and entertained them royally. He also asked Mozart to write a new symphony for a private concert he had planned for the fifth day after their arrival.

"When we arrived at the gates of Linz," wrote

Mozart to his father, "a servant was waiting there to conduct us to the old Count Thun's where we are still living. I can't tell you how they overwhelm us with kindness in this house. On Thursday, November 4th [1783], I am going to give a concert in the theatre, and since I haven't a single symphony with me, I am up to my ears writing away at a new one which must be finished by then."

As a matter of fact, it was finished the day before the concert, which would be unbelievable if we didn't know that Mozart thought out a great deal of his music in his head before putting a single note on paper. Once Mozart had such a composition in his mind, writing it out was a fast mechanical process, which he liked to perform in the most congenial company possible. He could sit down in a room full of dancing, playing, chattering people and, with a glass of punch handy, enjoy their fun while his pen flew across the page and a new masterpiece unfolded before his enthusiastic friends.

But in spite of the gay atmosphere in which it was written, the Linz Symphony is more than merely playful or sentimental society music of the kind that had been traditional in symphonies up to then. New emotions of manly fire and thoughtful melancholy break through the polite old forms, and they seemed very disturbing to conservatives of Mozart's day.

The opening of the first movement is majestic, almost portentous. Then there is a sudden transition to a reflective, almost pessimistic mood, with sliding, chromatic scales that lead into the mettlesome allegro of the first movement proper. This is the earliest symphony in which Mozart introduces his first movement with a slow passage of the kind Haydn had used for many years.

The second movement is unusually somber.

It is dangerous and sometimes foolish to try to read Mozart's personal experiences into his works. But it is quite possible that the disappointment of his visit to Salzburg contributed to the melancholy with which he sings in this movement. Of course his father had preserved all the outward forms of politeness, but he never really became reconciled to Konstanze. In his heart he always felt Mozart's young wife an intruder. Nor was Mozart's beloved sister ever able to feel friendly toward her, and this threw a dark shadow over the hearty understanding that brother and sister had always had. Konstanze was deeply wounded by her reception in the Mozart household and she never forgot it.

The visit had been a failure. But the symphony which came of it is still alive.

We hear echoes of Haydn in the good-humored minuet and again in the finale, which begins in a festive mood. There are joyous outbursts of the full orchestra, brilliant rushing figures in the violins, bright contrasts and catchy rhythms. But for all the gaiety with which the movement begins and ends, it touches in the middle on the pessimism of the slow movement, like the memory of a hurt that cannot quite be banished. Toward the end, the music takes heart again. The festivity returns and the symphony closes on a note of hearty affirmation.

It is interesting that Mozart's greatest symphonies were composed after he became acquainted with Joseph Haydn. And it certainly is no coincidence that Haydn produced his finest works after meeting Mozart. Mozart was twenty-five and Haydn was nearly fifty when they met in Vienna. Mozart had always admired Haydn's music, now he adored him. Haydn, too, recognized Mozart's genius. "I declare to you before God and as a man of honor," he said later to Mozart's father, "that your son is the greatest composer I know, either personally or by reputation. He has taste and beyond that the most consummate knowledge of the art of composition."

That was high praise from a man of high reputation, and it shows that Haydn stood as far above the petty jealousies of the day as Mozart did. Unfortunately the two men did not have much time to be together, for Haydn spent most of the year away from Vienna. But when he was there, he came often to Mozart's house to play quartets with him and other friends, and from this time dates one of the most fruitful friendships in the history of music. Mozart declared it was from Haydn that he learned how to write quartets. Haydn acclaimed Mozart's superiority in opera. And in their symphonies each influenced the other.

Haydn's G major Symphony, the eighty-eighth of his long career, is typical of the best he wrote during his friendship with Mozart. It has a slow introduction of the kind Mozart adopted in the Linz Symphony and the fast part of the first movement is based on a merry little theme whispered first by the strings and then shouted aloud in the brilliant voice of the full orchestra.

The wonderful song of the slow movement has a depth of emotion that is near to melancholy and it is curiously akin to the opening of the aria, "Porgi amor," from Mozart's opera, "The Marriage of Figaro," which was written in the same year. Since this sort of melody was even more typical of Mozart than it was of Haydn, and we know that Haydn particularly loved "The Marriage of Figaro," this may be one of the cases in which Haydn was enriched by his young admirer.

There is a simple, rustic minuet and the finale is a

witty little rondo with a lilting, dancing refrain that will
set you laughing for pleasure each one of the countless
times it returns.

⚜   ⚜

MOZART: Jupiter Symphony (K. 551)
HAYDN: Symphony #98 (B. & H.), B flat

We don't know who gave Mozart's great last Symphony in C major the name of Jupiter. Certainly it wasn't
Mozart, and there is little in the music to suggest the Jupiter who threw the lightning-bolts, or the thunderer or the
god of rain. On the contrary, its beauty is intensely
human.

It was written in 1788 at the time of a heartbreaking
series of letters to Mozart's merchant friend, Puchberg,
begging for one loan after another. Neither Mozart's fame
nor his artistic triumphs earned him enough to escape
what had become a crushing burden of debt, or to achieve
any real peace of mind for himself and his fragile, sickly
wife. His appeals to Puchberg are frantic, humiliating
documents and yet the Jupiter Symphony is serene as
sunshine.

Mozart did write one tragic symphony at this time,
the famous G minor, but it had nothing to do with his
practical woes. Nor on the other hand, did the pride and
strength and joy of the Jupiter mean that Puchberg had
paid the bills. Puchberg gave what he could, but it was
never enough. No, the Jupiter Symphony was simply

Mozart's healthy spiritual reaction to the desperation and tragedy of the G minor.

Its very first bars establish the fundamental mood. The heroic opening figure for full orchestra is followed by a quiet, reflective phrase for the string instruments alone. Among the other themes of the first movement, is a tune which Mozart took from a little aria he had written the year before to be inserted into a comic opera. It is an amiable, mocking scrap of melody, but what Mozart distills from it in his symphony is pure poetry. It emphasizes again the joyful character of the whole symphony, and it is interesting incidentally as one of hundreds of examples of how strongly Mozart's melodic thought was influenced by the opera buffa, the comic opera of the day. The first movement has its moments of drama and contrast too. Twice there is an outburst of dark, threatening C minor, but only for a moment, as if to call attention to the sunshine that follows.

The second movement is an andante cantabile, with the accent on the cantabile—the songful flow of melody.

The third movement is a minuet that recalls the playful serenity of parts of the first movement, and it has a droll trio in the middle that will remind you of Haydn.

The last movement is not a fugue, in spite of the fact that this symphony is sometimes spoken of as the Symphony in C major with a Fugue. The finale is as symphonic as the rest of the symphony, and Mozart uses fugal passages and contrapuntal sleight of hand only to emphasize the joyful play of forces that characterize the rest of the symphony, and to bring them together to a great climax of beauty and light and power.

One day when Haydn was quietly at work in his house in Vienna, he was confronted by a strange man. "I am Salomon from London and I have come to fetch you," he announced unceremoniously. "We will agree upon the job tomorrow."

Haydn was highly amused by the word "job." He was a man of fifty-nine, with a long and honorable career behind him, regarded all over Europe as the greatest living composer beside Mozart. He had a comfortable pension from the Esterházy family, and had no particular need of a job.

But Salomon's offer proved to be very attractive. And the job turned into the twelve greatest symphonies of Haydn's already illustrious career.

Haydn engaged himself first to write six entirely new symphonies for Mr. Salomon's concerts in London and to preside himself during their performance at the piano or harpsichord. For in those days orchestral concerts were still such an uncertain business that there had to be some instrument like the piano to fill in and reinforce the body of sound, and uphold the players if they began to falter.

The first of the Salomon concerts took place in 1791 in the famous Hanover Square Rooms. The orchestra consisted of forty players (as against nearly a hundred today) ; Haydn presided and Salomon stood as leader of the band.

Next year Haydn left England full of fame, about twelve hundred pounds to the good, and with an invitation from Salomon in his pocket to return and compose six more symphonies.

So, in February, 1794, back he came. And this time the public enthusiasm for him was even greater. We may not think of Haydn's symphonies today as calculated to rouse anyone to a frenzy, but "frenzy" is the word we hear time and time again from the people of that day, when they try to describe the effect of Haydn's music.

One enthusiastic listener wrote home: "It is truly wonderful what sublime and august thoughts this master weaves into his works. Passages often occur which make it impossible to listen without becoming excited. We are altogether carried away with admiration and forced to applaud with hand and mouth. This is especially the case with Frenchmen, of whom there are so many here that all the public places are filled with them. [London was over-flowing at this time with refugees from the Reign of Terror, which was at its height in the period of the Haydn concerts.] You know that they have great sensibility and they cannot restrain their transports, so that in the middle of the finest passages in the soft adagios, they clap their hands in loud applause, and thus mar the effect.

"In every symphony of Haydn the adagio or andante is sure to be repeated after the most vehement cries of 'encore'! The worthy Haydn conducts himself in the most modest manner. He is indeed a good-hearted, candid man, esteemed and beloved by all."

Haydn not only cut a swathe among the ladies of London, but the royal family took a great fancy to him. The Prince of Wales commanded his presence at Carlton House twenty-six times, and the king and queen asked him to spend the summer at Windsor Castle; so automatically, of course, Haydn was lionized by all the "best people" of London. That meant money. For England in that day was the same kind of gold mine for musicians that America is today.

The twelve symphonies which Haydn wrote for Salomon's concerts show Haydn's ripest mastery of symphonic form. In his youth he had pioneered in the development of the symphony and had influenced, among others, young Mozart. Then Mozart's meteorlike career had influenced him. Finally in London Haydn took up the evolution of the symphony again and brought it to the point where Beethoven was to begin with his First Symphony in 1800.

It was during his first London visit that Haydn received the news that his friend Mozart had died. Some musicians believe that the slow movement of the B flat Symphony written during that visit is a lament for the man he admired so much, for there are passages in it which could have been intended as quotations from Mozart's last symphony, the Jupiter. If they are not, then they show all the more clearly how much Haydn had absorbed from his younger colleague.

The B flat Symphony, the eighth of the Salomon or London Symphonies and the ninety-eighth of Haydn's long career, opens with a slow introduction in B flat minor. Its stark, almost tragic motive is transformed in the fast part of the movement to a bright and vigorous main theme. This whole section of the symphony has a special nobility and loftiness of utterance which sets it apart from the usual gay allegro.

We shall never know whether Haydn thought of Mozart in his slow movement, but he could not have spoken with deeper or stronger feeling if he had.

In the minuet Haydn's high humor returns. And the finale is a rondo full of laughter, cracking jokes right and left, and telling us, in Haydn's inimitable way, that all's well with the world again.

HAYDN: Symphony #104 (B. & H.), D major
BEETHOVEN: Symphony #1, C major

Haydn was sixty-three when he took leave of London with a farewell concert for his own benefit. The symphony he chose for this program was his 104th in D, the last of the London series and the last of his career. The performance took place on May 4, 1795. "The hall was filled with a picked audience," wrote Haydn in his diary. "The whole company was delighted and so was I. I took in this evening 4000 gulden. One can make as much as this only in England."

Haydn had been happy and successful as a liveried servant at the Esterházy castle in Hungary. In London he was the honored guest of the English royal family and the idol of English concert audiences. He took this too in his stride, appreciated it for what it was worth, no more and no less. Haydn was able to take whatever his place might be in the society of his day without feeling hampered in his independence. And the same was true of his music. We seldom feel there is anything revolutionary about Haydn; yet he experimented with symphonic form as freely as anyone before or after. Nothing could be further from fact than the popular picture of Papa Haydn as a cheerful, periwigged conventionalist, whose emotions never ran any deeper than what Berlioz called "the innocent joys of the fireside and the pot-au-feu."

The introduction alone to Haydn's last symphony gives the lie to that phrase, for it is solemn, almost tragic. The body of the first movement is built almost entirely on its graceful, lively opening theme.

The variations of the slow movement are freely strung together, ending in a codetta of great depth and simplicity. The energetic minuet is followed by one of the richest of Haydn's finales. His themes develop as ingeniously as many of Brahms, who was evidently influenced by this symphony. Brilliant and imaginative, there isn't a page of it you could foretell by rule of thumb. The surprises continue up to the sudden shift of rhythm in the final cadence.

Five years later, Beethoven, who had had a few lessons from Haydn, picked up the development of the symphony where his master had laid it down. There are few more amusing comparisons in music than you can make between Haydn's last and Beethoven's First Symphony. Of the two, Beethoven, the future revolutionist, seems more bound by tradition. Only under the surface do you sense the lurking power and virility, the breadth and sweep that distinguish him from Haydn.

This First Symphony is like Beethoven himself at the time he was writing it. He was then a very different man from what he later became. Instead of the uncouth giant, whose eccentric manners, slovenly dress, unshaven face and domineering conduct were tolerated because of his genius, he was a man with pretentions to elegance, to the world of high society which of course meant conservative society.

He already had the self-assurance which characterized him the rest of his life but he was also rather a man of the world. His popularity as a piano soloist was at its height and his circle of aristocratic friends, patrons and pupils opened wide to him the doors of the most influential houses in Vienna. He was financially secure since one of the great Austrian aristocrats, Prince Lichnowsky, had assured him support as long as he was without an official position worthy of his talents. He had more commissions than he could fill and an excellent income from his compositions. In these happy circumstances he presented his First Symphony at a concert for his own benefit in the Austrian National Court Theatre on April 2, 1800.

Just as Beethoven himself was conforming for the time being to the social patterns of his surroundings, so his symphony follows the established symphonic patterns of the day. There is a slow introduction à la Haydn, with ambiguous shifting harmonies, before the first movement settles down to its quiet, purposeful first theme. This bustles along with a good deal of simple humor, is followed by a simple melodic second theme, and the two are worked out quite according to the rules of the game.

The graceful slow movement is balanced against a real scherzo which Beethoven calls by the older, conventional name of a minuet. But it moves faster, with more drive than the minuets of Mozart and Haydn.

The last movement begins with an amusing trick. A simple scale creeps slowly upward through the violins, reaching one note further with each repetition, until in a sudden flurry of impatience it rushes ahead into the dancelike theme of the finale. The wit and laughter that follow are as infectious as anything Haydn ever wrote.

This First Symphony is not only in a rather light and comic vein; it shows all possible deference to Mozart and Haydn in form and style. Yet it is almost like a masquerade. It wears an eighteenth-century pigtail, it speaks the courtly language and behaves with the restraint expected of a well-bred symphony. But not for a minute did it deceive Beethoven's contemporaries. The pedants smelled a revolutionist and they were rightly alarmed. Their indignation shows how frightened they were.

One called it "the confused explosions of the outrageous effrontery of a young man." And ten years later a Parisian musician could still write that the "astonishing success" of this symphony was "a danger to the musical art." "It is believed," he added, "that a prodigal use of the most barbarous dissonances and a noisy use of all the instruments will make an effect. Alas, the ear is only stabbed; there is no appeal to the heart."

III. *Music and Politics*

"REVOLUTION may be contained within the four walls of a symphony," wrote Robert Schumann, "and the police be none the wiser." Or it can be contained within a tone poem. Even the police knew this when they forbade performances of Sibelius' "Finlandia" at the time Finland was agitating for independence from tsarist Russia. It may be contained in an opera too, as Verdi proved, to the joy of his Italian countrymen and the constant anxiety of the Austrian police. Verdi's very name came to be a hidden battlecry in the struggle for Italian independence. "Viva VERDI" scrawled on streets and doorways signified "Viva *V*ittorio *E*manuele, *R*e *D'I*talia"—"Long Live Victor Emmanuel, King of Italy"—king of the free Italy of their dreams.

But composers have not been merely revolutionists.

Lully glorified Louis XIV and the absolutist pomp of Versailles, Beethoven hymned the dawn of democracy, and Shostakovitch exalts the defense of Leningrad. "Music," claims Shostakovitch, "cannot help having a political basis —an idea the bourgeoisie are slow to comprehend. There can be no music without ideology. . . . Good music lifts and heartens, and lightens people for work and effort. It may be tragic but it must be strong. It is no longer an end in itself, but a vital weapon in the struggle."

BEETHOVEN: Overture to "Egmont"
Symphony #5, C minor

No one, it seems to me, could listen to the triumphant exaltation of the intensely dramatic overture to "Egmont" without feeling that it is a mighty paean of victory. It is just that. The finale of the overture is identical with the music which ends the drama. After Goethe has sent his hero to death at the hands of tyrants, after he has told us that Egmont's death is the spark that will fire the Netherlands to desperate revolt and a battle that will restore their lost freedom, after the eloquence of a great poet has said all that words can say, he calls on music, and asks literally for a "symphony of victory" to say what is beyond the power of words.

No one in the world could have been better fitted to fulfill Goethe's request than Beethoven, whose music was a conscious embodiment of Goethe's ideal of freedom and heroism. And one reason why this overture has become one of the enduring masterpieces of music is that the ideas behind it—freedom and the willingness to die for it—did not exist only in Goethe's drama. Like most great plays, "Egmont" is a parable, and the struggle of the Dutch against the Spanish was a story of oppression repeating itself in Beethoven's time as surely as it is being repeated in Europe today.

When I hear this music, I sometimes wonder about our glib saying that art and politics should not be mixed.

57

It seems to me that only a person who has an extremely shallow view of art, who thinks of it only as an escape from life, could believe that art and politics should be kept apart. Beethoven obviously didn't think so, nor did Goethe, nor Dante, nor do the finest minds among our living artists. To these people art never has been an escape from life, but rather an intensification of life.

Now it so happens that the overwhelming issues of Beethoven's day have become again the issues which every single one of us is forced to face in our own time—only that we have to face them in more violent form, in infinitely more dangerous form, and we have to face them much more quickly. We have suddenly been wrenched out of a comfortable life and forced to risk our lives in an ancient battle which we sweetly imagined had been settled long ago.

And that is why the music of that battle, the symbols that Beethoven used, move us more deeply now than they may have before, say, December 7, 1941, or the rape of Norway or France. It is all happening over again. Suddenly we realize that in the deepest sense Beethoven was talking about us. Or, as the Latin line has it: "De te fabula narratur"—"Of thee the tale is told."

The same holds true of Beethoven's Fifth Symphony. Of course, it's just an accident that the rhythm of the letter V for Victory, in Morse code, should happen to be the rhythm of the chief motive of the Fifth Symphony. But the choice of that motive as the musical banner of the victory campaign had a better justification than that. The music itself speaks with overwhelming eloquence of everything the V campaign stands for.

You remember the story that Beethoven said of that first motive: "Thus fate knocks on the door." If he didn't

actually say those words, he might well have said something similar, for there is obviously a strong symbolic
meaning in those first four aggressive notes, and in the way
they not only dominate the whole first movement, but
come back again and again at the most dramatic moments of the whole symphony.

The first movement is one savage onslaught of
rhythm, the rhythm of the motive of fate, sometimes in a
whisper, sometimes in a roar, sometimes as an ominous
throbbing in the depths of the orchestra. Even the relatively lyric second theme is built on it, and it brings the
movement to a close with one final shout of defiance.

The second movement is a series of variations on two
alternating, contrasting themes. The first, which is sung
in A flat major by the violas and cellos, is a smooth-flow-
ing melody of feminine grace and charm. The second,
square-shouldered and masculine, sounds in a blazing C
major.

The third movement has nothing of the traditional
dance form about it except, perhaps, for the rather ele-
phantine gambols of the double basses in the middle part.
But even that sounds more like an earthquake than a
dance. The beginning and end are shadowy and haunted,
with an atmosphere of terror that has seldom been
equaled in music. In the midst of the suspense the motive
of fate sounds softly, in slightly altered form. It is answered by whispered, plucking sounds of the string instruments, and the whole orchestra falls back, as if exhausted,
onto a softly sustained chord of uncertain tonality. The
music seems in a state of suspended animation except for
one muffled drum that throbs underneath it like a slow,
persistent heartbeat—beating in the rhythm of the motive
of fate. The suspense grows with the challenge of that

rhythm, fragments of the scherzo theme weave through the orchestra, the uncertain harmonies shift more and more towards the C major, which you feel is waiting there, like the sun to burst out of the clouds. Just at the moment when the suspense seems absolutely unbearable the orchestra pulls itself together with a sudden tremendous crescendo and strides forth into the light with the magnificently heroic theme of the last movement. This finale has a surge and drive, and its themes are broad and massive and blunt, like Beethoven himself. There are passing reminders of the scherzo, but only enough to point out that the terrors of the scherzo have been banished. The final presto and the exultant C major chords at the end are confident and powerful and shining with the promise of victory.

Haydn: Harpsichord Concerto, D major
Beethoven: Piano Concerto #5, E flat. Emperor

Having survived half a dozen governments and as many revolutions, that cynical old diplomat, Talleyrand, once declared in a burst of nostalgia that no one who had not been alive before 1789 would ever know the true joy of living. That world before the fall of the Bastille, safe, charming and happy for its privileged few, the world for which Talleyrand sighed, is embodied in the D major Harpsichord Concerto of Joseph Haydn, just as the turbulent grandeur of a later day is reflected in Beethoven's Emperor Concerto.

At the time he wrote his concerto Haydn was still a sort of glorified domestic servant in the household of the Hungarian Prince Esterházy. He wore livery just like any butler or footman, but he didn't mind, because that was the generally accepted position of musicians in Haydn's world, and because livery or no livery, he was admired as an artist and loved as a man.

Prince Esterházy and consequently his staff, including Haydn, spent most of the year at his splendid summer residence, Esterház. Originally Esterház had been just a small hunting lodge way off by itself in the Hungarian countryside, but the family had transformed it, at a cost of seven million gulden, into a summer palace which à French traveler declared had "no place but Versailles to compare in magnificence."

Not only was the palace surrounded by flower gardens, artificial grove, deer park, hothouses, elaborately furnished summerhouses, grottoes, hermitages and temples, there were also two beautifully ornamented little theatres for private performances of opera, drama, marionette shows and concerts of orchestral and chamber music. The orchestra, part of the prince's retinue, was under Haydn's regular direction. But Haydn did not compose and conduct for the prince alone. A constant stream of cultivated aristocrats and royalty from all over Europe poured through the gates of Esterház to enjoy both its fabulous hospitality and the music for which Haydn had made it famous.

"My prince was always satisfied with my works," said Haydn. "I not only had the encouragement of constant approval, but as conductor of an orchestra, I could make experiments, observe what produced an effect and what weakened it, and was thus in a position to improve, alter, make additions or omissions, and be as bold as I pleased. I was cut off from the world, there was no one to confuse or torment me, and I was forced to become original."

This particular concerto was·composed toward the end of Haydn's service at Esterház, around 1784. It is in the usual three movements: fast, slow and fast. In the first, the main theme is introduced by the orchestra, then repeated by the harpsichord alone, and finally developed in a lively dialogue between soloist and orchestra. The harpsichord is at somewhat of a disadvantage in the slow movement because it has no sustained, singing tone like the piano. But it makes up for that lack by dressing up the slow melody in an enchanting profusion of ornament: grace notes, trills, scale passages and so on. The finale is a rondo "all'ungarese" with a recurring theme in the Hungarian manner. It is brilliant, witty and full of such high spirits that you know the music at Esterház was fun.

Twenty-five years later when Beethoven wrote his Emperor Concerto, Haydn's world was crumbling to pieces under the cannon of Napoleon Bonaparte. Vienna was besieged. The house where Beethoven lodged was built on the city walls, so when the noise got too loud, he would take refuge in the cellar of his brother Karl's house and cover his head with pillows—not out of cowardice, but to protect his ears and save what little hearing he had left. "What a wild, disturbing life around me," he wrote, "nothing but drums, cannon, men and misery of all sorts."

The French took Vienna. Beethoven was furious and defiant. "If I were a general and knew as much about strategy as I know about counterpoint, I'd give you fellows something to think about," he cried, doubling his fist at the back of a French officer in the street. Once before,

when Beethoven was visiting his friend, Prince Lichnowsky, at his country estate, there had been French officers
quartered in the house. His host had asked him to play
for the foreigners, but Beethoven would have no truck
with them; and when he was jokingly threatened with
being locked up in the house till he did play, there was a
terrible scene. He stole away in a towering rage, took the
night post back to Vienna, and when he got home he was
still so angry he smashed a bust of the prince—an amusing contrast to Haydn's treatment of princely patrons.

Beethoven's first great successes in Vienna he had
won as a pianist playing his own works. He had taken the
solo part in the first performances of all four piano concertos so far. But now he was too deaf to play. Perhaps
that is the reason that his Fifth Concerto, the Emperor, is
also his last.

When it had its première (with Carl Czerny as soloist) the French were still in Vienna and there is a story
that it was a French officer in the audience who acclaimed
it as "an emperor among concertos." Be that as it may,
the name has stuck and it still seems appropriate to the
majesty and power of the music.

The first movement begins with a decisive chord of
the full orchestra, and the piano enters unconventionally
with a sweeping cadenza—the kind of thing customarily
reserved for the close of a movement. There are two more
such chords, the piano continuing its rhapsodic outburst
after each, then the orchestra spreads before us the various themes of this movement. Now they are taken up by
the piano alone and together with other instruments.
They are developed stormily, restated and brought back
again for a triumphant coda which replaces the conventional cadenza.

The slow movement is romantic, personal and deeply thoughtful. The melody is sung mostly by the orchestra while the piano surrounds it with garlands of graceful figuration. Toward the end there are hints of the principal theme of the finale, which follows without pause, in a sudden joyous outburst. It is a rondo with a jaunty, vigorous refrain almost like a folk dance. There is a wealth of contrasting episodes including a sort of hunting-call figure for the horns. The reckless drive of the movement appears to subside toward the end with a long series of descending chords for the piano, while underneath the timpani softly sustain the rhythm of the theme. But the whole is rounded off with one more burst of the exuberant refrain.

SIBELIUS: "Finlandia"
Symphony #2, D major

One reason the Finnish people worship Sibelius is that they associate him with the winning of their independence. At the end of the last century when Sibelius was young, Finland was a part of Russia, but a very restless and unhappy part. For more than eight hundred years the Finns had been under the political domination of first Sweden and then the tsars. But spiritually and culturally the Finns had always been independent, and now, following a series of tsarist decrees to curb Finnish liberties, free speech, the right of assembly and the bit of political representation they enjoyed, the old longing for complete independence again burst into flame.

Whether a new national consciousness strengthened the feeling for Finnish culture, or the romantic interest in Finland's past stimulated the national consciousness would be hard to say. Probably it worked both ways. At any rate, in the closing years of the nineteenth century when Sibelius returned to his native land, Finnish art, folk music, the Finnish language itself and the Finnish legends of the Kalevala were experiencing a great renaissance. Sibelius was immediately caught up in an enthusiastic group of patriotic young writers, painters, poets, musicians, men of the theatre, students and critics, who had rediscovered their ancient Finnish heritage. And for many years his music showed their influence.

In the years around 1900 one tone poem of his used to excite the Finns to such demonstrations that the police forbade performances under its patriotic title of "Finlandia." Yet "Finlandia" is said to have contributed more than a thousand pamphlets to the cause of Finnish liberation. There is a tragic undertone to this music, but not a note of resignation. It opens in sullen anger and menace. After a prayerful, hymnlike interruption, which has become popular in this country in choral arrangements, the agitation grows to a blazing defiant climax.

But we should bear in mind that "Finlandia" refers to emotions of four decades ago, and does not refer to contemporary political events. In later years, Sibelius has withdrawn further and further into the field of so-called absolute music, which has no concrete program or message at all, except the impact of its own emotion. It is as if the dream were much more capable of firing a composer's imagination than the fulfillment, which being reality, can never have the purity and idealism of that first vision.

It is interesting that a somewhat similar thing happened to the other two great musical prophets of national unity and independence: Wagner and Verdi. Wagner's most "national" operas were written when German unity was a far-off dream and a still unsullied ideal. After German unity was achieved the reality of the thing lost its inspiration for Wagner, and the only other opera he produced was the deeply religious "Parsifal."

Verdi, too, had sung all his life with passionate conviction of the liberation and unification of Italy, but that achievement was disappointing to him also. Not of course the unity and independence itself, but the way in which it was used. Verdi's feeling was one of humiliation and often even of disgust. He turned away from the subjects of his youth and produced only two more great masterpieces, both based on Shakespeare: the tragedy of "Otello" and the comedy of "Falstaff."

If politics were the only reason why the Finns feel the way they do about Sibelius, he might have been forgotten in the kaleidoscope of post-war developments. But there are deeper reasons. For example, his uncanny musical intuition has led him to write melodies so much like Finnish folk music that some commentators simply assumed they were folk songs. Yet we have Sibelius' own word for it that he has never used a folk tune in any of his big orchestral works. Actually, it was not until after he was an established figure in the field of European music that Sibelius first heard, on a visit to Karelia, the ancient Finnish melodies which are still sung to the runes of the great national epic, the Kalevala. It was only then that he realized with astonishment and delight how near his own music came to the thousand-year-old musical speech of his country-men.

Sibelius' Second Symphony belongs to the same period as "Finlandia." The same musical intuition is at work here and the same political feelings. In Finland the Second Symphony is accepted as a symphonic drama of liberation. According to Georg Schneevoight, an intimate friend of Sibelius, the first movement was intended to depict the quiet, pastoral life of the Finns. The second movement, which is marked lugubre, is a lament, charged with patriotic feeling. The scherzo, which is like a bleak, snow-scurried landscape, portrays the awakening of national feeling. And at the end of this agitated scherzo, a long crescendo leads without pause into the fourth movement. This finale is a mighty chant of triumph, the dream of the fatherland which has burst its shackles. It is bold, spacious music of monumental simplicity. The simple, elemental theme of the finale climbs slowly and inexorably from the bottom of the orchestra to a climax of staggering power.

⚶ ⚶

RIMSKY-KORSAKOFF: Coq d'Or Suite
"Dubinushka"
SHOSTAKOVITCH: Symphony #1

Today when we see the amusing pageantry of Rimsky-Korsakoff's opera, "The Golden Cockerel," or when we hear its exotic, brilliant music, most of us think of it simply as a charming legendary fantasy—a sort of musical fairy tale, and nothing more. It is hard to imagine that this sort of thing once played a political role in Russian life, just as does the music of Shostakovitch. But it did.

During the revolutionary disturbances in Russia in 1905, Rimsky-Korsakoff had been openly sympathetic with the unruly students who caused much of the trouble. As a result the performance of one of his operas was postponed, and he himself was dismissed from the St. Petersburg Conservatory, where he had been a popular professor. Immediately he became a sort of martyr-hero of liberal Russians and he was flooded with expressions of sympathy in letters and in speeches and by the visits of deputations. Rimsky stood his ground and replied to his persecutors by arranging the revolutionary song, "Dubinushka," as a short orchestral piece. The government answered back by forbidding all performances of his works in Petersburg and various smaller cities for two months.

Later, Rimsky-Korsakoff was reinstated at the conservatory, but that by no means put an end to the violent disagreements between him and his superiors, and "The Golden Cockerel," which he composed in 1907, was a satire on the stupidity of the autocratic Russian government. It has even been said that the opera was intended to poke fun at the conduct of the Russo-Japanese War in which the Russians got a terrible trouncing. In any case, the government had its revenge by banning "The Golden Cockerel" until two years after Rimsky-Korsakoff's death.

Dimitri Shostakovitch was born just about the time that Rimsky-Korsakoff started work on "The Golden Cockerel." He was only eleven when the government that caused Rimsky so much annoyance collapsed in Russia, so that most of his education and upbringing have taken place under the Soviet regime.

He was born too late to be a pupil of Rimsky-Korsa-koff, but he studied at the same conservatory—now called the Leningrad Conservatory—where the elder master had taught, and his First Symphony was composed as his graduation piece. He was only nineteen at the time and the symphony was performed in the same year, 1926, by the Leningrad Philharmonic with great success. It quickly spread to the other music centers of the world and it has remained his most popular symphony.

The Russians were swift to recognize that Shostako-vitch was the most gifted of their younger composers and he became their official composer laureate, so to speak. Shostakovitch has composed greater music since then, par-ticularly in his Fifth Symphony, and his Seventh Sym-phony, written during the siege of Leningrad, has been given far wider publicity. But this First Symphony has a freshness and spontaneity that make it particularly ap-pealing.

There is the jaunty little theme of the first move-ment, for example, which scampers along in the clarinet, like a sort of cross between a quick march tune and a bit of old-fashioned ragtime. This theme is particularly inter-esting because it returns later in a much slower version as a subject of the third movement, and again, in another transformation, in the finale. The first movement really has three themes: the angular, grotesque figure announced by the trumpet at the very beginning; then the clarinet theme we have just spoken of; and finally a lovely lyric phrase played by the flute. These themes are worked out pretty much according to the classical symphonic tradi-tion. As a matter of fact, the whole symphony and the orchestra Shostakovitch uses are really quite conserva-tive, though his style and harmonies are modern.

The second movement is a perky little scherzo, with

a theme that is full of quicksilver and mocking laughter. It has a slow and rather melancholy middle section, which might have been labeled religioso, if it hadn't been composed in Soviet Russia.

The third movement, you remember, is based on one of the themes of the first, which is sung here much more slowly and mournfully by a solo oboe against an accompaniment of strings. Then the strings themselves take up the melody which becomes more and more impassioned and rises to a great climax against a strong countermelody in the brass.

A dramatic roll of the drums opens the slow introduction to the finale. The finale itself is fast with agitated whirling figures, building toward the climax with its famous passage for the kettledrums alone. There are interesting transformations of the various themes and the closing measures are frantic and brilliant with a great fanfare of the brass instruments.

PROKOFIEFF: Classical Symphony
SHOSTAKOVITCH: Symphony #5

The word classical tells us only part of the spirit in which Prokofieff wrote this witty little symphony way back in 1916 and 1917. Of course, the classicism to which he refers had flourished more than a century earlier, and even if he had wished to do so, it could hardly have been revived in the Russia of World War I. But Prokofieff wasn't interested in reviving. Long before neo-classicism became a fad in western Europe, he made this half-mocking, half-affectionate bow to an age he deeply revered.

He limited himself precisely to the orchestra of Mozart and Haydn, and condensed the four movements of his Classical Symphony to thirteen minutes. There is a glittering technique in his instrumentation; the thematic development is dextrous, but not pedantic. It has been said that Prokofieff's idea was to catch the spirit of Mozart and to put down what Mozart might put into his scores had he been alive in 1917.

Twenty years later, when Shostakovitch produced his Fifth Symphony, the musical climate of Russia had changed. There was no more escape into a polite eighteenth century. Music was expected to be a political force.

"In the western world," wrote a Soviet critic, Gregori Schneerson, "the object of the avant-garde is presumably the overthrow of old artistic foundations, the breaking out of 'new paths,' however meaningless, at any cost. For us in the Soviet however, the avant-garde is held to express progressive ideas only when it talks to the people in a new, powerful and intelligible language. The demands of the wide masses of people, their artistic tastes, grow from day to day. The 'advanced' composer is therefore one who plunges into the social currents swirling about him and, with his creative work, serves the progress of mankind."

There is not much use our delving too deeply into the political background of Shostakovitch's Fifth Symphony. Like so many other things in Russia, it is complicated and enigmatic to the outsider. According to mysterious Soviet spokesmen, young Shostakovitch had fallen to imitating the corrupt and effete bourgeois music of the western world. For this the newspaper, *Pravda,* gave him a sound beating, and dubbed his work "un-Soviet, unwholesome, cheap, eccentric, tuneless and [of all things] leftist." He was advised to return to an art which would appeal to the masses.

Apparently Shostakovitch took the hint. All the first performances of his new Fifth Symphony, written to celebrate the twentieth anniversary of the October Revolution, were sold out far in advance; newspapers outdid each other in praise. Probably we shall never know what, if anything, Shostakovitch did to change his musical style; whether he gave in to pressure, whether he had a real change of heart, or whether he just kept on composing and let nature take its course.

Without wishing to compromise Shostakovitch's position as a Soviet artist, we can put down his Fifth Symphony as a descendant of the great line of symphonic rhapsodies that runs from Berlioz through Liszt, Strauss and Mahler. Like Strauss, Shostakovitch uses many themes which are banal and flat enough in themselves, and depends on his dazzling virtuosity in orchestrating them, or on sheer temperament to carry him through.

"The first movement," asserts Schneerson, "unfolds the philosophic concept of the work, the growth of the artist's personality with the revolutionary events of our time." But that is Schneerson, not the composer speaking.

The symphony opens with a bold, uncompromising theme and the unfamiliar listener may need several moments before the logic and direction of the music becomes clear. Shostakovitch is in no hurry to get started, and the heart of the movement lies deep in the development, where clashing harmonies and rhythms bring the themes to their emotional climax.

Ideas come so fast to Shostakovitch that you can't call it mere fertility—it is a volcanic eruption of ideas.

But like all volcanoes, this one is unselective, and along with the pure fire of inspiration it casts up a great deal of slag and ashes. Alongside passages of true grandeur and power, there are others of brassy bombast that are just embarrassing. The dramatic and the theatrical are all mixed up together. Even at a second or third hearing, it isn't always easy to tell the gilt from the gold; the musical diamonds from paste.

The scherzo is short and brutal, but it provides an indispensable contrast to the beautiful slow movement that follows.

The third is perhaps the most stirring of all four movements—the most original, the most sincere, and the most effective as well. Shostakovitch shows his greatest strength just where so many other modern composers prove weakest: in melody. This great brooding song could not have been put together by a mere craftsman, however sleek and skilled. It seems to grow out of itself. The melody arches grandly and it reaches an almost unbearable pitch of intensity before subsiding back into the deep calm of the beginning.

The first and last movements may have their derivative moments, but they detract little from the heroic stature of the work as a whole. Shostakovitch emerges as one of the few vital symphonists of our day. And his Fifth Symphony, already popular in our concert halls, may yet live to be called a twentieth-century classic.

IV. *Concertos and Virtuosos*

I N THE CONCERTO, symphonic music becomes a highly
personal affair. Not only will a virtuoso of mettle tend
to dominate interpretations with his own characteristic
feeling for color, architecture and drama—many composers, far from finding this an evil, have written concertos
with a particular virtuoso in mind. And if, as was often
the case, the composer and the performer he had in mind
were one and the same person, then we catch our symphonic artist in a peculiarly self-revealing mood. His music may reflect his own particular style of performance, as
was probably true in the concertos of Mozart and Bee-
,thoven, or it may reflect the way he aspired to play, as
in the great B flat Piano Concerto of Brahms. The latter
work, by the way, in spite of the extreme difficulty and
brilliance of its solo part, has been called a symphony

with piano obbligato, and the same might be said of many more modern concertos. But the personal element is too deeply rooted in the solo concerto for it ever to disappear. Just as we still profit from the fact that Shakespeare and Molière were once actors, so we must be thankful that Mozart and Beethoven were among the great virtuoso performers of their day.

BACH: Harpsichord Concerto, D minor
MOZART: Violin Concerto, D major (K. 218)

In his own day, Bach was best known as an incomparable organ and harpsichord player. His greatness as a composer was almost unknown except to little local groups of admirers at the court or in the congregations where he served. Most of his music was written for immediate performance by himself or under his own direction, and it was doubtless for his own use that he arranged the famous D minor Harpsichord Concerto.

This work has a curious history. It began as a violin concerto, but the original was lost. Since very little of Bach's music was published during his lifetime, and most of his works were written for special occasions, it seemed only sensible when he had a good idea to use it several times. Like many other composers of the day, Bach was constantly rearranging his own and other people's compositions for different combinations of instruments or even instruments and voices. And in this D minor Concerto he knew he had a good idea.

He liked it so much that he not only turned it into a harpsichord concerto, he also used it in a church cantata for voices and orchestra. The cantata begins with the words: "We must pass through much tribulation into the kingdom of God." Bach rearranged the first movement of his concerto as a great instrumental overture. He gave the violin part to the organ an octave lower, added three oboes to his orchestra and behold: he had an eloquent musical picture of the tribulations of the faithful in their struggle for the kingdom of God.

Then comes one of the most amazing stunts in the history of music. Or it would be a stunt, if Bach had done it just to show how clever he could be. The slow movement of the concerto is rearranged in the same way as the first movement, but the whole thing is used here merely as the accompaniment for a completely new and independent four-part chorus! The miracle is that the voice parts sound completely fresh and spontaneous, and the concerto fits in so well you would never dream it had been composed as anything but an accompaniment to this particular chorus. There have been plenty of composers who could perform polyphonic tricks like this, and even harder ones. But most of them are so preoccupied with technical artifice that they forget the music. With Bach, the chorus grows out of the concerto as naturally and beautifully as the branches of a tree spring from the trunk.

Wolfgang Amadeus Mozart belonged to a generation which had revolted against the complicated art of Bach and his contemporaries. Simplicity and good taste were the catchwords of this new school. But one thing Mozart did have in common with his great predecessor: they both started their careers as virtuosos. Mozart was only seven when he amazed his father and two friends with his uncanny gift for the violin. One of the men who was present, a trumpeter from the orchestra of the Archbishop of Salzburg told the story many years later to Mozart's sister.

"Just after you returned from Vienna, where Wolfgang had been presented with a small-sized violin, our good fiddler, the late Herr Wentzel, who was learning to compose, came to your father with six trios that he had written and asked for his opinion on them.

"We played the trios. Papa played the bass part on the viola, Wentzel played the first violin and I was to play the second violin. Little Wolfgang asked to be allowed to play the second violin, but Papa turned down his silly request, because he had never had the least instruction in playing the violin, and Papa thought he would be incapable of doing anything at all. Wolfgang said: 'But you don't really have to be taught, to know how to play the second violin.' And when Papa insisted that he leave the room immediately and stop bothering us, Wolfgang began to cry bitterly and tumbled away with his little violin. I begged them to let him play along with me, and at last Papa said: 'Well, you may play your fiddle with Herr Schachtner, but you must play so softly we can't hear you, or else you'll have to go away.' It was done, and Wolfgang fiddled along with me. To my astonishment, I soon noticed that I was completely superfluous. I put away my violin quietly and glanced at your father. Tears of admiration and happiness were streaming down his face. And thus Wolfgang played through all six trios. When we were through, our applause made him so bold that he maintained he could even play the first violin part. So we tried him out, for the fun of it, and nearly died with laughter, when he actually did play it, and in spite of a whole mass of mistakes and irregularities, got through it without once breaking down."

That was how, at the age of seven, Mozart began his short but brilliant career as a violin virtuoso. Later on that year, when the family went on tour again, little Wolfgang was already appearing as violin soloist. Everywhere he went, he listened and learned. In Italy he discovered more about violin technique. In France he picked up brilliance of style, and in Vienna he heard Austrian melodies that echo through all five of the concertos he wrote when he was nineteen. As he grew older, Mozart began to lose interest in his own violin playing, perhaps because in Salzburg one of his official jobs was to play in the orchestra of the archbishop, whom he thoroughly detested. His father thought it was because he had no real confidence in his own abilities, which must have been tremendous.

"You don't realize yourself," he wrote him once, "how well you play the violin when you are on your mettle and play with confidence, spirit and emotion—as if you were the greatest violinist in all Europe."

Mozart's D major Violin Concerto is one of five that he composed for himself during the summer of 1775. They were neither Austrian nor German nor French nor Italian in style, but a combination of all the styles he had absorbed during his travels. They were a musical mirror of all rococo Europe: graceful, aristocratic, humorous and wonderfully melodious. They are not by any means the greatest music he produced, but these outpourings of youthful genius have such an irresistible appeal that it is safe to say they will be heard as long as there are violinists to play them.

The concerto opens with a stock figure which Mozart borrowed from the Neapolitan opera. But though he begins with a conventional theme, the richness and variety of effects he draws from the violin are surprisingly original. The slow movement is more serious in its manner, but no less witty in detail. The finale is a rondo with a wistful, questioning refrain that alternates with more vivacious episodes, by turns skittish, grave and masterful. The mastery and inspiration of the whole are astonishing in a nineteen-year-old boy, even in a nineteen-year-old genius.

Two years later Mozart left Salzburg for a long trip. While he was away his father wrote him: "Always on my way home a feeling of melancholy steals over me. And as I approach our house I seem to hear you still—playing the violin."

⊱⊰   ⊱⊰

MOZART: Piano Concerto, A major (K. 488)
BEETHOVEN: Piano Concerto #4, G major

Strong emotion, so important to us in a great work of art, was considered rather bad taste by the world in which Mozart was brought up. Music in those days was written for polite entertainment in which any too personal griefs or joys would have been out of place. Music was a commodity produced for immediate consumption by a certain definite public and geared to that public's taste and imagination. To these people, the nineteenth-century romantic conception of a composer writing only for himself or for an abstract posterity would have been quite incomprehensible.

But as Mozart grew older his personal feelings began to struggle more and more for expression. And at the same time other people became increasingly interested in the individual artist and his personal emotions.

Jean-Jacques Rousseau with his famous "Confessions" had already pointed the way in literature which, as usual, was far ahead of music. The time hadn't come yet when a musician could put his personal confessions into music, or write a symphony exclusively about himself, as Berlioz did later, when he composed a whole Fantastic Symphony about his own love affair. But it was already on the way.

And Mozart's piano concertos are the perfect compromise between the delightful, impersonal amusement of rococo society music, and the romantic, subjective emotions which became so eloquent in the music of Schubert and Schumann.

Mozart's A major Piano Concerto, number 488 in the Köchel listing of his works, was written in the single month of March, 1786. For all its apparent simplicity and friendly nods to polite convention, it succeeds in telling us a lot about Mozart personally. "Give me the best piano, or clavier in Europe," he once said, "and at the same time listeners who understand nothing . . . who don't understand with me what I play, and all my joy is gone."

The concerto begins quite regularly with the orchestra announcing a large group of lively, graceful themes, which are later taken up and developed along with new material by piano and orchestra together. It is brilliant, happy music and shows us the sunniest side of Mozart's nature.

The slow movement is in the relative key of F sharp minor and a mood of the most touching melancholy. Notice how beautifully the piano sings; how all through the music Mozart has the human voice in mind, that most personal of all instruments; how personally and directly the keyboard sings to you. Listen to the exquisite ornamentation of the song, which never disturbs the simple flow of melody. Listen also, to the wonderful, silvery coloring of the orchestra, how the flutes and other wind instruments mingle with the tone of the piano. It is one of Mozart's loveliest slow movements.

The finale is a rondo of endless contrast, wit, melody and rejoicing.

Within a year after he had finished this concerto Mozart received a visit from an awkward sixteen-year-old boy who had come all the way from Bonn on the Rhine. The boy extemporized for him, but noticed that Mozart, thinking he had played a prepared piece, was not particularly impressed. So he begged Mozart to give him a theme of his own to improvise upon. The result was so extraordinary that Mozart slipped out of the room and whispered to some friends who were standing by: "Keep your eyes on that fellow. One day he will give the world something to talk about."

The boy's name was Ludwig van Beethoven. Mozart gave him some lessons during that short visit to Vienna and probably would have continued them had he been alive when Beethoven came back to stay. And for the rest of his life Beethoven cherished what he had learned from Mozart and his works.

Like Mozart, Beethoven wrote most of his piano concertos to be played by himself, and he made his first big success in Vienna as soloist in his own works. His early piano concertos were extremely Mozartean and even in his great G major Concerto, the Fourth, we still hear echoes of Mozart, transfigured with the stress and drama of his own personality.

From Beethoven's sketchbooks we know that the serene motive at the beginning of this concerto grew out of the same thought which supplied the tempestuous opening of his Fifth Symphony—the motive which has been called fate knocking on the door. But how gentle and ingratiating it sounds here, and how it can sing! One graceful phrase chases another across these melodious opening pages, and in spite of the stormy grandeur with which they are all developed—the sweeping arpeggios, the brilliant scales and sudden dynamic contrasts—it is supremely lyrical music from beginning to end.

The romantic dialogue of the second movement was once compared by Franz Liszt to Orpheus taming the wild beasts. Beethoven's orchestra may not be exactly a wild beast, not in this movement anyway, but the harsh peremptory octaves in which it speaks, and the soft, pleading phrases with which the piano replies might easily have been inspired by the thought of Orpheus supplicating the powers of the underworld. Gradually the stern voice of the orchestra melts, the octaves dissolve into harmony, and at the very end, orchestra unites with solo in a tragic little sigh of acquiescence.

The melancholy spell of the andante is broken by a whispering, vivacious theme, the refrain of the rondo finale. But after this discreet beginning, the rondo turns out to be rough in spirit as well as form. Following the deep shadows of the slow movement, the violence of this gaiety recalls the stories of Beethoven's sudden fluctuations of mood when improvising for his friends. Sometimes when he had finished and turned around to find his listeners shattered, overwhelmed with emotions, he would burst into a roar of laughter. "We artists don't want tears," he would mock, "we want applause."

The finale is rich in such contrasts. It charms, it blusters, it crackles, and after the grand flourish of the cadenza and some humorous afterthoughts, it launches into a triumphant presto with the obstinate refrain still dominating the glorious orchestral frenzy.

BEETHOVEN: Violin Concerto, D major
PAGANINI: Violin Concerto, E flat (finale)

For sheer melodic beauty, for loftiness of expression and grandeur of proportion, Beethoven's Violin Concerto stands today without rival. Yet, curiously enough, early audiences complained on one hand of its insignificance and on the other, of its heavy, noisy orchestra. Both critics and amateurs were agreed that it was the function of a concerto to display the solo instrument. Conservative critics expected something more like a Mozart concerto and audiences wanted more spice, fireworks that left them gasping, technical magic à la Paganini—though Paganini himself had not yet made his conquering appearance in Vienna.

Franz Clement, the violinist for whom Beethoven wrote, was not above a certain amount of circus play. For example, at the first performance of this concerto he inserted between the movements a sonata of his own— played on one string with the violin upside down. Contemporaries agree on his technical mastery.

But when he wished, Clement was an artist of true distinction, purity and nobility of style. "His performance is magnificent," says one contemporary, "in its way probably unique. It is not the bold, robust, powerful playing of the school of Viotti, but it is indescribably graceful, dainty, elegant." Another adds that "gracefulness and tenderness were its main characteristics."

Now all these qualities are reflected in Beethoven's music. He certainly did not ignore the concerto's function of displaying the soloist. He gave him plenty of technical difficulties, but he also paid him the compliment of writing music which placed Clement's highest artistic gifts in the foreground.

Needless to say, Beethoven slaved over the music. He always did. Sometimes one single theme would be hammered and pounded in his mind for years until it emerged in the perfect form that we hear today. In composing the Violin Concerto he left four staves open for the solo part simply to have room for the changes he knew he would make, and in many parts of the manuscript all four lines are filled. He dedicated it with a dubious bilingual pun: "Concerto par Clemenza pour Clement." Unfortunately with all the alterations it was not finished in time even for the last rehearsal, and poor Clement had to play from the manuscript, corrections and all, at sight. Since the concerto is difficult technically, and many violinists today consider it a work of decades to scale its artistic heights, we can imagine what that first performance on December 23, 1806, was like.

The fundamental mood of the music is happy and serene and interestingly nearer to the spirit of Mozart than Beethoven had come in those early works when he was actually imitating. It opens with five soft drum strokes introducing the wonderfully calm first theme. But those five beats startle when they are taken up by the orchestra and repeated as a D sharp, a note drastically foreign to the key of the concerto, which is D major. It all resolves in the most natural way in the world, however, and those five beats haunt the thematic development.

The sublime song of the slow section is a theme and variations, with the violin weaving exquisite garlands of melody about the theme in the orchestra. The finale, which follows without pause, is an exuberant rondo, simple seeming, but rich in contrasts, and it ends in an irrepressible outburst of high spirits.

Paganini, who was already revolutionizing the technique of violin playing, appeared in Vienna the year after Beethoven's death, a legendary figure with piercing dark eyes sunk deep in an emaciated face, long scarecrow arms and legs and skeletonlike frame. His playing had inexplicable, unearthly brilliance. There seemed no limit to what he could do with a violin, and he never practiced!

It was a common rumor that he had bartered his soul to the devil for this superhuman skill. And one member of his Viennese audience explained quite flatly that Paganini's wizardry was not to be wondered at, for he had seen the devil himself at his side, directing his arm and guiding the bow.

For fear of revealing his secrets Paganini published very few of his compositions. One of his secrets was this E flat Concerto, the first movement and finale of which in particular are full of feats impossible to perform in E flat. Paganini was careful never to let anyone hear him tuning his violin. It never seems to have occurred to anyone that he simply played the concerto as if it were written in D major, with his instrument tuned a half-tone high so that it sounded in E flat. The whole thing would have been incredible enough in D major anyhow!

Certainly he exaggerated the sensational aspects of his playing. But he was a remarkable musician. "One would have to write a volume," said Berlioz, "to indicate all the finds he has made in his works of novel effects, ingenious procedures, noble and imposing forms, orchestral combinations not even suspected before him.

"His melody is the great Italian melody, but alive with an ardor generally more passionate than one finds in the most beautiful pages of the dramatic composers of his country. His harmony is always clear, simple, and of an extraordinary sonority."

After Paganini, violin playing and violin writing could never be quite the same again. Hardly anyone escaped his influence. Yet he himself had no precedent.

To quote Berlioz again: "Paganini is one of those artists of whom it must be said, 'They are because they are, and not because others were before them.'"

LISZT: Piano Concerto #1, E flat
CHOPIN: Piano Concerto #2, F minor

These two concertos, Chopin's F minor and Liszt's Concerto in E flat major, were written by two friends: both of them great romantic figures of the nineteenth century. Famous for their love affairs, for the revolutionary imaginativeness of their music, they remain today the two most renowned pianists who ever lived. But apart from that, they were vastly different men.

Chopin was the dreamer and poet. He was fragile physically and his piano playing, even in his own most heroic works, was on an intimate scale. Liszt, though he learned much from Chopin, was more dynamic, brilliant and aggressive, as pianist, composer and as a man. He developed the technique of piano playing to where it seemed sheer wizardry. He was an impressive figure both in society and on the platform and he knew it. He was worshiped in all the capitals of Europe. In an age when

ladies fainted more easily than they do nowadays, no concert of Liszt seemed complete unless some high-born dam-
sel swooned from surfeit of emotion. And men carried
their hero worship so far that even his cigar butts were
treasured as precious relics.

Like any other human being, Liszt couldn't help enjoying a certain amount of adulation, but there are few
men who would have had the strength of character, as he
did, to give up his career as a virtuoso with all the fanfare
and acclaim attached to it, and devote his life to composing, conducting and helping other talented musicians.
Richard Wagner is only the most famous of a long list of
composers who had to thank Liszt for giving them opportunities to be heard. And many of them not only borrowed
money from Liszt—they borrowed his harmonies and
themes as well. Even in Wagner's greatest and most mature works, there is more of Liszt than Wagner ever cared
to admit.

Liszt's E flat Concerto is the perfect example of a virtuoso concerto. It is not only brilliant music to show off
a brilliant technique but a special type of music which has
to be played boldly and recklessly, with a sort of swash-
buckling nobility and a lordly disregard of the limitations
of ten fingers.

It is written in one continuous whole, uniting the several movements of the traditional concerto, much as Liszt
and his romantic contemporaries tended to unify the
sonata and symphony into one movement.

The main theme is an imperious, commanding rhythmic figure given out at the very beginning by the strings,
and punctuated by chords of the wood-wind and brass
instruments. This is the exulting theme to which Liszt
used to sing, as he played it: "Das versteht ihr alle nicht!"

(None of the rest of you know how to do this!) And it was true: no one else could have written such music, or played it with such dash and grandeur as Liszt.

There is a slow second theme sung by the cellos and basses, which might correspond roughly to the traditional melodic slow movement. This concerto was for a long time ridiculed as the "triangle concerto," because of the triangle which introduces the sparkling scherzo section. The motto theme of the beginning keeps bobbing up through the music, and there is a final, martial allegro that quickens into a headlong, flashing presto.

Chopin was only nineteen when he wrote his F minor Concerto. He was still living in his native Poland, and hadn't yet ventured forth to conquer the sophisticated salons of music and fashion in Paris. This music is simpler, but perhaps more exquisitely sensitive and tender than Chopin appeared in his later works.

He was nineteen, delicate, poetic, and desperately in love—for the first time. And like a true romantic he poured his most intimate feelings into his concerto. To a friend he wrote: "I have—perhaps to my own misfortune—already found my ideal, whom I worship faithfully and sincerely. Six months have elapsed and I haven't yet exchanged a syllable with her of whom I dream every night." Not only did he dream of her at night, as he confessed to his friend: he dreamt of her in the wonderful slow movement of his F minor Concerto, which is almost like a long nocturne, interrupted in the middle by a dramatic passage of recitative. Later, after Liszt and Chopin had met in Paris, Liszt used to speak of "the almost ideal perfection" of this movement, "now radiant with light and anon full of tender pathos."

Two years after this music was written, Chopin's ideal

married a rich Warsaw merchant, and we don't know whether Chopin had even had the courage to declare his love. So nothing came of his timorous passion except this immortal piano concerto.

The first movement begins according to tradition with a rather long orchestral introduction, which announces the main themes. But from the moment the piano takes over, the orchestra becomes its humble servant and remains so to the end. Chopin's instrument was the piano. He never felt particularly at home with the orchestra. Not that there is anything awkward or inelegant about the orchestration—there never was in any of Chopin's music —but it takes its natural place here as discreet support for the soloist.

The finale is crystal-clear brilliance and melody, with an occasional hint of a mazurka about it. It has none of the rich chromaticism of the later Chopin, but in return it has a pristine freshness that even he never found again. It was Anton Rubinstein who later said of the composer of the F minor Concerto: "The piano bard, the piano mind, the piano soul is Chopin."

⚜   ⚜

WEBER: Konzertstück
BRAHMS: Violin Concerto, D major

Whether Weber was writing an opera or a piano concerto, he was always at his best when he had a dramatic program in mind for his music. His charming, old-fashioned Konzertstück is really a romantic piano concerto, and as you might guess from the music alone, it has a plot —a very simple plot, but enough to fire Weber's imagination. He wrote the Konzertstück at the time his most famous opera, "Der Freischütz," was being prepared for its première at the Berlin Opera House in 1821. In fact he put the finishing touches on the Konzertstück on the morning of the opera's première, and played it over immediately to one of his pupils, who wrote down the story of the Konzertstück as Weber explained it to him, then and there.

A lady, a chatelaine, sits alone in her tower, gazing away into the distance. Her knight has gone on a crusade to the Holy Land. Years have passed and battles been fought. She wonders whether he is still alive and whether she will ever see him again. In her excited imagination she sees a vision of her knight lying wounded and forsaken on the battlefield. If she could only fly to his side and die with him! She falls back unconscious. And then from the distance there is a sound of a trumpet, there is a flashing and glittering in the forest coming nearer and nearer. It is the crusaders, knights, and squires, with banners waving and people shouting. And he is among them. She sinks into his arms. Love is triumphant. The very woods and waves sing of their love, and a thousand voices proclaim his victory.

That's hardly a story that would excite a modern audience. But all that matters is that it excited Weber. And since he wrote down his excitement in music instead of words, it is as stirring today as it was 120 years ago. Its freshness and simplicity are irresistible. The naïve pomp and chivalry of the march, the frantic rejoicing of the finale make us forget for a moment the sophistications of modern music, and exult with Weber over the rescue of his poor foolish chatelaine.

The "Freischütz" that evening was a triumph, and a week later, before leaving Berlin, Weber gave a concert to benefit himself. It netted him only the equivalent of $87.50, but it was an historic occasion because Weber played the solo part in his new Konzertstück. Probably as an act of kindness, he allowed a French violinist by the name of Boucher also to take part in the program. Boucher was an eccentric fellow, who had been exiled from France because of an unfortunate resemblance to the deposed Emperor Napoleon. He was supposed to play Weber's "Variations on a Norwegian National Air," and he stipulated only that he be allowed to contribute a short cadenza of his own toward the end of the Variations. Weber, who accompanied him at the piano, good-naturedly consented.

But he was as dumbfounded as the audience when the cadenza came and Boucher (according to Weber's son), "after various gambols, arpeggios, trills and mysterious chords, launched into a regular potpourri of motives from 'Der Freischütz,' dished up à la Boucher. In vain the tortured composer tried to cut short these flights of fancy of his would-be interpreter; on he went in spite of Weber's supplicating glances, until at last, after an attempt to represent the Wolf's Glen tempest from 'Der Freischütz' on the fourth string, he laid down his violin, rushed to the piano, and clasped Weber in his arms, exclaiming: 'Oh, master, great master! How I adore you, how I admire you!'"

The audience, which also adored Weber, instead of being offended at this scene, overwhelmed both men with storms of applause and cries of "Long live Weber."

Styles in violin-playing had changed considerably by 1878, when Brahms came to write his Violin Concerto. Violinistic gambols à la Boucher were no longer the fash-

ion. And Brahms, like the Schumanns, from whom he had
learned so much, particularly frowned on virtuoso display which was not demanded by the music. He never
hesitated to write music that was difficult to play, either
in his piano concertos or in his one violin concerto. But
he never indulged in fireworks for their own sake. On the
contrary his most difficult passages are seldom the most
spectacular or effective from the audience's point of view.
Still he did want to keep within the bounds of what was
possible on the violin. So he consulted his friend, the
famous violinist, Joachim.

With characteristic humility Brahms wrote: "It was
my intention, of course, that you should correct it, not
sparing the quality of the composition, and that if you
thought it not worth while scoring you should say so. I shall
be satisfied if you mark those parts which are difficult,
awkward or impossible to play."

Joachim, it seems, took a great deal of trouble, going
over the solo part, and pointing out technical details,
which he felt should be changed. Brahms listened sol-
emnly and then, in spite of his humility, changed almost
nothing in his music but bow markings and fingerings.
However he did dedicate the concerto to Joachim.

In form, it is fairly orthodox, with three separate
movements, the traditional tuttis, solos, cadenzas and so
on. It is the spirit of the music which makes it different
from any other violin concerto that had yet been written.
The first movement is extraordinarily rich in its orchestral
development, with a solo part which never obtrudes too
far into the foreground, for all that it makes cruel technical demands on the performer. The slow movement is an
exquisite pastorale and the finale is a brilliant, irregular
rondo in the Hungarian style.

Brahms's concerto has taken its place alongside the Beethoven as one of the two greatest concertos ever written for violin. But Joachim wasn't the only one to be disturbed about its technical difficulties. The great conductor, Hans von Bülow, once declared it was not a concerto for violin, but a concerto against the violin. Perhaps another musician came nearer the truth when he amended that remark: "Brahms's concerto is neither against the violin, nor for violin with orchestra. It is a concerto for violin against orchestra—and the violin wins."

☙ ❧

BRUCH: Violin Concerto, G minor
TCHAIKOVSKY: Piano Concerto, B-flat minor

When Bruch sent his G minor Concerto to Joachim for advice and criticism, he told the great violinist that because of the freedom of the first movement, he felt he ought to call the whole work a fantaisie. But Joachim maintained that the title, concerto, was fully justified. "For a fantaisie," he argued, "the last two movements are too completely and symmetrically developed. The different sections are brought together in beautiful relationship, yet—and this is the principal thing—there is sufficient contrast."

Bruch was not a violinist and he was more than glad to adapt the long list of alterations which Joachim offered along with his praise. Indeed, this was not the first revision. The sketches were written when Bruch was nineteen, but the first version was only completed nine years later when he himself conducted the first performance. Immediately after the première he revised it thoroughly and forwarded the score to Joachim. Then, after further changes, the version we know today was dedicated to Joachim who played it for the first time in 1868, again with Bruch conducting. The concerto was not, even then, considered revolutionary, and it had no difficulty establishing itself in the popular position it holds today with violinists and their audiences.

For all its brilliance, the first movement has a melancholy strain. Its deliberate avoidance of monumental form, which made Bruch hesitate to call his work a concerto, gives us the impression we are hearing merely an elaborate introduction to the slow movement, which follows appropriately without pause. The languorous melodies of this movement lead gradually to a poignant, dramatic climax and die away to a quiet close. The principal theme of the finale is a vigorous figure which Brahms may have remembered when he came to write the finale of his own violin concerto. There is also passionate declamation for both violin and orchestra, but the dominating mood is one of exuberance and fire.

As much of a virtuoso war horse as Bruch's Violin Concerto is the B minor Piano Concerto of Tchaikovsky. Interestingly enough, just as Bruch, not being a violinist, had asked expert advice on his concerto, so Tchaikovsky, who was not a pianist, sought advice for his, but with less happy results. Tchaikovsky was sensitive to criticism. He felt the need of "a severe critic, but at the same time of one friendlily disposed toward me."

In his uncertainty he went to see an old and affectionate, if rather domineering friend, Nicholas Rubinstein, a distinguished pianist, brother of the famous Anton

Rubinstein, and head of the Moscow Conservatory where Tchaikovsky taught. On Christmas Eve, 1874, before a party to which both men were invited, Rubinstein suggested that they play over the new concerto in one of the classrooms of the conservatory.

After the first movement Rubinstein said not a word. "If you only knew how uncomfortably foolish you feel," wrote Tchaikovsky to a friend, "if you invite a friend to share a dish you have prepared with your own hands, and he eats and—is silent. At least say something. If you like, find fault, in a friendly way, but for heaven's sake speak— say something, no matter what! But Rubinstein said nothing. He was preparing his thunder. . . . As a matter of fact I did not require any opinion on the artistic form of my work; it was purely the technical side which was in question. . . . I took patience and played the concerto to the end. Again silence.

" 'Well?' said I, as I arose. Then there burst from Rubinstein's mouth a mighty torrent of words. He spoke quietly at first, then he waxed hot, and finally he resembled Zeus hurling thunderbolts. It seems that my concerto was utterly worthless, absolutely unplayable. Certain passages were so commonplace and awkward they could not be improved, and the piece as a whole was bad, trivial, vulgar. I had stolen this from somebody and that from somebody else, so that only two or three pages were good for anythihg and all the rest should be wiped out or radically rewritten. . . .

"An unbiased spectator could only have thought that I was a stupid, ignorant spoiler of music paper, who had had the impertinence to show his rubbish to a celebrated man. . . .

"I left the room without a word and went upstairs.

I was so excited and angry I could not speak. Soon afterwards Rubinstein came up to me and seeing that I was very depressed, called me into another room. There he repeated that my concerto was impossible and pointed to several places that required a thorough revision, adding that if these alterations were completed within a certain fixed time, he would play my concerto in public. I replied that I would not alter a single note, and that I would have the concerto printed exactly as it then stood. That is, in fact, what I have done."

Tchaikovsky did more. He erased the intended dedication to Rubinstein and inscribed it instead to the famous German pianist, Hans von Bülow, who he had been told was a great admirer of his works. Flattered, and delighted with the concerto, Bülow wrote a warm letter, praising the originality, nobility and power of the music. "The form is so mature, ripe, the style so distinguished, and labor and intention are everywhere concealed. I should weary you if I were to enumerate all the virtues of your work."

Since Bülow was leaving for a tour of North America, he took the concerto with him and so it came to have its première in Boston. It was enthusiastically received there and in other American cities and Bülow sent Tchaikovsky clippings from the press. "Think what healthy appetites these Americans must have," Tchaikovsky commented. "Each time, Bülow was obliged to repeat the whole finale of my concerto! Nothing like that happens in our country."

The concerto opens with a vigorous four-bar prelude, the horns anticipating the theme to follow. Then against the crashing D flat major chords of the piano, the orchestra flings forth a nobly arched melody which is later taken up by the soloist. But we have not yet come to the main theme, a vivacious tune Tchaikovsky had heard sung by blind beggars at a fair. There are two other melodies of typical Tchaikovskian appeal and the whole is worked out with great brilliance and power.

The lyric slow movement includes a scherzo middle section. The bright opening dance theme of the finale contrasts with a melodic second theme which flows tenderly at first but later soars with true majesty over the orchestral storm of the closing pages.

BLOCH: "Schelomo"
SIBELIUS: Violin Concerto, D minor

It's a curious paradox that although the two men who wrote the music on this program, Ernest Bloch and Sibelius, are still living and working among us, the music itself seems to belong to a remote past. Not that either "Schelomo" or the Sibelius Violin Concerto is withered or old fashioned. Far from it. But the world they represent is further away than can be measured in years. "Schelomo" was written in 1916. That means not a mere twenty-eight years ago, it means two wars ago. And the Sibelius Violin Concerto was written before that in the mythical days of security and plenty which were taken for granted as the normal state of affairs before World War I. Under the very eyes or ears of present-day concertgoers, both works have become classics of the past, as much as any concerto of Schumann or Mendelssohn.

And there is another thing that anchors them even

more firmly in the past. They are both late products of a once fruitful idea: the glorification of national and racial characteristics (perhaps I should say the affectionate emphasis on such characteristics) an idea that ran through much nineteenth-century art and politics. Today, now that we have seen the glorification of race carried to a point where it would be preposterous if it didn't threaten our entire civilization, we aren't likely to feel so romantic about our own or other people's racial origins, or about local color in music, which can so easily be perverted into national color.

Yet that needn't blind us to the greatness of the art those ideas once produced. Ernest Bloch consciously looked for his inspiration in the memories of the Jewish race, and his greatest music has been composed on that endlessly fascinating theme. "It is the Jewish soul that interests me," he has said, "the complex, glowing, agitated soul, that I feel vibrating throughout the Bible; the freshness and naïveté of the Patriarchs; the violence that is evident in the prophetic books; the Jews' savage love of justice; the despair of the preacher in Jerusalem; the sorrow and immensity of the Book of Job; the sensuality of the Song of Songs. All this is in us; all this is in me. And it is the better part of me. It is all this that I must endeavor to hear in myself and to transcribe in my music; the venerable emotion of the race, that slumbers way down in our soul."

In Bloch's Hebrew Rhapsody for Cello and Orchestra, he not only paints the richness and pomp of the court of King Solomon, or Schelomo,—he also lets us hear the introspective voice of the philosopher-king who, having known all the power and pleasures of man, meditated and found that everything was futile, that all was vanity. In between the moments of exultant jubilation and the barbaric splendor of his orchestra, we hear the pessimistic voice of the cello,—skeptical, despairing and ending on a deep, unanswered question.

In the Sibelius Violin Concerto there is also exaltation and pessimism, but the voice is a voice of the north, and the splendor that surrounds it seems not man made. It is like the ghostly splendor of northern lights, and its majesty is the majesty of the storm. As far as we know, there is no Finnish mythology, or painting of the Finnish landscape here, as there is in so much of Sibelius' music. But the language he speaks is the same, he uses the same vocabulary, and his melody has the same turns that hark back to the ancient Finnish runes.

The concerto is in three movements. Over the murmurings of muted violins, a melancholy, rhapsodic theme is sung by the solo violin. This is the principal melody of the first movement, which is soon echoed and developed by the darker wood-wind instruments. There is a second, more forceful, plodding theme, ending with the characteristic drop of a fifth, which also is painted in the dark colors of cellos and bassoons. As these themes begin to grow and sprout new phrases and themes, as simply and logically as a tree thrusts out new branches, there is plenty of opportunity for virtuoso display of the solo violin. But the solo part never seems ostentatious passage work or cadenzas; it remains an organic part of the growth of the music.

The second movement begins with a poignant little phrase in thirds for the wood winds, like the rise and fall of a sigh. It is echoed bleakly by other wind instruments, and then the violin takes up a deep-throated song of almost Tchaikovskian melancholy. The movement works up to a great climax of interweaving orchestral voices built around this theme, and then suddenly breaks off and dies away with a few nostalgic phrases.

The finale is a wild, dance movement, with a savage, lumbering main theme which Donald Tovey said was evidently a polonaise for polar bears. It begins with a sort of stamping figure in the drums and low string instruments, but I defy any polar bear to continue that dance with the dizzy leaps and whirls and somersaults in the air that Sibelius gives to his solo violin.

There are moments when the dance themes rumble about heavily enough in the depths of the orchestra, but always the solo part shoots up out of that whirling mass, like a rocket into the night sky, sputtering sparks as it soars aloft, to do its own infinitely more agile version of the same dance. There are incredibly difficult passages of thirds, arpeggios, harmonics, double-stops and the whole battery of violinistic fireworks, without there being a single bar of display for mere display's sake. The dance gathers momentum as it passes from one climax to another, and the end comes with a series of brilliant skyward sweeps of the violin, punctuated by sharp, decisive chords of the full orchestra.

V. *Music and Legend*

L EGENDS HAVE been called the dreams of the human
race, revealing its memories of things past, its fears
and longings for the future. Just as there is nothing more
personal, more typical of you than your dreams, so the
great racial dreams of saga and myth reveal racial character far more deeply than external appearances. Elmer
Davis once said that much of German history from Bis-
marck to Hitler could be explained by the fact that the
Germans are a people who admire a hero like Siegfried.
Yet there are many interpretations of Siegfried. St. George
with his dragon is probably a christianized version of the
story. Bernard Shaw has discussed Wagner's Siegfried
as a protestant and socialist. The slaying of Siegfried
wakened in Thomas Mann associations with Tammuz
and Osiris and even Golgotha. And Wagner himself re-

fused to be tied down to any one interpretation. The fasci·
nation of legend lies in this very dream quality, the fact
that it deals in symbols more profound than words. And
since the dream world beyond logic appeals most strongly
to the romantic artist, it is small wonder that the nineteenth century, with its revolt against the Age of Reason,
brought the magnificent outpouring of legendary music
which is still so popular in our opera houses and concert
halls.

Rimsky-Korsakoff: Symphonic Suite, "Scheherazade"
("After the Thousand and One Nights")
Borodin: Polovtsian Dances from "Prince Igor"

Stories that are older than the memory of man, the ancient dreams of a dozen races, speak from the fairy-tale pages of Rimsky-Korsakoff's suite, "Scheherazade."

Where did these stories come from? For centuries before they were told in Europe, the incredible yarns were spun by poets and beggars in the market places of Egypt. Polite Moslems considered them coarse or depraved. But they were popular. A thousand years ago they were already famous as the "Thousand Nights and a Night." And they were not new then. Of course each man added his bit . as he passed them along. But some of the stories and their framework had been heard before in Persia. And before that, probably in India. No one knows where they began.

In the nineteenth century the stories were told again in words, in colors and in music by Rimsky-Korsakoff, who mastered as no Russian had before him the magic of the nineteenth-century orchestra. He could conjure up strange perfumes and colors with the tone of a flute or a trumpet, and his "Scheherazade" unfolds like a vast dream panorama of the Arabian Nights we read as children—sometimes a rather jumbled dream, but always full of gorgeous colors and exciting adventure.

The background of the dream, as Rimsky-Korsakoff explained on the flyleaf of his score, is this:

"The Sultan Schahriar, persuaded of the falseness and faithlessness of all women, has sworn to put to death each one of his wives after the first night. But the Sultana Scheherazade saved her life by interesting him in tales which she told him during one thousand and one nights. Pricked by curiosity, the Sultan put off his wife's execution from day to day and at last gave up his bloody plan entirely.

"Many marvels were told Schahriar by the Sultana Scheherazade. For her stories the Sultana borrowed from poets their verses, from folksongs their words; and she strung together tales and adventures."

Hints of the stories the composer had in mind are given us in the titles of the various movements. But Rimsky-Korsakoff was careful to warn his listeners that they are disconnected episodes and pictures only. Even the recurring motives do not always have the same significance. "I meant these hints to direct but slightly the hearer's fancy on the path which my own fancy had traveled. . . . All I desired was that the hearer, if he liked my piece as *symphonic music,* should carry away the impression that it is beyond doubt an oriental narrative of some numerous and varied fairy-tale wonders, and not merely four pieces played one after the other and composed on the basis of themes common to all four movements."

The opening movement describes the Sea and Sindbad's Ship. Heavy, forbidding octaves proclaim the principal theme, the motto, as it were, of the symphony. This might be the ferocious Sultan himself except that, as Rimsky pointed out, it recurs in other movements where there is no thought of the Sultan. Some people have called it the sea motive, others the motive of Sindbad. But give it your own name. Soft wood winds introduce the voice of

Scheherazade: a high, wheedling violin. Then the story begins and it has two principal themes: the vigorous motto of the opening and another, which suggests the billowing rise and fall of the waves.

The second movement is the Story of the Kalandar Prince. But which one? There are several in the Arabian Nights. At the outset we hear again the beguiling solo violin. A meandering bassoon begins the fantastic tale which is interrupted by trumpet calls from near and far. These fanfares develop into a story of their own before we are led back into the tale of the Kalandar.

The third movement is an exotic love song, the Young Prince and the Young Princess. Again Rimsky does not tell us which prince and which princess. But no matter! We hear the languorous voice of the violins set off by rippling scales of flutes and clarinets. We hear the tingling, glittering rhythms, and the sentimental phrases that follow, and we can imagine what we will.

The finale is entitled: Festival at Baghdad; The Sea; The Ship Goes to Pieces against a Rock Surmounted by a Bronze Warrior. A nervous transformation of the symphony's main theme is followed by the voice of Scheherazade. The festival begins with light, whirling figures. Gradually you gain the impression of a dancing crowd. There are shouts from the onlookers, abrupt changes of rhythm as one group interrupts the other. The excitement increases. The dancing becomes more and more agitated, the rejoicing more frenzied until it has an undertone almost of desperation. Suddenly the merrymaking seems to be on shipboard. The sea rides higher and higher and the ship crashes upon the magic rock. The wood winds scream against the overwhelming waves. Slowly the storm and the sea subside and the story is told. The lovely voice of Scheherazade's violin fades away into the highest reaches of the orchestra like the passing of a dream.

Rimsky-Korsakoff's orchestral wizardry fortunately was not confined to his own works. He also used it to round out compositions which were left unfinished by gifted friends such as Borodin.

Like many other talented Russian composers of his day, Borodin did not start life as a musician. He was a physician, and though his real love was for music, his career was divided between his profession and his avocation. His greatest opera, "Prince Igor," based on the half-legendary, half-historical Epic of the Army of Igor, deals with the struggles between the Russians and Tartars in the eleventh century. Borodin had made a special study of the songs and poems that had come down from the time of Igor and he wrote his own libretto for the opera. He delighted in the musical opportunities offered by the struggle between Russian and Asiatic nationalities, for he himself was a native of the Caucasus and well acquainted with oriental melodies.

The Polovtsian Dances are taken from the second act, where the Polovtsi chieftain, Khan Kontchak, organizes a festival of dances in honor of his royal prisoner, Prince Igor. There are dances of wild men, of young girls and boys, of slave girls, of prisoners; dances in honor of the great Khan. The savage rhythms and the exotic color of the eastern melodies Borodin knew so well are the more effective for being clothed in the brilliant and masterly orchestration of his friend, Rimsky-Korsakoff.

WAGNER: Selections from "The Ring of the Nibelung"
1. "Das Rheingold": Entrance of the Gods into Valhalla
2. "Die Walküre": Spring Song and Duet from Act I
3. "Die Walküre": Ride of the Valkyries
4. "Die Walküre": Wotan's Farewell and Magic Fire Music
5. "Siegfried": Forest Murmurs

To some people, a legend is a story of something that didn't happen—a long, long time ago. To Wagner, a legend was a story of something that was happening to him, that very minute. It was also, of course, about things that had happened in the past and would happen again in the future. But primarily it was about me, now. And that is what makes Wagner's great legendary cycle, "The Ring of the Nibelung," as disturbing and fresh as this morning's headlines. Or perhaps it *is* this morning's headlines. In the last opera of the "Ring," "The Twilight of the Gods," many people have seen a prophecy of what is happening today: The passing of the old gods in a world conflagration caused by an inhuman lust for power, with the flower of mankind as innocent victims of the catastrophe.

The old gods would be the rulers who, like Wotan, really meant well, but hadn't hesitated to practice a little imperialism in their youth, and then became compromisers and appeasers when they were threatened. The villain of the piece, a man begotten in hate, whose lust to rule the world causes the catastrophe, is called by Wagner, Hagen. The innocent victims, Siegfried and Brünnhilde, were Wagner's symbols of the best that is in mankind. And after the conflagration? Well, Wagner doesn't tell us in words, but his music seems to say that, though Siegfried is murdered and Brünnhilde sacrifices herself, it is they or their kind who inherit the earth.

"The Ring of the Nibelung" with its four operas: "Das Rheingold," "Die Walküre," "Siegfried" and "Die Götterdämmerung," occupied Wagner's immensely fertile mind for over a quarter of a century. And there is everything in this "Ring" from Karl Marx to psychoanalysis, and a deeply Christian philosophy hidden under the pagan trappings. It started fairly simply as a sketch for a single opera, "Siegfried's Death," which ended with Brünnhilde taking Siegfried up to Valhalla where they lived happily ever after. Then the legend began to unfold in Wagner's mind and take on new meanings. He added another opera, and Siegfried became the ideal revolutionist, who was going to sweep away the capitalist system and substitute the rule of love. Finally, when Wagner had grown in wisdom, and no longer believed that the rule of love was a practical substitute for the capitalist system, the "Ring" became a vast tragedy of the entire human race. Its various symbolical meanings went deeper than even Wagner could explain, though the central idea remained a simple one: that the lust for power can end only in destruction and death.

Our first excerpt from the "Ring" shows the stage set for tragedy. Valhalla, the new home of the gods, stands shimmering in the glow of sunset. The god, Froh, has built a rainbow bridge across the valley to the castle gates, and the Valhalla theme swells up majestically from the orchestra. But this new power and glory have been bought at a terrible price. Wotan, himself, the king of the gods, has stooped to deception and theft. He has stolen the ring of the Nibelung, Alberich. Alberich had stolen the gold to make the ring from the depths of the Rhine. By the tragic act of foreswearing love, he won the strength to take the Rhinegold and forge it into a ring which gave him power over the whole world. But as he won the ring through a curse, so he curses it again as it leaves his hand. Henceforth all those who do not have its evil power shall long to possess it, and once they touch it, they are doomed to destruction through the envy of others.

To be sure, Wotan has used the ring only to pay for Valhalla, yet he is filled with fears and foreboding. Then suddenly he foresees a salvation: he will cleanse the world of the curse through a great hero, a human being, who shall return the ring to its rightful home in the Rhine. At this thought, the theme of the redeeming hero's Sword blazes forth from the orchestra, and with a new assurance, Wotan leads the gods toward Valhalla. But as they are about to set foot on the rainbow bridge, the mournful call of the Rhinemaidens comes from the valley below, imploring the great gods to return the gold they treasured and guarded. Wotan starts guiltily, but one of the gods throws back a mocking answer, and they continue on their way. The lament of the Rhinemaidens is soon swallowed up in the pomp of the Valhalla motive, joined now to the motive of the Sword. Finally the great arching theme of the Rainbow flashes and glitters in the orchestra and the curtain falls as the gods are crossing the bridge.

Some of the tenderest love music Wagner ever wrote is contained in the Spring Song and duet from the first act of "Walküre." Here we meet Wotan's hero, Siegmund, and his twin sister, Sieglinde, the children of Wotan by a mortal woman. They have been separated since early youth. Siegmund does not know that Sieglinde is his sister, nor that he has been guided to her by Wotan. He knows only that his father once promised him a sword in his hour of greatest need, and that now he is guided to the sword by a woman he has quickly come to love. Suddenly a gust of wind bursts open the door to the hut. Outside the forest glistens, the moonlight pours in through the door, Siegmund draws Sieglinde tenderly to his side, and the music soars with the ecstasy of his Spring Song.

Sieglinde replies that he himself is the spring, come to free her from the bondage of winter, from a forced marriage to her savage husband, Hunding. In the caressing phrases that follow, the lovers wonder at their resemblance to each other, and Sieglinde discovers they are children of the same father. She jumps up in excitement: "Then it was for you he thrust the sword into the tree!" Siegmund seizes the hilt and the motive of the Sword crashes and echoes through the orchestra like a mighty fanfare, as he wrenches the blade from the tree trunk.

Exultantly Sieglinde tells him she is his own sister, whom he has won with the sword. "Bride and sister be to thy brother," he cries, "and thus may the Volsungs be blest." Sieglinde falls into his arms as the motives of the Sword and of their love rush to a furious climax and the curtain falls quickly.

But laws and conventions must be upheld if the power of the gods is to survive. In the battle that follows between Siegmund and Hunding, Wotan sadly bids his Valkyrie daughter, Brünnhilde, give victory to Hunding. Instead of living to redeem the world, Siegmund must die to preserve the rule of the gods. But at the last moment Brünnhilde is overcome with pity for the son Wotan has deserted and she disobeys his command. Wotan himself intervenes, Siegmund is slain and Brünnhilde flees, with Sieglinde in the saddle of her horse.

The introduction to the third act of "Die Walküre," the Ride of the Valkyries, describes the storm that plays about a mountaintop, where the nine Valkyrie sisters gather after battle, each carrying a slain hero in her saddle. Through the realistic gale of swishing violins and trilling wood winds, you hear the galloping rhythm of the Valkyries' winged steeds. You can almost see the storm they ride with its scudding clouds and the lightning flashes about them.

Brünnhilde arrives last of all and sends Sieglinde on ahead while she remains behind to brave Wotan's anger. In a great thundercloud, Wotan arrives. Wrathfully he pronounces judgment on Brünnhilde and dismisses her pleading sisters. She has disobeyed his commands in battle, therefore she must be punished by becoming a mortal woman. She shall be put to sleep and the first man to find and waken her shall be her husband.

The curse of power! First it was his son that Wotan had to sacrifice. Now it is his best-loved daughter from whom he must take eternal farewell. Brünnhilde reminds him of his love for Siegmund, and pleads that in defending Siegmund, she did only what he himself wished to do but could not. "Yes," says Wotan bitterly, but still she must be punished. Brünnhilde adds that she knows Sieglinde will bear a son, Siegfried, the mightiest hero of all. But Wotan wishes to cut short this agony of leave-taking. In a last despairing prayer, Brünnhilde begs that if she must leave her father forever, if she must sleep here on the mountain peak, then let him at least protect her slumber with a sea of fire so terrible that no coward will ever approach the rock to make her his bride.

In a great burst of emotion, the god grants her wish. He describes the scorching tempest that will surround her rock, and when he speaks of the hero who will end her slumber, the orchestra softly entones the Siegfried motive. Father and daughter gaze silently into each other's eyes, while the orchestra sweeps up to a great climax on the motive of Brünnhilde's Sleep. Then the theme subsides into a softly rocking accompaniment figure, and Wotan sings a last farewell to the Valkyrie's lustrous eyes, with a melody that occurs often again throughout this scene and in the following operas, "Siegfried" and the "Götterdämmerung."

He puts Brünnhilde to sleep with a long kiss on the eyes, while the orchestra breathes the strange descending harmonies of the Magic Ban. Now the strings sing the melody of the Farewell, accompanied by variations of the theme of Brünnhilde's Sleep. Wotan covers her with her shield and helmet and turns away.

With the bold, descending octaves in the brass, Wotan seizes his spear, the symbol of his power, and orders Loge, the fire-god, to encircle the rock with flames. The music hisses and crackles as the flames grow until they completely surround the peak. Wotan stretches out his spear in a charm, so that only a hero who fears neither that spear nor its charm may ever penetrate the wall of fire. The Siegfried motive, thundering through the orchestra, reminds us again who that hero will be. Once more we hear the yearning melody of the Farewell as Wotan glances back at his sleeping child. The motive of Fate sounds questioningly in the orchestra—another glance back, and Wotan turns slowly to disappear in the flames.

While Brünnhilde sleeps, young Siegfried, after whom the next opera is named, grows to manhood. The scene of the Forest Murmurs takes place deep in a legendary wood, near the den of the dragon Siegfried is to slay. It is early morning, and as the sun filters through the thick roof of branches, the leaves begin to stir, the birds begin to chirp, first one and then another, until the air is filled with the soft, murmuring voice of the woodland.

Here the concert version of Forest Murmurs skips over the killing of the dragon to the place where Siegfried tastes the dragon's blood and suddenly understands the speech of the birds. With rising agitation he hears one of them sing of the beautiful half-goddess, Brünnhilde, who lies on a fire-girt mountaintop, waiting for a hero who knows no fear to stride through the flames and claim her as his bride. Siegfried jumps up. The orchestra fairly laughs for joy; we hear the fluttering of the bird as it darts ahead to show the way to the mountain, and Siegfried's jubilation as he disappears into the forest in quest of his bride.

❧❦   ❧❦

WAGNER: Selections from "The Ring of the Nibelung":
1. "Siegfried": Introduction to Act III
2. "Siegfried": Fire-Music
3. "Götterdämmerung": Siegfried's Rhine Journey
4. "Götterdämmerung": Waltraute Scene
5. "Götterdämmerung": Siegfried's Funeral Music
6. "Götterdämmerung": Immolation Scene

We take up the music of the "Ring of the Nibelung" at the point where Wagner took it up again after an interruption of a dozen years, during which he wrote "Tristan und Isolde" and "Die Meistersinger," and had passed through a hundred other adventures and calamities including the fiasco of "Tannhäuser" in Paris. These years had enormously enriched his style. One of the most fascinating comparisons I know is to listen to the Ride of the Valkyries, with all its elemental rhythmic excitement, and then to hear the Introduction to Act III of "Siegfried" where Wagner brings us back to the Valkyries' Rock and uses some of the same material. But how differently!

Here the galloping figure of the Valkyries is only one of a great panorama of musical ideas that Wagner spreads before us as the drama approaches its climax. Underneath it in a great orchestral groundswell we hear the motive of Erda, the Earth Mother, whom Wotan has come to consult in storm and lightning at the foot of the Valkyries' Rock. At its peak the Erda motive is transformed into a descending figure, which has magically become the theme of the Twilight of the Gods. We hear the short, tortured theme of Wotan's Despair and then as a vast harmonic framework for all these themes, the motive of Wotan as the Wanderer—the king of the gods, stripped of his power, and doomed to wander over the face of the earth as a passive spectator of the events which he himself has set in motion. And then, as the final irony, the theme of Wotan's Spear, the symbol of the power he no longer possesses.

The Fire-Music from Siegfried accompanies the change of scene from the foot of the Valkyries' Rock to the peak where the sleeping Brünnhilde lies. Siegfried has brushed aside Wotan, spear and all, and as he turns to climb the mountain the fire upon the summit rushes down to envelop him. You will hear his horn call exulting through the orchestral flames and combined at times with the motive of the Rhinegold. Gradually the fire dissolves into the rosy mist of dawn on the mountaintop and the music tells of the serenity and beauty which Siegfried found there.

Siegfried's Rhine Journey from "Götterdämmerung" begins with another dawn on the Valkyries' Rock—the dawn before Siegfried's leave-taking of Brünnhilde. We hear the ominous, questioning motive of Fate, and the motive of Siegfried's Horn Call stirs sleepily in the orchestra. Then Brünnhilde's graceful melody gives more animation to the music. As the light grows these two themes work up to a great climax and Siegfried and Brünnhilde emerge together from their cave.

In parting Siegfried gives Brünnhilde the fateful ring as a pledge of his love, from the depths of the valley we hear the merry flourish of his horn, and as the curtain closes on this prologue, the orchestra takes up the theme of the Horn and weaves it into the story of his journey down the Rhine to the castle of Gunther. We hear the surge of the Rhine itself and then, in a burst of orchestral glory, the cry of the Rhinemaidens for their lost gold. Toward the end the music becomes gloomy and foreboding, prophesying the evil that is to come. The motives of the Ring and the curse-laden gold warn us of the outcome of Siegfried's adventures.

At Gunther's castle Siegfried meets Gunther's half-brother, Hagen, who is plotting to win the ring by stealth. Hagen gives Siegfried a potion which makes him forget Brünnhilde and fall in love with Gunther's sister, Gutrune. They strike a bargain: Siegfried may have Gutrune as his wife if he will win Brünnhilde for Gunther.

Meanwhile, Brünnhilde is visited by one of her Valkyrie sisters, Waltraute, who begs her to throw the ring back into the depths of the Rhine, whence it was stolen, and thus save the gods and the whole world from its curse. In Valhalla the gods and heros are waiting, she says, waiting with silent, stony faces for the message of their doom which now only Brünnhilde can avert. But Brünnhilde no longer belongs to the world of Valhalla. She knows the ring only as the pledge of Siegfried's love, and rather than give that up, she will see Valhalla and all the old gods destroyed.

What Brünnhilde cannot know is that she and Siegfried and the gods themselves are already doomed. In the background stands crafty Hagen, playing off one innocent victim against the other, and all against the tottering gods of Valhalla.

Siegfried tears his ring from Brünnhilde's finger, marries her to Gunther, so that he may himself marry Gutrune. In her despair and humiliation, believing that Siegfried has betrayed her of his own free will, Brünnhilde joins Hagen in a plot to murder him. A hunt is planned for the day after the wedding, and Brünnhilde confides to Hagen that Siegfried can be slain only by a spear thrust in the back—by treachery.

The deed is well prepared. While they are resting from the hunt, Hagen asks Siegfried to tell the story of his youth. Siegfried describes the slaying of the dragon and how he won the ring. Then, in the midst of the narrative, Hagen gives Siegfried a potion that restores his memory, so that he now unwittingly betrays himself. He goes on to tell how he climbed the flaming mountain and won Brünnhilde for his bride.

Thereupon Hagen, with a bloodcurdling show of indignation, plunges his spear into Siegfried's back. Gunther and the vassals gather in pity and terror around the broken body, while Hagen disappears into the darkening forest. Siegfried dies with a last greeting to his true bride, Brünnhilde. Gunther bids the vassals raise Siegfried on his own shield and bear him back to the castle.

A mist steals up from the Rhine and gradually fills the stage. The dark harmonies of Fate are answered in the orchestra by the angry crash of the Death motive. The moon breaks through the mist for a moment and illumines Siegfried's upturned face, and the orchestra unleashes a flood of memories. It weaves together the poignant themes of Siegmund and Sieglinde, the melodies of their tragic love, and of the whole unhappy Volsung race. Higher and higher over them all swirls the Death motive until the sharp, shining theme of Siegfried's Sword cuts through the orchestra: the sword which was his and his father's before him, and which once had meant hope of salvation. Then suddenly we realize that this mighty dirge is not just for one man's death. All the world of slain beauty and light and hope is being borne away into the mist, murdered by the powers of stealth and darkness. One last blaze of light in the orchestra: the Siegfried motive, and the gloom returns for the final scene of the twilight of the gods.

Too late, Brünnhilde has come to understand the whole tragedy. As she looks down on the dead hero's face, she muses on his great innocence and his great betrayal. Then she turns to the guilty gods, to Wotan, her father, whose weakness caused Siegfried's death and the catastrophe which at last will engulf them all. The Valhalla motive, the motive of Death, of Wotan's love for the Volsungs and the motive of Fate sound softly as Brünnhilde announces to Wotan that his hour of release, the twilight of the gods, is near.

She takes the Nibelung's ring from Siegfried's finger

and bequeaths it to the bed of the Rhine, while Siegfried's body is carried to the funeral pyre. Then she seizes a torch from one of the men and throws it onto the pyre which bursts into flame. Those flames, she knows, will rise to Valhalla itself where the gods await their doom.

Siegfried's horse is brought in. To the combined strains of the Siegfried motive and Redemption through Love, she sings a last, exalted greeting to Siegfried, mounts the horse and rides it into the flames. The fire leaps and seizes on Gunther's castle. When it crashes to the ground, the Rhine overfloods its banks and sweeps forward to recover the ring. But meanwhile the flames have mounted to the sky which seems to be on fire. It is Valhalla itself and all the gods of corruption and compromise that sought to rule the world. The Valhalla motive piles up to a climax of great orchestral splendor as they are completely enveloped in flames. We hear once more the motive of Siegfried and the passing of the old gods, and the last ecstatic, soaring melody tells of the birth of a new and cleaner world.

⚜   ⚜

BERLIOZ: "Damnation of Faust" Selections
WAGNER: Faust Overture
LISZT: "Mephisto Waltz"
RICHARD STRAUSS: "Don Juan"

Legends are not only a favorite subject for opera—they have also provided an inexhaustible inspiration for symphonic composers.

Both Don Juan and Faust were creations of the folk imagination of the sixteenth century, and it's perhaps significant that each represents a revolt against the commands of a church that had never been seriously threatened until the Reformation of that time. Both men were probably historical characters, though the legends that grew up about them soon surpassed reality, and they both became so popular with tellers of folk tales and strolling players all over Europe that they began to gather to themselves stories that had been told in the past about other, less popular mythical persons. The central motive of the Faust story, for example, the idea of a man selling himself to the devil or to evil spirits in order to gain superhuman knowledge, goes back at least to certain Jewish tales that are older than Christianity itself.

But evidently there was some real person by the name of Faust or Fust, who lived somewhere in Germany at the beginning of the sixteenth century, and soon became famous enough for the great religious leader Melanchthon to denounce him as "a disgraceful beast and a sewer of many devils." Fantastic adventures began to cluster about his name and before the end of the century the Faust legend had been published not only in German, but Danish, French, Dutch, Flemish, Czech and English, as the "History of the Damnable Life and the Deserved Death of Dr. John Faustus." The great Elizabethan dramatist, Marlowe, was the first to raise the legend to the realm of literature, but most of the modern treatments of the story, including both Berlioz' "Damnation of Faust" and Wagner's Faust Overture are based on Goethe's tragedy.

Goethe, over the course of his long career, changed the fate of Faust. He saved him by having his quest for knowledge lead finally to a realization that it is only by working for and with one's fellow men that even the most selfish man can make himself truly happy. Mephistopheles he treated from an extremely modern point of view—as a symbol of the negative, cynically intellectual side of Faust's own nature. And it is interesting to see that to musicians, Mephisto has seemed more interesting than Faust himself.

The Minuet of the Will O' the Wisps and the Dance of the Sylphs from Berlioz' "Damnation of Faust" are examples of Mephisto's glistening, deceptive magic. In Liszt's "Mephisto Waltz" the Evil One mocks Faust's sentimental adventures at a dance. In Wagner's Faust Overture, which was originally intended as the first movement of an entire Faust Symphony, there is more emphasis on the theme of salvation—which was quite according to Wagner's own nature. But even Wagner outdoes himself with the demoniac snarls of Mephisto.

Don Juan may have been a well-known folk-tale personality in many lands before he finally received his name in Spain at about the same time the Faust legend was growing up in Germany. It's not hard to see why Don Juan became a popular character, in spite of the fact that he left a wake of broken hearts behind him. The picture of a man who was irresistible to all women has been as fascinating to his prospective victims as it has to the men who fancied themselves potential Don Juans. And lest people have a bad conscience for admiring such a person, there was the handy ending to the story, the visit of the stone guest: the statue who came to dinner with Don Juan and dragged him down to hell to do eternal penance for his sins.

Purcell and Gluck and half a dozen forgotten com-

posers used the legend before Mozart and Da Ponte made
it into their operatic masterpiece, "Don Giovanni." Then
a long line of French writers, including Mérimée, Dumas,
Alfred de Musset and Flaubert developed the theme. But
Richard Strauss's tone poem, "Don Juan," is based on
still another version of the story by the Austrian poet,
Lenau. In this version, Don Juan is not merely the aristocratic rake and sensualist. His long succession of conquests
represent his search for the ideal woman. This Don Juan
is a dreamer and philosopher as well as lover, and his
desertion of one victim after another represents his suc-
cessive disappointments in his search for the ideal. Disillusionment and contempt for life grow in his heart and at
the end, instead of meeting retribution from the stone
guest and demons and hell-fire, his own dissatisfaction
with life brings about his death. Existence has become in-
tolerable to him and he purposely allows himself to be
stabbed in a duel.

With a rush of pride and gallantry the opening
phrase of the tone poem shows us the Don on his impetuous way to adventure. This is a theme that recurs later in
the music, seeming each time to represent the start of a
new episode. There are several passages of love music and
each one describes the character of the woman in whom
Don Juan hopes to find the ideal. First there is the tender,
ecstatic voice of a solo violin, sweet and confiding, yet with
something aristocratic about it.

Then the music whips off again and the search is
renewed. Perhaps this is the goal. Over a murmuring accompaniment of strings and horns, the oboe sings a song
of forgetfulness and bliss. But once more the orchestra
rouses itself, the dream disperses, and then, through a
brilliant tremolo of the high strings there flashes a theme

of such knightly pride and magnificence as has hardly been equaled in all music. More than any other, this theme, which Strauss gives to six horns in unison, proclaims the essentially noble nature of this Don Juan. There is even a touch of scorn about it, as though for a moment the hero stood above his own fate.

But there follow moments of frivolity. I believe it was here that Strauss many years ago, when he was rehearsing "Don Juan" with the Boston Symphony Orchestra, stopped the players and said to them: "Gentlemen, I must admit that I had not conceived this passage as being so beautiful. She was an ordinary sort of wench." Once again the Don is off on adventure. The orchestra approaches another tremendous climax and then suddenly stops dead in its tracks. There is a terrible pause. The music fades suddenly, and as it subsides a dissonant trumpet note cuts through—the rapier thrust of death. There is no lamenting peroration. But stoical acceptance of the end of all man's searching, and—silence.

VI. *Nature in Music*

JUST AS NO two painters ever see the same colors in a tree, so each musician will catch different overtones from a whispering forest, an echoing thunderbolt, the cadence of waves on a calm beach, the orchestration of color in a sunset, or the shadow of a cloud. Indeed, like the painter, the composer may not see the thing in itself at all, but as a symbol of something else. A river may become the symbol of his country; a stormy sea may stand for a stormy fate ; or nature tamed to the uses of man, as in the Roman fountains, may suggest legend and history of a city.

There was a time in the eighteenth century when philosophers declared that the true function of music was to imitate nature. But fortunately our ideas of nature, both scientific and artistic, change from age to age and man to man. There are a baroque and a rococo conception of nature, there is romantic pantheism, and a naturalist and impressionist view of nature, to name but a few. Debussy's description of his own Nocturnes shows how close he sometimes felt to the impressionist painters of his day. But bare realistic imitation is rare. And the greatest composers, like Beethoven in his Pastoral Symphony, have been first of all concerned with their own emotional reaction to the sights and sounds of changing, changeless nature.

MENDELSSOHN: Hebrides Overture
WAGNER: Overture to "The Flying Dutchman"
RIMSKY-KORSAKOFF: The Sea and Sindbad's
    Ship from "Scheherazade"
DEBUSSY: "La Mer"

"Age cannot wither her nor custom stale her infinite variety" could have been spoken of the sea as well as a beautiful woman. For the poetry of the sea is as old as the memory of man. From Homer's "wine-dark sea" to the shuddering open fifths that begin "The Flying Dutchman" or Debussy's resplendent Dialogue of the Wind and the Sea, there must be as many descriptions as poets who knew the ocean.

The Hebrides Overture (or "Fingal's Cave" as it is also called) was inspired by Mendelssohn's trip to the Islands of the Hebrides off Scotland. A good part of the music came to him when he saw Fingal's Cave. It describes not only the great pillared vault itself but also the cries of the sea birds that inhabit it, the wail of the wind and the lonely waste of sea.

Mendelssohn's trip to the Hebrides was essentially sightseeing. Wagner's experience of the sea was terrifyingly in earnest. The trip across the North Sea which inspired "The Flying Dutchman" threatened to end in shipwreck and drowning for all aboard. For many reasons, Wagner's overture was bound to be different from Mendelssohn's.

Wagner's is a wild, nightmarish, ghost-ridden sea, with a phantom ship that defies the elements and an unhappy human being whose curse is that he cannot die. This man, the Dutchman, and his shadowy crew are doomed to sail the ocean until the Last Judgment. Once every seven years he is allowed to go ashore to search for the only person who can release him from that curse: a woman who shall be true to him till death. At the beginning of the music stands the demoniac figure of the Dutchman, surrounded by a tremolo of the strings like a whistling gale. Then we hear the melody of the gentle, faithful Senta. At the end of the overture light breaks through the storm, the wrathful sea is appeased, and Senta and the Dutchman are united in death and redemption.

The sea which Rimsky-Korsakoff describes in the first movement of his "Scheherazade" is yet another: a sunlit, perfumed sea, colored like a jewel, traveled by legendary barks of the East. The story of the Sea and Sindbad's Ship is told by the Sultana Scheherazade, whose voice we hear in the high, florid notes of the solo violin. The music opens with a powerful, mottolike theme perhaps meant to personify the sea itself and another figure which obviously suggests the rise and fall of the waves in long and graceful cadence—the fairy-tale waves of the "Thousand and One Nights."

Rimsky-Korsakoff had known the sea as a young officer of the Russian Navy. Debussy knew and loved the sea off the coast of France. "You may not know," wrote Debussy once, "that I was intended for the fine career of a sailor, and that only the chance of life led me away from it. Nevertheless I still have a sincere passion for the ocean." The sea music of "Pelléas et Mélisande," his third nocturne, "Sirènes," "La Mer," and many passages in his letters all bear out his words.

"Here I am again," he wrote in 1906, the year after finishing "La Mer," "with my old friend, the sea; it is always endless and beautiful. It is really the thing in nature which best puts you back in your place. But people don't respect the sea sufficiently. . . . In the sea, there should be only sirens, and how do you suppose those estimable persons would consent to return to waters frequented by rather low company?" And again later he speaks of "the sea which is stirred up, wants to dash across the land, tear out the rocks, and has tantrums like a little girl, singular for one of her importance."

"La Mer" consists of three symphonic sketches: From Dawn till Noon on the Sea; Play of the Waves; and Dialogue of the Wind and the Sea. There would be little point in analyzing the score even if that were possible and Debussy had not pronounced himself unalterably against it. First we have an impression of the immense resting power of the ocean at dawn. Gradually the waters awaken. A lazy wisp of foam is cast aloft. A simple two-tone figure from "Sirènes" is the starting point of a development of astonishing imagination and mastery. Debussy is less concerned with conventional melody than with the play of minute fragments of rhythm and tonality, ever-changing reflections of sky, clouds and sunlight on his flashing, tossing orchestral sea. Toward the end, the depths themselves are set in motion with a brief but impressive chorale phrase, which is to return at the climax of the last movement.

In the Play of the Waves the ocean lashes itself into a sportive fury. Rainbow colorings appear and vanish in the fountains of spray.

A deep, threatening voice, as of approaching storm, opens the Dialogue of the Wind and the Sea. A shiver of anticipation runs through the orchestra; there is a swift gathering of forces and the tempest seems about to break. Instead, there is a sudden lull, and from afar we hear a nostalgic call, like the sirens of Debussy's imagination. The siren song is repeated and now it is answered by Tritons' horns; the clamor grows and the creatures of the deep hold high carnival. The chorale of the first movement returns in an exultant climax till at last a curious, unresolved harmony ends the never-ending tale of the sea.

❧❧   ❧❧

WEBER: Overture to "Der Freischütz"
BEETHOVEN: Symphony #6, F major. Pastoral

The Overture to Weber's "Der Freischütz" used to be one of the old stand-bys of symphony programs. Somehow nowadays we don't hear it so often in the concert hall. But how wonderfully fresh it is! It's fresh like the forest air after a storm, and clear as the sunlight, which the horns describe so beautifully at the beginning of the overture. It might be an overture to one of Grimms' fairy tales. As a matter of fact, the "Freischütz" is a fairy tale and it sprang from exactly the same atmosphere as Grimms' tales and from the same source of German folklore. It's a typical fairy story, set in the forest, with ghosts, evil spirits, seven charmed bullets—with which the devil tempts huntsmen's souls—a loving couple, a friendly hermit, and a happy end. But the real hero of the opera is the forest itself, and so the overture, which is a sort of epitome of the opera, reflects the hundred moods of the forest.

What could be more poetic than those serene sunlit bars of the opening, with the tranquil weavings of the strings and the lovely chant of the horns? Then a shadow passes through the forest. The shuddering tremolo of the strings and the mysterious plucked basses are Samiel, the evil tempter with the seven charmed bullets, with which he buys men's souls. The pandemonium in the middle of the overture is the wild midnight storm in the Wolf's Glen, where the bullets are cast, and the ghosts and goblins appear and finally Samiel himself, the Wild Huntsman. Was the Wild Huntsman Wotan or the devil? Probably he was a little of both. For when Christianity came to Germany, instead of banishing the old gods altogether which might have been hard or impossible, it turned them into evil spirits, and Wotan fell from his throne in Valhalla to storm through the forest at midnight with a ghostly pack of hounds and strike terror into the hearts of simple-minded peasants.

But after the storm comes the sunlight again and the jubilant air of Agatha as she greets her beloved Max. The forest is cleansed of evil spirits, and the joyous impetuosity of the music says, as only music can, that "they lived happily ever after."

Beethoven's Pastoral Symphony is also descriptive music, nature-painting by a man who loved nature as much if not more than Weber did. How different from Weber's terrifying, haunted storm, is the storm of the Pastoral Symphony! It seems almost a friendly thunderstorm, which interrupts the merrymaking in the country only long enough to give you perhaps a good dousing, and which gives rise, in Beethoven's words, to "happy and thankful feelings" afterwards.

Beethoven's feelings about all of nature were friendly. He may have had his conflicts, and wild ones too, with human beings, but with nature he felt at ease. More than that, he worshiped the fields and the forest, and he liked best to compose during long walks through the country-side near Vienna.

From Beethoven's sketches for the Pastoral Symphony, we know that he originally planned a much more detailed explanation of the symphony's meaning than was finally published with the score. "Anyone who has an idea of country life," he noted in his sketches, "can make out for himself the intentions of the author, without a lot of titles." And he warned his listeners that the symphony was "more an expression of feelings than painting."

Still, he did indicate in a general way what he had in mind. The first movement describes the "awakening of serene impressions on arriving in the country"; the second a "scene by the brookside"; the third, a "jolly gathering of countryfolk, a thunderstorm and tempest"; and the fourth movement a "shepherd's song, and gladsome and thankful feelings after the storm."

With the arrival in the country, the first movement opens in the sunny key of F major with simple, lively, melodic themes that keep repeating themselves in a sort of naïve joy at their own beauty and charm. There are no labored thematic developments, but rather subtle variations of color and tonality, like the play of light and shade in nature itself. This is music that, like Shakespeare's Master Fenton, "smells April and May."

In the second movement you can hear how Beethoven heard the song of the birds. It opens with the soft murmuring of the brook which continues throughout. Over this accompaniment there is a lovely winding melody, interrupted now and then, particularly towards the end, by the twittering of the birds.

The "jolly gathering of the countryfolk" is the scherzo of the Pastoral Symphony, and here Beethoven rung in some passages imitating a rustic band, which he often heard at the Tavern of the Three Ravens in the country outside Vienna.

But the dancing of the countryfolk is interrupted by a very realistic storm. Notice how wonderfully Beethoven has caught the atmosphere of suspense of the last few seconds before a storm breaks. You can almost see the ominous quiet broken by the first timid scurries of wind and the splash of the first big drops of rain. Then the tempest roars out in its fury. The clouds open and there is thunder and lightning and a screaming wind. It is violent, but not frightening, like the storms in the Overtures to "Der Freischütz" or "The Flying Dutchman." It disappears almost as quickly as it came, and the last echo of the receding thunder is answered by the piping of the shepherd's song of thanksgiving. When the orchestra takes up the shepherd's theme, it is as if the whole world were exulting in the miracle of the fresh-washed sky and air and the return of the sun.

*   *

DEBUSSY: "Prelude to the Afternoon of a Faun"
                  Nocturnes: "Nuages," "Fêtes," "Sirènes"
RESPIGHI: "Fountains of Rome"

Debussy's popular "Afternoon of a Faun" is one of the most sensitive and revealing scores he ever produced. His musical vision of the faun, basking in the gentle warmth of the afternoon sun, is almost symbolic of an age and of a people that had few deep worries, basking in a security and comfort which seem as remote as a fairy tale to us today. Since his early youth Debussy had been fascinated by artistic and literary currents of his time. In the 1880's when he was emerging from his teens, he began frequenting the famous Tuesday evenings at Mallarmé's home, where he was enabled to meet a whole world of people with ideas and feelings sympathetic to his own: Mallarmé himself, Verlaine, Monet, Rodin, Pierre Louys, Gustave Kahn, Paul Claudel, Camille Mauclair, André Gide, Paul Valéry, and celebrated foreigners such as Whistler, Maeterlinck or the German poet, Stefan George.

"Impressionism, symbolism, poetic realism were all merged in a great current of enthusiasm, curiosity, and intellectual passion," writes Dukas, the composer. "Painters, poets, sculptors were all bending questioningly over the material of their mediums, dissecting or recomposing them according to their desires—all trying to give to words, sounds, color and design, new nuances and significance."

Debussy was caught up in this current and his compositions of the ensuing years were influenced more deeply by the men of Mallarmé's salon than by purely musical factors. His painter friends, the impressionists, had discarded the clear outlines and the objectivity of the preceding generation, for misty impressions, dissolved in light. His poet friends, headed by the symbolist, Mallarmé, dissolved the logic of language into a musically suggestive succession of words. Verlaine sought in his poetry "de la musique avant toute chose." It was no accident that Debussy chose Mallarmé's famous poem, "L'Après-Midi d'un Faune," as a subject for his own music. Performed at Paris in 1894, the "Prelude to the Afternoon of a Faun" was his first big public success.

Mallarmé's poem, which doesn't make, and probably wasn't intended to make much logical sense, even when read in French, has been interpreted as follows:

"A faun—a simple, sensuous, passionate being—wakens in the forest at daybreak and tries to recall his experience of the previous afternoon. Was he the fortunate recipient of an actual visit from nymphs, white and golden goddesses, divinely tender and indulgent? Or is the memory he seeks to retain, nothing but the shadow of a vision, no more substantial than the 'arid rain' of notes from his own flute? He cannot tell . . .

"Were they, are they swans? No! But naiads plunging? Perhaps! Vaguer and vaguer grows the impression of this delicious experience. He would resign his woodland godship to retain it . . . Ah, the effort is too great for his poor brain . . . the delicious hour grows vaguer; experience or dream, he will never know which it was."

Debussy's miniature tone poem, while catching the mood of Mallarmé's elusive words, is considerably more understandable. It begins with a single strand of languorous, capricious melody—perhaps the flute of the faun himself. Then touch by touch Debussy adds orchestral color, more and more exotic harmonies and more fantastic transformations of the melody. There is a suggestion of sunlight and warmth, the glitter of water, the hush of a passing breeze, the drowsing forest—and the dream vanishes into thin air.

In his Nocturnes Debussy again takes nature—slow-moving clouds, dancing lights, the sea—as his subject. The title, he explains, does not have the traditional significance of a nocturne. Here, it has "a more general and above all a more decorative meaning."

The first nocturne, "Clouds," reflects, in Debussy's words, "the unchanging aspect of the sky, with the slow and solemn passage of clouds dissolving into a vague grayness tinged with white." The high wood winds weave soft, fluctuating patterns, which repeat and yet change as imperceptibly as the clouds. Underneath, the solitary voice of an English horn chants a melody of loneliness and contemplation.

The second nocturne, "Festivals," reflects (again in Debussy's words) "the restless dancing rhythms of the atmosphere, interspersed with brusque bursts of light. There is also the episode of a procession—a wholly visionary pageant—passing through and blended with the argent revelry. But the background of uninterrupted festival persists—luminous dust participating in the rhythm of all things." It opens with a dazzling burst of light and excited rhythm and vivacious little scraps of melody miraculously derived from the first nocturne. Debussy's orchestration is delicate and spare and it achieves its greatest effects by its reticence. It has always seemed to me that the most marvelous moment of the "Festivals" comes when, after a moment of silence, we hear the almost inaudible, throbbing rhythm of a march, and over it the muted fanfare of distant trumpets. Debussy is the great master of the half-spoken word. And he can make a silence speak with more eloquence than the loudest roar of the orchestra.

For the third nocturne, "Sirens," Debussy asks for a chorus of eight women's voices, which may be why this one is more rarely heard than the other two. It describes "the sea and its endless rhythm. Then amid the billows

silvered by the moon, the mysterious voice of the sirens
is heard. It laughs and passes." The song of the sirens is
without words for, as Philip Hale once said, "To each
hearer on the ship of Ulysses, or to each hearer of Debus-
sey's music, the sirens sang of what might well lure him."

Among the few composers strongly influenced by
Debussy is the Italian Respighi. His "Fountains of Rome,"
composed in 1916, was first performed under Toscanini's
direction at a concert for the benefit of artists disabled in
World War I. In this music Respighi has tried, according to his note in the score, to express "the sentiments and
visions suggested to him by four of Rome's fountains at
the hour in which their character is most in harmony with
the surrounding landscape, or in which their beauty appears most impressive to the observer." They are the
fountain of the Valle Giulia at dawn; the Triton Fountain in the morning; the fountain of Trevi at noonday;
and the Villa Medici fountain at sunset.

The music opens with an impressionist picture of a
pastoral landscape in the soft twilight of morning. "Droves
of cattle pass and disappear in the fresh, damp mists of
a Roman dawn."

A sudden blast of horns and brilliant flourishes of
the whole orchestra introduce the Triton Fountain in the
bright sunshine of morning and the composer imagines a
frenzied dance of Naiads and Tritons between the jets of
water.

This merges imperceptibly into the music of the
great baroque Trevi Fountain at noonday. Trumpets peal
and all the pomp and majesty of the baroque age of Rome
are conjured up before our eyes. Then, as this climax dies
away, we are transported to the gardens of the Villa
Medici, where the fountain glows in the light of sunset.

The melodious clamor of distant church bells merges with the twittering of birds and the rustle of leaves. As the light dies away, there are gleaming pinpricks of sound in the orchestra, like the twinkling of the first stars that usher in the silence of night.

☙☙   ☙☙

WAGNER: Siegfried's Rhine Journey from "Götterdämmerung"
SMETANA: "The Moldau"
JOHANN STRAUSS: "The Beautiful Blue Danube"
KERN: Scenario from "Show Boat"

From the first river that flowed out of the Garden of Eden, to the Mississippi and the Volga the life of men has clustered about their great rivers. Economists tell us we loved rivers because they were an easy path for trade. But much more than trade has centered around them: men's dreams, their legends, poetry, novels, even religion, and their music. There are thousands of river folk songs and both serious and popular composers have added the symphony orchestra to the chorus of praise.

Many years before the Nazis tried to pervert the old German legends into political propaganda, Richard Wagner wrote some of his most romantic and colorful music about Siegfried's journey down the river Rhine. Today the Nazis would hardly make such a fuss about Wagner if they understood what his Siegfried stood for. Siegfried's fight represents the war against the old gods of political power and corruption and against the dragon of greed.

Siegfried's Rhine Journey from "The Twilight of the

Gods," paints the dawn on a mountaintop, Siegfried's leave-taking from his Valkyrie bride, Brünnhilde, and then his journey down the Rhine. The dawn begins to break, the Siegfried motive begins softly in the orchestra and is answered by the appealing melody of Brünnhilde. As the music grows in light and warmth the couple emerge from their cave, take leave of each other, and Siegfried disappears down the side of the mountain, blowing his horn as he goes. Brünnhilde catches one last glimpse of him in the depths of the valley, his horn call echoes once more to the mountain peak. Then the curtains rush together and the orchestra takes up the theme of the Horn Call and weaves it into a picture of Siegfried's journey. The music grows livelier and livelier until we hear the mighty surge of the Rhine and finally, over it all, the cry of the Rhinemaidens, mourning for their lost gold—the gold which was stolen from the bed of the Rhine to make all men slaves of the holder. And now the music takes on a darker hue, for Siegfried is journeying down the Rhine to his death. Only after that tragedy is accomplished can the gold be restored to the maidens, and the world be cleansed of greed and power-seeking men.

After they had occupied Czechoslovakia, one of the first "cultural" decrees of the Nazis was to forbid the performance of Smetana's tone poems, for they express the deep love of the Czechs for the scenery and legends of their country.

In a preface to "The Moldau," Smetana indicates the scenes through which that great river passes in his native land. The Moldau is made, he tells us, from two streams, one cool and calm, the other warm and vivacious, that meet far away in the Bohemian forest. It courses through the woods which echo with hunters' horns, through groves where merry peasants dance and sing at a wedding feast; it rushes through tempestuous rapids, where at night-time the water sprites play in the foam, and finally it comes to the magnificent city of Prague, where it broadens in its march to the sea.

"The Moldau" belongs to a cycle of six symphonic poems entitled "My Fatherland" which closes, perhaps prophetically, with a description of a famous mountain where · Czech heroes are reported to sleep, biding their time until they pour forth and rescue their country in time of direst need.

What the Moldau is to the Czechs, the Danube is to Austria. Strictly speaking, the "Blue Danube" waltz is not a symphonic work, yet the music is so great that the most famous conductors have not hesitated to put it on their programs, and Brahms, one of the most serious composers of the nineteenth century, when he was asked for an autograph, jotted down the first bars of the "Blue Danube" and wrote underneath: "Alas! *Not* by Brahms!"

That waltz itself has created a legend. It doesn't matter if you've been to Vienna, and seen that the Danube is really a sort of nondescript brownish gray—it remains the beautiful blue Danube because of the genius of Johann Strauss. The music is a symbol of the gaiety and grace and charm that were Vienna, and a promise of the day when the waltz will again ring out with the happiness and freedom and laughter that once inspired it.

Just as Strauss's waltz has become a symbol of the Danube, so does Jerome Kern's "Ol' Man River" mean the Mississippi—even to people beyond the borders of our country. In 1941 when Kern wrote his Scenario on Themes from "Show Boat" at the request of the conductor, Artur Rodzinski, he prefaced his music with a quotation from one of Winston Churchill's international broadcasts: "The British Empire and the United States. . . . together. . . . We do not view the process with any misgivings. I could not stop it if I wished. . . . Like the Mississippi it just keeps rolling along. . . . Let it roll on in full flood, inexorable, irresistible, benignant, to broader lands, better days."

Kern, of course, is not a symphonic composer, so when Rodzinski asked him for an orchestral fantasy on "Show Boat," he wisely did not try to write in a symphonic vein which would hardly have corresponded to his themes anyway. Instead, he strung the tunes loosely together in what he called scenario form, roughly outlining the story of his musical comedy.

He begins with a soft melody labeled: "The Mississippi River (Natchez) in the late 1880's." Then an English horn sings the lament of the Negroes on the levee, "Misery's Done Come," and "Ol' Man River" makes his first appearance. Suddenly the orchestra crackles: we hear the roustabouts loading the busy river steamboats and the songs of the Negroes as they work. There is a passage marked Tempo di Blues, an imitation of the calliope of the good ship, *Cotton Blossom,* and a parade of near-folk songs: "Can't Help Lovin' Dat Man," "Make Believe," "Why Do I Love You?" and so on back to "Ol' Man River." More than most of the serious music our country has produced these tunes have the jaunty self-assurance, the gusto and sentimentality and deep underlying sense of power that say America. On the last page of the score, the composer has written:

"He jes' keeps rollin' alon'."

HANDEL: "Water Music"
ROBERT SCHUMANN: Symphony #3, E flat major. Rhenish

One of the most diverting and hotly contested of musical anecdotes centers about the Water Music of George Frederick Handel.

It was in the reign of Good Queen Anne that Handel first visited London. Though only twenty-five, he had already made a brilliant name for himself in Italy. In England he was received with open arms, his music acclaimed by the public and smiled upon by the court. Such was his success that on his second visit he was commissioned to write a birthday ode for the queen as well as the official Te Deum celebrating, among other things, the acquisition of the Rock of Gibraltar. These works won him a yearly stipend of 200 pounds from the queen and such prestige that he stayed on in fashionable, cosmopolitan London, instead of returning to the provincial German court of Hanover which still claimed his services.

The Elector of Hanover was peeved with Handel, not only for overstaying his generous leave of absence, but also for glorifying the birthday of his enemy, Queen Anne, and the Peace of Utrecht, which was disliked in Germany. Now, the elector's feelings need have concerned Handel but little, except for the fact that the elector was heir to the English throne. When Queen Anne died shortly after, and the disgruntled elector arrived in London as George I of England, Handel found himself in disgrace. He wisely kept out of sight of the king until a road to reconciliation seemed clear.

The king, like all London society of the day, loved

pleasure trips on the Thames in the richly caparisoned sailboats and barges, which were often followed by boat-loads of musicians who gave "water serenades" and whole "water concerts." Handel wrote a series of graceful pieces, well suited to play in the open air, and left it to powerful friends at court to find the proper use for them.

One fine summer day, probably August 22, 1715, King George was having himself rowed down the river from Whitehall to Limehouse, enjoying the playing of royal musicians aboard his own boat. Suddenly another bark appeared close by from which ravishingly beautiful music was wafted to the royal ear. George, who was fond of music, inquired, and heard that Handel himself was conducting.

The ruse succeeded. The king was in a good mood. Handel was brought before him. There were excuses, apologies; royal melting and clemency, finally ending in congratulations—and Handel was back in the good graces of the English court.

Some recent scholars have attempted to explode this story which is told us by Handel's first biographer, Main-waring. But it has been accepted by even more modern research and there seems little reason now to doubt its authenticity.

"The King entered his barge at about eight o'clock," writes a contemporary of another such water fete. "By the side of the royal barge was that of the musicians to the number of fifty, who played all kinds of instruments: trumpets, hunting horns, oboes, bassoons, German flutes, French flutes à bec, violins and basses, but without voices. This concert was composed expressly for the occasion by the famous Handel, native of Halle, and the first composer of the King's music. It was so strongly approved by His Majesty that he commanded it to be repeated, once before and once after supper, although it took an hour for each performance.

"The evening party was all that could be desired for the occasion. There were numberless barges and especially boats filled with people eager to take part in it. In order to make it more complete, Mad. de Kilmanseck [the King's mistress] had made arrangements for a splendid supper at the pleasure house of the late Lord Ranelagh at Chelsea on the river, to where the King repaired at an hour after midnight. He left there at three and at half past four in the morning His Majesty was back at St. James's. The concert cost Baron Kilmanseck 150 pounds for the music alone."

Strings and oboes were the backbone of this orchestra, calculated to make its effect in the open air. A miniature overture introduced an abundance of contrasting numbers: dance movements, singing adagios, even fugato pieces, airy minuets, jigs, merry hornpipes and pieces for double orchestra. The version of the "Water Music" most frequently heard today is a selection from probably more than one such water concert, arranged for modern orchestra by the English musician, Sir Hamilton Harty.

But the Thames has not been the only river to inspire music. Schumann composed his Rhenish Symphony as a glorification of the landscape and life of the Rhineland. It was intended primarily for the Rhenish city of Düsseldorf where he was conductor of the civic orchestra, a position for which he was poorly fitted and where he met many disappointments, including the cold reception of this symphony.

The Rhenish is more frankly tone-painting than any of the other three symphonies Schumann wrote. It is cast in five movements instead of four, but this break with tradition is less remarkable if you think of the two last movements as forming a two-part finale.

The festive opening theme is sounded immediately without the formality of an introduction. It dominates the whole first movement, which is among the most brightly colored music Schumann has given us.

The naïve and humorous second movement resembles a swinging peasant dance, the ländler, from which the modern waltz is descended. There is an enchanting sentimental middle section to contrast with the beginning and end.

The third movement is a romanza. Over his fourth movement Schumann originally wrote: "In the character of an accompaniment to a solemn ceremony." But later he struck out this label and remarked: "One should not show his heart to people, for the general impression of a work of art is more effective. At least then the listeners don't make any absurd comparisons in their minds." Yet we do know that this impressive music was inspired by the ceremony of the elevation of a cardinal in the ancient cathedral of Cologne, which Schumann witnessed while he was writing the symphony. The finale opens with a brilliant folk-festival scene and ends with the triumphal return of the cathedral music.

VII. *The Suffering Artist*

T HE ROMANTIC halo with which we surround suffering genius is fairly new. Little more than a century
has passed since Byron dieted on crackers and salts to
preserve his pallid complexion—when face powders of
green-blue hue proclaimed a sorrow-eaten soul—and Berlioz wrote his exhibitionistic masterpiece, the Symphonie
Fantastique. To Berlioz there was no doubt that the story
of his unhappy love would fascinate perfect strangers in
the concert hall. And he was right. For his contemporaries
were not only interested in suffering artists, they expected
artists to suffer as the price of greatness. Naturally all this
public preoccupation with his emotional life influenced
the artist's attitude toward himself and his music. Thus
from Berlioz' day down to our own there runs a romantic
strain of musical autobiography.

But society has not always been interested in the woes of musicians and in such times composers acted differently in their music. Haydn suffered. But he was far from announcing it in his symphonies. Mozart suffered perhaps more. But it never occurred to him that music should lament his tragic fate. And out of the blackest private despair, when he himself was near to suicide, Beethoven wrote a Second Symphony so full of light and joy that it has been called "an heroic lie." Of course it is no lie, nor is it necessarily more heroic than Tchaikovsky's gloomy Pathetic, for example. Each symphony reflects the attitude of the man and hence of the society from which it grew.

MOZART: Symphony #39, E flat (K. 543)
Symphony #40, G minor (K. 550)

To any person who believes that music is a reflection of the mood of the man who wrote it, the music of Mozart must remain forever a riddle. Of course no man can write great music without sincerely feeling what he puts down on paper, but the mood he puts himself into for composing may have nothing in the world to do with the momentary circumstances of his life, or the way he feels about them.

At the very time that Mozart wrote a heartbreaking series of begging letters to his friend Puchberg—letters which show how he was sinking deeper and deeper into a morass of debt and misery—the composer produced one of the greatest miracles of his own amazing career. In the space of about ten weeks, he wrote, aside from other works, his three last and greatest symphonies: the one in E flat major, the one in G minor, and the Jupiter.

On June 17, 1788, apparently in the midst of the E flat Symphony, he moved out of town to cheaper lodgings in the suburbs of Vienna. His old landlord wouldn't let him go until he had paid up all the back rent—which meant more struggles and more begging letters to the faithful Puchberg. Mozart's pitiful explanations of why he couldn't pay back the last loan and why, if Puchberg will only lend him a little more, he can really straighten out his affairs this time, and produce enough music to pay it all back—all this apparently moved Puchberg as much as any present-day reader. Puchberg kept these pathetic and humiliating letters, and though he was too good a business man to be able to believe all the rosy promises of repayment, most of the letters still bear the mark in Puchberg's hand: "Sent so and so much that same day." They were modest sums, most of them. But sometimes the letters asked for more than Puchberg could give. Then there would be a silence, followed by an abject apology from Mozart and a request for a tiny bit of cash to placate some threatening tradesman.

Nine days after Mozart and his ailing wife moved into their cheap suburban quarters, Mozart set his signature to the finished E flat Symphony, which was a flood of golden melody, one of the most cheerful and innocently beautiful symphonies ever written.

The long introduction establishes a mood of wonderful, quiet dignity, a spiritual harmony and serenity, which show how high Mozart's emotions could rise above the care and suffering so soon to destroy his body. The main part of the first movement, which is fast, opens with a graceful, singing theme that is the essence of Mozartean charm and simplicity. But for all its simplicity, it is richly developed. There are brilliant passages for full orchestra tutti, a lively second theme, and endless variety and imagination in this movement—a perfect example of classical symphonic form. It is perfect because it just seems to have grown that way naturally, without any coaxing or goading from the composer's pen.

The songful second movement is pensive and quiet, but not wanting in inner drama, and it is gorgeously colored with the small orchestra Mozart had at his disposal.

The beginning of the minuet recalls the festive joyousness of the first movement. It is cast in strictly symmetrical three-part dance form, and the middle part, the trio for wood winds, is an enchanting musical idyll, with its little echoes, where the flutes take over the melody at the end of each phrase.

The finale is full of witty quips, energetic humor, and high good spirits which convince you, if convincing were needed, that at the moment he conceived this music, Mozart was one of the happiest men alive. The sensitive wounded pride, the humiliation and despair seem to have dissolved into thin air, and the symphony is pure sunlight.

But if anyone should be tempted to think that Mozart's music was all sunshine, or that Mozart was incapable of expressing pain and struggle in his music, he need only listen to the G minor Symphony. One of the most tragic works Mozart ever wrote, it is full of restless agitation, even in the melancholy slow movement. It is full of dramatic contrasts, and yet so compact that there isn't one superfluous note in the score.

You may have noticed the particularly warm, golden color of the orchestra in the E flat Symphony. That was due to Mozart's skillful use of the clarinets, which he particularly loved, and to the fact that in the E flat Symphony he completely left out the somewhat acid tone of the oboe. In the G minor Symphony, on the other hand, Mozart did just the opposite thing. He left out the smooth clarinets, and emphasized the dark, tragic mood of the music by giving great prominence to the oboes. It's true that he did later add clarinets for another performance, in order to make the orchestra sound fuller. But the original version is the one which most conductors prefer today.

The E flat Symphony, you remember, begins with a long and impressive introduction in slow tempo. The first movement of the G minor dispenses entirely with an introduction, the throbbing main theme enters immediately and is punctuated as it goes along by sharp blows of the full orchestra. After a pause, the graceful, drooping melody of the second theme sounds in the wood-wind instruments, and out of these two the whole movement is built. Following this exposition of the thematic material, there is a violent harmonic wrench into a distant and foreign tonality. Here the first theme is chopped up into little pieces, and tossed back and forth from one part of the orchestra to another, and repeated, now in a shout, now in a whisper. Then the excitement dies down and the first part of the movement returns—but with a difference. This time the second theme too sings in the minor key, with unforgettable poignancy.

The slow second movement has all the typical rococo frills we associate with Mozart's time, and usually with music of the lighter sort. But what a different language they speak here! There is a restless, pulsing undertone all through this section of the symphony, which rises to a sharp, agonized climax in the middle.

The third movement is a minuet—in name—but it is far from the quaint, courtly nonchalance and the polite laughter we associate with a minuet. It is an aggressive, straightforward, square-toed piece, with a hearty, thumping rhythm. In the pretty little trio in the middle comes the only glimpse of sunshine we have in the whole symphony.

The last, very fast movement is full of grim, hectic humor, which is next door to tragedy. A theme of the kind that was compared to a skyrocket in Mozart's day skips up through the orchestra. It skips lightly and gaily enough at first, but soon there are wild, rushing figures in the violins and the rest of the instruments join the fray. Not even the singing second theme can hold up the dynamic drive of this finale. Sharp harmonies clash and for a moment chaos seems loose. There is a quick, tragic climax like the one in the first movement. Then order is restored. The themes return in clearer form, and the work closes with insistent, almost despairing reiterations of that dark fundamental: G minor.

BEETHOVEN: Symphony #2, D major
SCHUBERT: Symphony #8, B minor. Unfinished

Beethoven's Second Symphony has been called "an heroic lie"—not because the music is particularly heroic, but because Beethoven was able to write such a witty, carefree work while he himself was passing through the most terrible agony of soul. The symptoms of Beethoven's approaching deafness had begun a few years earlier with a roaring in his ears, but he had not yet faced the idea that he might lose his hearing altogether. It seemed to him that deafness was a ridiculous and shameful malady for a musician, and he did his best to keep the secret from his friends. "I shall, as far as possible, defy my fate," he wrote, "although there must be moments when I shall be the most miserable of God's creatures. . . . I will grapple with fate. It shall never pull me down!"

In order to protect his ears as much as possible, Beethoven's doctor advised him to spend the summer of 1802 outside of noisy Vienna. The little village of Heiligenstadt was one of his favorite country haunts for composing. So he took rooms in a large peasant house which stood alone outside the town in high fields where his windows looked out far over the plain, across the Danube and beyond to the Carpathian Mountains that lined the horizon.

In the midst of these idyllic surroundings, in the midst of the lighthearted music of the Second Symphony Beethoven realized with crushing certainty what was in store for him: total deafness. To be merely hard of hearing was a bearable misfortune. That could be passed off among his friends—or so he thought—as absent-mindedness. But now a terrible silence was closing in upon him, slowly cutting him off from the world, from the sound of music, and from his friends.

Beethoven used to take long walks into the woods about Heiligenstadt. "On one of these wanderings," says his pupil, Ferdinand Ries, "I called his attention to a shepherd who was piping very agreeably in the woods on a flute made of a twig of elder. For half an hour Beethoven could hear nothing, and though I assured him it was the same with me (which was not true), he became extremely quiet and morose. When he occasionally appeared to be merry, it was generally to the point of boisterousness; but even that happened seldom."

It may have been this very incident which suddenly showed Beethoven the suffering that lay ahead for him, and which inspired that gloomy document, the Heiligenstadt Testament.

"What a humiliation," he wrote, "when one stood beside me and heard a flute in the distance and *I* heard nothing, or someone heard *the shepherd singing* and again

I heard nothing, such incidents brought me to the verge of despair, but a little more and I would have put an end to my life—only art it was that withheld me, ah, it seemed impossible to leave the world until I had produced all that I felt called upon to produce, and so I endured this wretched existence."

Still he dined and joked and played music with his friends. Not until after his death did the record of the Heiligenstadt Testament reveal the anguish he had gone through during that apparently serene summer.

The Second Symphony opens with a slow introduction, which may remind you of Haydn except for the new note of virility it contains. The gay themes that follow might also have been written by Haydn. But instead of trotting docilely down the path which Haydn and Mozart laid out, Beethoven's themes suddenly take the bit in their teeth and gallop off in a burst of excitement. Conservatives of the day clutched their seats in terror lest the whole symphonic buggy be overturned before they got home to the final cadence. They needn't have been afraid or indignant. For Beethoven's themes, strong and self-willed as they are, follow a discipline of their own.

The lovely melody of the slow movement is followed by a tiny scherzo that foreshadows the bearish humor of Beethoven's maturity.

A bold orchestral somersault opens the finale: a boisterous, explosive rondo.

A critical bigwig of Beethoven's time characterized the Second Symphony as "a gross monster, a pierced dragon, which will not die, and even in losing its blood [in the last movement], wild with rage, still deals furious blows with its tail, stiffened in the last agony." To us it is a touching farewell to the half century of Haydn and

Mozart classicism, and at the same time a prophecy of the later, greater Beethoven.

Franz Schubert, who worshiped Beethoven like a god, shared little with him except misfortune. Schubert's Unfinished Symphony, which breaks off midway, like his own tragic life, is music from another world, yet modesty and simplicity itself. For Schubert was a simple, modest man. Unlike Beethoven, who could domineer the great aristocracy of Vienna or scold Goethe for doffing his hat to them, Schubert had humble friends and a shy manner. He never succeeded in attracting serious notice from the great society in which Beethoven moved with such assurance. He was truly at home only when he could escape from the neighborhood of aristocrats to the company of housemaids and his jolly tavern companions, whom he entertained with practical jokes, with improvised waltzes on a wheezy old piano, and with performances of his immortal song, "The Erl-King" on a hair comb.

But whether he played on a comb or a symphony orchestra, Schubert's music was always a song. That was his weakness and his strength. It is what makes the two movements of his Unfinished Symphony so intensely individual. He says things here which no one had yet said with an orchestra, and which no one after him was ever to repeat.

The poetic and introspective first movement grows out of the mysterious introductory phrase for cellos and basses. In ten short measures the mood is established and the thematic foundation laid. Then over a murmuring accompaniment of the strings the oboe sings a song of unforgettable melancholy. The second theme is another melodic fragment given to the cellos. Parts of the devel-

opment are stirringly dramatic and at the end, the introduction is brought back with a phrase of laconic tragedy.

Like the first movement, the second has a short introductory phrase, the seed from which springs the whole
luxuriant growth of melody.

"My music is the product of my genius and my misery," said Schubert, "and that which I have written in
my greatest distress is that which seems best to the world."
After the funeral of Beethoven, Schubert drank a toast to
the one of his company who should be next to go. That
one was Schubert himself. And his misery followed him to
the end. A few days before his death, he sent out one of
his friends to sell some of his recently completed songs,
among the greatest he had written. The friend came back
with the money in his hand. The songs had brought six
cents apiece.

SCHUBERT: Overture to "Rosamunde"
Symphony #7, C major

"Mr. Schubert displays originality in his compositions, but unfortunately bizarrerie as well. The young man
is in a stage of development in his art which we hope may
proceed satisfactorily. On this occasion he received too
much applause."

The occasion on which Schubert received too much
applause was the first performance of the play "Rosamunde," for which he had written the incidental music,
and the man who delivered that solemn verdict was critic

of the Viennese paper, the *Sammler*. "Rosamunde" must have been a very bad play. It survived exactly two performances and then Mr. Schubert's incidental music was tucked away in a dark corner and forgotten. But it's good to know that he once received too much applause.

Some forty years after Schubert's death, Sir George Grove, the editor of the famous music dictionary, unearthed a few scattered pieces of the "Rosamunde" music in Vienna. He set his heart on finding the rest, and the following year he returned to Vienna with Arthur Sullivan (of Gilbert and Sullivan) to continue the search. Up to the last moment of their stay, they hadn't found a trace of the music, and they felt it would be a cruel failure to leave without accomplishing the main object of their trip.

"It was Thursday afternoon," writes Grove, "and we proposed to leave for Prague on Saturday. We made a final call on Dr. Schneider, to take leave and repeat our thanks and also, as I now firmly believe, guided by a special instinct. The doctor was civility itself; he again had recourse to the cupboard and showed us some treasures that had escaped us before. I again turned the conversation on the 'Rosamunde' music; he believed that he had at one time possessed a copy or sketch of it all. Might I go to the cupboard and look for myself? Certainly, if I had no objection to being smothered in dust. In I went; and after some search, during which my companion kept the doctor engaged in conversation, I found, at the bottom of the cupboard, and in its farthest corner, a bundle of music books two feet high, carefully tied round, and black with the undisturbed dust of nearly half a century. . . . When we dragged the bundles into the light, we found that . . . these were the part books of 'Rosamunde,' tied up after the second performance in December, 1823, and probably never disturbed since. Dr. Schneider must have been amused at our excitement. . . ."

That, of course, was the trouble. Dr. Schneider was like the rest of the world, which had patronized Schubert when he was alive, patronized him after his death and even today isn't fully aware of the riches he left.

When Brahms produced his First Symphony, his admirers liked to call it the Tenth, meaning it was the only symphony written up to then worthy to place beside the immortal nine of Beethoven. Again, they were forgetting the modest, tragic little man—Schubert. For just as he was neglected during his lifetime, so were his symphonies neglected and undervalued later on. Yet his Seventh Symphony, which poor Schubert never heard performed, is worthy to stand beside Beethoven.

It is long: when played without cuts it fills nearly a full hour with glorious music. And for Schubert's day it was considered difficult. There is no good reason to doubt the traditional story which says he wrote this symphony for the Musikverein of Vienna, that they accepted it and even began rehearsals, but when it seemed too long and difficult to them they finally discarded it in favor of an earlier and easier symphony by the same composer.

Beethoven had the tragedy of his deafness to bear. He could never hear his last and greatest works. But at least they were performed and he received, by and large, the admiration and affection he deserved. Schubert's tragedy was even crueler: he could have heard his last symphony, had anyone during his lifetime been interested enough, or thought the work important enough to overcome the slight difficulties it offered. After his death it was performed twice, and then lay forgotten for ten long years until Schumann visited Vienna. Schumann looked through a whole mass of manuscripts in the possession of Schubert's brother, Ferdinand, and found the great symphony in C major which had never been published. He had a copy made and sent to his friend, Mendelssohn, who performed it several times at the famous Gewandhaus Concerts in Leipzig. Mendelssohn even tried—in vain—to get the London Philharmonic to perform it. Later, when he went to London as guest conductor of that orchestra, he wanted to put it on his own programs, but the players were laughingly and openly contemptuous, and so once more Schubert's masterpiece was shelved.

This Seventh Symphony has come up the hard way, from neglect, contempt and misunderstanding, to the place it deserves among the greatest symphonies ever written. One reason it had to wait so long is that musicians and music lovers have tended, ever since Beethoven, to regard Beethoven as the eternal standard of what a symphony should be. There is no eternal standard of what a symphony should be, any more than Gluck, or Rossini, or Verdi, or Wagner, or Richard Strauss have given us an eternal standard of what an opera should be. The word "symphony" is nothing more than a name or a tag given to a piece of music, and originally it meant nothing more than that: a piece of music. It can have and has had a thousand forms and styles.

As a matter of fact, Schubert was a passionate admirer of Beethoven, and he was deeply influenced by him. But what makes his Seventh Symphony great is not its resemblance to Beethoven; it is its resemblance to Schubert.

Its inspiration never flags from the foursquare theme that opens the first movement to the overwhelming coda of the finale. That first theme is not only the basis of the

leisurely, Olympian introduction; it is the thematic kernel of the whole first movement. As the tempo quickens,
its bold, dotted rhythm sets the whole orchestra swinging
with exuberance and power. There is another, delicious,
rocking figure which Schubert gives to the wood winds in
the melancholy relative key of E minor. And now, instead
of a traditional development of these two themes, there
follows one of Schubert's most marvelous breaks with tradition, a break that Schubert made, not because he didn't
know the tradition, but because he had something more
important to say. In a wonderfully imaginative passage
the trombones very softly take up a fragment of the introduction. The theme grows and swells and takes hold of
the whole orchestra and mounts to a blazing triumphant
climax. The rest of the movement is more along orthodox
lines, and in spite of its length, there is not one note too
many.

After a few introductory bars, the slow movement begins with a pathetic little tune, piped by the oboe, in a
sort of march rhythm that is like the pitiful courage and
persistence of Schubert himself in the face of his own
despair. Later on there is a dreamy phrase for the strings
leading into some of the most romantic music ever written for horns. It was probably this spot that Schumann
referred to when he said that "it seems to come from another sphere, while everything listens, as though some
heavenly messenger were hovering around the orchestra."

The scherzo begins in a robust, burly mood, but it
has a middle section full of the nostalgia and sentiment
that we all associate with Schubert's Vienna.

And the finale is an apotheosis of the driving power
and impetus of rhythm. It is on a vast scale, but it is full
of concentrated might. Here Schubert shows us that Bee-

thoven was not the only one who could laugh and exult with the elements. What might have come afterward if Schubert had only lived? Over his grave they wrote: "Music has buried here a rich treasure, but still fairer hopes."

❧❧   ❧❧

BERLIOZ: Symphonie Fantastique

Hector Berlioz was a martyr and a symbol. In all the strange history of music, you must look hard to find a more fantastic figure than that heroic, unreasonable, pathetic man. By great good fortune, he was also slightly mad. No one in his right senses would ever have begun such an impossible project as Berlioz' Symphonie Fantastique. And no really sane man could have left such a fitting monument to the topsy-turvy world in which Berlioz lived.

It was an age of revolution. One bastion after another toppled before the onslaught of the younger generation: old canons of behavior, old political dogma, and ancient artistic traditions. Eighteen-thirty, the year that Berlioz' Fantastic Symphony burst on an astonished world, saw three different revolutions. It was the year of the political revolution that swept Louis-Philippe, the Citizen-King, into the throne of France. It was the year of the literary and theatrical revolution that swept Victor Hugo onto the spiritual throne of France, with a triumphant performance of his romantic melodrama, "Hernani." And finally it was the year of the musical revolution that established Berlioz as the father of a grand line of romantic orchestral composers that runs through Liszt and Wagner to Mahler and Strauss and even to the young Soviet composer, Dimitri Shostakovitch.

Berlioz, of course, can have had little idea of the tremendous influence he would have over a century of European music, but that doesn't mean he didn't recognize the importance of his symphony—even before it was written. He had just fallen in love with the Irish actress, Henrietta Smithson. He knew her only from the stage, but he declared: "That woman shall be my wife, and on that story I shall write my greatest symphony."

The extraordinary thing was not that Berlioz should make such a prophecy—after all, other young men have made such prophecies before and after—the extraordinary thing was that the prophecy came true. Berlioz was only twenty-four when he first saw Miss Smithson as Ophelia, and his musical training at the time was of the sketchiest. He had arrived in Paris three years before, not to study music but to take courses in medicine. But the spirit of the times was too much for Berlioz. He soon deserted the laboratory to take his place among the incredible collection of geniuses that walked the streets of Paris. There were Victor Hugo, Balzac, Musset, Gautier, Dumas, Heine, Liszt, Chopin, Meyerbeer, Rossini, Paganini —and a hundred other romantic artists—and Berlioz knew he was predestined to be one of that illustrious company.

There was little time to lose. He studied at the Paris Conservatory, learning nothing but contempt for the pedants, but much from the sympathetic spirits he found there. He came to know the orchestral instruments at first hand from the men who played them. And within the space of a few months, his wild enthusiasm for orchestral effects and his completely uninhibited imagination made him the greatest living master of descriptive music.

But with Miss Smithson he had harder sledding. He wooed her with such impetuosity that at first he seemed little but a burden to her. She said she liked him "well enough," which was an insult to his volcanic heart. Then two years after he had first seen her in "Hamlet," she returned to London. While she was gone, the slanderous stories Berlioz heard about her drove him nearly insane and it is said that for two whole days he wandered desolate, without food and without sleep, through the countryside about Paris, meditating his betrayal and the perfidies of Miss Smithson.

Meanwhile the symphony grew. The plot of the symphony—for you remember he had decided to write the story of his love—was a masterpiece of exhibitionism and self-pity.

But in Berlioz' day, such outpourings didn't seem as strange as they would today. He belonged to a generation when no artist, or would-be artist, could afford not to be suffering from some grand passion: political, amorous, or otherwise. And if you were reticent about it, people concluded you had no feelings to express. It was probably the only age which could have made a fad of suicide. That may sound flippant, but it's true. Fortunately, Berlioz didn't commit suicide. He produced a symphony instead.

It was prefaced with this thinly veiled explanation: "A young musician of morbid sensibility and ardent imagination poisons himself with opium in a fit of amorous despair. The narcotic dose, too weak to result in death, plunges him into a heavy sleep, accompanied by the strangest visions, during which his sensations, sentiments and recollections are translated in his sick brain into musical thoughts and images. The beloved woman herself has become for him a melody, like a fixed idea, which he finds and hears everywhere."

The symphony itself, which is more like a symphonic poem than a conventional symphony, is divided not into four, but five parts. Part One is called Dreams, Passions, and according to Berlioz' program it recalls first the uneasiness of soul which he experienced before meeting her whom he loves, then the frantic love with which she inspires him, his moments of delirious anguish, of jealous fury, his returns to loving tenderness, and his religious consolations.

In Part Two he sees his beloved at a ball, in the midst of the tumult of a brilliant fete. Part Three is a pastoral scene in the fields, with two shepherds playing to each other on their pipes. But even in these calm surroundings, his heart stops beating as she appears once more, and he is overcome with anxious presentiments: what if she were to betray him?

Now the musician dreams that he has slain his beloved. He is condemned to death and led to execution. Part Four is the march to the scaffold, and the finale is a gruesome Walpurgis Night's dream. He sees himself at the witches' Sabbath. A horrifying clan of ghosts, magicians, witches and nameless monsters have gathered to celebrate his obsequies. Even here he is not safe from the torments of the beloved woman. Her melody reappears, but it has lost its noble, modest character. It has become a trivial, grotesque dance tune. There are howlings of joy at her arrival, funeral bells and a burlesque of the ancient religious chant, Dies Irae.

The original program of the Symphonie Fantastique was even more open than the one it bears today, and Berlioz hoped the wretched woman would be there to hear the first performance. "But I do not believe she will," he declared. "She will surely recognize herself in reading the program of my instrumental drama, and she will take care not to appear."

Fortunately Miss Smithson was away. But two years later, after she had failed in London and in desperation had returned to Paris, hoping to open her own theatre there, she was invited to another performance of this Symphonie Fantastique. She went and read the program, which Berlioz had toned down considerably in the meantime, she remembered his incredible wooing, was flattered at the thought he had taken poison for her, and her heart softened. The audience was a brilliant one. It included Alexandre Dumas, Hugo, Paganini and Heine. And Berlioz presided at the kettledrums. Heine tells us that every time Berlioz caught Miss Smithson's eye he gave a furious roll on the kettledrums. Be that as it may, he certainly caught her eye, and they were married.

The marriage was a failure, but the symphony was a tremendous success. It is difficult to perform—not because the notes are hard to play, but because there are few conductors who have the imagination and passion to transport themselves and their audience into the fantastic world of Berlioz' dreams. But to those who have the flair, and to their fortunate listeners, it is a world of unforgettable drama and music that will not die.

Robert Schumann: Overture to "Manfred"
                  Symphony #2, C major

The great melancholy god of romanticism, on the continent at least, was Byron. "The English may think of Byron as they please," wrote Goethe, "but this is certain that they have no poet who is to be compared with him." His masterpiece, "Manfred," so excited the romantically minded that it was translated thirty-one times: into French, German, Italian, Spanish, Russian, Czech, Roumanian, Romaic, Danish, Hungarian, Polish and Dutch.

Byron himself, in a letter to his publisher, declared his dramatic poem to be "of a very wild, metaphysical and inexplicable kind. Almost all of the persons—but two or three—are spirits of the earth and air, or the waters; the scene is in the Alps; the hero is a kind of magician, who is dominated by a species of remorse, the cause of which is left half unexplained. He wanders about invoking these spirits, which appear to him and are of no use; he at last goes to the very abode of the Evil Principle, in *propria persona,* to evoke a ghost, which appears and gives him an ambiguous and disagreeable answer; and in the third act is found by an attendant dying in a tower, where he had studied his art."

Like so many of his contemporaries, Schumann was deeply impressed by "Manfred." His overture paints the gloomy passion and pride of Byron's hero almost more eloquently than the play itself. The instrumentation is highly original and the music tense with conflicting emotions.

"It really matters very little," as Donald Tovey wrote, "that Schumann himself was so un-Byronic. The particular Byronic trait that he lacked was nothing but the bluff of a mysterious and mythological wickedness. Schumann had a reverence for sorrow of all kinds, as the root of his appreciation of romantic poetry; and romantic poetry attains great heights in 'Manfred'."

Schumann's Second Symphony is the only one of his four directly connected with the tragedy that ended both his career and, two years later, his life. His was a frail and sensitive genius. So sensitive that he suffered from little things an ordinary person would have taken in his stride; so sensitive that he eventually collapsed in his struggle with the material world and the mental and emotional struggles of composing.

For the first few years, Schumann's ecstatically happy marriage to Clara Wieck seemed not only to have restored him to complete calm and happiness. It seemed to have given him immense new resources of strength. But after a trip to Russia in his thirty-fourth year Schumann was troubled by a growing nervousness. At times his memory would desert him, and he was exhausted by composing. Finally he had to give up work of all kinds, including his editorship of the progressive *Neue Zeitschrift für Musik* which he had founded. Schumann had always had a peculiar dread of insanity and that summer he appeared to be on the verge of it.

In the fall he and Clara moved back to the quiet atmosphere of Dresden where he gradually recovered his health. It was in the course of this convalescence that he wrote his so-called Second Symphony. Actually this is his third. For his real second symphony, composed the same year as the first, was withdrawn after performance, revised and only published several years later as Number Four.

Although Dresden was a quieter city than Leipzig where the Schumanns had been living, there were at least two interesting people whose acquaintance he made here. One was the widow of Weber, the composer of "Der Freischütz," who had shared certain romantic traits with Schumann. The other was Richard Wagner. It was at this time that Wagner's "Tannhäuser" was first performed at the Dresden Opera, where Wagner was the leading conductor. Schumann of course heard it, but although he spoke highly of it, he deplored Wagner's lack of melody. Probably because of Schumann's faint appreciation of Wagner, and the tremendous difference in the two men's temperament, they never became close friends.

Schumann was not only in poor health; he had never been an expansive conversationalist, and now he spoke less than ever. Wagner afterwards said of him that he was a highly gifted musician, but an impossible person. It seems that when he visited Schumann he tried every subject he could think of—music, literature, politics and so on— but during a whole hour Schumann uttered hardly a word. "One can't always speak alone," said Wagner afterwards.

Schumann on the other hand, remarked of this one-sided conversation that Wagner was a well-informed and talented man, but that he talked incessantly, and one couldn't put up with it for long.

Of the symphony he composed at this time Schumann said: "I wrote the symphony in December, 1845, when I was still half sick. It seems to me that one must hear this in the music." And again: "I sketched it when I was in a state of physical suffering. I may even say that it was, so to speak, the resistance of the spirit, which exercised a visible influence here, and through which I sought to contend with my bodily state. The first movement is full of this struggle and is very capricious and refractory."

And it's true that the feverish first movement seems a reflection of the troubled fancies that were eventually to overthrow Schumann's mind completely. It begins with a slow introduction that is like a troubled dream. At the very opening stands a dominating horn motive or motto, which is to reappear in two of the remaining three movements and again at the end of the first.

The second movement, a scherzo, uses at the beginning a figure based on the motto we have just been talking about, except that here the mood is more agitated and wilder, and the harmonic background is sharper and more vivid. And again we hear the call of the horn.

The third movement is by far the most appealing, at least at first hearing. It is a melancholy, romantic song, sung first by the violins, then by the oboes, and it grows in yearning and passion to an ecstatic climax in the wood-wind instruments against poignant trills of the violins descending semitone by semitone. There is a short passage of staccato counterpoint for the sake of contrast, and then the song returns, to close in the sweeter major mode.

"In the finale," Schumann wrote, "I first began to feel myself; and indeed I was much better after I had completed the work." It begins brilliantly with an introductory passage of chords and scale passages leading into an impassioned theme for solo wind instruments. For the moment, at least, Schumann seemed to have won out over the dark powers that threatened him. And the final sounding of the ominous horn is transformed into the exultation of victory.

TCHAIKOVSKY: "Francesca da Rimini"
Symphony #4, F minor

The tragedy of Francesca da Rimini was not of Dante's invention, though most of the artists who have put it into words or music have taken their inspiration from the famous episode in the fifth canto of Dante's "Inferno." The story is a true one which was well known in Dante's day.

Francesca was sought in marriage by Gianciotto, an elderly nobleman of Rimini. But Gianciotto wooed her by proxy through his handsome young brother, Paolo. Francesca, believing Paolo to be her future husband, fell in love with him. When she came to Rimini and found herself married to Gianciotto it was too late; she and Paolo were unable to restrain their love. One day Gianciotto surprised them together and murdered them both.

The interesting thing about this story is the sympathy which Dante shows for the guilty lovers, in spite of the fact that the church considered their souls eternally damned. His romantic attitude toward forbidden love was typical of the age of chivalry and "amour courtois," which proclaimed real love to be possible only outside the marriage bond. The power of this tragic conception of love is proved by a dozen contemporary legends like those of Launcelot and Guinevere or Tristan and Isolde, many of which have retained their popularity undiminished to our own day.

Tchaikovsky's music describes Dante's meeting, in the second circle of the Inferno, with the souls of Paolo and Francesca. They are in illustrious company: Helen of

Troy, Paris, Cleopatra, Achilles, Tristan. Here according to the medieval concept of hell, punishment is meted out for the sins of the flesh. Just as in life these souls were driven by storms of passion, so now they are forever tossed on the winds of an infernal tempest which fills the second circle of hell.

As the ghosts of the unhappy couple approach through the air, Dante calls out to them. In the name of their love he begs them to pause and tell him how they first lost their hearts.

It is Francesca who tells the story, briefly, in words of the utmost poignance. She begins with the famous lines, which Tchaikovsky used as the motto for his score: "There is no greater pain than happiness remembered in time of misery." They were reading one day quite innocently the story of the loves of Launcelot, when their eyes met over the book. They came to the place where Launcelot kissed his love and "Then he," says Francesca, "who ne'er

"From me shall separate, at once my lips
All trembling kissed. The book and writer both
Were love's purveyors. In its leaves that day
We read no more."

While the one spirit speaks, the other falls to weeping so grievously that Dante is overcome with pity and sinks unconscious to the ground.

Tchaikovsky's symphonic fantasy suggests first the grandeur and terror of the infernal landscape, the blasting winds. The tender, melodious middle section is the voice of Francesca's love. Then we hear the screaming of the wind again as the two souls are swept away on the storm, each the eternal torment and the eternal consolation of the other.

It is not surprising that Tchaikovsky was drawn to such a subject as "Francesca da Rimini." The anguish, grief and loneliness of his life had prepared him well.

"Fate, the mocker," he wrote in 1875, "has arranged so that for the past ten years all whom I most love in the world are far from me. I am extremely lonely in Moscow. . . . Perhaps this is partly my own fault. I don't make friends easily. . . . Nearly all winter I was constantly unhappy, sometimes to the very edge of despair. I longed for death. With the coming of spring these attacks have ceased, but I know that with every winter they will return stronger than ever."

Tchaikovsky dedicated his Fourth Symphony, which he composed the year after "Francesca da Rimini," to his best friend. And it is typical of Tchaikovsky that his best friend, to whom he poured out his soul in long, passionate letters of confession, was a woman he never met. For a man who lived in his own world of fantastic dreams, even more than most artists do—for a man of Tchaikovsky's emotional instability, to whom existence was a cruel, incomprehensible tragedy, this shadowy, idealistic intimacy with his "beloved friend," Nadejda von Meck, was a wonderful boon. Their friendship was shadowy only in the sense that it involved Tchaikovsky in none of the difficulties of a direct human relationship. But it was very real in the sense that Mme. von Meck supported him, or partly supported him with her own money for many years.

Mme. von Meck, who belonged to a completely different world both socially and financially, had fallen under the spell of his music. She began tactfully by giving him several commissions which finally grew into a yearly stipend that relieved him of most material worries. But at the same time she had the intuitive good sense to stipulate that they should never meet.

Hardly had Tchaikovsky begun his Fourth Symphony when his loneliness and melancholy drove him, as they had before, to thoughts of marriage. "I am very much changed," he wrote to one friend, "especially mentally. Not a kopeck's worth of fun and gaiety is left in me. Life is terribly empty, tedious and tawdry. My mind runs toward matrimony or indeed any other steady bond."

The temptation of a steady bond was nearer than he knew. It took the form of Antonina Ivanovna Milukova, who was young, pretty, attractive and madly in love with Tchaikovsky. She had seen him first at the Moscow Conservatory and though Tchaikovsky had never noticed her, she wrote him ardent, frantic love letters. She persuaded him to see her, then threatened to commit suicide if he wouldn't see her again and so on until finally it was a question of marriage. Tchaikovsky made it perfectly plain that he did not love her; all he could offer was friendship and solicitude. But she persisted and so, partly because he felt guilty of encouraging her, partly out of pity, and partly out of his own desire to settle down, Tchaikovsky gave in and they were married.

It ended as anyone who knew either Tchaikovsky or his wife could have predicted—in an explosion. Within a month Tchaikovsky in the most frightful agitation rushed out of their Moscow home and spent the summer away from his wife. In the fall he made one more attempt to take up their life together, and this time his mistaken chivalry brought him to the verge of madness.

He fled to St. Petersburg, had a complete nervous breakdown on the way, was taken to the hotel nearest the station there, where he lay unconscious for two days and then passed into a high fever. His doctors ordered him to go to Switzerland, and gradually, in a quiet village on Lake Geneva, he won back his peace of mind and strength. And then, with the help of Mme. von Meck, he went back to his interrupted Fourth Symphony. It was to her that he wrote a description of the symphony which reveals so much of the workings of his tortured mind.

The subject of the symphony is pitiless fate. "The introduction is the kernel, the quintessence, the chief thought of the whole symphony. This is fate, the fatal power which hinders one in the pursuit of happiness from gaining the goal. This might is overpowering and invincible. There is nothing to do but submit and vainly complain." The fast part of the movement Tchaikovsky calls "a sweet dream." "A radiant being promising happiness floats before me and beckons me. But the dream disappears."

In the second movement he describes "the melancholy feeling that enwraps one, when he sits at night, alone in the house, exhausted by work. The book which he had taken to read has slipped from his hand. A swarm of reminiscences has arisen." The famous pizzicato third movement, with its pluckings of the string instruments, expresses no clear idea. There are, says Tchaikovsky, "vague figures that slip into the imagination, when one has taken a little too much wine. The mood is now gay, now mournful. . . . Suddenly the picture of an intoxicated peasant and a street song rush into the imagination. Military music is heard passing by in the distance. These are disconnected pictures, which come and go in the brain of the sleeper." In the fourth movement Tchaikovsky says: "If you find no pleasure in yourself, look about you. Go to the people. See how they can be jolly, how they surrender

themselves to gaiety. Scarcely have you forgotten yourself, scarcely have you had time to be absorbed in the
happiness of others, before untiring fate announces its
approach. The other children of men are not concerned
with you. They neither see nor feel that you are lonely
and sad. How they enjoy themselves, how happy they are!
And do you still maintain that everything in the world is
sad and gloomy? There still is happiness! Simple, naïve
happiness!"

TCHAIKOVSKY: Symphony #6, B minor. Pathetic

Tchaikovsky let it be known that there was a story
behind his Pathetic Symphony. But what that story was,
he never told. It is possible that the break with his beloved
friend and protectress, Mme. von Meck, had a great deal
to do with it. For that was one of the cruelest blows he had
ever had to suffer.

Though they had never met, both he and Mme. von
Meck had sworn eternal friendship a thousand times in
their letters, and each of them had meant it deeply and
sincerely. By now Tchaikovsky was famous enough to be
quite capable of supporting himself, but through the years
he had come to value the affection of Mme. von Meck far
more than her money. Then unexpectedly, curtly, she had
broken with him on the pretext that she could no longer
help him.

Tchaikovsky inquired anxiously what was to become
of her in reduced circumstances, repeated that her friend-

ship and faith were more important to him than anything else. But he never heard from her. What was worse, she seemed to have lost all interest in him. Never again, even through third persons, did she inquire about him. And to crown his injury, Tchaikovsky learned that she had lost little or nothing of her fortune. She was as rich as before.

Now he felt doubly humiliated. Bitterly he recalled her extravagant protestations of friendship and suspected that it had all been a pose, the passing whim of a wealthy woman. But characteristically, instead of blaming Mme. von Meck, he came to much more depressing conclusions about human nature in general.

"All my faith in people," he said, "all my trust is turned upside down."

Tchaikovsky was a chronic self-doubter. But he seems to have felt, even while he was writing it, that the Pathetic would be the greatest of his works. "It is hard for me to tear myself away from it," he wrote to his brother Anatole. "I believe it comes into being as the best of my works. . . . I told you I had completed a symphony which suddenly displeased me and I tore it up. Now I have composed a new symphony *which I certainly shall not tear up*." And to another friend: "I myself consider it the best, and especially the most open-hearted of my works. I love it as I have never loved any other of my musical creations."

And the world has agreed with him. In spite of the power and splendor of the Fourth and Fifth Symphonies, there can be no doubt that the Pathetic introduces us to a Tchaikovsky who is at last complete master not only of symphonic form and idiom, but of the wild and tragic emotions he poured into them. Instead of fitting his music to an established pattern, he lets his emotions mold their own pattern for themselves. The last movement, for example, instead of being brilliant and festive, is a song of farewell and despair. And there is no slow movement, but instead an uneasy dance in the disturbing rhythm of five-four—like a waltz, which for some mysterious reason, is incomplete.

In the slow introduction we hear the main theme of the first movement, a figure that twists and turns and grovels in the depths of the orchestra. As the tempo quickens, this theme is chopped up and thrown from instrument to instrument. The pace is nervous and it rises at times to a pitch of near hysteria. Again, there are echoes of the Russian Requiem. Then the excitement dies down to prepare for the famous melody of the second theme, which is like a memory of vanished happiness. The development opens with a crash. It is tortured and intricate and rises to a tremendous tragic climax. Then the songful second theme returns, and the whole closes on a solemn cadence for trumpets and trombones, with inexorably repeated descending scales of the pizzicato strings.

We have already spoken of the strange restlessness of the second movement, which is due to its peculiar, unsymmetrical five-four beat. Its beauty has an undercurrent of melancholy and doubts that cannot be quite forgotten.

The third movement is one of the most original Tchaikovsky ever wrote. It begins in confusion. There are wild, whirling figures and then, through the chaos, we hear a hint of a march, like the distant vision of an approaching procession. As this march takes form it is proud, almost arrogant, and full of courage—but a false courage, the courage of despair. For the moment it sweeps everything before it, but there is a terror behind this brave masquerade, and for all its defiance and swagger, you feel that it is the last, desperate sortie of the fighter who knows that the battle cannot be won. There is a furious climax and then a last crash to destruction.

The finale could be called a requiem for the passing soul, except that this soul sees no eternal rest and no hope or life beyond the grave. The repeated opening phrase is like a pathetic sigh for the lost hopes, the joys fled forever, and for the blackness and nothingness of the end. The beautiful melody of the second theme resembles an affectionate, lingering farewell. It leads into a great climax of despair which dies away to the tolling of a gong. The second theme returns in melancholy minor and the song disappears slowly and reluctantly into shadow and then darkness.

MAHLER: Symphony #9, D major

Mahler's Ninth Symphony is probably his greatest. It is his last, and it reflects the pessimism of a morbidly sensitive artist who knew bitterly that he had but little time to live. Mahler had looked upon life as a cruel, torturing enigma, but he was more deeply attached to it than he knew until it was time to go. Then, like so many people before and after, he was torn at the thought of leaving behind the little things: a patch of blue sky with clouds in it, a tree, a brook in the countryside. His Ninth Symphony is a lengthy farewell to the world he so suddenly found he loved, as well as the things that had martyred him through his agitated life.

Mahler's whole career was a struggle between his

desire to compose and the necessity to earn a living as a conductor. With amazing speed he worked his way up from provincial cities to become head of the Vienna Philharmonic Orchestra and the foremost opera company of Europe, the Vienna Hofoper. He made Vienna the greatest opera center of the world. Then he was called, with Arturo Toscanini, to conduct the Metropolitan Opera in New York. Those were golden years for opera in this country. But in his frantic desire to put by enough money to retire and give himself up solely to composing, Mahler undertook simultaneously the reorganization and direction of the New York Philharmonic concerts. The strain was too great. He collapsed during a concert of the third season and was taken back to his beloved Vienna to die. His friend, Bruno Walter, took up the crusade for Mahler's works.

In his book on Mahler, Walter writes: " 'Der Abschied'—Farewell—might well have been used as the heading for the Ninth Symphony. Born of the same mood, but without musical connection with 'Das Lied von der Erde' . . . the first movement grew to be a tragically moving and noble paraphrase of the farewell feeling. A unique soaring between farewell sadness and a vision of the Heavenly Light . . . lifts the movement into an atmosphere of celestial bliss. The second movement . . . is remarkable for its varying moods. A tragic undertone sounds in the joy and one feels that 'the dance is over.' In the defiantly agitated third movement Mahler once more furnishes proof of his stupendous contrapuntal mastery. In the last movement he peacefully bids farewell to the world, the finale being like the melting of a cloud into the ethereal blue."

Fortunately for music lovers we have not only Bruno Walter's words; his magnificent performance of the music was recorded on an historic occasion. This was the last concert in which he conducted the Vienna Philharmonic. Only a few weeks later, Nazi tanks and squadrons extinguished forever the Vienna of Mahler and Bruno Walter. The symphony was banned, the orchestra purged, and the conductor fled. So this performance had been a farewell in many—too many—senses of the word.

Until you are familiar with it, Mahler's Ninth may seem too long. And there are places where it falls victim to that straining after monumental effects which Spengler long ago noticed to be typical of late cultures. A great heritage can be a burden. Mahler himself knew he stood at the end of a great line of romantic composers. And he speaks the tortured, introspective, oversensitive, oversubtle language of a man who is perhaps too conscious of the great tradition he must carry on.

The four movements of the Ninth Symphony are not cast in classical form or sequence. The first and last movements are slow: andante and adagio. Two quick movements come in between. And the key relationships are free: the first movement in D major, the second in C major, the third in A minor, the finale in the distant tonality of D flat.

Imaginative people may hear in the brooding, foreboding parts of the music, in its feeling of having reached an end, a premonition of the catastrophes which were to sweep away this old culture—World War I, which followed closely after Mahler's death, and the present war which has meant death to artistic Germany and Austria.

But in spite of all his premonitions, Mahler had a

redeeming sense of humor, which also appears in his music. He knew that the end of romanticism wasn't the end of music, but only of a particular epoch and style.

One day he was climbing the banks of a mountain stream with another musician. His friend, in a lugubrious mood, lamented that no more great music was being written. Its possibilities seemed exhausted; nothing more could possibly come after Beethoven, Wagner, Bruckner and Mahler. Suddenly Mahler stood rooted to the spot, pointed wildly to the stream and cried: "Great God, look there!"

"What is it?" asked his anxious friend.

"The last wave," was Mahler's reply.

Nevertheless, though he could joke about it and poke fun at himself, Mahler made of his last symphony a subtle homage to death. Like the series of old German woodcuts and engravings, the Totentänze or Dances of Death, which show a grinning skeleton in a hundred friendly and unfriendly guises, the movements of this symphony might have been called Death as a Liberator, Death as Fiddler for the Dance, Death as the Opponent in Battle, and the finale: Death, the Consoling Friend.

VIII. *Humor in Music*

J UST AS laughter and tears are often close together and from the sublime to the ridiculous is said to be but a single step, so the exalted language of the symphony lies close in its origins to comic opera. Italian opera buffa invented a new melodic speech. Satirical texts with their rapid-fire barrage of puns, repartee and epigram, demanded quick-witted melodies, brief, pointed phrases— the very kind of thematic epigram which was to prove so useful to composers of symphonies. Now whether symphonic composers consciously adapted this language because they realized such short, pregnant phrases would suit their purpose of musical contrast and conflict, or whether they fell into the language of opera buffa simply because it was new and exciting, we do not know. Anyhow they used it. Mozart even went so far in both his Jupiter and Prague Symphonies as to make direct quotations from his own comic-opera tunes. On the other hand, certain slow movements were influenced by the melodic pathos of *serious* Italian opera and we have seen how the form of the symphony grew out of the overture to Italian opera seria. Thus the symphony with its tremendous range of human emotion was born, appropriately enough, in an operatic no man's land between tears and laughter. But humor in symphonic music did not end there. Since then we have had all kinds, from the orchestral horseplay of "Till Eulenspiegel," the delicate fantasy of the "Midsummer Night's Dream" music, the impudent gallicisms of Dukas, to the open-hearted laughter of Beethoven and back again to the sublime irony of Strauss's "Don Quixote."

"Papa" Haydn is a nickname that has stuck to the composer of the Farewell Symphony and the Surprise Symphony for more than a century now. And it's a very good name for him too, if we take it to mean the kind, fatherly, humorous, adult sort of person he really was. He was a fatherly admirer of Mozart, and Mozart was frank to say what he had learned from Haydn. But Haydn was no stuffed shirt, and he wasn't too proud to learn a lot in his turn from the young genius of Mozart.

He was a father also to the domestic musicians of Prince Esterházy, at the magnificent palace of Esterház, where they all spent most of the year together in the service of the prince. Esterház was set way off by itself in the plains of Hungary, a sort of miniature Versailles, where marionette shows, plays, operas, symphonies and quartets were the everyday amusement of the prince and his guests. Its isolation threw all the singers, actors and musicians together into one big family. They were all fond of Haydn, and always eager to carry out his wishes. Haydn, in his turn, was always trying to improve their position for them, interceding with the prince on their behalf, and so you can imagine that he didn't have to wait till he was dead to be known by the affectionate nickname of Papa Haydn.

The Farewell Symphony was one of the many occasions when Haydn came to the assistance of his men. Prince Nicholas always spent as much of the year as he could at Esterház, even though it was supposed to be a summer palace. And since most of his staff were not allowed to bring their wives and families the long season was sometimes hard on them. The object of the Farewell Symphony was to persuade the prince, tactfully, to shorten his stay in order that the musicians might go home to their families again. Haydn arranged his music so that in the last movement the players, one by one, stopped playing. Each one snuffed out the candles at his music stand and quietly left the orchestra until at the end only two violins were left softly playing in the half-light. It was a pretty broad hint. But it was meant humorously, and Prince Nicholas took it well. "If everybody is leaving," he said, "we may as well go too." And the musicians got their vacations.

There is an impish humor about a lot of Haydn's music, but it is never thoughtless or shallow, and Haydn was capable of very deep emotion. He knew not only the salons of the aristocracy, but the peasants of the countryside. He knew poverty and the seamy side of life in Vienna, and all these things gave his music a depth and reality which is far from the superficial optimism that certain people hear in it. Even some great musicians like Rubinstein have been very condescending about Papa Haydn. But one of Rubinstein's friends prophesied that when Rubinstein had become "great-grandfather Rubinstein," Haydn would still be Papa Haydn. And he was right. Already few people remember Rubinstein, even as a great-grandfather, but Haydn gets younger every day.

Nearly twenty years after his joke of the Farewell Symphony, Haydn played another joke on a much larger audience than Prince Esterházy. He was in London, at the height of his fame and fortune, feted by the Prince of Wales, invited to spend the summer at Windsor Castle with the king and queen, and automatically, of course, a lion of London aristocracy. But Haydn had no use for social fripperies, and he noticed that though the ladies gushed over him, when they could get him to dinner, they had a way of going to sleep during the soft slow movements of his symphonies.

Another man might have cursed the frivolity of the London audiences and decided on the spot that he was a misunderstood genius. But, being Haydn, he made a joke out of it instead. The slow movement of the symphony he wrote then begins very quietly and proceeds in a manner of subdued good-breeding until the moment when the audience might be comfortably settled for its little nap, and then bang! the orchestra explodes with a great fortissimo chord. "That'll make the ladies jump," he said, and it probably did.

Nowadays, since the symphony has been christened the Surprise Symphony, there isn't much surprise left, but there is the music and it is some of the greatest Haydn ever wrote. We hear the slow movement as an enchanting series of variations that grow out of that first harmless theme, with a simplicity and variety that seem as natural and inevitable as nature itself.

The wonderful broad introduction to the first movement has a romantic tinge quite unlike the conventional idea of Papa Haydn and the first and last movements set off the waggish joke of the surprise with brilliant originality and absolutely irresistible gaiety.

And even the gaiety was more than mere fun to Haydn as he showed once in answering a compliment

that was payed him toward the end of his career. He said:
"Often, when contending with the obstacles of every sort
opposed to my work, often when my powers both of mind
and body failed, and I felt it a hard matter to persevere
in the course I had entered on, a secret feeling within me
whispered: 'There are but few contented and happy men
here below. Everywhere grief and care prevail. Perhaps
your labors may one day be the source from which the
weary and worn, or the man burdened with affairs may
derive a few moments' rest and refreshment.' What a
powerful motive to press onwards! And that is why I now
look back with heartfelt, cheerful satisfaction on the work
to which I have devoted such a long succession of years,
with such persevering efforts and exertions."

MOZART: Overture to "The Marriage of Figaro"
         Duet, "Aprite presto" from "Figaro"
         Prague Symphony (K. 504)
BEETHOVEN: Symphony #8, F major

Mozart's "Marriage of Figaro" and his Prague Symphony take us back to a city and to a date that were
among the happiest of Mozart's life. For Prague was a
town where Mozart was loved and understood more than
anywhere else in the world. In Vienna he had his wealthy
and aristocratic circle of admirers. But their enthusiasm
was divided between Mozart and a dozen other composers
who are nothing but a name today. In Prague, on the other
hand, the whole population adored Mozart. There he was

a god. In Vienna his "Marriage of Figaro" was a big success, that's true, but it was soon shelved to make room for
operas of other intriguing composers. And "Figaro's" success wasn't even enough to land Mozart a good job at the
Viennese court, which would have given him at least some
financial security. So the greatest composer in Vienna went
back to giving music lessons and an occasional concert.

But in the meantime "The Marriage of Figaro" had
been put on in Prague. There it was a tremendous, un-
heard-of success, and it played on and on and on without
interruption. Finally friends in Prague wrote Mozart asking
whether he couldn't come himself and enjoy some of the
fruits of his popularity. There didn't seem to be any good
reason why he couldn't, so in January, 1787, he and his
wife, Konstanze, arrived in the capital of Bohemia where
the music season was at its height and all the Bohemian
nobility were in their town palaces. Mozart and Konstanze
were the guests of Count Thun, one of the most influential
music lovers of Prague, and soon they were caught up in
a whirl of concerts, balls, opera, receptions and dinners
and parties. Mozart was a very sociable person, and he
had the time of his life. He arrived about noon and was
immediately head over heels in fun. "At six o'clock," he
wrote to a friend, "I drove with Count Conac to the so-
called Breitfeld Ball, where the cream of the beauties of
Prague are wont to assemble. That would have been something for you, my friend. . . . As for me, I didn't dance
and I didn't flirt. The first because I was too tired and the
second because of my native bashfulness. But with the
greatest joy, I watched all the people hopping around to
their hearts' content to the music of my 'Figaro' turned
into contratänze and teutsche. For here they talk about
nothing but 'Figaro'; they play nothing, sing nothing,

whistle nothing but 'Figaro'; they go to no opera but 'Figaro' and forever 'Figaro.' Truly this is a great honor for me."

On January 17th he went himself to hear "Figaro." During the overture, the news of Mozart's presence spread like wildfire through the house, and as soon as it was finished the whole audience overwhelmed him with welcoming applause. Three days later he conducted a performance of "Figaro," which was an even greater triumph.

In between these two performances Mozart gave a concert for his own benefit at which he conducted the first performance of a new symphony. For the last number on the program Mozart sat down at the piano and improvised a free fantasy, which excited his audience so much that he had to do two more improvisations, one of them a series of variations on the air, "Non piu andrai," from "The Marriage of Figaro."

"Never before had the theatre been so crowded," wrote an eyewitness. "Never was there greater, more unanimous enthusiasm than his godlike playing awakened. We actually could not tell which to admire more: the extraordinary composition, or his extraordinary playing. The two of them together made an impression upon our souls, that was like the sweetest magic."

The Prague Symphony, as it has been called ever since, is in three movements, so that it is also known as "the symphony without a minuet."

A slow introduction, full of tension and drama leads into an agitated, syncopated figure in the violins, and brilliant, clear-cut descending scales. There are vigorous, marchlike passages and darkly pessimistic moments. The whole first movement is built out of this conflict, and finally the reconciliation of these two moods.

The slow movement too, songful as it is, is not without its moments of inward conflict and drama.

The finale is full of laughter, and well it might be, because it grows right out of one of the themes from Mozart's comic opera, "The Marriage of Figaro." You will hear that theme in the tiny duet between Susanna and Cherubino—"Aprite presto"—repeated again and again throughout the duet in a sort of breathless whisper, while Susanna hurriedly rescues Cherubino from his hilarious predicament. It consists of the first five notes you hear. But you will have to listen carefully, for it sounds only in the orchestral accompaniment—not in the voices. The whole finale of the Prague Symphony is infected with the hectic merriment of that duet. The instrumentation sparks and glows, the melodies dance for joy and the whole laughing world of eighteenth-century comic opera comes to life again before us in this memento of the happiest days of Mozart's life.

Many years were to pass before even so great a master as Beethoven was able to write music of such effortless zip and humor as Mozart's Prague Symphony. All the while that Beethoven wrote music echoing the thunder of the French Revolution, his critics warned and implored him to go back to the eternal spirit of Mozart and Haydn. But when he did, in his Eighth Symphony, they failed to recognize the spirit, and the public complained that the symphony was too small. When Beethoven was told that it had been less favorably received than his Seventh he growled: "That's because it's so much better."

Beethoven's humor could be brash and startling—at least to the periwigs of the day, and in his Eighth Symphony he uses the old forms to crack some of his maddest jokes. For a moment he appears to take on the rococo elegance from which he had burst free. But he is juggling with the style he had left so far behind. And never is his own mastery of form surer than when, to the academic eye, he appears to be breaking sacrosanct tradition.

The symphony begins with a simple, lively theme that seems to presage a dapper, well-mannered, little first movement. Then all of a sudden the symphony appears to have put on seven-league boots and it surges ahead with the easy stride of a giant. But Beethoven thinks better of it and he lays aside the boots with a chuckle. The orchestra can hardly contain its laughter as Beethoven toys about with the old classical formulae, and pretends to be a good boy again. I wonder if there ever was such a combination of naïve joy and complete urbanity in music.

In place of the traditional slow movement there is a delicious little allegretto scherzando, with the theme that Beethoven later improvised into his famous joking round: "Ta, ta, ta, lieber Mälzel." The "Ta, ta, ta," which you will hear in the music, was suggested by the metronome, or rather its predecessor, the musical chronometer, which Mälzel had invented. Years later Beethoven remembering the second movement of the Eighth Symphony said: "Ta, ta, ta, the canon on Mälzel. It was a jolly evening when we sang that canon. Mälzel was the bass and that time I sang the soprano."

And now, because a vigorous scherzo of the kind Beethoven had developed in his other symphonies would have been out of place here, he relaxes the pace by going back to the old tempo di menuetto. At the beginning of the minuet we hear a horn call which is said to recall the post horn of the coach that drove Beethoven from Teplitz that summer, where he had met Goethe.

The glittering, dancing finale is a sort of cross between a rondo and the symphonic sonata form. It is full of surprises that were once outrageous, full of irreverent giggles and cosmic laughter. It is the laughter of a great artist who has discovered that he cannot only hurl thunderbolts, but can be witty and charming as well.

＊＊　＊＊

Rossini: Overture to "La Gazza Ladra"
Mendelssohn: "A Midsummer Night's Dream" Selections
Dukas: "The Sorcerer's Apprentice"

Rossini's career began almost simultaneously with the Battle of Waterloo. The whole European continent heaved a great sigh of relief and turned away from the horror and grandeur and the fierce tragedy of the Napoleonic era and tried to remember what it was like to be happy and laugh again.

Rossini's music, like the overture to his opera, "La Gazza Ladra," is typical of that reaction, of the reaction which comes after all wars, when people are sick and tired from the strain of heroism, and ask only to be amused as easily and painlessly as possible. That is what made Rossini the man of the hour and enabled him to overshadow Beethoven for a while even in Beethoven's own home, Vienna.

Rossini, you remember, was a famous cook and a famous wit, and I think you can hear that in his music. He could dish up an opera, even an immortal master-

piece like "The Barber of Seville," as easily and spicily as
he made an omelet. He wrote it down as fast as he could
make the pen go. What if he did repeat himself sometimes? It was good enough to hear twice. They nicknamed
him Monsieur Crescendo because he got to abusing those
long, exhilarating crescendos, beginning in a whisper and
rising to a flashing, glittering tempest. He did it everywhere: in arias like the famous "Calumny" aria in "The
Barber of Seville" and in his operatic overtures. It was a
trick. But it was a good trick, and it still works. And if the
tempest was sometimes more like a tempest in a teapot,
remember that was the only kind of storm people were in
a mood to hear for many years. Napoleon had given them
enough deadly lightning and thunder to last for a long
time.

Like Rossini, Felix Mendelssohn had an incredible
musical facility which developed early. And at the age of
seventeen, with the Overture to "A Midsummer Night's
Dream," he grew from an astonishing talent to full-fledged
genius. Together with his beloved sister, Fanny, he had
just made the acquaintance of Shakespeare, and his enthusiasm boiled over into this immortal overture. He
wrote it first as a piano duet, which he and Fanny played
to delighted friends in the garden house of their parents'
Berlin estate.

At that time Felix was already enrolled at the University of Berlin and he later told how he used his spare
time between lectures to improvise the music of the overture on the piano of a beautiful lady who lived close by
the university buildings. "For a whole year I did hardly
anything else." Then, during the summer vacation he
orchestrated the overture, working in the great Mendelssohn garden, and the first orchestral performance was

given in the garden house that winter before several hundred guests.

Four lovely chords of the wood winds summon the fantastic creatures of Shakespeare's comedy. First we hear the fairy music given out by the high violins and viola pizzicati. As the overture develops there are more references to the play, including the bray of Bottom, the clown, who has been endowed with an ass's head. And there is a quick descending passage for the cellos said to have been suggested not by Shakespeare but by the buzzing of a big fly in the garden where the score was written. The music has a romantic freshness, an elfin imagination and humor which Mendelssohn never surpassed though he sometimes recaptured the mood.

One time he recaptured it completely when, twenty years later, the King of Prussia asked him to write some incidental music for a Berlin production of Shakespeare's comedy. Among the twelve new numbers which Mendelssohn wrote for this performance are the Nocturne, Scherzo and Wedding March usually heard in the concert hall with the Overture. With wonderful felicity, the themes of twenty years back are woven into the new pieces. The Nocturne, with its dreaming solo horn, describes the magic slumber of the characters at the end of the third act. The Scherzo, with its whispering, laughing fairy music, and its echo of Bottom's bray, follows Act I; and the festive Wedding March brings up the close of Act IV. There was more that was grotesque and humorous in the numbers we seldom hear. "Never did I hear an orchestra play so pianissimo," wrote a friend after the performance. "The dead march for Pyramus and Thisbe is really stupendous; I could scarcely believe that Felix would have the impudence to bring it before the public, for it is exactly like the mock preludes he plays when you cannot get him to be serious."

Mock-serious too, is the introduction of "The Sorcerer's Apprentice" of Dukas. Then, with outrageous gallic merriment and as much gusto as if the story were new, the music proceeds to tell us that a little learning is a dangerous thing. The plot of this brief tone poem, based on Goethe's ballad, "Der Zauberlehrling," which in turn goes back to an ancient tale in "The Lie-Fancier" of Lucian, concerns a master sorcerer and an envious apprentice.

Despite all his wondrous teachings this conjurer would never part with the secret of one favorite trick. He would take a broom, clothe it, mutter a spell, whereupon the broom turned into a human being ready to perform a servant's duties, order meals, carry water and so on.

However one day the apprentice manages to overhear the spell and as soon as his master is out of the way, decides to try it for himself. The mysterious harmonies of the introduction are an impressive hocus-pocus. Soon three bassoons begin a grotesque jumping figure which suggest the broom hobbling out to fetch water at the bidding of the apprentice. He quickly has more than enough water and orders the broom to stop and become a broom again, but to his horror he cannot remember the words to stop the magic.

The room is overflowing. In desperation he seizes an ax and strikes the broom in two. There is a tremendous crash in the orchestra. Silence. Then both halves of the broom start fetching water at once, faster and faster, until the flood in the orchestra becomes a tidal wave. At the height of the rumpus dreadful blasts of brass announce the appearance of the master sorcerer. He pronounces the spell and the room is still. The themes of the beginning return quietly, simply, with an air of false innocence. But in anger the master has vanished.

※ ※

RICHARD STRAUSS: "Till Eulenspiegel's Merry Pranks"
"Don Quixote: Fantastic Variations on a Theme of Knightly Character"

Who was Till Eulenspiegel that Richard Strauss should have written a tone poem about him? And what were the merry pranks the music describes? Evidently some of them defy description, for when Strauss was pressed for details he begged off, saying: "Were I to put into words the thoughts which the various incidents suggested to me, they would seldom suffice and might give rise to offense. Let me leave it therefore to my hearers to crack the hard nut which the rogue has prepared for them. By way of helping them to a better understanding, it seems enough to point out the two Eulenspiegel motives which, in the most manifold disguises, moods and situations, pervade the whole up to the catastrophe when, after he has been condemned to death, Till is strung up to the gibbet. For the rest let them guess at the musical joke which a rogue has offered them."

So we have to guess from the music and from the various legends which have cluttered about Till's name. We know that he was a wandering jack-of-all-trades who lived by his wits, an insolent prankster who never stayed long in any one town because it soon became too hot to hold him. Till had an irresistible desire to show up the stupidity and shams of honest people. And since the one unforgivable thing you can do to any man is make a fool of him, Till left a great wake of enemies in his path. Sometimes they caught up with him, and there are desperate moments in the music while Till squirms and wiggles in the hands of his captors. Then suddenly he's off again, thumbing his nose as he scampers out of reach, and the music fairly dances for joy.

With the saucy theme of the French horn Till's adventures begin. We hear him disguised in a monk's clothes, uttering oily platitudes to a gaping throng; we hear him upset all the pushcarts in the market place. He is pursued; there is pandemonium; he escapes; is pursued again, caught and condemned to death with ridiculous ferocity. He squeaks a last jest and is strung up. Society and its pompous conventions have won. The orchestra shudders and Till hangs loosely in the noose.

And what was the musical joke which we were to solve? Well, the final, unbearable joke that Till played on his enemies in the legend was to escape from the gallows and to die finally at peace in his own bed. Even after he was dead he tormented his heirs by refusing to lie quiet, as a dead person should, in his grave. Perhaps that is what Strauss had in mind, for after the mock majesty of Till's execution, we hear first the peaceful Eulenspiegel motive of the introduction, and the end is a roistering, impudent version of Till's second theme, suggesting that he is not dead, even in his grave, and that his irrepressible spirit lives on forever.

After "Till Eulenspiegel" the next person on whom Strauss turned his now famous sense of humor was Cervantes' Don Quixote. Don Quixote was an old-fashioned, impoverished gentleman of La Mancha, who spent all his time reading books on the age of chivalry and meditating the adventures of ancient knights, villainous giants, magicians and enchanted princesses. Till at last "through his little sleep and much reading, he dried up his brains in such sort, as he wholly lost his judgment." Thereupon "he fell into one of the strangest conceits that a madman ever stumbled on in this world, to wit, it seemed to him very requisite and behooveful . . . that he himself should become a knight errant, and go throughout the world with his horse and armour to seek adventures, and practice in person all he had read was used by knights of yoare. . . ."

Strauss opens the introduction to his variations with a gallant, prancing theme associated with the bookish chivalry which ensnared the imagination of Don Quixote. As his mind weakens, the theme begins to wander and the harmonies go awry. Then over a harp accompaniment the solo oboe presents a rather timid, noble melody—Don Quixote's ideal of womanly beauty and virtue, the fair Dulcinea in whose name the coming exploits are performed. At once his excitement increases. He imagines her endangered and his theme sounds heroically in the brass, only to degenerate into a series of insane discords, indicating clearly enough his state of mind.

The themes: We have already heard the motive of Dulcinea. Don Quixote is now to himself the personification of chivalry. So the theme of knight-errantry becomes his own, played by the instrument henceforth associated with him: a solo cello. He is followed down the road by the lumbering theme of Sancho Panza in the bass clarinet and tenor tuba.

I. The first variation describes the adventure of the windmills. In spite of Sancho's frantic warnings, the Don takes their vast waving arms, creaking and groaning in the wind, for evil giants. Lance set, he charges, is whirled up to the heavens and back to earth where he lands with a resounding thump.

II. The second variation brings another enemy: an immense army made up of all the nations of the earth led by the Great Emperor Alifanfaron. The army moves slowly down the road in a great cloud of dust accompanied by a distinct sound of baaing from the muted brass. Sancho insists that it is only a flock of sheep, but already the Don has charged into their midst. A bold, military fanfare clashes with the panic bleating of the army, and our knight would have been left victor on the field, except for the shepherds who unloosed their slings "and began to salute his pate with stones as great as one's fist."

III. Don Quixote and his servant discuss the ways of knight-errantry. A garrulous viola (Sancho) questions the point of such a life. His master rebukes him for his irrelevant stupidities and describes his ideal with waxing enthusiasm. Three times his theme is repeated. With the last repetition it ends on a note one degree higher than normal and we are magically lifted into the land of Don Quixote's chivalric dreams. The instruments shimmer, a glow spreads through the orchestra. The melody of the ideal soars and sings with a nobility which tells you better than any words that this is the true reality—a thousand times more real than the fat, querulous Sancho Panza and his world of eat and drink. The radiance grows and the transfigured voice of the Don mounts to a gallant, rapturous climax. Sancho makes one last flat-footed remark and the orchestra, in a burst of irritation, bids him hold his tongue.

IV. A doleful ecclesiastical chant announces the approach of several penitent pilgrims. To Don Quixote they are marauding desperadoes and he throws himself upon them. They knock him senseless and go their prayerful way.

V. While Sancho sleeps, the Don keeps vigil beside his weapons. Amid fantastic glissandos of the harp a vision of Dulcinea appears.

VI. Next day they meet three coarse country wenches, one with a tambourine, whom Sancho points out to his master as Dulcinea. The melody of the ideal woman has become a foolish, banal ditty. The Don concludes that a magician has transformed his princess and vows vengeance.

VII. The knight and his servant, being blindfolded, mount a wooden horse which is to carry them through the air. The vertiginous speed of their courser, the terrible heights and the wind that howls between the planets sound vividly enough in the music, but one low note sustained throughout in the depths of the orchestra suggests that the pair have never left the ground.

VIII. A deserted boat lying oarless on the river bank appears to have been sent to their aid by some kindly spirit. The knight's theme turns into a barcarole as they career crazily downstream, capsize and manage to scramble ashore. They say a brief prayer of thanksgiving for their miraculous escape, and go on to the next adventure.

IX. A whining counterpoint of two bassoons represents two Benedictine monks whom Don Quixote takes for magicians. This time the Don tastes victory. The two monks are put to flight, scared out of their wits by his warlike cries.

X. Finally, to rescue Don Quixote from his own folly, a kindly neighbor from La Mancha masquerades as the

Knight of the White Moon, and challenges him to single combat. If he loses, Don Quixote shall be obliged to retire to his home for a full year. After a swift and crushing defeat the homeward march begins. Over a desolate, throbbing pedalpoint of the timpani, like the tread of the broken hero, there rises a mighty dirge for defeated ideals and shattered illusions. Don Quixote resigns himself to the simple life of a shepherd, and we hear phrases of pastoral melody in the wood winds. Then gradually his mind clears.

The finale is Don Quixote's farewell to his dreams and to life. His sanity returns, his theme leaves off its cavorting and melts into warm, diatonic melody. Here it is naïvely forthright and tinged with greatness. But his strength ebbs. The voice of the cello grows fainter and fainter as wisps of the original theme echo through the orchestra. It falters and is silent. The final cadence is like a smile of serene understanding.

"All the house was in a confusion and uprore; all which notwithstanding the neece ceased not to feede very devoutly; the maid servant to drinke profoundly, and Sancho to live merrily. . . . The notary was present at his death and reporteth how he had never read or found in any book of chivalry that any errant knight died in his bed so mildly, so quietly, and so Christianly as did Don Quixote. Amidst the wailefull plaints and blubbering teares of the bystanders, he yeelded up the ghost, that is to say, hee died."

IX. *Composers in Love*

Unhappy love, both in fiction and as personal experience, has inspired so many artists that one is tempted to believe that poets and painters and music-makers are as bored as the rest of the world by felicity. It may be true that all the world loves a lover. But we prefer them unhappy. The luckless couples are the ones we remember, whose stories are told and sung through the centuries: Romeo and Juliet, Héloïse and Abélard, Paolo and Francesca. In such surroundings the very idea of a happy marriage seems grotesque. The thousand-year glamour which has accompanied Tristan and Isolde from the song of ancient Celtic bards to the diamond horseshoe of the Metropolitan Opera, would scarcely endure if Isolde had lived out her days becalmed as Mme. Tristan.

One could build up a very plausible argument that

the essence of romanticism lies in frustration and suffering, and possibly deduce that great music is a compensation for the heartaches of the composer. But there are exceptions enough to upset such facile theories. Think of the blissful domestic serenity reflected in Wagner's Siegfried Idyll; of Beethoven's heroic drama, "Fidelio," glorifying the faith of married lovers; or the ecstatic courtship of Robert and Clara Schumann, which released such a flood of immortal music. The secret of the relation, if any, between love and artistic creation lies beyond our analysis. Wagner, whose psychological insight at times ran very deep, may have hinted at it when, in his allegorical "Ring of the Nibelung," he used love as a symbol of all beneficent creative power.

Beethoven's Fourth Symphony and his Third Leonore Overture were written during one of the happiest years of his life: 1806. Beethoven was in love. Not that that was anything unusual for him; Beethoven was always falling in and out of love, and sometimes with women who were marvelously unsuited to him. But this time he was in love with a woman of the same noble intelligence, human sympathy and high ideals as himself: Therese von Brunswick.

Therese's brother, the Count von Brunswick, was a close friend of Beethoven's, and in the spring of 1806 he went to visit the two of them on their estate in Hungary. Beethoven was a difficult man, moody, often violent, given to sudden fits of anger and equally sudden fits of repentance. He seems to have prided himself on his boorish manners with the aristocracy, because that was one way of asserting his independence. His sense of humor was strong but not always very tactful, and if he were not in exactly the right mood he could be a very difficult guest.

But when he spoke to Therese in the language of his art he was irresistible. He wooed her while the moonlight streamed through the window, playing Bach's tender air: "If thou wilt give me thy heart, let it first be a secret, that our hearts may commingle and none may divine it."

Whether the joy and lightness and exquisite sentiment of the Fourth Symphony had to do with Beethoven's
love is a question which has never been answered. But it is
not impossible.

There is a slow introduction of great simplicity and
depth. But it is thoughtful, rather than brooding or portentous, and it culminates in six sharp, insistent repetitions of the same chord, that launch one of the gayest,
most carefree, skipping allegros in all Beethoven. The
second theme is a little melodic conversation between the
oboes, bassoon and flute. And as the movement develops
these scraps of melody and the skipping first theme are all
churned up together with enchanting symphonic sleight of
hand.

Like all great composers, Beethoven can turn a simple
scale into the most eloquent song in the world. The theme
of the second movement consists of almost nothing but
the slow, descending notes of the E flat major scale, over
a gently rocking accompaniment. Berlioz wrote that "its
form is so pure, its melodic expression so angelic and of
such irresistible tenderness that the prodigious art of work-
manship completely disappears."

The main theme of the third movement is a jolly,
robust figure for full orchestra. And the finale is a whirl of
gaiety, which requires no analysis at all but only ears to
hear, and a mind to laugh with Beethoven and enjoy the
endless sparkle and variety of his musical wit.

There were two barriers in the way of Beethoven's
marriage to Therese von Brunswick. One was that she
belonged to the Austrian aristocracy, where to marry a
commoner meant social ostracism. But she was ready to
disregard that. The other was Beethoven's own lack of
decision, and that seems to have been the obstacle on

which their plans shattered. They parted with high regard for each other and neither of them ever married. Therese lived to be eighty-six and died as a canoness in a convent.

But neither Beethoven's indecision in this case, nor the frequency with which he formed passionate attachments for other women before and after, should be taken to mean that he was in any way frivolous or promiscuous. On the contrary, he was a person of almost puritanically strict ideals and his lofty conception of the relationship of men and women is obvious from his famous letter "To the Immortal Beloved," which was found after his death in a secret drawer of his room. From that day to this, scholars have disputed as to who the Immortal Beloved was. We shall probably never know. But there is a good deal of evidence to show that she was Therese von Brunswick.

"My angel, my all, my very self," he wrote, ". . . You are suffering—ah, wherever I am there you are also. I shall arrange affairs between us so that I shall live, and live with you, what a life! ! ! ! thus! ! ! ! thus without you. . . .

"No one can ever again possess my heart—none— never— Oh God, why is it necessary to part from one whom one so loves . . . ? Your love makes me at once the happiest and the unhappiest of men. . . . Be calm, only by a calm consideration of our existence can we achieve our purpose to live together—be calm,—love me—today— yesterday—what tearful longings for you—you—you—my life—my all—farewell— Oh, continue to love me—never misjudge the most faithful heart of your beloved L.

"Ever thine
"Ever mine
"Ever for each other."

Courage, faith, sacrifice, calm—his message to the Immortal Beloved is also the theme of Beethoven's one opera: "Fidelio," or "Leonore," as it was originally called. It is a hymn to the strength and devotion of married lovers.

Florestan has been imprisoned by his powerful enemy, Pizarro, in the lowest dungeon of a fortress near Seville. Word is given out that he has died, and when Pizarro hears the fortress is to be inspected by a minister from Seville, he decides Florestan must perish before his presence is discovered. Meanwhile Florestan's wife, Leonore, has disguised herself as a boy and entered the service of old Rocco, the jailor. Rocco takes her with him down into the dungeon to help dig the grave. There she recognizes her own husband and at the crucial moment she throws herself between him and his would-be murderer. The desperate Pizarro resolves to kill both husband and wife, but Leonore draws a pistol. At that moment a trumpet call is heard from the ramparts of the castle announcing the arrival of the minister from Seville, and Florestan is saved.

In the course of his several revisions of "Fidelio," Beethoven wrote four overtures. The first, second and third bear the opera's original title, "Leonore." The fourth is the one which is used nowadays as the Overture to "Fidelio."

The Third Leonore Overture is really a symphonic poem which tells all the essentials of the drama to come. It is so tremendous and complete in itself that Beethoven decided it was too much to put at the beginning of the opera, and wrote another simpler overture in its place.

It begins, after the famous slow descending octaves, with Florestan's lament in prison, and works gradually up to a tremendous climax which is cut short by the trumpet call that announces his liberation. There are few more moving moments in all opera than the soft, hesitating measures that follow that trumpet—those first seconds after the danger is past, while Florestan's mind gropes through the horror and darkness, almost afraid to believe that he is still alive, that his savior is the Leonore who stands at his side. Once more the trumpet sounds, the door to the dungeon is thrown open from above. The light streams down, his enemy disappears like a shadow, and the couple are alone. The finale of the overture is filled with a cosmic jubilation which transcends even the rejoicing of Leonore and Florestan. It is Beethoven himself singing his great hymn to the liberation and freedom of all mankind.

ROBERT SCHUMANN: Symphony #1, B flat major. Spring
Piano Concerto, A major-minor

Like a true romantic, Robert Schumann received the inspiration for his First Symphony from a poem—a spring poem, whose final couplet became the motto for the score:

"O wende, wende deinen Lauf,
—Im Tale blüht der Frühling auf!"
(Oh turn, oh turn aside thy course,
For the valley blooms with spring!)

"I wrote the symphony toward the end of the winter of 1841," wrote Schumann, "and if I may say so, in that flush of spring which carries a man away even in his old age and surprises him again each year. I did not intend to describe or paint, but I firmly believe that the time when it came into being influenced its character and form, and made it what it is."

The "flush of spring" which moved the thirty-year-old composer, existed in his own emotions. The Spring Symphony was actually composed during the first two snowy months of the year, but since these were the early months of married life with his beloved Clara, they were to Schumann, spring. What a bridal gift! It was Robert's first venture with an orchestra in this large form. Yet the draft took shape in four days and nights of intensive labor, in one single burst of inspiration.

The orchestration itself took longer, of course, and when it was finished, Robert wrote in the diary which he and Clara kept together: "The symphony has given me many happy hours. But now, after sleepless nights, comes exhaustion. I am like a young wife after a confinement—so light, so happy, and yet so ill and weak. My Clara understands this and treats me with double consideration and kindness which I will repay. But I would never come to the end, if I were to tell all the love Clara has shown me during this time. I might have sought through millions without finding anyone who would treat me with such thoughtfulness and understanding."

Schumann did not exaggerate. There can be no question that it was Clara with her delicate artistic intuitions and the emotional security she brought him, who unleashed the pent-up energies of Schumann's frail genius. He took strength from his love returned. The agonies and uncertainties of their long-drawn-out engagement, the humiliating battles they had fought against Clara's father, who was determined to prevent their marriage at any cost, had hampered Robert's inspiration, and prevented him from producing anything more than exquisite miniatures. Now his confident spirit soared.

Clara was delighted and she wrote timidly in their diary that she would like to say a little about the symphony too, "but I should never finish talking about the buds, the scent of violets, the fresh green leaves, the birds in the air—all of which one hears living and stirring through it in youthful strength. Don't laugh at me, dear husband," she said. "If I can't express myself poetically, still the poetic spirit of this work has reached my inmost heart."

The slow introduction to the symphony begins with a fanfarelike motive in the horns and trumpets, which Schumann wanted to sound as if from on high, "like a call to awaken. In what follows of the introduction," he said, "there might be a suggestion of the growing green of everything, of a butterfly taking wing, and in the allegro of the gradual assembly of all that belongs to spring. But these are fantastic thoughts that came to me after I had finished the work."

The theme of the allegro, of the first movement proper, is a quick transformation of the opening trumpet call. There is another gentle rocking figure in the wood winds, and the oboe plays a new melody. All these are developed rather elaborately, and Schumann took the usual romantic liberties with the classical symphonic form.

The intimate larghetto is one of the loveliest moments in all Schumann. Its graceful, far-flung melodic arch, in a slightly changed version, becomes the subject of the third movement, the scherzo, which follows without any break. The transition is pure magic. Toward the end of the slow movement, the orchestral color begins to change, the trombones enter softly, the melody we have spoken of is transformed so subtly you hardly realize it, until with an abrupt change of tempo, we are in the scherzo, whose theme is a vigorous, stamping version of the same lovely melody. This scherzo is full blooded and masculine—the perfect counterpart to the feminine charm of the larghetto.

The finale begins with a majestic flourish of the full orchestra, and then comes an enchantingly light-footed, tripping figure in the violins. So delicate is this theme of the finale that a heavy-handed conductor can make it sound inconsequential or banal. Schumann was thinking of this danger when he wrote: "I like to think of it as the farewell of spring, and so I shouldn't want it to be played too frivolously."

But the Spring Symphony was not all Robert produced during that momentous year of 1841. There followed, during the spring and early summer months, a Fantasy in A minor for piano and orchestra, which eventually became the first movement of his Piano Concerto; the D minor Symphony, afterwards revised and published as his Fourth; and his Overture, Scherzo and Finale.

Schumann had planned a piano concerto at Vienna in 1839, probably even then with Clara in mind. For his fiancée was already a famous pianist in her own right, with a serious and poetical turn of mind which made her the ideal interpreter of his works. He wrote her: "My concerto is a compromise between a symphony, a concerto, and a huge sonata. I see I cannot write a concerto for the virtuosos—I must plan something else."

When the Leipzig Gewandhaus Orchestra was rehearsing Robert's Spring Symphony, Clara took the chance to try over the Fantasy with them and she saw at once that it was "magnificent" music. "Carefully studied, it must give the greatest pleasure to those that hear it," she wrote in the diary. "The piano is most skillfully interwoven with the orchestra—it is impossible to think of one without the other."

Four years later Robert added an intermezzo and finale so that, as Clara wrote in her diary: "It has now become a concerto which I mean to play next winter. I am very glad about it, for I have always wanted a great bravura piece by him." And a month later, on July 31st: "Robert has finished his concerto and handed it over to the copyist. I am happy as a king at the thought of playing it with the orchestra."

It is hard to imagine today how puzzling this simple, poetic work seemed to Schumann's contemporaries. For in those days a concerto was considered completely inadequate which did not give ample room to show off a brilliant technique.

The dramatic introduction leads into a plaintive melody for oboe which forms the basis of the entire first movement. We hear it again in tender dialogue between the piano and orchestra, in various impulsive melodic transformations, and in a brilliant marchlike version at the close.

A playfully lyric intermezzo leads directly into the finale, which is another treasure-trove of melody, full of delightful rhythmic twists, and crowned with an irresistibly light-hearted, exultant coda.

Clara, of course, was the soloist at the first performance, which took place at one of her own concerts in Dresden. She played it again that winter in Leipzig with Mendelssohn conducting, and next year in Vienna with Robert on the conductor's stand. In the following years they joined hands many times again in this concerto. And

all during the unhappy years after Robert's death Clara
continued bravely to spread the gospel of her husband's
music. The public had listened to her before they had to
him, but as a revered, elderly artist she had the joy of
knowing that through her efforts Schumann was respected
and loved everywhere as she herself had loved him.

TCHAIKOVSKY: "Romeo and Juliet"
Symphony #2, C minor. Little Russian

The list of composers who have been inspired or who
thought they were inspired by Shakespeare, is endless. And
in that endless list, Tchaikovsky is one of the very few
whose music speaks with the elemental passion and strife
that grip us as do the words of Shakespeare. Yet incredible
as it may sound, the "Romeo and Juliet" fantasia is only
the fourth of Tchaikovsky's published orchestral works. He
wrote it when he was twenty-nine, but it stands out among
the works of those years—a sudden blaze of genius, fore-
telling a unique inspiration which, though it never burned
with a steady flame, was to touch peaks of intensity such
as few composers have equaled.

The slow, solemn harmonies of the introduction to
"Romeo and Juliet" recall the peace and friendly counsel
of Friar Laurence's cell. But the charm is soon broken.
The ancient feud of Montagues and Capulets rages
through the orchestra. Then after a long hesitation there
begins very softly the love music of Romeo and Juliet. At
first its mood is reminiscent of Tchaikovsky's song which

has become popular under the title of "None But the Lonely Heart."

In a duet from "Romeo and Juliet" found among Tchaikovsky's papers after his death, this marvelous, soaring melody builds the climax, the phrase on which Romeo sings: "O nuit d'extase, arrête-toi! O nuit d'amour, étends ton voile noir sur nous." (Oh, tarry, night of ecstasy! Oh, night of love, stretch thy dark veil over us.)

But the tender song of Romeo and Juliet is interrupted again by the fury of the street brawls. Finally both of them are heard in combination with the theme of Friar Laurence. All these opposing forces rise to a great outburst of orchestral fury, and then die away in broken sorrowing phrases to silence.

We hear Romeo's song, now lamenting, and the end comes with sharp, tragic chords of the orchestra.

Perhaps some of the passion of this music may have been due to actual experience, for in 1868 and in 1869, the year he wrote it, he was going through the only real love affair of his life. He had fallen deeply in love with the great singer, Désirée Artôt, and wished to marry her. "Never in my life have I met such a sweet, such a warmhearted, such an intellectual woman," he wrote. And again, later, to his brother Modeste: "How thoroughly delighted you would be with her exquisite gestures, her grace of movement, her artistic poise!"

But Tchaikovsky was poor and as yet he hadn't made much of a reputation for himself, and he dreaded living on his wife's money, perhaps having to give up composing to follow her around Europe on her operatic tours, and becoming only his wife's husband.

"And so, dear father," he wrote in a confidential letter, "you will see that I am somewhat in a fix. On the one hand, I am, I may say, attached to her, body and soul, and my life seems a blank without her. On the other hand, cold, stern philosophy compels me to reflect upon the disastrous consequence which may ensue, and which my friends continue earnestly to impress upon me."

Unfortunately the affair was settled within a month. The lady married a popular baritone in Warsaw, without offering a word of explanation. A short time later, Artôt appeared at the Moscow Opera, and Tchaikovsky, whom she had caused so much suffering, sat in the audience with the tears streaming down his face. But it was twenty-five years before they met again, as old friends, in Berlin.

Meanwhile Tchaikovsky continued teaching at the newly founded Moscow Conservatory, which was his chief source of income, and he went on composing. His First Symphony, entitled "Winter Dreams," which he had completed the year he met Désirée Artôt, had already shown him what agonies composing could cost. While he was working on it, his nerves were almost pathologically overstrained, he suffered from insomnia, a hammering in the head, and even hallucinations. But he persisted. The First Symphony, though it was a success in its day, has long since been forgotten. But the Second Symphony is an extremely colorful work, which is still occasionally performed. It is interesting for many reasons: one because it is already so typically Tchaikovskian in its spirit; another, because it is based largely on Russian folk tunes; and finally, because Tchaikovsky himself, even in later years, considered the finale of this symphony one of his finest works.

It was given the nickname of the Little Russian Symphony by one of Tchaikovsky's friends, because most of the principal themes are folk tunes of Little Russia. It opens with the solo horn chanting, very softly, a melody of characteristic Slav melancholy, which dominates the whole introduction. The main part of the movement, the allegro, is built on one of the many Russian songs associated with the rebel Stenka Razin, who according to the legend, was beheaded in the Red Square in 1671.

The second movement, an andantino marziale, is based on a swinging little tune Tchaikovsky had used in the Wedding March from his opera "Undine," completed in the same year as "Romeo and Juliet."

The third movement is an agitated scherzo with a wonderful rhythmic drive.

The brilliant finale is built around the Little Russian folk song, "The Crane." It is certainly the most powerful movement of the symphony, the most masterly and original, and when you listen to it now, you will understand why it kept Tchaikovsky's affection through the many tortured years that lay ahead.

WAGNER: Overture to "The Flying Dutchman"
　　　　 Prelude and Love-death from "Tristan und Isolde"
　　　　 Siegfried Idyll

The three most important women in Wagner's life were his wife, Minna; Mathilde Wesendonck; and Cosima von Bülow, who became his second wife. Wagner was still deeply in love with Minna when he composed "The Flying Dutchman" and he gave her name to the heroine of the opera who later became Senta. Mathilde Wesendonck was the muse of "Tristan und Isolde" and the Siegfried Idyll was written as a present for Cosima.

As a young and relatively unknown composer, Wagner resolved to seek his fortune with Minna in Paris. On the way they took a small Norwegian ship across the North Sea. In mid-voyage the tiny vessel was caught in a terrifying storm. The Norwegian sailors were superstitious, and they began telling of an ancient legend, which they half believed, of a phantom ship that rode the storm and could not be sunk. The master of the ship was a real man, a Dutchman doomed to sail the seas until the Last Judgment. Once this Dutchman had been trying to round the Cape of Good Hope in the teeth of a gale, and in his fury at the opposing elements, he had vowed he would round the Cape, even if heaven or hell itself should oppose him.

Then, the sailors said, the fiend was heard in a loud laugh from the deep, and the rash Dutchman was doomed to fight the gale from that very moment to the sounding of the last trumpet. His crew had long since become ghosts, but the Dutchman lived on, unable to find peace or rest, unable to find death by his own or any other man's hand, always driven, and driving through the storm.

The terrors of the northern sea and the grim tale of the Norwegian sailors took hold of Wagner's imagination, and the Dutchman became the hero of an opera. In Paris, Wagner was desperately unhappy and unsuccessful and homesick. He took to identifying himself with the wandering Dutchman, longing for a haven and rest, and forever tossed on the stormy seas of an unfriendly world.

Every seven years the Dutchman was allowed to go ashore and look for a woman who would be true to him until death. If ever he succeeded in finding such a woman, he would be released from the curse, could return to the world and become a happy man again. That idea appealed particularly to Wagner, for one of his dearest wishes, through all of his fantastic, storm-tossed career, was to be able to live a happy, normal, domestic life. Needless to say he never achieved his goal, but he poured out all his longing for it in this music.

The overture is built around the tormented figure of the Dutchman, whose motive is heard at the very beginning, and around the idea of his redemptress, the faithful, loving Senta. Her theme is the soft, prayerlike passage of the wood winds which follows the first outburst of the storm. There are echoes of the Norwegian sailors' songs, more storm music and finally at the end of the overture the themes of Senta and the Dutchman, as the redeemed couple rise heavenwards together.

Twenty years later the storms of Wagner's life had still not abated, but he no longer hoped for salvation from Minna. They had long ceased to understand each other, and they parted in a spat over Mathilde Wesendonck—the woman who had captured Wagner's imagination while he was writing "Tristan und Isolde." But Mathilde was faithful to her worthy merchant husband.

Now whether Wagner wrote "Tristan und Isolde" because he was in love with Mathilde, or whether he fell in love with Mathilde because he was writing "Tristan," is a question which Wagner himself probably couldn't have answered. At any rate, his version of the ancient legend tells of the suffering of two lovers who could never belong to each other.

The Prelude to "Tristan" opens with a prolonged sigh of unfulfilled passion, which is repeated, each time with rising intensity. Since in this world they are doomed to separation, the desire of Tristan and Isolde for each other becomes a longing for death. "The world, power, fame,

splendor, honor, knighthood, fidelity, friendship, all,"
writes Wagner, "are dissipated like an empty dream. One
thing only remains: longing, longing, insatiable longing,
forever springing up anew, pining and thirsting. Death,
which means passing away, perishing, never awakening,
their only deliverance . . ."

Notice how the harmonies of the prelude never seem
to come to rest. There is not one single, simple, satisfying
cadence that reaches a definite end. That is Wagner's
way of symbolizing a passion which, by its very nature,
cannot be consummated this side of the grave. The interweaving voices, the themes of the Love Potion, the Love
Glance, Longing and Death, reminded him of the legend
of the ivy and the vine, which grew out of the graves of
Tristan and Isolde and entwined in loving embrace.

The Love-death is the finale of the opera. Tristan
has expired in the arms of Isolde. King Marke, who has
heard the story of the love potion, arrives to forgive and
unite the lovers. But too late. Isolde no longer sees or hears
the people about her. As she looks down upon Tristan's
body a light shines from his face, and a song which she
alone can hear: the wonderful melody of their love duet
from the second act. It begins in a tender whisper and as
it rises higher and higher and floods on to its magnificent
climax, Isolde is swept on the crest of the song, past the
sorrowing onlookers, to join Tristan "in the vast wave of
the breath of the world." Night and death and love are
one.

Eleven years later, with the Siegfried Idyll, we find
Wagner in a state of happy if illegitimate domesticity.
Wagner's unconventional family life was of a complexity
which we won't try to unravel here. Suffice it to say that
Cosima, though still legally married to Hans von Bülow,

had left him several years before to become the wife, protectress and muse of Richard Wagner. Their son, Siegfried, was born in 1869 in Villa Triebschen, their Swiss home near Lucerne, where Wagner was composing his music drama, "Siegfried," in exile.

"She has defied every disapprobation," wrote Wagner, "and taken upon herself every condemnation. She has borne me a wonderfully beautiful boy, whom I can boldly call Siegfried. He is now growing, together with my work. He gives me a new long life, which at last has attained a meaning. Thus we get along without the world, from which we have wholly withdrawn."

The Siegfried Idyll was written the following year as a combination birthday and Christmas present for Cosima, whom he had finally been able to marry. It is filled with allusions to Wagner's and Cosima's life and to their son, Siegfried, after whom it is named.

Cosima's birthday fell on December 25th. Wagner completed the score in November, and he took the greatest precautions to surprise Cosima with the first performance of the Idyll. Orchestra players from Zürich instead of near-by Lucerne were engaged and the first rehearsal took place in the foyer of the old Zürich Theatre. Among the few listeners were Mathilde Wesendonck and her husband.

Wagner himself conducted the last rehearsal in Lucerne on December 24th. Early the next morning, the musicians assembled at Triebschen. They tuned their instruments in the kitchen, so as not to wake Cosima. Then they took up their places silently on the stairs of the villa, with Wagner who was conducting, at the top. The performance began at 7:30 A.M.

If you have ever seen the stairs at Villa Triebschen,

you know that they are very narrow and winding. Wagner couldn't see the cello and double bass at the bottom of the stairs, but the performance was faultless, and they repeated it several times that day.

Aside from an old German lullaby, "Schlaf, mein kind, schlaf ein," all the themes of the Siegfried Idyll were supposed, until very recently, to have been taken from Wagner's music drama, "Siegfried."

It begins with the peaceful melody that introduces Brünnhilde's words in the last act: "Ewig war ich, ewig bin ich." (Deathless was I, deathless am I.) But this melody does not come originally from the opera, as Ernest Newman, the great English authority on Wagner, has shown. It comes from sketches for a string quartet which Wagner had intended as a present to Cosima, several years earlier at the time when they were falling in love. So this reference to their first attachment, in the work celebrating the birth of their son, had a symbolical and sentimental meaning for both Wagner and Cosima, over and above the beauty of the music itself.

A group of soft caressing themes lead to an old German cradlesong, which is piped quite simply by the oboe. Then the first theme returns, the violins put on their mutes, the music shifts dreamily into a distant key. The rhythm changes and the wood winds give out the theme of "Siegfried, hope of the world," the melody which Brünnhilde sings to Siegfried in their great love duet. But it takes on a new and infinitely touching meaning here as Wagner addresses it to his and Cosima's son.

Soon this melody too combines with the undulating first theme. They work up to a brief climax which is suddenly cut off and a solitary horn intones the more energetic theme associated with Siegfried as a young man.

The clarinet and flute break in with the song of the birds from the forest scene in "Siegfried." Other themes from the love duet return and finally the triumphant song of the bird that Siegfried understood, the one that led him to the Valkyries' Rock and the sleeping Brünnhilde. But this climax too is brief, and the hushed mood of the lullaby returns, the first themes sound again clothed in even more glowing poetry. The orchestra subsides, the horns croon the old cradlesong and the "hope of the world" is safe in sleep. It is perhaps the most beatifically tender and contented music that Wagner ever wrote.

SCHÖNBERG: "Verklärte Nacht"
BERG: Violin Concerto

We are so used, nowadays, to thinking of Arnold Schönberg as a sort of Mephistopheles of modern music, the man who invented atonal music—that it always comes as something of a surprise to hear his early, romantic work, "Verklärte Nacht." For Schönberg started his career as a full-fledged romantic. Like Richard Strauss and a good many other young German and Austrian composers of his day, he fell deeply under the spell of Wagner. It was especially "Tristan und Isolde" that fascinated Schönberg, and I think you can hear that influence in his "Verklärte Nacht." This music was originally composed as a string sextet, when Schönberg was only twenty-five, in 1899. Later he rearranged it for string orchestra.

It was inspired by the poem, "Verklärte Nacht,"

from a poetic series entitled "Woman and the World" by the German poet and dramatist, Richard Dehmel. The poem tells of two lovers wandering through the moonlight. The woman's voice, heavy with guilt, confesses to her husband. Before she met him, before she knew what love could be, she had longed at least to know the joy of being a mother. And in despair she had given herself to a strange man. Now she bears his child. Then the husband's voice is heard. "The power of our love," he says, "will change the child, and you will bear the child to me. It will be ours." And the night which had seemed empty and cold, is transfigured by the warmth of understanding love and forgiveness.

But this romantic atmosphere soon lost its fascination for Schönberg, and gradually he developed his own new aesthetic world: the twelve-tone system of so-called atonality. In its most extreme form, the twelve-tone system seems to the layman and to most musicians a rather negative, intellectualized theory, which has very little to do with musical emotion. It is a system which appears to deny not only the classical laws of harmony which are the basis of the music of the past few centuries, but all laws of harmony. And the result of this highly artificial theory has often been music which looked very fascinating on paper, but which sounded merely like a clever intellectual game when it was played or sung.

But there is no denying Schönberg's immense influence on the composers that followed him. Probably the most gifted of his pupils was Alban Berg, the composer of the opera, "Wozzeck," and the Violin Concerto.

Neither life nor art ever conforms completely to any ironbound theory, and no more does a gifted musician like Alban Berg when he writes so deeply emotional a piece as his Violin Concerto. And so we find that his music has a more natural sound than we would expect from so-called atonal music. Actually, there is a basic feeling of tonality throughout this concerto, and the beautiful chord with which it ends, gives a greater feeling of satisfaction and rest than the close of many a more conventional composition.

As a matter of fact, if we forget all the theories for a moment, and think only of the development of music, we can see that a gradual evolution leads straight from the passionate chromatic harmonies of "Tristan und Isolde" to the bolder dissonances of Richard Strauss, to the startling unresolved dissonances of Alban Berg. A great deal of the vivid impression that "Tristan" makes upon us, the restless passion and unsatisfied longing, is due to the fact that the dissonances Wagner uses are seldom completely resolved. Even so popular a concert piece as the Prelude to "Tristan" never once, from beginning to end, sounds the fundamental chord of its home key—in other words, it never comes to rest. And yet we always have a very definite feeling that that fundamental home key is there, giving unity to the whole work. Alban Berg simply goes several steps further along the same road. But when you listen to this concerto, I'm sure you will feel, especially toward the end, that the old-fashioned tonality is there—only hinted at perhaps, and carefully disguised. But it is there—whatever the theorists may say.

Berg wrote his best music when he was inspired by a program, a drama or some human sentiment, and this concerto was composed in memory of a very dear friend, Manon Gropius, who had died after a tragic illness, which she fought with sweetness and calm and real heroism. It is inscribed "To the memory of an Angel," and was finished only six months before Berg's own death on Christmas Eve, 1935.

There is a quiet introduction with a theme built on the perfect fifths that sound naturally from the unstopped strings of the violin and which return at the end of the concerto. During the whole first part of this movement, the solo violin moves rhapsodically, sometimes almost as if it were improvising. The second half of the movement, which might correspond to the scherzo of a conventional concerto, is said to recall the cheer and gaiety of Manon when she was alive, and it uses elements of a Viennese waltz and a Carinthian folk song. But the gaiety is overcast with melancholy, and there is little that will remind you of a real waltz.

The second and final movement is also in two parts: the first may well have been intended to portray the struggle with death. There is a sharply rhythmic, threatening theme in the horns, and the violin courses in tortured, agitated figures up to a tragic climax. And out of the main melody there grows amazingly the chorale theme "Es ist genug" from Bach's cantata, "O Ewigkeit, du Donnerwort," which Bach used to express the resignation and peace of the longing for death. Gradually fragments of the chorale take shape. The solo violin continues with a touching elegy for the soul that has passed, in which it is joined by the first violins of the orchestra. Finally the first violins drop away again. The solo ascends to a long-held, ecstatic high G, the strings of the orchestra descend into the depths, sounding the perfect fifths of the opening, the cycle is complete, and in the final chord there is reconciliation and peace.

X. *Symbolism in Music*

THE MUSICAL LEITMOTIV was not invented by Richard Wagner. The use of musical symbols to represent an object or an idea goes back at least a thousand years. When we consider the symbolism underlying all religious art, it isn't surprising to find it in religious music too. Just as the great cathedrals of the Middle Ages are laid out on a vast sign of the cross, so the religious compositions of that day are built over vastly magnified musical phrases of deep symbolical importance. Centuries passed and techniques changed, but for eight hundred years, through the time of Bach, there is an unbroken tradition of symbolism in music, associated largely with religion. After Bach it died out for a few years, but Mozart revived it toward the end of his life in a work of high ethical significance, "The

227

Magic Flute." Beethoven took it in the service of his exalted ideals; romantic composers used it for both mystical and picturesque ends; Wagner developed it to undreamed-of psychological subtlety in his music dramas, and in our own day Richard Strauss has used it with dazzling effect in his popular operas and tone poems.

One night when Beethoven was having a fish dinner with his friend, Kuffner, in a little tavern called Zur Rose, Kuffner asked him which of his symphonies was his favorite. Beethoven had already written eight of his nine symphonies, but he replied: "Ah ha! the Eroica."

"I should have guessed the C minor [the Fifth]," said Kuffner.

"No," answered Beethoven, "the Eroica."

There are more reasons than one why Beethoven felt the way he did about his Third Symphony.

If you're familiar with the Eroica, and you don't happen to know the gay little contradances, you may be surprised to recognize one of them as the theme of the Eroica finale. Evidently, that beautiful swinging melody meant a great deal to Beethoven, because he used it not only in those early dances. He used it three times again in the course of his career, each time in a work that was of great significance, not only in his musical development, but in a symbolical sense—symbolical of the things which were most important to Beethoven in his own life and in the world about him, which was groping its way through upheaval and revolution to the ideals we are still fighting for today.

Heroism, which is the subject of the Eroica Symphony, was to Beethoven one of the vital shaping forces in human destiny—not mere animal courage, but the heroism of the divine creative impulse, whether it appears in political life or in art.

The first great work in which Beethoven used the theme we are talking about, was his ballet, "The Creations of Prometheus." Prometheus, you remember, was the heroic figure of Greek mythology, who stole fire from heaven to bring it to mankind—and to Beethoven he was certainly a symbol of beneficent creative power. We don't know what thoughts Beethoven had in the back of his mind when he used this theme for the third time in his important Piano Variations, Opus 35. But we find the theme for the fourth time as the crowning glory of the Eroica Symphony.

In this symphony he had in mind a person who must have seemed to him a modern Prometheus: Napoleon Bonaparte. For at the time Beethoven was composing his Eroica Symphony, Napoleon still appeared to be the great defender of the French Revolution and the message of freedom, which was intended not for France alone, but for all humanity. He was still regarded as the great liberator, the smasher of ancient tyrannies and conventions, which was exactly the role Beethoven played in music. Of course Beethoven felt this, and he named his Third Symphony after Napoleon. Then came the news that Napoleon had had himself proclaimed Emperor of France. Beethoven flew into a rage. "Then he's nothing but an ordinary man," he cried. "Now he'll trample on all the rights of men to serve his own ambition. He'll put himself above all others and turn out a tyrant."

On the manuscript of the symphony's title page you can still see the place where the name, Bonaparte, has been blotted out.

The symphony received a new name: "Sinfonia Eroica, composed to celebrate the memory of a great man." For the Napoleon Beethoven had admired was dead. Beethoven had seen him as a symbol of freedom, but now the symbol was perverted, and the symphony was re-dedicated to the spirit beyond symbols: the spirit of heroism.

The Eroica Symphony has no introduction. There are two sharp staccato chords and the orchestra sails ahead with its energetic swinging theme. The theme is so simple that it might have been a reminiscence of a military trumpet call, and perhaps, indirectly, a reference to Napoleon's triumphs as a defender of the French Revolution. Of course, this isn't the only theme of the movement. There is a tremendous wealth of ideas that swell and clash against each other in a dramatic development section. Then, as the orchestra prepares to return to the first part of the movement, Beethoven plays a trick on his listeners, which upset all the pedants of his day, and all the rule-of-thumb musicians for decades to come. A soft tremolo of the violins is hovering in suspense over a chord obviously meant to lead back into the main theme, when suddenly one lone horn plays the theme we are waiting for, before the harmony has changed, creating a peculiar dissonance—as if the horn player had missed his cue, and come in two measures too soon.

At a rehearsal for the Eroica a friend of Beethoven's, who was standing near him, heard this spot and exclaimed indignantly: "Why can't that horn player keep his wits about him. It sounds horribly false!" Beethoven merely glowered at the unfortunate man, and crushed him with a glance. It hadn't been a mistake.

The tremendous funeral march, the second movement

of the Eroica, has puzzled some people who thought that the only reason Beethoven had his funeral march come second instead of last was that tradition put slow movements in second place. But Beethoven wasn't writing a biography. If he had, there wouldn't have been any funeral march at all, because Napoleon wasn't dead yet. He was erecting a monument to the spirit of heroism, and no one can say that this funeral march does not express an heroic attitude toward death.

There is no pessimistic whining or petty personal grief in this music. Its step seems to falter as the shuddering rhythm starts, but its tread becomes firmer and firmer. There is no luxury of self-pity here, but rather a sort of cosmic woe. It is an epic lamentation over heroes slain in the defense of freedom, anyone's freedom, or all freedom. They could have been Leonidas and his Spartans at Thermopylae. And there is a proud exaltation in grief.

But neither death nor sorrow could have the last word in Beethoven's faith. The scherzo which follows is full of light and laughter and outbursts of wild humor.

And as if to symbolize the indomitable life and creative vitality of the heroic spirit, Beethoven uses the magnificent theme from "Prometheus," the contra-dance theme on which to build his finale. Naturally, it is developed into something infinitely greater than a dance tune. For example, there is a grand contrapuntal development of a strange, angular theme, which later proves to be the bass part of the dance theme. But the fundamental idea is there throughout. And as befits Beethoven's conception of the hero's spirit, the symphony ends in a burst of triumph.

BEETHOVEN: Symphony #9

Beethoven was only sixteen years old when he first thought of composing Schiller's "Ode to Joy." At various times during his career the idea returned and finally, four years before his death, it took form in the last and greatest of his symphonies. What was it in Schiller's ode that attracted him so and which seemed as important to the fifty-five-year-old master as it had to the boy of sixteen? It can hardly be that he thought the text particularly singable, for Beethoven never paid much attention to the limitations of the human voice. And it can't have been the beauty alone of the poetry, for Schiller had written better verse. No, what fired Beethoven's imagination was the thought behind the poetry, the thought which had taken political form in the slogan of the French Revolution: "Liberty, Equality, Fraternity," and which was given artistic form here by one of the greatest of German poets.

Schiller and Beethoven belonged roughly to the same generation. Both were deeply stirred by the French Revolution and its ideals of freedom and democracy. The brotherhood of man, which is hymned in the finale of the Ninth Symphony was a goal for which each of them fought in his own way as long as he lived. Schiller's death came in the midst of that epic struggle, shortly after Napoleon had perverted the French Revolution into an instrument for tyranny and proclaimed himself Emperor of France. But Beethoven lived on to see the fall of Napoleon, the restoration of order in Europe, and the close of one chapter in the fight for freedom.

So in the Ninth Symphony, which took him six years

to complete, he was able to look back on the battles, the defeats and victories with a long perspective, to sum them up, and crown his nine symphonies with the prophetic vision and the optimistic faith of the great chorale finale.

In the very first measures you sense the vastness of the design that lies ahead. Those mysterious open fifths of the introduction are like the darkness and void before creation. Gradually, fragments of the first theme emerge from the darkness until suddenly the theme itself blazes forth like a flash of orchestral lightning. It is followed by a wealth of new ideas. The development, as imaginative and varied in detail as it is overpowering in the breadth and splendor of its conception, mounts to a tremendous climax with the return of the first theme. The coda, with its ominous, muttering ostinato, is like a voice from the grave.

The octave hammer blows which open the scherzo are said to have struck Beethoven's mind as he stepped from darkness into light. The puckish exuberance, the brusque but delicate humor of the music that follows is interrupted by a trio of exquisite serenity.

In the third movement, a set of variations on two themes, melody reigns supreme. For warmth and depth of feeling it is unsurpassed even by Beethoven.

There have been many interpretations of the symbolism in the Ninth Symphony. One of the most popular calls the first movement Destiny, the inexorable pattern of the universe; the second, Physical Exuberance and Power; the third, Love. In the finale there is no doubt. Its theme is Joy—joy in the brotherhood of man. "Be embraced, ye countless millions," cries Schiller's poem, "with one kiss to all the world." But Schiller's words and Beethoven's music go far beyond the political slogans of the

French and American Revolutions, back to the deep religious thought from which they sprang.

The last movement has a lengthy introduction, a bridge between the first three movements and the finale, where Beethoven is among the stars. Between fierce clamorings of the orchestra, each preceding movement is recalled and then abruptly dismissed. The chorale theme of the finale has a friendlier welcome. Then once more the orchestra bursts into rebellion, but it is answered by the admonishing baritone solo in words written by Beethoven himself: "Oh, friends, no more of these tones. Let us sing more pleasant ones and full of joy."

Beethoven's rejoicing transcends even the "saintly shout and solemn jubilee" of a Milton. It is the vision of a liberated, united mankind, toward which we still strive. Chorus and soloists call upon the Goddess of Joy:

> "Let thy magic bring together
> All whom earth-born laws divide;
> All mankind shall be as brothers
> 'Neath thy tender wings and wide."

Beethoven was the only person not to hear the torrent of applause which followed the first performance of his Ninth Symphony on May 7, 1824. He had been deaf since middle life but he followed the score. His eyes were still glued to the page when one of the singers, finally noticing his pathetic isolation, turned him gently toward the audience that he might at least see the adoring faces and hands, silently clapping for the work he would never hear.

Mozart: Overture to "The Magic Flute"
Wagner: Prelude to "Lohengrin"
Hindemith: Symphony, "Mathis der Maler"

All three of these operatic selections by Mozart, Wagner and Hindemith are essentially religious music. Not that they were written for the church, or have anything at all to do with narrow dogma, but they are religious in the sense that they deal symbolically with the core of all our great philosophies and religions: man's love for his fellow man.

The Overture to "The Magic Flute" has a relatively easy symbolism. It opens with three solemn chords which appear later in the opera as part of the ritual of Sarastro's Temple of Wisdom. We know that the number three, to musicians of the middle ages, symbolized the Holy Trinity. But here it has another significance. For this number also played a great role in the mysteries of the idealistic order of Freemasons, to which both Mozart and Schikaneder, the librettist of "The Magic Flute," belonged. The action of "The Magic Flute" plays in ancient Egypt, the land where Freemasonry was said to have originated, and the teachings of Sarastro and his priests are closely associated with the humanitarian doctrines of the Freemasons.

In the introduction following the three solemn chords, there is a slow damming up of energies, which then burst forth in a stream of glittering, dancing counterpoint. But even this gossamer web of counterpoint has its symbolical purpose—to recall the only contrapuntal scene of the entire opera, where Tamino and Pamina are prepared for their trial by fire and water before being admitted to

the mysteries of Isis and Osiris. At the climax of the overture, as if to emphasize his meaning, Mozart repeats his
three solemn chords—this time in exactly the rhythm
used to greet new members at their initiation into a Ma-
sonic lodge. But for all its impressive symbolism, Mozart
preserves a delicate, fairy-tale atmosphere throughout.
There's Puck and quicksilver in the music; grace and
laughter in its moral.

The Prelude to Wagner's "Lohengrin" is a vision of
the Holy Grail, the supreme symbol of loving self-sacrifice.
Wagner pictured this vision as appearing to a world overwhelmed by its own selfishness in a ruthless struggle for
power. His own description of the music is still the best we
know.

"Out of the clear blue ether of the sky," he wrote,
"there seems to condense a wonderful, yet at first hardly
perceptible vision; and out of this there gradually emerges,
ever more clearly, an angel host, bearing in its midst the
sacred Grail. As it approaches the earth, it pours out exquisite odors, like streams of gold, ravishing the senses of
the beholder. The glory of the vision grows and grows,
until it seems as if the rapture must be shattered and dis-
persed by the very vehemence of its own expansion. The
vision draws nearer and the climax is revealed in all its
glory, radiating fiery beams and shaking the soul with
emotion. The beholder sinks on his knees in adoring self-
annihilation. The Grail pours out its light on him like
a benediction and consecrates him to its service. Then the
flames gradually die away, and the angel host soars up
again to the ethereal heights in tender joy, having made
pure once more the hearts of men by the sacred blessings
of the Grail."

Wagner had written "Lohengrin" at the time of the

revolutions which convulsed Europe around 1848. Mozart composed his "Magic Flute" at the time of the French Revolution. Hindemith wrote his opera, "Mathis der Maler," in the midst of another great European crisis. World War I, the hectic post-war years were past, Hitler had come to power, and life was in deadly earnest, particularly for Germans like Hindemith, who hated Hitler. The vicious political and military forces that are now grinding Europe to pieces had already begun their work. It was becoming more and more difficult for an artist who saw and understood what was going on around him to concentrate on a mere painting or an opera. How could a man go on writing music when the whole civilization to which his music belonged was tumbling down about his ears? How could a musician bear to go on composing, if he felt he should be straining every muscle to beat off the barbarism that threatened us all? Wasn't it the duty of every thinking person to drop what he was doing and take part in the struggle of world affairs?

Hindemith found an answer, or at least a partial one, in the life of another great artist who had once been confronted with the same problem. Matthias Grünewald, the painter of the famous Isenheim altarpiece, lived at the time of the Reformation, when the struggle between Catholic and Protestant forces rent Germany to her foundations. Little is known of Grünewald's personal life, so Hindemith was able to shape his own story for the libretto, without violating history. He chose one of the darkest moments of the Reformation, the terrible Peasant War of 1524—that volcanic upsurge of democratic forces which ended in scenes of appalling slaughter.

His social conscience aroused by one of the leaders of the peasants, Mathis gives up his painting and joins the battle to free his oppressed countrymen. In the background of the scene where he takes leave of his past, we see the threatening glow of a bonfire of heretical books in the market place of Mainz. Was Hindemith thinking of the Nazi book-burnings?

But the painter finds he is powerless to prevent either the injustices of the nobles or the plundering and slaughter of the peasants, some of whom forget the very cause for which they are fighting. Confusion and doubt grow in his mind. In an allegorical scene he experiences the temptations of St. Anthony, which he himself had painted as a part of the triptych for the Isenheim altar at Colmar in Alsace. Demons rise to plague him and call him to account for his actions. Finally he recognizes that artistic creation too is part of the good fight. Out of the struggle and confusion come clarity and confidence in the mission of the artist to which he returns.

From this opera, Hindemith has taken three instrumental episodes to form a symphonic whole. Each movement was inspired by a separate panel of the Isenheim altarpiece: The Angelic Concert, The Entombment of Christ, and The Temptation of St. Anthony.

The opening of the Angelic Concert has about it something of the atmosphere of the Prelude to "Lohengrin," but the following recalls the old technique of Bach's religious music, with a slow, choralelike theme, about which he weaves elaborate strands of contrapuntal ornament.

The Entombment is a brief interlude of exalted religious calm and mysticism.

The Temptation of St. Anthony paints a parallel to the temptation of Mathis himself. It opens with a boldly sculptured unisono melody. There are agitated rhythmic figures of the brass instruments and fierce clashes of contrapuntal forces. One sharp climax follows another and finally, over the harmonious commotion, there soars another chorale melody fragment. There is a last massive proclamation of the chorale ending in a blaze of spiritual illumination.

ᚼᚼ   ᚼᚼ

FRANCK: Symphony in D minor
LISZT: "Les Préludes"

There are few works in the entire symphonic repertory that are more popular today than César Franck's D minor Symphony, and it's hard to imagine that it could have been a failure when it was first performed in Paris, only a few months before the composer's death. But the failure was partly Franck's own fault, for he had never troubled to thrust himself or his music before the public. Either he didn't know how to use his elbows, or he just didn't want to. He had none of the commanding manner of Beethoven, who had made it a policy to be rude to the Austrian aristocracy, just to show them their place in the presence of genius. And he had none of the aggressive egotism of Wagner, though he learned much from Wagner's music.

Franck was content to be a saint. He was even willing to pay the penalties which the world exacts from those people who perversely refuse to get ahead by stepping on other people's necks. In Franck's case the penalties were almost complete obscurity, rare and usually bad performances of his works, and hence the wildest misunderstanding of his music, both among the public and among trained musicians. From the point of view of the outside world, Franck's career, almost up to the last year of his life, was one failure after another.

When his D minor Symphony was first played, neither the audience nor the professors of the Paris Conservatory, where the performance took place, could make head or tail of it. After the première one of Franck's pupils, Vincent d'Indy, asked a head of the conservatory what he thought of the new symphony.

"That, a symphony?" was the contemptuous answer. "But, my dear sir, who ever heard of writing for the English horn in a symphony? Just name me a single symphony by Haydn or Beethoven that uses an English horn. There, well, you see: Your Franck's music may be whatever you please, but it will certainly never be a symphony!"

At another door of the concert hall, Gounod delivered his solemn judgment to a flock of admirers. Franck's symphony, he said, was the affirmation of incompetence pushed to dogmatic lengths! However, since then, this symphony has done almost as well in the concert hall as Gounod's "Faust" has in the opera house. And that's saying a great deal.

The opening theme of Franck's symphony is a phrase that has fascinated composers for more than a century: a sort of musical question of just three notes. Beethoven used it in one of his last quartets where he wrote over the notes: "Must it be?" Wagner used it in his "Ring of the Nibelung" as the questioning theme of Fate. And Franz Liszt used it again as the main theme of his symphonic poem, "Les Préludes."

César Franck doesn't give the motive any label, but

he places it as a slow portentous question at the very opening of his symphony. Again and again, with rising insist-
ence, the orchestra asks this question till we come to the
main part of the first movement, an allegro. And suddenly this question is itself turned into a reply, an energetic, aggressive version of the same theme, which seems
to say that the answer is life itself with its agitation and
struggle. Higher and higher the orchestra surges until suddenly all yearning and straining resolves into soaring
melody. The rest of the movement is taken up with the
conflict between these two moods, and at the end the solemn question is answered in a blaze of affirmation.

This symphony has only three movements instead of
the usual four, but the allegretto which follows now,
seems to unite the characteristics of both slow movement
and scherzo. It begins with soft pluckings of the harp and
other string instruments. And soon there rises above it
the melancholy song of the English horn, which so upset
the pedants of César Franck's day. The middle part of
this movement lets through a gleam of light, a gayer, more
care-free atmosphere, but at the end, the sad lay of the
English horn returns.

The finale hasn't the dash or drive of the classical
symphony, but it is festive music. There are reminiscences
of the melancholy and the struggles of the past, but they
give way to a mounting wave of assurance and strength.
The sad theme of the second movement is transformed into
a song of joy and the answer to all the questionings is triumph, not despair.

In Franz Liszt's symphonic poem, "Les Préludes," the
question which Franck asked in his symphony, and which
had been asked before him by Wagner and Beethoven, receives an even clearer answer. For Liszt took more pains

than the other composers to say exactly what his use of that theme signified. His title, "Les Préludes," is taken from some verses of the French poet, Lamartine, and the music itself is intended to reflect Lamartine's emotions and thought.

"What is our life," asks Liszt in a preface to the score, "but a series of preludes to that unknown song, the first solemn tone of which is sounded by death? Love forms the enchanted dawn of all existence. But in whose destiny are these first ecstasies of happiness not interrupted by some storm . . . which blasts his fond illusions. . . . And after the passing of the tempest, what cruelly wounded soul does not seek to rest his memories in the sweet calm of rural life? And yet when the trumpet signals the alarm, he hastens again to the post of danger, be the war what it may. . . . And there in combat he regains himself and full possession of his forces."

Technically speaking, this symphonic poem is a series of variations on the famous theme we have mentioned above. It begins with a soft, slow introduction. Plucked strings and wood winds echo each other, building up to a climactic portrait of the hero. And the great theme is thundered out by the brasses with brilliant, sweeping arpeggios of the violins and violas above.

Then the music becomes tender, and violins and cellos sing a more lyric version of the theme. A new section and a new theme tell us that the "enchanted dawn of every life is love." Horns and violas chant a rhapsodic melody which mounts to a climax of passion. As the excitement dies down again, soft chords of the flutes recall us to the principal theme of the poem.

Then again the orchestra is convulsed with the storms of disillusionment. As this subsides, the hero takes refuge in the "sweet calm of rural life." The love theme returns, but the hero has still to gird his loins for further struggle. Both his own theme and that of love reappear in martial guise.

In the final coda, andante maestoso, the hero theme returns in its complete, original form. This at last is the full glory of day, the reality to which the episodes of life were only a series of preludes. The theme is shining and majestic. The orchestra suggests to us the power and grandeur of a light which is too bright for mortal eyes.

＊＊　　＊＊

BEETHOVEN: Overture to "Coriolanus"
TCHAIKOVSKY: Symphony #5, E minor

Each of these works is in its own way a confession of faith. And the price of faith, in each case, is a titanic emotional struggle, reflected in the clash of great musical symbols.

Beethoven's Overture to "Coriolanus" is a portrait of a hero much like himself: one proud, uncompromising, quick to anger, but equally quick to sacrifice himself for a great principle. It matters little that it was composed not for Shakespeare's great tragedy but a contemporary "Coriolanus" by one Heinrich Joseph von Collin. Shakespeare dominated both Collin and Beethoven. And as Richard Wagner long since pointed out, Beethoven certainly took his cue from the greater play.

Coriolanus, having been banished from Rome, returns at the head of a victorious enemy army, fully intending to annihilate the city which has humiliated and rejected him. To his camp outside Rome comes one friend and ambassador after another pleading for mercy, but Coriolanus haughtily rejects them all. At last, confronted by his mother, his wife and little son, he wavers, his hard resolution is cracked, his pride is broken. He returns to his old allegiance and his old faith. For though Rome is in the hands of the mob, it is still Rome. Coriolanus gives up his revenge and with it, as he knows, his life, for something that is greater.

The overture begins with an imperious gesture of triumph. Or you may think of it as the contemptuous conqueror himself. You can hear the tide of indecision rising in the hero's mind, his angry defiance, then the collapse of pride and the uncompromising, self-destroying victory as the last murmurs of the orchestra drop away into silence.

Beethoven's overture tells the faith of a fighter, a doer of high deeds, full of strength and courage, even for self-sacrifice.

Tchaikovsky's Fifth Symphony is the intimate confession of a man who is afraid. Afraid of the world and of himself. His is the hardest fight of all, for he fights alone against his self-doubt and torture of soul. And perhaps, for just that reason, his victory is the more poignant.

There have always been people who sneered at Tchaikovsky. And, unfortunately, most of them have been musicians. The aesthetes and the high priests of art (self-appointed high priests, of course) sneered when Tchaikovsky's works were first performed, and there are still a good many of these gentry around today. They are the people who will tell you gravely that it was in bad taste for Tchaikovsky to unpack his emotions in the market place—that he is cheap, tinselly, an applause-catcher, or

Heaven knows what, but certainly nothing that a real musician would take seriously.

Well, Tchaikovsky has been doing very nicely, thank you, without the help of any of the musical snobs, because, fortunately, the public has a sound instinct which refuses to take their advice.

Tchaikovsky was a Slav, and when he broods and wails over personal tragedy, or exults in triumph, as in the last moment of the Fifth Symphony, he does it without reserve and without regard for the conventions of polite society, musical or otherwise. And it was not just a romantic pose. When Tchaikovsky brooded, he fell into the blackest depths of pessimism.

After the first performance of this Fifth Symphony, which took place in 1888, he was convinced, in spite of the applause, that the work was a failure. He wrote to Mme. von Meck, his "beloved friend" and protectress: "There is something repellent, something superfluous, patchy and insincere, which the public instinctively recognizes. It was obvious to me, that the ovations I received were prompted more by my earlier work, and that the symphony itself did not please the audience." But the next time he heard the symphony he liked it better, and it slowly dawned on him that all the applause was not just a polite tribute. It came from the depths of his listeners' hearts.

The core of the Fifth Symphony is the slow, foreboding theme which begins the first movement. It recurs in each of the four movements and binds them together in a way that suggests that there may have been a story or program behind this symphony, a story that Tchaikovsky chose to keep to himself. Eminent scholars have specu-

lated as to what that story might be. But in the end, your
guess is as good as theirs.

The opening theme may be a symbol of fate, ominous and melancholy. The main body of the first movement, as in the classical symphony, is a fiery allegro.

The second movement, andante cantabile, is a sort of
romanze, which allows the conductor great freedom of interpretation. After a brief introduction on the deeper
strings, the horn sings the principal melody, a sound of
haunting nostalgia. It is answered by a melancholy oboe,
and the voices intertwine. Suddenly this idyll is interrupted by the threatening main theme of the symphony.
But the melody returns, and, as if in protest, the longing
grows and swells to a passionate lyric outpouring. Then,
once again, there is a terrifying interruption of the motive
of fate. This time, the clash of the brass instruments is
catastrophic and imperious. The dream is shattered. And
the movement dies away with pleading, broken phrases. It
is the triumph of Slavic pessimism.

On the surface, the third movement seems a gay and
simple waltz, but there is an undertone of melancholy
which never completely disappears. And it is confirmed
by the reassertion of the motive of fate at the close.

Then in the last movement a miracle happens. That
same slow theme of gloom and defeat grows gradually
and imperceptibly into a song of affirmation. A roll of
kettledrums leads in the fast part of the movement. Rapid,
joyous figures course through the orchestra. The theme
returns transformed, with the majestic stride of a conqueror. The music shouts and exults. All doubts and fears
are banished. The pace increases and the orchestra plunges
into a headlong presto and a final paean of victory with

brilliant fanfares of the brass—all derived from that first tortured theme of fate.

It is a work of shattering dramatic impact. And the story it tells could have been told only in music.

❧❦   ❧❦

RICHARD STRAUSS: "Thus Spake Zarathustra"
"Death and Transfiguration"

Symbols can mean many different things at the same time. Perhaps that is the very secret of their power. We are always finding new interpretations of familiar musical symbols and many or all of them may be true. Richard Strauss himself gave two different explanations of his own tone poem, "Thus Spake Zarathustra," and who can say that one was right and the other wrong?

Strauss wrote his tone poem at the time of the great Nietzsche fad in Germany, he named it after Nietzsche's philosophical masterpiece, "Also sprach Zarathustra," and carefully labeled each section after certain chapters of the book. Then, having made it clear to the blindest person what his music was about, he blandly denied the whole business. "I did not intend to write philosophical music," he wrote, "or to portray in music Nietzsche's great book. I meant to convey by means of music the idea of the development of the human race from its origin through the various phases of its development, religious and scientific, up to Nietzsche's idea of the superman."

Nietzsche had never been popular while he was alive.

But when he was safely dead and buried, the German public began to think he was quite wonderful. There was
something almost masochistic in their uncomprehending
adoration of a man who despised the mass of Germans
above all others. Nietzsche was a classical philologist, an
admirer of Mediterranean culture—above all the Greek
and the French. With typical arrogance, he gave his
"Zarathustra" the subtitle of "A book for all and for
none." Which may have been just a high-sounding way of
saying: "Take it or leave it." His book has nothing to do
with the mythical-historical Zarathustra, the warrior-
king and wise man who was also known as Zoroaster.
Nietzsche's Zarathustra is Nietzsche himself, dispensing
his wisdom to the ignorant multitude in epigram, apho-
rism and paradox.

While Strauss was still working on his tone poem the
following program was published: "First movement: Sun-
rise. Man feels the power of God. Andante religioso. But
man still longs. He plunges into passion (second movement) and finds no peace. He turns toward science and
tries to solve life's problems in a fugue (third movement).
Then agreeable dance tunes sound and he becomes an
individual and his soul soars upward while the world sinks
far beneath him."

This program may sound a little high flown today,
but the music itself has true grandeur. The elemental
main theme of "Zarathustra" blazes forth in the trumpets.
Philip Hale once said of this opening that it was like the
gates of eternity swinging slowly asunder. For once, the
pomp of the full organ does not sound out of place in an
orchestra.

Each section of the score, which is played without
pause, has a heading from Nietzsche's book: Of the Great

Yearning; Of Joys and Passions; Grave Song; Of Science; The Convalescent; Dance Song [in which the great Zarathustra dances to something suspiciously like a Viennese waltz]; and The Night Wanderer's Song [which you can easily recognize by the twelve strokes of the bell with which it begins]. The conclusion is in two keys, soft, mystical and enigmatic—perhaps symbolizing the riddle of the universe which, as Hale remarked, is unsolved by Nietzsche, by Strauss and even by Strauss's commentators.

The opening measures of "Death and Transfiguration" are an excellent example of how strongly Strauss was influenced by Richard Wagner. They are descended direct from one of the most touching moments of the last act of "Tristan und Isolde," the passage which follows the climax of Tristan's long monologue when he falls motionless onto his couch. Kurwenal, afraid that he is dead, leans anxiously over his body. After a moment's silence, we hear a faint throbbing in the orchestra, like the uneven flutter of a heart, or the barely perceptible breathing of an unconscious man who lies near death.

Strauss's tone poem, "Death and Transfiguration," begins with the same realistic portrayal of the faint breath and the weakly pulsing heart. There follows a deep sigh of exhaustion. According to Alexander Ritter's poem which Strauss had printed in his score, and which was written *after* the music, it depicts the thoughts and dreams of a half-conscious man lying in a dimly lit, poverty-stricken room waiting death. A candle that flickers as fitfully as his own fast-ebbing life, casts fantastic shadows through the room, and in his fever the man's dreams go back to pictures of his childhood, the battles of his youth, the hopes, the illusions and the ideals that sustained him against his foes. Then the last foe strikes and the man falls.

But behold, his dreams and ideals go on, rising from climax to climax of triumph.

Notice that first sigh of exhaustion, which is repeated many times, even through the dreams of childhood. For that very sigh later becomes the triumphal chant of the close. You will hear a hint of it in the first dramatic outburst of the orchestra, like an incomplete vision of the ideal, seen through the struggles of youth. The serenity returns for a moment, then the struggles of manhood break out afresh. There is a terrible climax which dissolves into thin air, and then the tolling of a gong. It throbs slowly in the depths of the orchestra and then magically the tolling of the passing bell is transformed into a song of victory. Higher and higher it rises through the orchestra, clearer and clearer to a last climax of blinding light. Not the man himself, but his dreams are immortal.

XI. *The Other Romanticism*

IN A romantic century, two mighty quarreling camps gathered about the names of Wagner and Brahms. One dynasty of giants led from Berlioz and Liszt to Wagner and in our own day to Richard Strauss. They were the aggressive romantics, the men who reached out to embrace philosophy, politics, literature, the whole drama of human life in their music—the revolutionists and publicists of romanticism. The opposing camp, headed by Mendelssohn, Schumann and Brahms, had a quieter, more introspective turn of mind, though Schumann was an influential writer on music. Their impulse was not revolution but evolution. In their symphonic writing they were less dependent on external description or story-telling, and so perhaps truly closer to the spirit of Mozart, Haydn, or Beethoven. Another bond was their rediscovery of Bach which had a deep influence, on Brahms in particular. Indeed, as he matured, Brahms's music developed more and more of the severity and restraint of Bach and the balance of the classical symphonists. And Sibelius, perhaps the nearest heir to Brahms in our own day, had a somewhat similar experience. In spite of their literary and political allusions and the lavish orchestration of his early works, Sibelius was never sympathetic to Wagner. And as the years passed his music too grew more and more compact, laconic and essentially classical in spirit.

BACH: Brandenburg Concerto #6, B flat
ROBERT SCHUMANN: Symphony #4, D minor

When Johann Sebastian Bach died in 1750 he was almost a forgotten man. His life's work was like a great mountain peak of an evolution that had been going on for the past three hundred years. But already the river of little talents in the valley had flowed around and beyond him, and the mountain was left behind. The mountain was as great and awe-inspiring as it had ever been, had anyone chanced to turn back and look at it, but the sons of Bach and their contemporaries rushed boldly on, their eyes straining toward new and more exciting musical horizons. And Bach disappeared into the mists of an almost legendary past.

It was another three generations before men got far enough away so that they were able to turn back and see the mountain in its true perspective, and then a great revival of Bach began, which is still going on today. Curiously enough, the men who were most responsible for the revival of Bach were the ones you would least expect: the romantics.

Bach, who had been accused for so long of writing musical mathematics, was revived by the men to whom feeling was everything and mathematics were nothing. Mendelssohn led the way, and Schumann, whose poetic and introspective Fourth Symphony we hear next on our program, called Bach the source of all wisdom. He declared that Bach, like the Bible, was for daily use. "I myself," he said, "confess my sins daily to that mighty one and endeavor to strengthen and purify myself through him."

Not only that, but Schumann believed that "the poetry and humor of modern music originated chiefly in Bach." That is why, though their music may seem poles apart, it is particularly interesting to hear these two men on the same program.

Schumann's so-called Fourth Symphony is actually his second. It was composed immediately after his First Symphony, during the first, ecstatically happy year of his marriage to Clara Wieck. With his extremely sensitive and excitable nature, Schumann had suffered agonies trying to overcome the opposition of Clara's father to their wedding. But then the immense spiritual well-being, the tranquillity, love and understanding that Clara brought into his life resulted in a great wave of creative activity.

In May, 1841, soon after the First or Spring Symphony was finished, Clara wrote in the diary which she and Robert kept together: "Yesterday Robert began another symphony which will be in one movement, but still contain an adagio and finale. As yet I have heard nothing of it, but from seeing Robert's bustling and hearing the D minor chord sounding wildly in the distance, I know in advance that another work is being wrought in the depths of his soul. Heaven is kindly disposed toward us: Robert cannot be happier in the composition than I am when he shows me such a work." And a few days later: "Robert is composing steadily; he has already completed three movements, and I hope the symphony will be ready by his birthday."

It was finished not for Robert's but for Clara's birth-

day, in September, the day on which they christened their
first child, Marie. When he presented Clara with the
score, Robert wrote in their diary: "One thing makes me
happy: the consciousness of still being far from my goal
and being obliged to keep doing better, and then the feeling that I have the strength to reach it."

But the first performance that year was not very successful, and Schumann himself seemed dissatisfied. So he
put the symphony aside. Ten years later, after he had
published two more symphonies, he revised the score and
had it printed as his Symphony #4. In the meantime
he had altered the orchestration, made important changes
in the thematic development—cutting out elaborate contrapuntal work to gain a broader, simpler line, especially
in the last movement, and he had changed the opening.
It was to be played as a continuous whole.

In its final form the symphony begins with a lovely
reflective theme which returns again and again in various
forms throughout the score. An agitated figure derived
from this introduction furnishes the central motive for the
remainder of the first movement.

The second movement, romanza, opens with a mournful melody sung by the oboe and cello, the melody of a
Provençal song, which alternates with the languorous
theme of the introduction.

Now the scherzo bursts out with another variation of
the introduction, but below this gust of energy there runs
a strain of romantic melancholy. There is a brooding
transition to the finale, with echoes of what is past. Then
the mood changes, and the sunlight bursts through the
clouds. The familiar themes take on a jaunty, almost
marchlike brilliance. An exultant, singing second theme

spreads through the orchestra. The pace increases, the agitation disappears and the symphony rushes on to its triumphant close.

ᗐᗏ   ᗐᗏ

MENDELSSOHN: Symphony #4, A major. Italian
Violin Concerto, E minor

Few great composers have led consistently happy and successful lives. But Mendelssohn is one of them. And I think you can hear it in his music. Unfortunately, Mendelssohn's reputation as a composer has been handicapped by this very fact. For a composer who came of a banker's family, who was handsome and popular, happy in his marriage, rich in friends, and pampered by the crowned heads of Europe—such a composer obviously didn't fit into the romantic picture of the suffering genius.

Mendelssohn had good manners and he was as elegant in looks as he was in his music—all of which is faintly enraging to the people who feel that the privilege of genius should be paid for, if not by financial need, then at least by morbid emotions or an unshaven appearance. But Mendelssohn did not have to pay, except possibly with anxiety about the quality of his works.

Young Mendelssohn set out on the trip which inspired his Italian Symphony with all the financial and social advantages one could wish for. He hobnobbed with the great and the wealthy on his way south through Germany. In Weimar he had the privilege of spending two weeks in delightful talks with that unapproachable grandee of German literature, Goethe. The poet was past eighty and was slowly putting the finishing touches on his colossal tragedy of Faust. He was revered as one of the towering figures of his century, but was almost more feared than loved. Yet he unbent to this twenty-one-year-old musician and spent long, happy hours talking with him, doubtless reminiscing and describing the Italy that he had known on his own famous trip so many years before.

In Munich again, Mendelssohn visited everywhere, flirted with all the pretty girls; and a friend wrote that it was "worth standing by, and watching how he is the darling of every house, the center of every circle. From early in the morning, everything concentrates on him." So it went: from Munich to Vienna and over the mountains to Venice. "Italy at last!" he cried. "What I have been looking forward to all my life as the greatest happiness is now begun, and I am basking in it. . . . The whole country had such a festive air that I felt as if I were a young prince making his entry."

And that is what we hear in the first movement of the symphony. The vibrant brilliance of the wood winds in the opening phrase is like the sparkle of the Italian sunshine, and over it the exultant cry of the violins, like a call to adventure. It expresses all the confidence and excitement of a young man off on his own to the promised land of new beauty. Mendelssohn's own words, "I felt like a young prince," are the real key to this movement, which unfolds with a rush of enchanting detail as the Italian landscape unfolded before him.

The mock-dolefulness and the plodding gait of the main theme in the second movement may have been suggested by a religious procession which we know Mendelssohn saw in the streets of Naples. And the third movement has a deftness and poetry that recall his music to the "Midsummer Night's Dream."

The finale is a saltarello, an old Italian dance form, with a skipping figure in triple time, which reflects the hectic fun of the Roman Carnival. "I arrived at the Corso," Mendelssohn wrote, "and was driving along, thinking no harm, when suddenly I was assailed by a shower of sugar candies. I looked up. They had been flung by some ladies whom I had occasionally seen at balls, but scarcely knew, and when in my embarrassment, I took off my hat to bow to them, the pelting began in right earnest. Their carriage drove on, and in the next was Miss T—, a delicate young Englishwoman. I tried to bow to her, but she pelted me too; so I became quite desperate, and clutching the confetti, I flung them back bravely. There were swarms of my acquaintances and my blue coat was soon as white as that of a miller. The B— family were standing on a balcony, flinging confetti like hail at my head. And thus pelting and pelted, amid a thousand jests and jeers and the most extravagant masks, the day ended with races."

Toward the end of the music, the merrymakers seem to be dispersing into the distance, but the close brings another brilliant surprise in the carnival spirit.

You wouldn't dream, to hear it, that that symphony cost Mendelssohn some of the bitterest moments of his life. At least that was what Mendelssohn said. But the bitterness came not from personal misfortune or professional neglect. It came from a self-conscious, over-critical attitude toward his own music. Even the fussiest of us today can hardly imagine anything we would like to change in the Italian Symphony, but to Mendelssohn his work was unfinished. Within a year after its first performance, he was going over the score, rewriting whole sections, and he died without having accomplished his purpose of revising the finale.

Like many other composers, Mendelssohn had a particular virtuoso in mind when he composed his popular violin concerto. In 1838, five years after completing the Italian Symphony, he wrote his friend, Ferdinand David: "I should like to write a concerto for you next winter. One in E minor keeps running in my head, and the beginning will not leave me in peace." Later, David visited Mendelssohn and when he saw the partially completed work, he exclaimed happily: "This is going to be something great!" "Do you think so?" asked Mendelssohn. "I'm sure of it," was David's reply. "There is plenty of music for violin and orchestra, but there has been only one big, truly great concerto [meaning the Beethoven Violin Concerto], and now there will be two."

But Mendelssohn objected. "No, no!" he said. "If I finish this concerto it certainly won't be with the thought of competing with Beethoven." And Mendelssohn was as good as his word. His concerto, after seven years' work, was far from a copy of either the form or the spirit of Beethoven's masterpiece.

Mendelssohn has too often been labeled as a man who merely accepted the classical forms handed down to him, filling them with music of unoriginal elegance and charm. In the concerto he not only avoided many of the traditional features of the classical concerto. He wrote with such originality and success that he pulled a whole century of composers in his wake. His concerto has been imitated so much that we often forget Mendelssohn was the first person to write this kind of work. Donald Tovey said he envied a person hearing the Mendelssohn Violin

Concerto for the first time, for he would discover that it was full of quotations, like Shakespeare's "Hamlet."

The very beginning is unconventional. The solo violin instead of the orchestra announces the passionate principal theme—a long, boldly arching melody, which works up to quite a climax before the orchestra interrupts with the transition to the second theme. The second theme itself is a drooping little melodic figure with a slight touch of melancholy. The cadenza for the violin alone, instead of coming as it usually does at the close of the movement, is very effectively placed just before the return to the first theme. In fact the first theme enters in the orchestra while the violin is still spinning out the rapid arpeggios of the cadenza, so that we have the impression that the violin is accompanying the orchestra, instead of the other way around.

All three movements of this concerto were meant to be played without pause. There is a mysteriously quiet transition to the second movement which has a broad melodic flow and an atmosphere of almost religious dignity. The last movement is light hearted, capricious and brilliant.

When Sterndale Bennett saw this music he said to Mendelssohn: "There seems to me something essentially and exquisitely feminine about it, just as in the Beethoven Concerto there is something essentially and heroically masculine. He had made the Adam of Concertos, and you have mated it with the Eve."

BRAHMS: "Variations on a Theme by Haydn"
Symphony #1, C minor

For centuries the name of Vienna has meant music.
And it has meant home to great musicians. Many of the
great musicians who made Vienna their home, were not
born there, but the city had a magic that drew them and
held them. There are many Viennas, and they are all
reflected in music, from the pompous Italian baroque
operas that entertained the ancient monarchs of the Holy
Roman Empire to bawdy little peasant verses sung over
a stein of beer. Marie Antoinette, while she was still a
spoiled young princess in Vienna, wrote songs that you
may hear any day at a concert in Town Hall, and the procession of great musicians who composed in Vienna is endless: from Gluck, Haydn, Mozart and Beethoven all the
way to Brahms, Mahler and the twelve-tone modernist,
Arnold Schönberg, who escaped from 'the Nazis to find
refuge in Hollywood.

Brahms and Haydn were born a century apart and
represent roughly the beginning and the end of what we
think of as Viennese classicism. When Brahms went to
live in Vienna, he was extremely conscious of the great
musical heritage he wanted to carry on, and in his first
large work for full orchestra alone, the "Variations on a
Theme by Haydn," he made his bow to the founder of
the Viennese classical school.

The theme Brahms chose is from one of Haydn's
divertimenti for wind instruments. Haydn called it the
Chorale of St. Anthony, and on the basis of this fact,
fanciful commentators have tried to interpret Brahms's

variations as the series of temptations to which St. Anthony was subjected. But Brahms was notoriously uninterested in stories for his music. And there is little in these healthy, vigorous variations, or in the powerful fugue that builds their climax, to suggest torture of the spirit or senses.

Brahms once said to his friend, the great conductor, Levi: "I shall never write a symphony. You have no conception how the likes of us feel, when we hear the tramp of a giant like *him* behind us." By "him" Brahms meant Beethoven. But when he said he would never write a symphony, he didn't mean it quite literally. For when he made that statement he had just finished the first movement of his First Symphony. It was in C minor. When his friends tried to make him get on with the symphony, he would reply that the world already had one symphony in C minor by Beethoven, and there was no hurry for another.

Brahms was forty-two before the score was completed and performed by the grand duke's orchestra at Karlsruhe. Nobody knows exactly when he began the First Symphony, but as far as we can tell, twenty-one years had elapsed between the first germ of the idea and the masterpiece in its final form.

Curiously enough, the beginning of the First Symphony as it stands today, the great surging introduction, was an afterthought. Over the deep insistent pounding of the kettledrums, there rises a gigantic procession of indistinct figures, which crystallize later into the chief themes of the first movement. The fast part of the movement begins stormily. Sometimes it is dramatic, with true Brahmsian gruffness, sometimes it is filled with tragic irony and pathos.

The slow second movement has tremendous breadth

and a magnificent, long melodic line. It begins in placid melancholy and rises to an impassioned climax with the violins soaring ecstatically above, and the strong basses tugging away at the bottom of the orchestra. There are brief, plaintive melodic interludes in the wood-wind instruments, and several dramatic surprises in the middle part, before the music returns to the meditating pathos of the beginning.

In place of a scherzo, Brahms has written a graceful little allegretto.

The finale has a long and very poetic introduction. After the first sweeping measures, there is a sudden quiet. Plucked notes of the string instruments stalk softly and ominously through the orchestra—slowly at first and then faster, until in a rush of panic they infect the whole orchestra with their agitation. The excitement comes to an abrupt end with a crashing roll of drums, followed by one of the most marvelous contrasts in all Brahms: through the rainbowlike shimmering of the strings, we hear the infinitely peaceful melody of a solo horn, an echo of a shepherd's horn that Brahms had heard in the Alpine country, where he loved to spend his summers. Then the silvery tones of a flute appear at the very top of the orchestra as a gleaming reflection of the horn. And then another contrast: a soft, majestic chorale for the brass instruments alone.

All this has been introduction. The main body of the finale begins with a bold, swinging theme, which recalls the finale of Beethoven's Ninth Symphony. When someone pointed this out to Brahms, he answered: "Any fool can see that!" But the resemblance is beside the point. Brahms was using Beethoven's language to say something very different. This and other themes are developed until the conflict and tension of the symphonic drama find an outlet in a headlong presto. This is interrupted to repeat the great chorale of the introduction, with the full splendor of the brass fortissimo, and then the symphony sweeps on to its exultant close.

❧❦   ❧❦

BRAHMS: Tragic Overture
Symphony #2, D major

The Tragic Overture, in spite of its brevity, is worthy to rank alongside Brahms's symphonies, as much for its magnificent tonal architecture as for depth of feeling. It combines the most powerful tragic emotion and a severely classical instinct for form with a triumphant mastery which recalls the spirit of ancient Greek tragedy. This music looks tragedy full in the face and accepts it as an overwhelming fact of life, without once breaking down and becoming merely pathetic in its mood.

But Brahms was not always stern. He could sing in the most personal and romantic mood, as he does in the Second Symphony. This music is filled with the breath of spring. It is the most light hearted of his four symphonies. One of Brahms's biographers has called it "a declaration of love in symphonic form."

Most of the Second Symphony was written during the summer of 1877 at a lovely spot called Pörtschach on one of the lakes of the Austrian countryside. Brahms was extremely happy there. Inspiration came easily and he wrote one of his friends: "So many melodies are flying about that one has to be careful not to tread them under-foot."

"Pörtschach is most exquisitely situated," he wrote, "and I have found a lovely and apparently pleasant abode in the castle. You can tell everybody that. It will impress them. But I may add in parentheses that I have only two little rooms in the housekeeper's quarters. They couldn't get my piano upstairs—it would have burst the walls."

As to the new symphony, Brahms was extremely reticent. He always loved to mystify and tease his friends when they asked him questions. And so he took particular pleasure in describing this gracious, sunny work as a gloomy, awesome piece. "The orchestra will play my new symphony with crepe bands on their sleeves," he wrote, "because of its dirgelike effect. It is to be printed with a black edge too."

When his devoted admirer, Elisabeth von Herzogenberg, tried to make him show her the music, he wrote that she could play it quite easily without the score. "You merely sit down at the piano, put your little feet on the two pedals in turn, and strike the chord of F minor several times in succession, then in the bass fortissimo and pianissimo and you will gradually gain a vivid impression of my latest."

As a matter of fact the Second was the most melodious, and long the most popular of Brahms's symphonies. Even its first theme, instead of being lively and dramatic according to classical tradition, is a great arch of melody. Notice those first few notes—how the thoughtful, tender introduction is built up on them; how later the violins take up the theme and weave it into a flowing garland of melody. Those first notes not only set the mood of the entire symphony; they are the thematic kernel of the first and last movements. Even the second theme of the first movement, which is sung by the cellos, seems somehow mysteriously derived from that first phrase.

Then the two melodies stream together and intertwine. There are gruffer passages of contrast, but essentially the whole movement is one of melody, right up through the coda, where the nostalgic theme of the introduction is sung once more by the mellow voice of the horn.

The second movement, too, is melodic, but this is Brahms in a more philosophical mood.

The third movement is built on a touching little pastoral tune which sounds first, very simply, on the oboe, but then undergoes a dozen whimsical transformations of rhythm, tempo and character. But the whole movement is light footed and humorous in tone—so light, in fact, that some of Brahms's contemporaries thought it undignified for a symphony.

The finale grows out of a brisk melody which you hear at the very beginning, played in unison by several instruments, and related to the main theme of the first movement. There are sudden explosive outbursts in an almost heroic mood, along with the wealth of melody. And in the closing bars the first theme is shouted aloud as a sort of joyous fanfare in the brilliant ringing voices of the trumpets.

WAGNER: Prelude to "Die Meistersinger"
Introduction to Act III, "Die Meistersinger"
BRAHMS: Symphony #3, F Major

"Die Meistersinger" is Wagner's only comedy. Conceived as a satirical companion piece to his early "Tannhäuser," it was completed many years later as a sort of antidote to the death- and passion-fraught score of "Tristan und Isolde." It is a triumphant affirmation of the goodness of everyday life and simple people, overflowing with good health, good spirits, good slapstick comedy and solid homespun wisdom, touched with nobility in the character of Hans Sachs.

The prelude, which is the epitome of the whole opera, was composed before the rest of the music and Wagner has described the moment when it took shape in his mind. After the fiasco of "Tannhäuser" in Paris and several vain attempts to have "Tristan" produced in Vienna and elsewhere, Wagner gave up trying to push performances of his operas and settled in a small town across the Rhine from Mainz, where he hoped to find the leisure and the peace of mind to compose. From his balcony, there, "in a sunset of great splendor, as I gazed upon the spectacle of 'golden' Mainz, with the majestic Rhine pouring along its outskirts in a glory of light, the Prelude to my 'Meistersinger' again made its presence closely and distinctly felt in my soul. Once before I had seen it rise before me out of a lake of sorrow, like some distant mirage. I proceeded to write down the prelude exactly as it appears today in the score, that is, containing the clear outlines of the leading themes of the whole drama."

The prelude opens with the magnificent pomp of the Mastersingers' Guild, followed by more tender, hesitating measures, associated with the love of Walter and Eva. These are the two poles of the drama and the music. At one point, chattering wood winds ridicule the pedantry of the Mastersingers with a parody of their opening theme, only to be swept away by more impetuous love music. We hear a sturdy march theme, taken from an authentic sixteenth-century Mastersinger tune; a theme which mocks Beckmesser, Eva's elderly wooer, and the melody of the Prize Song, with which Walter wins his love.

At the climax of the prelude all the elements of the drama are reconciled as the four themes sound together: the Mastersingers' theme plods along in the bass, the Prize Song soars above, and between the two we hear the Mastersingers' march and Beckmesser's skittery measures. It is a staggering feat of condensing drama into a few symbolical measures of music, and incidentally of contrapuntal science worthy of Bach himself.

The introduction to the third act of "Meistersinger" is a meditative, almost philosophical piece of music. It prepares a scene in the workshop of Hans Sachs, the shoemaker and poet who is the central figure of the drama. It opens with a broad melody for cellos alone, the theme of Sachs' famous monologue, "Wahn, Wahn," in which he laments the folly of never-ending squabbles between men, cities and nations, and ponders the riddle of this self-torture which humanity inflicts on itself. The warm humanity of Sachs and his philosophical turn of mind are eloquent in Wagner's music as one string instrument after another adds its voice to this grave, full-voiced orchestral quartet.

This passage is interrupted by a mellow chorale of

brass instruments, the chorale which Wagner composed to a poem by the historical Hans Sachs hailing the dawn of a brighter day. Once more the strings take over with a dreamlike transformation of the roistering shoemaker's song which Sachs improvised to disturb Beckmesser's unwelcome wooing of Eva in the second act.

Wagner and Brahms were once the idols of two great enemy camps of music. Wagnerites of fifty and sixty years ago despised the dullness and pedantry of Brahms; the Brahmsians denounced Wagner's sensationalism, his debauchery of the pure art of music. But Brahms himself was humorous and tolerant about his great rival. He admired many of his works, particularly "Die Meistersinger," perhaps because that opera came nearest to the balance between romanticism and classicism which characterized his own works. "Tristan und Isolde" he could not abide. "If I look at that in the morning," Brahms said, "then I'm cross for the rest of the day." But once when he and a friend were discussing Wagner, he pointed reverently to the score of "Meistersinger" and said: "*That* is where we meet."

In an age when composers were enthusiastically imitating the heroic manner of Wagner and Bruckner, using bigger and bigger orchestras and more and more overwhelming effects, it is interesting to see how Brahms kept his head and refused to be seduced into the lavish splashing of color and drama that was going on all around him. Take for example the exquisite middle movements of his Third Symphony. They are so intimate and restrained in style that they might almost have been conceived as chamber music. There is a German proverb: "Restraint proves the master." Brahms would have agreed with that.

Yet in the first and last movements Brahms shows he

could be as heroic as the best of his rivals. The symphony opens with a great sweeping motto theme which dominates the whole work, as well as supplying the basis of the first movement. The storm-ridden finale reminded Brahms's friend, Joachim, of the story of Hero and Leander. The end is serene as the moment between sunset and darkness.

This combination of strength and restraint, of self-confidence and humorous self-deprecation were typical of Brahms. He knew his own worth perfectly well, but he hated flattery or hero worship.

He particularly disliked the persistent and ingenious race of autograph hunters. Once an especially crafty fellow wired Brahms, hoping to get his signature at least in a telegram: "Your order for ten dozen rapiers, genuine Solingen make, will be dispatched in a day or two. We take the liberty of collecting payment through the post office." Brahms merely stuck the telegram in his pocket and waited for the rapiers.

At Baden-Baden he once lay stretched under the trees in a garden when a celebrity hunter approached him and began reeling off a sirupy speech of well-rehearsed praise. But Brahms interrupted. "My dear sir," he said, "there must be some mistake. I have no doubt you are looking for my brother, the composer. I'm sorry to say he has just gone for a walk, but if you hurry and run along that path, through the wood and up that hill over there, you probably can still catch up with him."

SMETANA: Overture to "The Bartered Bride"
DVOŘÁK: Symphony, E minor. From the New World

From the richness of Bohemian music—art music and folk music—have come two popular works, "The Bartered Bride" and the New World Symphony, that make up this program. The overture to Smetana's laughing masterpiece is brilliant, lively music which explains itself. Its lilting melodies have a typical Czech flavor, and the thoughtful middle section only makes the rest of the overture seem more exuberant by contrast. "The Bartered Bride" is a comic opera—and much more. Both inside and outside of Czechoslovakia it has become a musical symbol of the Czech people. The Czechs themselves adore it, both because it pictures the life of their own people and because it is associated historically with the rebirth of Czech culture, which began back in the middle of the nineteenth century, while they were still under Austrian rule.

From time immemorial, the Czechs, or the Bohemians as they used to be called, have been famous as musicians, not only in their own country, but as far as European music was made. In dusty chronicles from the Middle Ages, we find their names inscribed as pipers and fiddlers to the great dukes and kings of France and Germany. In the eighteenth century, Bohemian composers contributed richly to a startling new form of music called the symphony—many years before Haydn was given his misleading title of "father of the symphony." In later years they gave Mozart's "Marriage of Figaro" and "Don Giovanni" a warmer welcome than they ever had in Vienna. Mozart loved the Bohemian city of Prague and not only admired many Bohemian musicians, but passed on what he learned from them in his own immortal works.

Dvořák was following a tradition more ancient than he perhaps knew, when he accepted an important musical position in a far-off land, and came to teach at the National Conservatory of Music in New York City. He wrote his beautiful New World Symphony as a hymn to the folk spirit of two countries: the United States and Czechoslovakia.

When Dvořák was the penniless son of a village butcher, he and his viola had wandered among the little villages of Bohemia, playing for peasant dances at country weddings and fairs. He had drunk deeply from the rich springs of melody of his own people. So what could be more natural than that when he came to America, he should listen carefully to the songs of the simple people here? And the result was that, long before Negro songs became fashionable in our concert halls, he poured some of their spirit into his New World Symphony. The great pioneer in collecting Negro spirituals, Henry T. Burleigh, was a student at the National Conservatory when Dvořák was teaching there, and he sang many of them to Dvořák.

Just before the première of his New World Symphony was given in New York by the Philharmonic Orchestra, Dvořák wrote: "I am convinced that the future music of this country must be founded on what are called Negro melodies. These can be made the foundation of an original school of composition to be developed in the United States. When I first came here, I was impressed with this idea, and it has developed into a settled conviction. These beautiful and varied themes are the product of the soil. They are American. They are the folk songs of America and your composers must turn to them. All the great musicians have borrowed from the songs of the common people."

It is generally believed that Dvořák wrote the whole of the New World Symphony in this country, though there was a horrid rumor at the time that part of it had been written before he ever set foot on American soil. However that may be, a few months here couldn't be enough to make an American composer out of Dvořák, and he knew better than to try to be one.

Years later, when busy analyzers of the score thought they had discovered not only Negro themes, but Indian melodies as well in the New World Symphony, Dvořák was quick to repudiate them. When the symphony was performed in Berlin in 1900, he wrote to the conductor: "I am sending you Kretzschmar's analysis of the symphony, but omit that nonsense about my having made use of 'Indian' and 'American' themes—that is a lie. I tried to write only in the spirit of those American melodies."

He might have added that his homesickness made him introduce a great deal of Czech atmosphere into the score too. The slow introduction contains a dramatic, surging figure, which eventually becomes the main theme of the first movement proper, and keeps recurring even in the later sections of the symphony. In fact, it's typical of the New World Symphony that the themes are carried over from movement to movement, and the riches accumulate as we go. A plaintive little theme, played by the flutes and oboes, which Burleigh considered an echo of the spirituals he sang to Dvořák, leads into another melody, that sounds unmistakably like "Swing Low, Sweet Chariot." Whether or not Dvořák consciously used any Negro themes, we know that one of his favorite spirituals was "Swing Low, Sweet Chariot," and so we needn't bother much whether he was quoting the letter or the spirit of the American music he came to love.

A mysterious, solemn progression of chords leads to the wonderful song of the slow movement. The English horn sings a melody that has been adopted in this country almost as another spiritual.

The scherzo is full of Czech gaiety and abandon. The beginning and end are agitated, but in the middle there is a playful part, where you can almost see the Czech peasants dancing under the shade on a Sunday afternoon, you can hear the pipes tootling and the giggling laughter of the girls in between.

A finale of tremendous sweep and splendor brings the climax to this fresh and beautiful work—a symphony which speaks not only of a New World, but of new hopes, and is an enduring link between the unfortunate Czech people and their admirers in America.

※　　※

SIBELIUS: "En Saga"
Symphony #1, E minor

During his earliest years as a master composer, Jean Sibelius drew his main inspiration from the Finnish countryside and people and their ancient folklore. Though he dislikes Wagner and has never felt drawn to the field of opera, the Finnish sagas and runes which colored Sibelius' music are much like the Icelandic Eddas and German folk tales which Wagner used as the basis of his music dramas. This may have had something to do with the fact that as a young man Sibelius studied music in Germany, where Wagnerian romanticism was still at the high tide of its influence. But it had even more to do with the situation which Sibelius found when he returned to Helsinki.

The wave of nationalism which had been sweeping across Europe all during the nineteenth century had at last hit Finland with tremendous impact. Finland reacted, just as other countries had, with a new drive to political self-assertion and, in the artistic field, with a new enthusiasm for her own language and literature—particularly the ancient sagas of the Kalevala, the Finnish national epic.

This was the time when Sibelius wrote his tone poem, "En Saga," the first work to make him well known outside of Finland and the first published composition in which he really asserted his own character. In 1892 the conductor, Robert Kajanus, realizing Sibelius' extraordinary gifts, asked him to write a piece for performance by the Helsinki Conservatory Orchestra—something nice and short and easy to understand, which would promote his popularity. The result, "En Saga," was hardly what Kajanus expected, though it did become extremely popular.

Whether Sibelius had in mind any specific episode of his country's epic poems is beside the point. The title shows clearly enough where his imagination lurked. From out the mists and gloom of the long winter nights there emerge ghosts of the Kalevala, warrior heroes of Finland's legendary past, ancient symbols brought to life again in the artistic, political dreams of a new generation. One could think of the sorcerers' incantations which play such a role in the Kalevala, a barbaric war dance, and a dying lament as the vision fades back into the darkness of forgotten time.

This, says Cecil Gray, is the first work of Sibelius which one can unhesitatingly describe as a masterpiece. "From the very opening bars with the mysterious beckoning call of the horns, the bare open fifths of the tremolos and arpeggios of the muted strings, the strident dissonances of the wood winds, right through the catastrophic climax in the brass, and the sombre, whispered close in the lower strings—the whole work is one of astonishing power and originality, quite unlike anything previously written by any other composer."

The First Symphony grew out of the same romantic, nationalistic feelings as the other works of this time. And yet we also hear some of the flamboyant, Slavic emotionalism of Tchaikovsky. Though it has no official program or story, it is descriptive in its manner and there might well have been some unpublished poetic or dramatic idea behind the music. It can hardly be an accident, for example, that the theme of the lonely clarinet, which opens the first movement, over softly rolling drums, returns with slight changes at the beginning of the fourth movement.

But where Tchaikovsky pictures the struggles and the wild despair of one single soul, Sibelius sings for a whole nation in sorrow and in exaltation. There are enough melodies and themes in this score for a dozen symphonies and they have a sweep and passion that are irresistible. As he grew older, Sibelius became more laconic, perhaps greater as a symphonist. In his First Symphony he hadn't yet learned, as he did later, to use those small, pregnant themes, which can be so eloquent in symphonic development, when the orchestra tosses about the fragments, or transforms and expands a tiny melodic phrase.

Here Sibelius launches his themes with magnificent recklessness. The middle part of the movement is taken up with the clash and struggle between them. There is a mighty climax in the brass and then the movement subsides, to end quietly with two dramatic, plucked chords of the strings.

The slow second movement is melancholy and elegiac.

The third movement, the scherzo, is built almost entirely of two themes: one, a brutal rhythmic figure pounded out at the very beginning by the drums; the other, a melody like a folk song, though we have Sibelius' own word for it that he has never used any real folk music in his large orchestral works.

The finale opens with a reminiscence of the symphony's opening theme. The mood is first rhapsodic, then defiant and heroic. But this is the tight-lipped, tragic heroism of a people who have suffered much in the past, and though they are confident of ultimate victory, know that much suffering lies before them. There is an exultant climax, but it subsides, as in the first movement, to a moment of quiet intensity and ends on a repetition of the same two bleak pizzicato chords.

SIBELIUS: "Tapiola"
Symphony #5, E flat

Sibelius is one of the very few composers who is as great in so-called program, or descriptive music as he is in the purely symphonic field. His tone poem, "Tapiola," is a wonderful example of his descriptive powers. Tapiola was the ancient Finnish god of the forest, and to give the

listener a further clue to the meaning of his music Sibelius
had the following four-line stanza printed at the head of
the score:

"Widespread they stand, the Northland's dusky forests,
Ancient, mysterious, brooding savage dreams;
Within them dwells the forest's mighty God,
And wood sprites in the gloom weave magic secrets."

From the soft drum roll with which the work begins,
to the repose of the great final cadence, the whole work is
built around one theme, a theme which appears and reappears in a dozen different forms, that grow and expand
from the original thought. The entire work is as close knit
and organic as the trees of Sibelius' forest.

Sibelius wrote his Fifth Symphony in 1915 in the terrible pessimistic months of World War I. In September of
that year Sibelius wrote in his diary: "In a deep dell
again. But I already begin dimly to see the mountain that
I shall surely ascend. . . . God opens his door for a moment and his orchestra plays the Fifth Symphony."

It was completed after a period which had been particularly rich in descriptive music. But when Sibelius was
asked whether there was any program to the Fifth Symphony he replied emphatically that he would give no explanation of the symphony except to say that it was
absolutely symphonic, in contrast to the descriptive character of other works.

The first performance of the Fifth Symphony was
given in December, 1915, at Helsinki on the composer's
birthday. But a few months later he revised the music and
greatly condensed it. The new version was played one year
after the first, but Sibelius was still dissatisfied, and so
revised it once again, radically, in 1918. In the spring of

that year he wrote: "I am working daily at the Fifth Symphony in a new form, practically composed anew. The first movement is entirely new, the second movement is reminiscent of the old, the third movement reminiscent of the end of the old first movement. The fourth movement has the old themes, but stronger in revision. The whole, if I may say so, a vital climax to the end. Triumphal."

The symphony opens with a melancholy theme for the horn, which is carried on and developed by the wood winds. There is a contrasting theme in the wood winds, but the spirit of this movement broods deeper and deeper into blackest melancholy. The second movement, a scherzo-like passage, follows without any break, but in spite of this fact, Sibelius, as we have seen, regarded it as a movement in itself. Here the atmosphere is more agitated and the movement ends with great waves of string arpeggios surging up against a series of long-drawn-out chords in the brass instruments.

The third movement is calmer and more melodic, and consists largely of a theme and a set of variations.

The finale begins a rush of fantastic whispering figures in the strings. Presently, underneath these eerie whirrings, we hear a strong ostinato motive in the horns, rising and falling like the massive cadence of the sea. This recurrent figure dominates the whole finale: sometimes in its bold original form, sometimes like a shivering echo, high up among the strings. Toward the end the horns again take up the theme, piling climax upon climax with ever more clashing dissonances. The music broadens with tremendous majesty to the series of sharp, emphatic closing chords.

GRIEG: Piano Concerto, A minor
SIBELIUS: Symphony #7, C major

The great German pianist, Hans von Bülow, once called Grieg "the Chopin of the North." And after hearing the Grieg Concerto you may agree with him. Certainly, Chopin was one of the great influences in Grieg's life. For Grieg's mother, who was a very respectable pianist and from whom he inherited his talent, was an enthusiastic admirer of Chopin. She delighted in playing his music at a time when it was not widely understood. So Chopin's revolutionary harmonic discoveries were among the earliest, almost subconscious forces that molded Grieg's genius, and Chopin remained his favorite composer.

But there was something else, besides just harmonic innovations, that the two men had in common. Chopin's music was deeply colored by the tragedy of his murdered fatherland. In his mazurkas and polonaises the voice of Poland alternately lamented and exulted over the heroism of her enslaved people.

Although Norway had no such tragic history as Poland, Grieg became the voice of the Norwegian people, and his music spoke, for the first time, the clear, unmistakable accent of the North.

He was only twenty-five when he wrote his piano concerto and that same year he received a letter from Liszt with the warmest praise for his music. On the strength of such a recommendation, the Norwegian government gave Grieg the money for a trip to Rome to meet the master. Liszt was all encouragement and Grieg, who had brought his new concerto, was anxious to see whether Liszt would really play it at sight. "For my part," says Grieg, "I considered it impossible. Not so Liszt.

" 'Will you play?' he asked. And I made haste to reply, 'No, I cannot.' (You know I have never practiced it.) Then Liszt took the manuscript, went to the piano, and said to the assembled guests with his characteristic smile, 'Very well, then I will show you that I also cannot.' With that he began. . . . His demeanour is worth any price to see. Not content with playing, he at the same time converses and makes comments, addressing a bright remark now to one, now to another of the assembled guests, nodding significantly to right or left, particularly when something pleases him. In the adagio and still more in the finale, he reached a climax both in his playing and the praise he had to bestow.

"A really divine episode I must not forget. Toward the end of the finale, the second theme is, as you may remember, repeated in a mighty fortissimo. In the very last measures, when in the first triplets the first tone is changed in the orchestra from G sharp to G, while the piano part, in a mighty scale passage, rushes wildly through the whole reach of the keyboard, he suddenly stopped, rose to his full height, left the piano and with big, theatrical strides and arms uplifted, walked across the large cloister hall, at the same time literally roaring the theme. When he got to the G in question he stretched out his arms imperiously and exclaimed, 'G, G, not G sharp! Splendid! That is the real Swedish Banko!' . . . He went back to the piano, repeated the whole strophe and finished. In conclusion he handed me the manuscript and said in a particularly cordial tone, 'Keep it up; I tell you, you have the stuff for it and—don't let them intimidate you.'

"This final admonition was of tremendous importance to me. There was something in it that seemed to
give it an air of sanctification. At times when disappointment and bitterness are in store for me I shall remember
his words, and the remembrance of that hour will have
a wonderful power to uphold me in days of adversity."

Fortunately there was little adversity or bitterness
in store for Grieg. He had a highly successful career and
for many years, in spite of his own protests, he was considered the voice not only of Norway, but of Scandinavia
in general. In vain Grieg tried to point out how different
Norway was from the other northern countries, but few
people in Europe or America were able to appreciate the
difference, until around 1900 when they began to hear the
music of the Finnish composer, Sibelius.

Jean Sibelius, like Grieg, came to be a symbol of his
country both at home and abroad. He too belonged to the
great nineteenth-century school of nationalist composers.
Wagner was constantly asserting how German he was;
Verdi had spoken for Italian nationalism; Chopin for
Poland; there were Czechs and Russians and Frenchmen, all of whom glorified their nation in their music, and
Sibelius was the last of the great line. I say "was" because
his most nationalistic music was composed before and
around 1900—works such as "Finlandia" and his Second
Symphony, said to be a drama of the liberation of Finland. But from then on Sibelius became more and more
international in his manner. During and after World
War I his style became not only more universal but more
classical in spirit. He started his career as a romantic
nationalist, with a large, picturesque orchestra that fairly
splashed local color. Then as he grew, his orchestra
shrank; as his thought grew stronger, he used fewer but

stronger words to express it; and the more universal his music became, the less use he had for local color.

Finally in his Seventh Symphony, he speaks with a simplicity and directness of appeal that have long since burst the bounds of Finland. Of course no man can deny his own character. Sibelius was a Finn, and the symphony could have been written by no one but Sibelius. But this music has less of the external markings of Finland and, paradoxically, perhaps more of the essential character of Sibelius.

It was planned during World War I, with a revolution going on, and with the roar of bombardment about him at one time. Originally it was to be in three movements, but when it was finished, in March, 1924, the three had been fused into one gigantic whole, which is played without pause from beginning to end.

So as far as the form of this symphony goes, you will have a hard time spotting the conventional sequence of allegro, slow movement, scherzo and fast finale. The Seventh Symphony begins slowly and ends slowly and there are many changes of tempo in between. Externally it appears to have more the free form of a symphonic poem. But it has no story or program like a symphonic poem; the orchestra is reduced to the proportions of the classical symphony and above all the style is completely symphonic.

It opens with soft mutterings of the drums, and the strings climb in a long scale from the depths of the orchestra up to a sharp chord of the wood winds. The atmosphere is lonely and meditative. Suddenly the orchestra is swept by a typical Sibelius gust of winter wind, a harbinger of storms to follow. A trombone chants the simple principal theme, which is transformed with mysterious logic throughout the symphony. You will notice another typical Sibelius figure, like a great ostinato wave, that rises and falls in the bottom of the orchestra. There is a quick section, a sort of scherzo, and there are many climaxes, each greater than the last, until the final one falls back upon itself, the melancholy mood of the opening returns, and the symphony closes in an atmosphere of resignation; but it is the resignation of overwhelming strength.

XII. *The New World*

ALWAYS AMERICA has been a shining gateway to the future. Even to millions who never set foot on our soil, it has been a religious hope, an economic hope, a political hope. And today it has become an artistic hope as well. Our symphonic composers have been late in coming. The Walt Whitman of American music may not yet be among us, or if he is we don't know his name. But where a few years ago it would have been difficult to build one symphony program of American music, we have an embarrassment of riches. Even before 1939, according to Serge Koussevitsky, the shadow of approaching war had merely hastened the musical twilight already settling over Europe and it is now to the new generation of this country that he and his colleagues look for the future. American music has come of age. It has its own individuality and style and the courage and enthusiasm of youth. Music is part of America's promise for the future. And the American dream is happily not ours alone.

CHADWICK: "Jubilee Overture"
GRIFFES: "The Pleasure Dome of Kubla Khan"
TAYLOR: "Through the Looking-Glass"
BARBER: "First Essay for Orchestra"

Here is American music of three generations. To people who believe that American music must smell of prairie grass or Chicago slaughterhouses, these works will be a disappointment. Yet they could have been written only in this country. One of the earliest of our composers who still appears on symphony programs, George Chadwick, speaks the American language more clearly than many who came later and made more fuss about their Americanism. In 1895 when he wrote his "Symphonic Sketches," Chadwick had been an instructor at the New England Conservatory for over a decade. The following year he was asked to become its director and he remained in that position until his death in 1931.

But for all his European, academic background, he writes with what Philip Hale called a "jaunty irreverence, a snapping of the fingers at Fate and the Universe." His "Jubilee Overture," the first movement of his "Symphonic Sketches," is nearly half a century old, yet the brilliance of its opening page has not dimmed, its rhythms are as vigorous, its sentiment and poetry are as beguiling as they were when the ink was fresh. Chadwick prefaced his overture with the following lines:

JUBILEE

No cool gray tones for me!
Give me the warmest red and green,
A cornet and tambourine,
To paint *my* jubilee!

For when pale flutes and oboes play
To sadness I become a prey;
Give me the violets and the May,
But no gray skies for me!

The life of Charles Thomlinson Griffes was tragically different from that of Chadwick. Griffes' death at the age of thirty-six deprived this country of a man who many believe might have become our greatest composer to date. Like Chadwick, he had studied in Germany, but he later came more under the influence of French impressionism and Russian orientalism. Up to the last months of his life Griffes received no public recognition on the scale he was entitled to. He earned a meager living as music master in a boys' school. In 1919 when Pierre Monteux decided to perform his "Pleasure Dome of Kubla Khan" with the Boston Symphony, Griffes was already overworked from his double occupation of composing and teaching. He was too poor to hire a professional copyist to copy out the instrumental parts of the score for performance, so he set himself to that additional drudgery. The strain was too much. He was able to enjoy the overwhelming success of his masterpiece both in Boston and a few days later in New York. But success had come too late. Pleurisy, finally pneumonia took hold and four months later he was dead.

At the time of the première in Boston Griffes wrote: "I have taken as a basis for my work those lines of Coleridge's poem describing the 'stately pleasure dome,' the 'sunny pleasure dome with caves of ice,' and the 'miracle of rare device.' Therefore I call the work 'The Pleasure Dome of Kubla Khan' rather than 'Kubla Khan'. . . .

"As to argument I have given my imagination free rein in the description of this strange palace as well as of purely imaginary revelry which might take place there. The vague, foggy beginning suggests the sacred river running 'through caverns measureless to man down to a sunless sea.' Then gradually rise the outlines of the palace, 'with walls and towers girdled round.' The gardens with fountains and 'sunny spots of greenery' are next suggested. From inside come sounds of dancing and revelry which increase to a wild climax and then suddenly break off. There is a return to the original mood suggesting the sacred river and the 'caves of ice.' "

In happy contrast to Griffes, Deems Taylor has had an extremely successful career as composer, writer, war correspondent, critic, translator, artist, editor and radio commentator. Two of his operas, "The King's Henchman" and "Peter Ibbetson" have been performed by the Metropolitan Opera Company and he is at present musical advisor to the Columbia Broadcasting System.

His best known work, "Through the Looking-Glass," was originally written for chamber orchestra, but later enlarged and revised for a full symphonic ensemble.

"The suite," wrote Mr. Taylor, when it was first performed by Walter Damrosch in 1922, "needs no extended analysis. It is based on Lewis Carroll's immortal nonsense fairy tale, 'Through the Looking-Glass and What Alice Found There,' and the five pictures it presents will, if all goes well, be readily recognizable to lovers of the book. There are four movements, the first being divided into two connected parts.

Ia. Dedication.

"Carroll precedes the tale with a charming poetical foreword, the first stanza of which the music aims to express. It runs:

> "Child of the pure unclouded brow
> And dreaming eyes of wonder!
> Though time be fleet, and I and thou
> Are half a life asunder,
> Thy loving smile will surely hail
> The love-gift of a fairy-tale.

"A simple song theme, briefly developed, leads without pause to—

Ib. The Garden of Live Flowers.

"Shortly after Alice had entered the looking-glass country she came to a lovely garden in which the flowers were talking:

"'O Tiger-lily,' said Alice, addressing herself to one that was waving gracefully about in the wind, 'I *wish* you could talk!'

"'We *can* talk,' said the Tiger-lily: 'when there's anyone worth talking to.' . . .

"'And can *all* flowers talk?'

"'As well as *you* can,' said the Tiger-lily. 'And a great deal louder.'

"The music reflects the brisk chatter of the swaying, bright-colored denizens of the garden.

II. Jabberwocky.

"This is the poem that so puzzled Alice, and which Humpty-Dumpty finally explained to her. . . . The theme of that fruitful beast, the Jabberwock, is first announced by the full orchestra. Then the clarinet begins the tale, recounting how, on a brillig afternoon, 'the slithy toves did gyre and gimble in the wabe.' Muttered imprecations warn us to 'beware the Jabberwock, my son.' A miniature march signalizes the approach of our hero, taking his 'vorpal blade in hand.' Trouble starts among the trombones—the Jabberwock is upon us! The battle with the monster is recounted in a short and rather repellent fugue, the double basses bringing up the subject and the hero fighting back in the interludes. Finally his vorpal blade [really a xylophone] goes 'snicker-snack,' and the monster, impersonated by the solo bassoon, dies a lingering and convulsive death. The hero returns, to the victorious strain of his own theme—'O frabjous day! Callooh! Callay!' The whole orchestra rejoices—the church bells are rung— alarums and excursions.

"Conclusion. Once more the slithy toves perform their pleasing evolutions, undisturbed by the uneasy ghost of the late Jabberwock.

III. Looking-Glass Insects

"Here we find the vociferous *diptera* that made such an impression upon Alice—the Bee-elephant, the Gnat, the Rocking-horse-fly, the Snap-dragon-fly and the Bread-and-butter-fly. There are several themes, but there is no use trying to decide which insect any one of them stands for.

IV. The White Knight

"He was a toy Don Quixote, mild, chivalrous, ridiculous and rather touching. He carried a mouse-trap on his saddle-bow because 'if they *do* come, I don't choose to have them running about.' He couldn't ride very well, but he was a gentle soul with good intentions. There are two themes: the first, a sort of instrumental prance, being the knight's own conception of himself as a slashing, daredevil fellow. The second is bland, mellifluous, a little sentimental—much more like the knight as he really was. The theme starts off bravely, but falls out of the saddle before very long, and has to give way to the second. The two alternate, in various guises, until the end, when the knight rides off, with Alice waving her handkerchief—he thought it would encourage him if she did."

With Samuel Barber's "First Essay for Orchestra" we come to one of the most talented of young Americans and, in a sense, to the future. For the men of Barber's generation have the better part of their creative lives before them. Yet in spite of his youth, Barber is already widely played by the leading orchestras of this country and was being performed abroad before the outbreak of the war.

He has been called a conservative. But in a way his music is younger, more modern than the grinding dissonances that were so fashionable ten and twenty years ago. Barber has no need to thumb his nose at dead conventions. There is little lure today in being the big bad boy of the concert halls. There is even a romantic tinge to this "Essay for Orchestra." It begins in a quiet, elegiac mood, with a simple, lyric theme, and swells to a strong emotional climax. There is a scherzolike middle section, delicate at first, but more and more agitated, which at its height surges back into the broad theme of the beginning. Then, instead of the conventional recapitulation, the orchestra suddenly subsides. The stress has vanished. The music fades on a phrase of the greatest brevity and poignance, and the tale is told.

MacDowell: "Indian" Suite
Hanson: Symphony #2. Romantic

The first American composer to write music which could stand comparison with his European competitors was Edward MacDowell. And even today it is safe to say that he is still the most widely known and loved of our serious composers. If he has not kept a prominent place on our symphony programs, the chief reason is that he wrote very little of his mature music for orchestra. But his Second (Indian) Suite, first performed by the Boston Symphony in 1896, is still played, and deservedly. It contains some of his greatest and most characteristic music.

In spite of the title MacDowell had no use for nationalism in music, though he had studied in France and Germany during the high tide of nationalism abroad. And he certainly did not feel that his use of authentic Indian melodies in his suite made it thereby American music. MacDowell knew his own indebtedness to Europe, and artificial attempts to create a national style simply by using folk themes he considered childish.

"No," he said, "before a people can find a musical writer to echo its genius, it must first possess men who truly represent it—that is to say men who being part of the people, love the country for itself: men who put into their music what the nation has put into its life. . . . What we must arrive at is the youthful optimistic vitality and the undaunted tenacity of spirit which characterizes the American man. That is what I hope to see echoed in American music."

MacDowell wrote his "Indian" Suite just before he

became professor of the newly created music department of Columbia University. At the end of his life he declared: "Of all my music the 'Dirge' in the 'Indian' Suite pleases me most. It affects me deeply and did when I was writing it. In it an Indian woman laments the death of her son; but to me, as I wrote it, it seemed to express a world-sorrow rather than a particularized grief."

Not so much local color, even less nationalism was his purpose, but rather suggestions of an ancient past, of an almost legendary race. The five movements: Legend, Love Song, In War-time, Dirge and Village Festival are all imaginative and impressive, but musicians have agreed with MacDowell's choice of the Dirge. Lawrence Gilman called it "the most profoundly affecting threnody in music since the 'Götterdämmerung' *Trauermarsch*. . . . The extreme pathos of the opening section, the wailing phrase in the muted strings under the reiterated G of the flutes (an inverted organ-point of sixteen adagio measures); the indescribable effect of the muted horn heard from behind the scenes, over an accompaniment of divided violas and 'cellos *con sordini*; the heart-shaking sadness and beauty of the succeeding passage for all the muted strings; the mysterious and solemn close: these are outstanding moments in a masterpiece of the first rank: a page which would honour any music-maker, living or dead."

Like MacDowell, Howard Hanson of our own day is conservative in his music. Like him he is a romantic. MacDowell has often been compared with Grieg. Hanson has absorbed certain influences from the great northern composer of today, Sibelius. Hanson like MacDowell is a teacher, but on a much vaster scale. Since 1924 he has been Director of the Eastman School of Music. He is also a conductor of standing and in his various musical capacities he has done more to further the cause of American composers than anyone, with the possible exception of Serge Koussevitzky.

Among most modern composers, romanticism has long been out of style. It is supposed to have died a lingering death about the time of World War I. Today it takes considerable courage for a composer to stick to the lush harmonies and orchestration and the expansive manner of romanticism. But Dr. Hanson has the courage of his convictions.

Romantic, the title which he gives his Second Symphony is thus a challenge to musical snobs and even more to listeners with open minds. Its first movement has a pensive introduction. A flourish of trumpets summons the main theme, an heroic figure announced by four horns together and echoed vigorously by trumpets and other instruments. Then a pastoral interlude leads to a warmly melodic second theme which will be recalled later in the symphony. There is the traditional energetic development, and a return of the original themes rising to a brilliant climax and dying away to a tender pianissimo.

The melody of the second movement has a glow and a beauty of line hard to forget. The finale uses themes from both preceding movements reworked, transformed and combined with new material to build a climax of great brilliance and staggering power.

"My aim in this symphony," wrote Hanson, "has been to create a work young in spirit, romantic in temperament and simple and direct in expression.

"I recognize, of course, that romanticism is at present the poor stepchild, without the social standing of her elder sister, neoclassicism. Nevertheless I embrace her all the more fervently, believing as I do, that romanticism

will find in this country rich soil for a new, young and vigorous growth."

⚜   ⚜

CARPENTER: "Skyscrapers"
HARRIS: Symphony #3

Mention American music to a European and nine
chances out of ten he will assume you are talking about
"le jazz hot." As a matter of fact, he may be righter than
you think, even if you had in mind a symphony or a symphonic ballet. For how could an American composer escape the influence of ragtime, jazz, swing, or whatever it
happens to be called at the moment? Ever since medieval
churchmen wove drinking songs into their devotional
motets, popular songs and dances have been finding their
way into the most austere compositions. Where they don't
appear as actual quotations, they have always influenced
the speech and style of serious composers.

Now the influence of jazz may be hard to follow
through Roy Harris' Third Symphony. In many works it
is subtle and hard to trace. But often, as in Carpenter's
"Skyscrapers," the influence is frank and obvious. Carpenter himself spoke of this music as jazz filtered through
the medium of a symphony orchestra. Yet if that were all
he had done, "Skyscrapers" would be merely imitation
hits of the 1920's played by a symphony orchestra, which
would be a sad business all around. Carpenter did more.
He filtered something of the essence of jazz through a crea-

tive imagination and so produced music which is as exciting today as when it was produced in 1926.

It was Serge Diaghileff, always on the hunt for fresh talent, who suggested that Carpenter write a new ballet on an American subject for his Russian Ballet. But when the music was done they could not agree on the production. So the Metropolitan Opera, hearing that the ballet was ready, asked Carpenter to follow his own ideas in staging it for them. Robert Edmond Jones was chosen to work with him on settings and a Broadway producer was called in to help work out the dances. The performance, in February, 1926, was a brilliant success.

"I have not tried to tell any story in 'Skyscrapers,' " said Carpenter. "In fact there is no story to it." The music proceeds, according to a note in the score, "on the simple fact that American life reduces itself essentially to violent alternations of work and play, each with its own peculiar and distinctive rhythmic character. The action of the ballet is merely a series of moving decorations reflecting some of the obvious external features of this life."

It begins with the nervous clangor of a big city, a suggestion of the skyscraper itself, "of the work that produces it—and the interminable crowd that passes by." Then the scene switches to an amusement park, "any Coney Island," with roller coasters, Ferris wheels, street shows, dance-crazy street cleaners, flappers, policemen, black-face comics and men of the skyscrapers in search of their violent relaxation. Whitewings, a Negro street cleaner, goes to sleep against a traffic sign. There is a shadowy interlude, a dream with lamenting voices, but he snaps back to the frenetic dance. Finally a return to the skyscraper. The listless crowd pours on. Two workmen with their sledgehammers throw gigantic shadows, phantoms of crushing power. These symbolic shadows grow and expand beyond the confines of the stage as the music rises to its pounding climax and the curtain falls.

"Skyscrapers" reflects metropolitan America. But not the America that has inspired Roy Harris. "This sullen, colossal thing," he writes, "is not us. We built it. We lent ourselves to its inhuman rhythm because it seemed to multiply the power and glory of our collective self. We made it click. But we never did accept it. For us millions of 'unknown' Americans this great commercial machine was never more than an experiment. Back of our spendthrift energies and giddy enthusiasms there was always a touch of atavistic wisdom stubbornly sifting and weighing the effects of our daily lives. Back of it all we realize that the universe still keeps faith with us, that the sun still shines, calling forth harvest from the earth; that our grains and fruits and animals still multiply, that we still possess the capacities for love and parenthood, that our tomorrows give promise. The good biological stuff in our blood and bones assures us that we will reconstitute our world with broader, more representative human values.

"In that reconstitution, music will probably play an important role, because it can most completely liberate and express those powerful, intangible, subtle feelings which motivate human impulses. . . .

"The tide seems to be turning in our favor. However it remains to be seen whether Walt Whitman's 'I hear America singing' will prove to be the dying echo of an over-confident hope, or the prophecy of strong voices arising from the lives of millions of Americans."

One of the strongest voices that has yet risen is that of Roy Harris himself. His Third Symphony, composed in 1938, is regarded by many musicians as the greatest symphony, and by some, as the greatest orchestra work in any form this country has produced. Harris was born in Oklahoma, which has led many enthusiasts to praise his music in terms of his "cowboy origins," "vast prairies," "open spaces" and so on. Actually Harris left Oklahoma at the age of five for California. Yet there is something about his Third Symphony which easily suggests the land of his origin, the spaciousness and violence of American nature, the intensity of its contrasts.

Like Harris' own estimate of America and the mission of American music, his symphony is deeply serious. There is no trickery about it, no appeal to facile popularity. It is straightforward sometimes to the point of awkwardness. Yet that very trait may one day stand out as a strength.

Contrary to the classical symphony, Harris' Third is written in one continuous movement, the succession of moods according to his own outline being: tragic, lyric, pastoral, dramatic and dramatic-tragic. The total effect is one of extraordinary organic unity. From the slow-moving, but boldly arched melody of the opening, it gathers momentum, the melodic line becomes more graceful, livelier, the spare colors grow in intensity. In spite of many contrasts by the way, the line rises inexorably to its climax: a fugal section with violent contrapuntal clashes of the brass instruments. Finally comes the soaring dirge of the violins, dominating the angry brass and tympani and subduing all struggle to the simple power of the final cadence.

GERSHWIN: "Rhapsody in Blue"
          "An American in Paris"
COPLAND: "Music for the Theatre"
WILLIAM SCHUMAN: "American Festival Overture"

"Make it good, George," said Pa Gershwin, poking his head into the room where the "Rhapsody in Blue" was being written, "it might be important."

Pa Gershwin was joking, for both of them knew how important the rhapsody was. Not that George wasn't already a famous man. He was—in musical comedy. But this rhapsody was something else again. This was supposed to be symphonic. This was the work on which Paul Whiteman was depending for a concert in which jazz was to crash the serious concert halls. It had to be good.

Of course, other people before Paul Whiteman had tried to make an honest woman out of jazz. But nothing much ever came of it. Eva Gautier had thrilled a sophisticated New York audience by singing Berlin, Kern and Gershwin on her program along with Bellini, Schönberg and Milhaud. Some modern composers (particularly Europeans) had flirted with jazz in their serious works. But no jazz composer had yet established a place for himself on our symphonic programs.

George worked fast. Some of it came to him, he said, "on the train, with its steely rhythms, its rattlety-bang that is often so stimulating to a composer. . . . I frequently hear music in the very heart of noise. And there I suddenly heard—and even saw on paper—the complete construction of the Rhapsody from beginning to end. No new themes came to me, but I worked on the thematic material already in my mind, and tried to conceive the composition as a whole. I heard it as a sort of musical kaleidoscope of America—of our vast melting pot, of our unduplicated national pep, of our blues, our metropolitan madness. By the time I reached Boston I had a definite *plot* of the piece, as distinguished from its actual substance.

"As for the middle theme, it came upon me suddenly, as my music sometimes does. It was at the home of a friend, just after I got back to Gotham. . . . Playing at parties is one of my strong weaknesses, as you know. Well, there I was, rattling away without a thought of rhapsodies in blue or any other color. All at once I heard myself playing a theme that must have been haunting me inside, seeking outlet. No sooner had it oozed out of my fingers than I knew I had found it. . . . A week after my return from Boston I completed the 'Rhapsody in Blue.'

"Completed? Not quite. A few piano figurations were left out of the score. I was so pressed for time that I left them to be improvised at the first concert. I could do that, as I was to be the pianist."

Indeed, such was the hurry, or such was Gershwin's inexperience, that a large part of the orchestration was done by Ferde Grofé, who aside from composing himself, was Whiteman's arranger.

The concert took place at Aeolian Hall on February 12, 1924, before an audience in which Whiteman detected "vaudevillians, concert managers come to have a look at the novelty, Tin Pan Alleyites, composers, symphony and opera stars, flappers, cake-eaters, all mixed up higgledy-piggledy."

Whoever these people were, they lifted Gershwin and symphonic jazz to the skies. Witness the letter from Carl

Van Vechten: "Dear George Gershwin: The concert, quite as a matter of course, was a riot; you crowned it with what, after repeated hearings, I am forced to regard as the foremost serious effort by any American composer. Go straight on and you will knock all Europe silly. Go a little further in the next one and invent a new *form*. I think something might be done in the way of combining jazz and the moving picture technique. Think of themes as close-ups, flash-backs, etc.! This is merely an impertinent suggestion; whatever you do, however, including playing the piano, you do so well that you need no advice."

Four years later when George went to Europe, taking with him sketches for what was to become "An American in Paris," he found himself a concert-hall celebrity, the man of the moment in advanced musical circles. He enjoyed himself hugely, working, between bows, on his new score. Fortunately the sights and sounds of Paris failed to overawe him. Leave the deeper interpretations of "la ville lumière" to the men whose home it is. George had no desire to be anything else in his music than a happy-go-lucky American, strolling the streets of an exciting new city where the taxi horns had a funny sound and there were plenty of Americans to cheer him up when he got the blues.

The first Walking Theme, which Henderson called "without doubt the sassiest theme of the century," immediately sets the pace. A sunny spring day in Paris was meant to be enjoyed out of doors, not in museums or churches. Irreverent tootlings of the Paris taxi horns greet our hero as he strides down the Champs-Elysées. You may imagine most of his itinerary as you like, for Gershwin didn't explain it too exactly. But about halfway along he gets homesick, and the orchestra has an authentic case of the blues.

"However," writes Deems Taylor in his authorized analysis, "nostalgia is not a fatal disease—nor, in this instance, of overlong duration. Just in the nick of time the compassionate orchestra rushes another theme to the rescue, two trumpets performing the ceremony of introduction. It is apparent that our hero must have met a compatriot; for this last theme is a noisy, cheerful, self-confident Charleston, without a drop of Gallic blood in its veins . . . and the orchestra, in a riotous finale, decides to make a night of it. It will be great to get home; but meanwhile, this is Paris!"

While Gershwin, apparently with no effort at all, had done more than any musician in decades to wipe out the artificial boundary between popular and serious music, other less publicized composers were absorbing the idioms of jazz in their own way. Gershwin may have speeded the process but it was inevitable. One year after the "Rhapsody in Blue," Aaron Copland produced his highly successful "Music for the Theatre" which certainly is not jazz, but which would be unthinkable without jazz.

The title, "Music for the Theatre," does not mean that Copland had any play or literary idea in mind. It simply implies, according to the composer, that "at times, this music has a quality which is suggestive of the theatre." It is divided into five movements, cunningly scored, entertainingly contrasted, set down with the hand of a master. From the brilliant fanfare which opens the Prologue, through the jerky, eupeptic rhythms of the Dance, the romantic song of the Interlude, the witty Burlesque to the poetic close of the Epilogue, this is music with something to say. And it says it quickly, clearly, in the American language.

With William Schuman we come again to the youngest generation of American composers. Schuman was born in 1910 in New York City. His "American Festival Overture," written for some concerts of American music which Koussevitzky conducted with the Boston Symphony Orchestra in the fall of 1939, is an exhilarating piece based, according to Schuman, on the "call to play" of the New York streets—the syllables "wee-awk-ee." This is the very simple theme of a descending and rising minor third heard at the beginning of the overture—a call to some high orchestral sport. It has no particular program—this is no musical street scene. And as far as the city is concerned there seems to be almost as much of Bach's Leipzig in it as LaGuardia's New York. Certainly it has a dash of vigorous fugal writing, along with its strong melodic vein. The harmonies are modern as you please, but never just noisy. "Wee-awk-ee" makes a splendid symphonic theme to be tossed back and forth through the orchestra and the whole thing has an energy and sweep and spontaneity which are Americanism at its best. The man who can write music like this in his twenties has an exciting future. He and his colleagues are American music come of age.

Index

"Abduction from the Seraglio, The" (Mozart), 40, 42
Abélard, Pierre (1079–1142), 203
Académie Nationale de Musique et de Danse (Paris), 18
Achilles, 172
Aeolian Hall (New York), 303
Afternoon of a Faun, Prelude to the, see Mallarmé
Agatha, 131
Alberich, 110–111
Alexander II, Tsar of Russia (1818–1881), 4
Alice, 292, 293, 294
Alifanfaron, Emperor, 200
'American Festival Overture" (Schuman), 302, 306
"American in Paris, An" (Gershwin), 302, 304–305
American Revolution, 235
Anhalt-Cöthen, Prince Leopold of, 68
Anne, Queen of England (1665–1714), 38, 142
"Aprés-Midi d'un Faune, L'" (Mallarmé), 134–135
"Arabian Nights, The," see "Thousand and One Nights, The"
"Armide" (Gluck), 21
  Gavotte, 21
Artôt, Désirée, see Padilla y Ramos, Désirée
Austrian National Court Theatre (Vienna), 53

Bacchanale (Paris version), see Wagner
Bach, Johann Christian (1735–1782), 37, 38–39
  "Lucio Silla," 37, 38
    Sinfonia (Overture), 37, 38

Bach, Johann Sebastian (1685–1750), 1, 6–7, 8, 9, 14, 15, 37, 77–78, 205, 227, 239, 253–254, 255, 256, 270, 306
  Brandenburg Concertos, 7, 255
    #6, B flat, 255
  Harpsichord Concerto, D Minor, 77
  "If thou wilt give me my heart," 205
  "O Ewigkeit, du Donnerwort," 226
  "Es ist genug," 226
  Passacaglia and Fugue, C minor, 14, 15
  St. Matthew Passion, 37
  Suite for Flute and Strings, B Minor, 6, 7, 8
  "We Must Pass Through Much Tribulation," 77–78
Ballerina, the, 28, 29–30
"Ballet de la Nuit" (Lully and others), 19
Ballet Russe de Diaghileff, 24, 31, 299
Ballet Suite #2 (Gluck-Gevaert), 18, 21
Balzac, Honoré de (1799–1850), 163
"Barber of Seville, The" (Rossini), 194
  "Calumny" aria, 194
Barber, Samuel (1910–   ), 289, 294
  "First Essay for Orchestra," 289, 294
"Bartered Bride, The" (Smetana), 273
  Overture, 273
Bastille (Paris), 60
"Beautiful Blue Danube, The" (Strauss), 138

Beckmesser, Sixtus, 270, 271
Bee-elephant, the, 293
Beethoven, Ludwig van (1770–1827), 1, 3, 4, 10, 11, 12, 13, 14, 15, 36, 50, 51, 52, 53, 56, 57, 58–59, 60, 62–63, 75, 76, 81, 83–84, 85–86, 87, 95, 126, 130, 131–133, 148, 153–156, 157, 159, 160, 161–162, 182, 184, 191–193, 204, 205–209, 228, 229–235, 240, 241, 242, 244–245, 253, 261, 263, 265
"Coriolanus" Overture, 244–245
"Creations of Prometheus, The," 230, 232
"Egmont," incidental music, 57
Eleven Viennese Dances, 10
"Fidelio," 204, 208–209
    Overture, 208 (see also "Leonore" Overtures)
"Leonore," see "Fidelio"
"Leonore" Overtures, 208–209
    #3, 205, 208–209
Piano Concerto #4, G major, 81, 83–84
Piano Concerto #5, E flat, Emperor, 60, 62, 63–64
Piano Variations, Opus 35, Eroica, 230
Symphony #1, C major, 36, 50, 51, 52, 53–54
Symphony #2, D major, 148, 153–156
Symphony #3, E flat major, Eroica, 229, 230–232
Symphony #4, B flat major, 205, 206
Symphony #5, C minor, 57, 58–60, 83, 229
Symphony #6, F major, Pastoral, 126, 130, 131–133
Symphony # 7, A major, 10, 11, 12, 13, 14, 191
Symphony #8, F major, 13, 188, 191–193
Symphony #9, D minor, Choral, 233–235, 265
Twelve Contradances, 229

Beethoven, Ludwig van (Cont'd)
    Violin Concerto, D major, 85–87, 261, 262
Bellini, Vincenzo (1801–1835), 302
Bennett, Sir William Sterndale (1816–1875), 262
Berg, Alban (1885–193o), 223, 224–226
    Violin Concerto, 223, 224–226
    "Wozzeck," 224
Berlin, Irving (1888–   ), 302
Berlin Opera House, 92
Berlin, University of, 194
Berlioz, Louis-Hector (1803–1869), 12, 51, 72, 81, 87–88, 120, 121, 122, 147, 162–166, 205, 253
    Fantastic Symphony, 81, 147, 162, 164–166
    "Damnation of Faust, The," 120, 121, 122
    Dance of the Sylphs, 122
    Minuet of the Will o' the Wisps, 122
    Symphonie Fantastique, see Fantastic Symphony
Bible, the, 255
Bismarck-Schönhausen, Otto Eduard Leopold, Prince von (1815–1898), 103
Blackamoor, the, 28, 29–30
Bloch, Ernest (1880–   ), 99, 100
    "Schelomo," 99–101
Bolibochki, 26
Bonaparte, Napoleon, see Napoleon I, Emperor of the French
Borodin, Alexander Porfiryevich (1833–1887), 105, 108
    "Prince Igor," 105, 108
    Polovtsian Dances, 105, 108
Boston Symphony Orchestra, 124, 290, 295, 306
Bottom, 195
Boucher, Alexandre-Jean (1778–1861), 93
Brahms, Johannes (1833–1897), 1, 14, 15, 16, 17, 35, 52, 75, 91, 93–94, 96, 140, 159, 253, 254, 263–268, 269, 271–272

Brahms, Johannes (*Cont'd*)
Piano Concerto #2, B flat major, 75–76
Symphony #1, C minor, 159, 263, 264–266
Symphony #2, D major, 266–268
Symphony #3, F major, 269, 271–272
Symphony #4, E minor, 14, 15, 16–17, 18
Tragic Overture, 266
"Variations on a Theme by Haydn," 263–264
Violin Concerto, D major, 91, 93–95
Brandenburg, Christian Ludwig, Margrave of, 7
Brandenburg Concertos (Bach), 7, 255
#6, B flat, 255
Bread-and-butter-fly, the, 293
Breitfeld Ball, 189
Bruch, Max (1838–1920), 95–96
Violin Concerto, G minor, 95, 96
Bruckner, Anton (1824–1896), 182, 271
Brünnhilde, 109, 110, 112, 113–114, 115, 116–120, 139, 222
Brunswick, Count von, 205
Brunswick, Therese von (1775–1861), 205, 206–207
Bülow, Hans Guido, Freiherr von (1830–1894), 95, 98, 220–221, 282
Burleigh, Henry Thacker (1866–), 274, 275
Byron, George Noel Gordon, Baron (1788–1824), 147, 167–168
"Manfred," 167–168

Carlton House (London), 49
Carpenter, John Alden (1876–), 298–300
"Skyscrapers," 298–300
Carroll, Lewis (Charles Lutwidge Dodgson) (1832–1898), 291, 292

Carroll, Lewis (*Cont'd*)
"Through the Looking-Glass and What Alice Found There," 291
Cervantes Saavedra, Miguel de (1547–1616), 198
Chadwick, George Whitefield (1854–1931), 289–290
"Symphonic Sketches," 289
"Jubilee Overture," 289–290
Charlatan, the, 28, 29, 30
Charlotte, Queen of England (1744–1818), 49, 187
Cherubino, 191
Chopin, Frédéric-François (1810–1849), 7, 25, 88–89, 90–91, 163, 282, 284
Piano Concerto #2, F minor, 88, 90–91
Chorale of St. Anthony (Haydn), 263
Churchill, Winston Spencer (1874–), 141
Classical Symphony, see Prokofieff
Claudel, Paul (1868–), 134
Clement, Franz (1780–1842), 85–86
Coleridge, Samuel Taylor (1772–1834), 290–291
"Kubla Khan," 291
Collin, Heinrich Josef von (1771–1811), 244
"Coriolanus," 244
Columbia Broadcasting System, 291
Columbia University (New York), 296
Conac, Count, 189
Cleopatra, Queen of Egypt (69–30 B.C.), 172
concertos, harpsichord
Bach
D minor, 77
Haydn
D major, 60, 62
concertos, piano
Beethoven
#4, G major, 81, 83–84
#5, E flat major, Emperor, 60, 62, 63–64

concertos, piano (*Cont'd*)
  Chopin
    #2, F minor, 88, 90–91
  Grieg, 282–284
  Liszt
    #1, E flat major, 88, 89–90
  Mozart
    #23, A major (K.488), 81, 82
  Schumann, A minor, 209, 212–213
  Tchaikovsky
    #1, B flat minor, 95, 96–99
  Weber
    Konzertstück, 91–92, 93
concertos, violin
  Beethoven, D major, 85–87, 261, 262
  Berg, 223, 224–226
  Brahms, D major, 91, 93–95
  Bruch, G minor, 95, 96
  Mendelssohn, E minor, 258, 261–262
  Mozart
    #4, D major (K.218), 77, 80
  Paganini
    E flat, 85, 87
  Sibelius, D minor, 99, 101–102
Concerts Spirituels (Paris), 39–40
"Confessions" (Rousseau), 81
Copland, Aaron (1900-   ), 302, 305
  "Music for the Theatre," 302, 305
"Coq d'Or, Le" (Rimsky-Korsakoff), 67–68
  suite from, 67
"Coriolanus" (Collin), 244
"Coriolanus" Overture (Beethoven), 244–245
"Coriolanus" (Shakespeare), 244
Couperin, François "the Great" (1668–1733), 9
"Crane, The," 217
"Creations of Prometheus, The" (Beethoven), 230, 232
Crescendo, Monsieur, see Rossini, Gioacchino
Czerny, Carl (1791–1857), 63

"Damnation of Faust, The" (Berlioz), 120, 121, 122
  Dance of the Sylphs, 122
  Minuet of the Will o' the Wisps, 122
Damrosch, Walter Johannes (1862-   ), 291
Dance of the Apprentices, see Wagner
Dante Alighieri (1265–1321), 58, 171, 172
  "Inferno," 171, 172
Daphnis, 31
"Daphnis and Chloë (Ravel), 30, 31
  Second Suite from, 30, 31
David, Ferdinand (1810–1873), 261
Davis, Elmer, 103
"Death and Transfiguration" (Strauss), 248, 250–251
Debussy, Claude-Achille (1862–1918), 126, 127, 128–130, 133–137
  "Clouds," see Nocturnes: "Nuages"
  "Festivals," see Nocturnes: "Fêtes"
  "Mer, La," 127, 128, 129
  Nocturnes, 126, 133, 135–137
    "Nuages," 133, 136
    "Fêtes," 133, 136
    "Sirènes," 128, 129, 133, 136–137
  "Pelléas et Mélisande," 128
  "Prelude to the Afternoon of a Faun," 133–135
  "Sirens," see Nocturnes: "Sirènes"
Dehmel, Richard (1863–1920), 224
  "Woman and the World," 224
  "Verklärte Nacht," 223–224
Diaghileff, Sergei (1872–1929), 24, 25, 27, 28, 31, 299
"Dido and Aeneas" (Purcell), 15
  "Dido's Lament," 15
Dies Irae, 165
"Don Giovanni" (Mozart), 123, 273
Don Juan, 121, 122, 123, 124
"Don Juan" (Strauss), 120, 123–124
Don Quixote de la Mancha, 198–202

"Don Quixote" (Strauss), 184, 197
Dragonetti, Domenico (1763–1846), 12
Dresden Opera, 169
"Dubinushka" (Rimsky-Korsakoff), 67, 68
Dulcinea, 199, 201
Dukas, Paul (1865–1935), 134, 184, 193, 196–197
    "Sorcerer's Apprentice, The," 193, 196–197
Dumas, Alexandre *père* (1802–1870), 123, 163, 166
Dvořák, Antonin (1841–1904), 273, 274–276
    Symphony #5, E minor, From the New World, 273, 274–276

Eastman School of Music (Rochester), 296
"Egmont," incidental music (Beethoven), 57
"Egmont" (Goethe), 57
"Eine Kleine Nachtmusik" (Mozart), 6, 8, 9
Eleven Viennese Dances (Beethoven), 10
"En Saga" (Sibelius), 276, 277–278
Entrance of the Gods into Valhalla, see Wagner
Epic of the Army of Igor, 108
Erda, 116
"Erl-King, The" (Schubert), 156
Eroica, Symphony, see Beethoven
Esterház, 51, 61, 62, 185, 186
Esterházy family, 48
Esterházy, Prince Miklós Jozsef (1714–1790), 61, 185, 186, 187
Eugénie, Empress of the French (1826–1920), 5
Eulenspiegel, Till, 197–198
Eva, 270, 271

"Falstaff" (Verdi), 66
Fantastic Symphony, see Berlioz
Farewell Symphony, see Haydn
"Faust" (Goethe), 121, 259

"Faust" (Gounod), 241
Faust Overture, A, see Wagner
Fenton, Master, 132
"Fidelio" (Beethoven), 204, 208–209
    Overture, 208 (see also "Leonore" Overtures)
Fingal's Cave, 127
"Fingal's Cave" (Mendelssohn), see Hebrides Overture
"Finlandia" (Sibelius), 55, 64, 65–66, 67, 284
Fire Bird, 25, 26
"Fire Bird, The," see "Oiseau de Feu, L'"
Fire-Music, see Wagner
"First Essay for Orchestra" (Barber), 289, 294
Flaubert, Gustave (1821–1880), 123
Flying Dutchman (Vanderdecken), 128, 218, 219
"Flying Dutchman, The," see Wagner
Fokine, Mikhail (1880–1942), 25, 28
Forest Murmurs, see Wagner
"Fountains of Rome, The" (Respighi), 133, 137–138
Francesca da Rimini, 171, 172, 203
"Francesca da Rimini" (Tchaikovsky), 171–173
Franck, César-Auguste (1822–1890), 240–242
    Symphony, D minor, 240–242
Freemasons, 236
"Freischütz, Der" (Weber), 92, 93, 130, 133, 169
    Overture, 130–131, 133
French Revolution, 4, 191, 230, 231, 233, 235, 238
Friedrich Wilhelm IV, King of Prussia (1795–1861), 195
Froh, 110

"Gaîté Parisienne" (Offenbach-Rosenthal), 18, 24
Gautier, Eva (1886–   ), 302
Gautier, Théophile (1811–1872), 163

"Gazza Ladra, La" (Rossini), 193
  Overture, 193
George I, King of England (1660–1727), 142–144
George III, King of England (1738–1820), 49, 187
George IV, King of England (1762–1830), 49, 187
George, Stefan (1868–1933), 134
Gershwin, George (1898–1937), 302–305
  "American in Paris, An," 302, 304–305
  "Rhapsody in Blue," 302–304, 305
Gershwin, Morris, 302
Gevaert, François Auguste, Baron, see Gluck, Ballet Suite #2
Gewandhaus (Leipzig), 160, 212
Gianciotto, 171
Gide, André (1869–   ), 134
Gilbert, William Schwenk (1836–1911), 158
Gilman, Lawrence (1878–1939), 296
Gluck, Christoph Willibald, Ritter von (1714–1787), 18, 20, 21, 39, 122, 160, 263
  "Armide," 21
    Gavotte, 21
  Ballet Suite #2 (arranged by Gevaert), 18, 21
  "Iphigenia in Aulis," 20, 21
Gnat, the, 293
Goethe, Johann Wolfgang von 1749–1832), 57, 58, 121, 156, 167, 192, 196, 259
  "Egmont," 57
  "Faust," 121, 259
  "Zauberlehrling, Der," 196
"Götterdämmerung, Die," see Wagner
"Golden Cockerel, The," see "Coq d'Or, Le"
Golgotha, 103
Goodman, Benny, 10
Gounod, Charles (1818–1893), 241
  "Faust," 241
Gray, Cecil (1895–   ), 278

Grieg, Edvard Hagerup (1843–1907), 282–284, 296
  Piano Concerto, 282–284
Griffes, Charles Tomlinson (1884–1920), 289, 290–291
  "Pleasure Dome of Kubla Khan, The," 289, 290–291
Grimm, Jakob Ludwig Karl (1785–1863) and Wilhelm Karl (1786–1859), 130
  tales, 130
Grofé, Ferde (1892–   ), 302
Gropius, Manon (?–1935), 225, 226
Grove, Sir George (1820–1900), 158
Grünewald, Matthias (fl. 1500–1530), 238–239
  Isenheim altarpiece, 238, 239
Guinevere, 171, 172
Gunther, 117, 118–119, 120
Gutrune, 117, 118

Haffner Symphony, see Mozart
Haffner, Sigmund, Burgomaster Salzburg (1699–1772), 40–41
Haffner Serenade (Mozart), 41
Hagen, 109, 117, 118
Hale, Philip (1854–1934), 137, 249, 250, 289
"Hamlet" (Shakespeare), 164, 262
Handel, George Frederick (1685–1759), 7, 37–38, 142–144
  "Rinaldo"
    "Lascia ch'io pianga," 7
  Te Deum, 142
  "Water Music," 142
Hanover, Elector of, see George I, King of England
Hanover Square Rooms (London), 48
Hanson, Howard (1896–   ), 295, 296–298
  Symphony #2, Romantic, 295, 296–298
Harris, Roy (1898–   ), 298, 300–301
  Symphony #3, 298, 300–301
Harty, Sir Hamilton (1879–1941), 144

Haydn, Franz Josef (1732–1809), 3, 10, 35, 42, 43, 44–45, 46, 47–48, 49–50, 51–52, 53, 60, 61–62, 71, 148, 155, 185–188, 241, 253, 263, 273
  Chorale of St. Anthony, 263
  Harpsichord Concerto, D major, 60, 62
  Symphony #45 (B. & H.), F minor, Farewell, 185, 186
  Symphony #88 (B. & H.), G major, 42, 45
  Symphony #94 (B. & H.), G major (Salomon #3), Surprise, 185, 187
  Symphony #98 (B. & H.), B flat (Salomon #8), 46
  Symphony #104 (B. & H.), D major, 51
Hebrides Overture (Mendelssohn), 127
Heiligenstadt Testament, 154–155
Heine, Heinrich (1797–1856), 163, 166
Helen of Troy, 171–172
Héloïse (1101?–1164?), 203
Helsinki Conservatory Orchestra, 277
Henderson, William James (1855–1937), 304
"Hernani" (Hugo), 162, 163, 166
Herod, 5
Herzogenberg, Elisabeth von (1847–1892), 16, 267
Hindemith, Paul (1895–   ), 10, 236, 238, 239–240
  Symphony, "Mathis der Maler," 236, 238–240
"History of the Damnable Life and the Deserved Death of Dr. John Faustus, The," 121
Hitler, Adolf (1889–   ), 103, 238
Holy Roman Empire, 263
Honegger, Arthur (1892–   ), 32
  "Pacific 231," 32
Hugo, Victor (1802–1885), 162, 163, 166
  "Hernani," 162

Humpty-Dumpty, 292
Hunding, 112

"If thou wilt give me thy heart" (Bach), 205
Igor, Prince, 108
Immolation Scene, see Wagner
"Immortal Beloved," letter to the, 207–208
"Indian" Suite (MacDowell), 295–296
Indy, Vincent d' (1851–1931), 241
"Inferno" (Dante), 171, 172
"Iphigenia in Aulis" (Gluck), 20, 21
Isenheim altarpiece (Grünewald), 238, 239
Isolde, 171, 203, 219–220
Italian Symphony, see Mendelssohn

Jabberwock, the, 292–293
Joachim, Joseph (1831–1907), 94, 95–96, 272
Jockey Club (Paris), 21–22
John the Baptist (Jochanaan), 4–5
Jones, Robert Edmond (1887–   ), 299
"Jubilee Overture," see "Symphonic Sketches" (Chadwick)
Juliet, 203, 214, 215
Jupiter Symphony, see Mozart

Kahn, Gustave, 134
Kajanus, Robert (1856–1933), 277
Kalandar Prince, 107
Kalevala, the, 65, 66, 277
Karsavina, Thamar Pavlovna, 25, 28
Kastcheï, 26, 27
Kern, Jerome David (1885–   ), 138, 140–141, 302
  "Show Boat," 138, 140–141
    "Can't Help Lovin' Dat Man," 141
    "Make Believe," 141
    "Misery's Done Come," 141
    "Ol' Man River," 141
    Scenario on Themes from, 138, 140–141
    "Why Do I Love You?" 141

Kikimoras, 26
Kilmanseck, see Kilmansegge
Kilmansegge, Baron, 144
Kilmansegge, Madame, 144
King Marke, 220
"King's Henchman, The" (Taylor), 291
Köchel, Ludwig, Ritter von (1800–1877), 82
Kontchak, Khan, 108
Koussevitzky, Serge (1874–   ), 287, 297, 306
Kretzschmar, Hermann (1848–1924), 275
"Kubla Khan" (Coleridge), 291
Kuffner, 229
Kurwenal, 250

LaGuardia, Fiorello (1882–   ), 306
Lamartine, Alphonse-Marie-Louis de (1790–1869), 243
Launcelot, 171, 172
Laurence, Friar, 214
Lenau, Nikolaus (1802–1850), 123
Leningrad Conservatory of Music, 69
Leningrad Philharmonic Orchestra, 69
Leonidas (5th century B.C.), 232
"Leonore" (Beethoven), see "Fidelio"
"Leonore" Overtures (Beethoven), 208–209
    #3, 205, 208–209
Levi, Hermann (1839–1900), 264
Lichnowsky, Prince Karl (1756–1814), 52–53, 63
Liebestod, 217, 220
"Lied von der Erde, Das" (Mahler), 180
"Lie-Fancier, The" (Lucian), 196
Linz Symphony, see Mozart
Liszt, Franz (1811–1886), 72, 84, 88–90, 120, 122, 163, 240, 241, 242–244, 253, 282–284
    "Mephisto Waltz," 120, 122
    Piano Concerto #1, E flat major, 88, 89–90

Liszt, Franz (Cont'd)
    "Preludes, Les," 240, 241, 242–244
Little Russian Symphony, see Tchaikovsky
Loge, 114
"Lohengrin," see Wagner
London Philharmonic Society, 160
Louis XIV, King of France (1638–1715), 8, 9, 19, 22, 56
Louis-Philippe, King of France (1773–1850), 162
Louÿs, Pierre (1870–1925), 134
Love-death, see Wagner
"Lucio Silla" (J. C. Bach), 37, 38
    Sinfonia (Overture), 37, 38
Lully, Jean Baptiste (1632–1687), 8, 18, 19, 20, 21, 22, 56
    "Ballet de la Nuit" (with others), 19
    "Proserpine," 18
    Minuet of the Happy Spirits, 18, 20

MacDowell, Edward (1861–1908), 295–296
    "Indian" Suite, 295–296
Mälzel, Johann Nepomuk (1772–1838), 192
Maeterlinck, Maurice (1862–   ), 134
Magic Fire Music, see Wagner
"Magic Flute, The" (Mozart), 9, 227–228, 236–237, 238
    Overture, 236–237
Mahler, Gustav (1860–1911), 72, 163, 179–182, 263
    "Lied von der Erde, Das," 180
    Symphony #9, D major, 179–182
Mainwaring, John (1735–1807), 143
Mallarmé, Stephane (1842–1898), 134
    "Après-Midi d'un Faune, L'," 134–135
"Manfred" (Byron), 167–168
"Manfred," incidental music (Schumann), 167–168
    Overture, 167–168

Mann, Thomas (1875–), 103
Marie Antoinette, Queen of France (1755–1793), 20, 263
Marlowe, Christopher (1564–1593), 121
"Marriage of Figaro, The" (Mozart), 10, 45–46, 188, 189–191, 273
  "Aprite presto," 188, 191
  "Non più andrai," 190
  Overture, 188
  "Porgi amor," 45
Marx, Karl (1818–1883), 110
Mastersingers, 270
"Mathis der Maler" (Hindemith), 236, 238–240
Mauclair, Camille, 134
Meck, Nadejda von (1831–1894), 173–174, 175, 176–177, 246
"Meistersinger, Die," see Wagner
Melanchthon, Philipp (1947–1560), 121
Mendelssohn-Bartholdy, Fanny (1805–1847), 194
Mendelssohn-Bartholdy, Felix (1809–1847), 99, 127, 160, 193, 194–196, 213, 253, 255, 258–262
  "Fingal's Cave," see Hebrides Overture
  Hebrides Overture, 127
  "Midsummer Night's Dream, A," 184, 193, 194, 260
    Overture, 194, 195
    Nocturne, 195
    Scherzo, 195
    Wedding March, 195
  Symphony #4, A major, Italian, 258–261
  Violin Concerto, E minor, 258, 261–262
Mephistopheles, 122
"Mephisto Waltz" (Liszt), 120, 122
Mérimée, Prosper (1803–1870), 123
Metropolitan Opera Company, 180, 203, 291, 299
Meyerbeer, Giacomo (Jakob Liebmann Beer), (1791–1864), 12, 163

"Midsummer Night's Dream, A" (Mendelssohn), 184, 193, 194, 260
"Midsummer Night's Dream, A" (Shakespeare), 195
Milhaud, Darius (1892–), 302
Miliukova, Antonina Ivanovna, see Tchaikovskaya, Antonina
Milton, John (1608–1674), 235
Molière (Jean-Baptiste Poquelin) (1622–1673), 19, 76
Monet, Claude (1840–1926), 134
Monteux, Pierre (1875–), 28, 290
Montpensier, Mlle. de, 19
Moscow Conservatory of Music, 97, 174
Moscow Opera, 216
Mozart, Konstanze (1763–1842), 42, 44, 189
Mozart, Leopold (1719–1787), 38, 42, 78–79, 80–81
Mozart, Wolfgang Amadeus (1756–1791), 1, 3, 4, 6, 8, 9, 10–11, 35, 37, 38–42, 43, 44, 45, 46–47, 50, 53, 71, 75, 76, 77, 78–79, 80, 81, 82, 83, 85, 86, 123, 148, 149–152, 155, 156, 184, 185, 188–191, 227, 236, 237, 238, 253, 263, 273
  concertos
    piano #23, A major (K.488), 81, 82
    violin #4, D major (K.218), 77, 80
  operas
    "Abduction from the Seraglio, The," 40, 42
    "Don Giovanni," 123, 273
    "Magic Flute, The," 9, 227–228, 236–237, 238
      Overture, 236–237
    "Marriage of Figaro, The," 10, 45–46, 188, 189–191, 273
      Overture, 188
      "Aprite presto," 188, 191
      "Non più andrai," 190
      "Porgi amor," 45

Mozart, Wolfgang Amadeus (*Cont'd*)
  orchestral works
    "Eine kleine Nachtmusik," 6, 8,
      9
    Haffner Serenade, 41
  symphonies
    #31, D major, Paris (K.297),
      37, 39
    #35, D major, Haffner (K.
      385), 37, 40, 41
    #36, C major, Linz (K.425),
      42–43, 45
    #38, D major, Prague (K.504),
      184, 188, 190–191
    #39, E flat major (K.543), 3,
      149–152
    #40, G minor (K.550), 149,
      151–153
    #41, C major, Jupiter (K.551),
      46–47, 50, 149, 184
"Music for the Theatre" (Copland),
  302, 305
Musset, Alfred (1810–1857), 123,
  163
"My Fatherland" (Smetana), 140
"Moldau, The," 138, 139–140

Napoleon I, Emperor of the French
  (1769–1821), 11, 62, 93, 193,
  194, 230, 231, 232, 233
Napoleon III, Emperor of the
  French (1808–1873), 5, 23
National Conservatory of Music
  (New York), 274
Neue Zeitschrift für Musik (Leip-
  zig), 168
New England Conservatory of Mu-
  sic (Boston), 289
Newman, Ernest (1868–   ), 222
New York Philharmonic Orchestra,
  180, 274
New World Symphony, see Dvořák
Nibelung, 110, 119–120
Nietzsche, Friedrich (1844–1900),
  248–250
  "Also sprach Zarathustra," 248–
  250
Nijinsky, Waslav (1889–   ), 28,
  33

"None But the Lonely Heart"
  (Tchaikovsky), 215

October Revolution, 72
"Ode to Joy" (Schiller), 233, 234
"O Ewigkeit, du Donnerwort"
  (Bach), 226
  "Es ist genug," 226
Offenbach, Jacques (1819–1880),
  18, 22, 23, 24
  "Gaîté Parisienne" (arranged by
    Rosenthal), 18, 24
  "Vie Parisienne, La," 23
"Oiseau de Feu, L'" (Stravinsky),
  24, 25, 27
Opéra (Paris), 25
Ophelia, 163
Osiris, 103
"Otello" (Verdi), 66
Overture, Scherzo and Finale (Schu-
  mann), 212

"Pacific 231" (Honegger), 32
Padilla y Ramos, Désirée (Artôt) de
  (1835–1907), 215–216
Padilla y Ramos, Mariano (1842–
  1906), 216
Paganini, Nicolò (1782–1840), 85,
  87–88, 163, 166
  Violin Concerto, E flat, 85, 87
Pamina, 236
Paolo, 171, 172, 203
Papageno, 9
Paris, 172
Paris Conservatory, 163, 241
Paris Symphony, see Mozart
"Parsifal," see Wagner
Passacaglia and Fugue, C minor
  (Bach), 14, 15
Pastoral Symphony, see Beethoven
Pathetic Symphony, see Tchaikovsky
Peasant War of 1524, 238
"Peter Ibbetson" (Taylor), 291
Petrouchka, 28, 29–30
"Petrouchka" (Stravinsky), 24, 27,
  28
Phrygian mode, 17
Piano Variations, Opus 35 (Beetho-
  ven), 230

Picasso, Pablo (1881–), 24
Piccinni, Niccola (1728–1800), 39
Pierné, Henri - Constant - Gabriel
    (1863–1937), 25
Pilgrims' Chorus, see Wagner
"Pleasure Dome of Kubla Khan,
    The" (Griffes), 289, 290–291
Ponte, Lorenzo da (1749–1838), 123
Prague Symphony, see Mozart
Pravda (Moscow), 71-72
"Préludes, Les" (Liszt), 240, 241,
    242–244
"Prince Igor" (Borodin), 105, 108
    Polovtsian Dances, 105, 108
Prize Song, see Wagner
Prokofieff, Sergei (1891–), 70–
    71
    Classical Symphony, 70, 71
"Proserpine" (Lully), 18
    Minuet of the Happy Spirits, 18,
    20
Puchberg, Michael, 46, 149–150
Purcell, Henry (1658–1695), 15, 122
    "Dido and Aeneas," 15
    "Dido's Lament," 15

Ranelagh, Lord, 144
Ravel, Joseph-Maurice (1875–1937),
    3, 5, 6, 9, 30, 31
    "Daphnis and Chloë," 30, 31
    Second Suite from, 30, 31
    "Tombeau de Couperin, Le," 6, 9
    "Valse, La," 3, 5
Razin, Stenka (?-1671), 217
Reformation, 238
Respighi, Ottorino (1879–1936),
    133, 137
    "Fountains of Rome, The," 133,
    137–138
"Rhapsody in Blue" (Gershwin),
    302–304, 305
"Rheingold, Das," see Wagner
Rhenish Symphony, see Schumann
Rhinemaidens, 111, 117, 139
Ride of the Valkyries, see Wagner
Riemann, Karl Wilhelm Julius Hugo
    (1849–1919), 11
Ries, Ferdinand (1784–1838), 154

Rimsky-Korsakoff, Nikolay Andreye-
    vich (1844–1908), 25, 27, 67,
    68, 69, 105–108, 127, 128
    "Coq d'Or, Le," 67–68
    suite from, 67
    "Dubinushka" (arrangement), 67,
    68
    "Golden Cockerel, The," see "Coq
    d'Or, Le"
    "Scheherazade," 105–108, 127, 128
"Rinaldo" (Handel)
    "Lascia ch'io pianga," 7
"Ring des Nibelungen, Der" (Wag-
    ner), 109–120, 204, 241
    "Rheingold, Das," 109, 110
        Entrance of the Gods into Val-
        halla, 109
    "Walküre, Die," 109, 110, 111,
        113
        Ride of the Valkyries, 109, 113,
        116
        Spring Song and Duet from Act
        I, 109, 111
        Wotan's Farewell and Magic
        Fire Music, 109, 114
    "Siegfried," 109, 110, 114, 115,
        116, 221, 222, 223
        Fire-Music, 115, 116
        Forest Murmurs, 109, 114–115
        Introduction to Act III, 115,
        116
    "Götterdämmerung, Die," 109,
        110, 114, 115, 117, 138–139,
        296
        Immolation Scene, 115
        Siegfried's Funeral Music, 115,
        296
        Siegfried's Rhine Journey, 115,
        117, 138
        Waltraute Scene, 115
Ritter, Alexander (1833–1896), 250
Rocking-horse-fly, the, 293
Rodin, Auguste (1840–1917), 134
Rodzinski, Artur (1894–), 140
Roland-Manuel (1891–), 33
Romantic Symphony, see Hanson
Romeo, 203, 214, 215
"Romeo and Juliet" (Shakespeare),
    214

"Romeo and Juliet" (Tchaikovsky), 214–215, 217
"Rosamunde" (Schubert), 157–159
Overture, 157
Rossini, Gioacchino Antonio (1792–1868), 160, 163, 193
"Barber of Seville, The," 194
"Calumny" aria, 194
"Gazza Ladra, La," 193
Overture, 193
Rousseau, Jean-Jacques (1712–1778), 20, 81
"Confessions," 81
Rubinstein, Anton Grigoryevich (1829–1894), 91, 96–97, 186
Rubinstein, Nicholas Grigoryevich (1835–1881), 96–97, 98
Russo-Japanese War, 68

St. James Palace (London), 144
St. Matthew Passion (Bach), 37
St. Petersburg Conservatory of Music, 68
Sachs, Curt (1881–   ), 7
Sachs, Hans (1494–1576), 269, 270–271
"Sacre du Printemps, Le" (Stravinsky), 2, 3, 5–6, 24, 27–28, 30, 31–32, 33–34
Sacrificial Dance, 3, 5–6
Salome, 4–5
"Salome" (Strauss), 3, 4–5
"Dance of the Seven Veils," 3, 4–5
Salomon, Johann Peter (1745–1815), 48, 49, 50
Salomon Symphony #8, see Haydn
Salomon Symphony # 3, see Haydn
Salzburg, Hieronymus von Colloredo, Archbishop of, 78
Samiel, 131
Sammler (Vienna), 158
Sancho Panza, 199, 200, 201
Sarastro, 236
Schahriar, Sultan, 106
Scheherazade, Sultana, 106–108, 128
"Scheherazade" (Rimsky-Korsakoff), 105–108, 127, 128

"Schelomo" (Bloch), 99–101
"Scherzo Fantastique" (Stravinsky), 25
Schikaneder, Emanuel (1748–1812), 236
Schiller, Johann Christoph Friedrich von (1759–1805), 233, 234
"Ode to Joy," 233, 234
"Schlaf, mein kind, schlaf ein," 222
Schneerson, Gregori, 71, 72
Schneevoight, Georg (1872–   ), 67
Schneider, Dr., 158–159
Schönberg, Arnold (1874–   ), 223, 224, 263, 302
"Verklärte Nacht," 223
Schubert, Ferdinand (1794–1859), 160
Schubert, Franz Peter (1797–1828), 4, 82, 153, 156–162
"Erl-King, The," 156
"Rosamunde," 157–159
Overture, 157
Symphony #7, C major, 157
Symphony #8, B minor, Unfinished, 153, 156–157
Schuman, William Howard (1910–   ), 302, 305–306
"American Festival Overture," 302, 306
Schumann, Clara (1819–1896), 17, 94, 168, 169, 204, 210, 211, 212, 213, 214, 256–257
Schumann, Marie (1841–1929), 257
Schumann, Robert Alexander (1810–1856), 55, 82, 94, 99, 142, 144–145, 159–160, 161, 167–170, 204, 209–214, 253, 255–257
Fantasy, A minor, see Piano Concerto, A minor
"Manfred," incidental music, 167–168
Overture, 167–168
Overture, Scherzo and Finale, E major, 212
Piano Concerto, A minor, 209, 212–213

Schumann, Robert Alexander
(*Cont'd*)
symphonies
#1, B flat major, Spring, 209–
212, 256
#2, C major, 167, 168–170
#3, E flat major, Rhenish, 142,
144–145
#4, D minor, 168, 212, 255–
258
Scott, Raymond, 10
Senta, 128, 217, 219
Shakespeare, William (1564–1616),
66, 76, 132, 194, 195, 214, 244,
262
"Coriolanus," 244
"Hamlet," 164, 262
"Midsummer Night's Dream, A,"
195
"Romeo and Juliet," 214
Shaw, George Bernard (1856–   ),
103
Shostakovitch, Dmitri (1906–   ),
56, 67, 68–69, 70, 71–73, 163
Symphony #1, 67, 69–70
Symphony #5, 69, 70, 71–73
Symphony #7, 69
"Show Boat" (Kern), 138, 140–141
Scenario on Themes from, 138,
140–141
Sibelius, Jean (1865–   ), 1, 10,
35, 55, 64, 65, 66, 67, 99, 101,
102, 254, 276–281, 282, 284–
286, 296
"En Saga," 276, 277–278
"Finlandia," 55, 64, 65–66, 67,
284
Symphony #1, E minor, 276, 278–
279
Symphony #2, D major, 64, 67,
284
Symphony #5, E flat major, 279,
280–281
Symphony #7, C major, 282, 285–
286
"Tapiola," 279–280
Violin Concerto, D minor, 99,
101–102

Siegfried, 103, 109, 110, 114, 115,
116–120, 138–139, 222
"Siegfried," see Wagner
"Siegfried's Death," 110
Siegfried Idyll (Wagner), 204, 217,
218, 220–223
Siegfried's Funeral Music, see Wag-
ner
Siegfried's Rhine Journey, see Wag-
ner
Sieglinde, 111–112, 113, 119
Siegmund, 111–112, 113, 119
Sindbad, 106, 128
"Skyscrapers" (Carpenter), 298–300
Smetana, Bedřich (1824–1884), 138,
139, 273
"Bartered Bride, The," 273
Overture, 273
"My Fatherland," 140
"Moldau, The," 138, 139–140
Smithson, Henrietta (Harriet)
(1800–1854), 163, 164, 166
Snap-dragon-fly, the, 293
Solomon, King, 100
"Sorcerer's Apprentice, The" (Du-
kas), 193, 196–197
Spengler, Oswald (1880–1936), 181
Spohr, Ludwig (1784–1859), 12
Spring Song, see Wagner
Spring Symphony, see Schumann
Strauss, Johann, Sr. (1804–1849),
4
Strauss, Johann, Jr. (1825–1899), 3,
4, 138, 140
"Beautiful Blue Danube, The,"
138
"Wiener Blut," 3
Strauss, Richard (1864–   ), 3, 4,
72, 120, 123, 124, 160, 163, 184,
197–202, 223, 225, 228, 248–
251, 253
"Death and Transfiguration," 248,
250–251
"Don Juan," 120, 123–124
"Don Quixote," 184, 197
"Salome," 3, 4–5
"Dance of the Seven Veils," 3,
4–5

Strauss, Richard (*Cont'd*)
"Thus Spake Zarathustra," 248–250
"Till Eulenspiegel's Merry Pranks," 184, 197–198
Stravinsky, Igor (1882–), 2, 3, 5, 10, 24, 25, 27, 28, 30, 31, 32
"Fire Bird, The," see "Oiseau de Feu, L' "
"Oiseau de Feu, L'," 24, 25, 27
"Petrouchka," 24, 27, 28
"Sacre du Printemps, Le," 2, 3, 5–6, 24, 27–28, 30, 31–32, 33–34
Sacrificial Dance, 3, 5–6
"Scherzo Fantastique," 25
Suite for Flute and Strings, B minor (Bach), 6, 7, 8
Sullivan, Sir Arthur Seymour (1842–1900), 158
Surprise Symphony, see Haydn
Susanna, 191
"Swing Low, Sweet Chariot," 275
"Symphonic Sketches" (Chadwick), 289
"Jubilee Overture," 289–290
Symphonie Fantastique, see Berlioz
symphonies
  Beethoven
    #1, C major, 36, 50, 51, 52, 53–54
    #2, D major, 148, 153–156
    #3, E flat major, Eroica, 229, 230–232
    #4, B flat major, 205, 206
    #5, C minor, 57, 58–60, 83, 229
    #6, F major, Pastoral, 126, 130, 131–133
    #7, A major, 10, 11, 12, 13, 14, 191
    #8, F major, 13, 188, 191–193
    #9, D minor, Choral, 233, 235, 265
  Berlioz
    Symphonie Fantastique, 81, 147, 162, 164–166

Symphonies (*Cont'd*)
  Brahms
    #1, C minor, 159, 263, 264–266
    #2, D major, 266–268
    #3, F major, 269, 271–272
    #4, E minor, 14, 15, 16–17, 18
  Dvořák
    #5, E minor, From the New World, 273, 274–276
  Franck
    D minor, 240–242
  Hanson
    #2, Romantic, 295, 296–298
  Harris
    #3, 298, 300–301
  Haydn
    #45, F minor, Farewell, 185, 186
    #88, G major, 42, 45
    #94, G major, Surprise, 185, 187
    #98, B flat major, 46
    #104, D major, 51
  Hindemith
    "Mathis der Maler," 236, 238–240
  Mahler
    #9, D major, 179–182
  Mendelssohn
    #4, A major, Italian, 258–261
  Mozart
    #31, D major, Paris, 37, 39
    #35, D major, Haffner, 37, 40, 41
    #36, C major, Linz, 42–43, 45
    #38, D major, Prague, 184, 188, 190–191
    #39, E flat major, 3, 149–152
    #40, G minor, 149, 151–153
    #41, C major, Jupiter, 46–47, 50, 149, 184
  Prokofieff
    Classical, 70, 71
  Schubert
    #7, C major, 157
    #8, B minor, Unfinished, 153, 156–157

Symphonies (*Cont'd*)
Schumann
  #1, B flat major, Spring, 209–212, 256
  #2, C major, 167, 168–170
  #3, E flat major, Rhenish, 142, 144–145
  #4, D minor, 168, 212, 255–258
Shostakovitch
  #1, 67, 69–70
  #5, 69, 70, 71–73
  #7, 69
Sibelius
  #1, E minor, 276, 278–279
  #2, D major, 64, 67, 284
  #5, E flat major, 279, 280–281
  #7, C major, 282, 285–286
Tchaikovsky
  #1, G minor, "Winter Dreams," 216
  #2, C minor, Little Russian, 214, 216–217
  #4, F minor, 171, 173–176, 177
  #5, E minor, 3, 4, 177, 244, 245–248
  #6, B minor, Pathetic, 148, 176–179

Talleyrand-Périgord, Charles-Maurice de, Prince of Benevento (1754–1838), 60
Tamino, 236
Tammuz, 103
"Tannhäuser," see Wagner
"Tapiola" (Sibelius), 279–280
Taylor, Joseph Deems (1885–   ), 289, 291–294, 305
  "King's Henchman, The," 291
  "Peter Ibbetson," 291
  "Through the Looking-Glass," 289, 291–294
Tchaikovskaya, Antonina Ivanovna (Miliukova) (1849–1917), 174
Tchaikovsky, Anatole Ilyich (1850–1915), 177

Tchaikovsky, Modeste Ilyich (1850–1916), 215
Tchaikovsky, Piotr Ilyich (1840–1893), 1, 3, 4, 10–11, 95, 96–99, 148, 171–179, 214, 244, 245–248, 278
  "Francesca da Rimini," 171–173
  "None But the Lonely Heart," 215
  Pathetic Symphony, see Symphony #6
  Piano Concerto #1, B flat minor, 95, 96–99
  "Romeo and Juliet," 214–215, 217
  "Romeo and Juliet," vocal duet, 215
  symphonies
    #1, G minor, "Winter Dreams," 216
    #2, C minor, Little Russian, 214, 216–217
    #4, F minor, 171, 173–176, 177
    #5, E minor, 3, 4, 177, 244, 245–248
    #6, B minor, Pathetic, 148, 176–179
  "Undine," 217
  Wedding March, 217
Te Deum (Handel), 142
Théâtre des Champs-Elysées (Paris), 31
Thermopylae, 232
"Thousand and One Nights, The," 105, 128
"Through the Looking-Glass" (Carroll), 291
"Through the Looking-Glass" (Taylor), 289, 291–294
Thun, Count, 42–43, 189
"Thus Spake Zarathustra" (Strauss), 248–250
Tiger-lily, 292
"Till Eulenspiegel's Merry Pranks" (Strauss), 184, 197–198
"Tombeau de Couperin, Le" (Ravel), 6, 9
Toscanini, Arturo (1867–   ), 180

Tovey, Sir Donald Francis (1875–1940), 102, 167–168, 261–262
Town Hall (New York), 263
Tragic Overture (Brahms), 266
Triebschen, 221
Tristan, 171, 172, 203, 219–220, 250
"Tristan und Isolde," see Wagner
Tsarevitch Ivan, 25–26, 27
Twelve Contradances (Beethoven), 229
Twenty-Four Violins of the King, 19
"Twilight of the Gods," see Wagner

Ulysses, 137
"Undine" (Tchaikovsky), 217
Wedding March, 217
Unfinished Symphony, see Schubert
Utrecht, Peace of, 142

Valéry, Paul (1871–), 134
Valhalla, 110, 111, 118, 119, 120, 131
Valkyries, 113
"Valse, La" (Ravel), 3, 5
Van Vechten, Carl (1880–), 33, 303–304
"Variations on a Norwegian National Air" (Weber), 93
"Variations on a Theme by Haydn" (Brahms), 263–264
Venusberg Music, see Wagner
Verdi, Giuseppe (1813–1901), 55, 66, 162, 284
"Falstaff," 66
"Otello," 66
"Verklärte Nacht" (Dehmel), see "Woman and the World"
"Verklärte Nacht" (Schönberg), 223
Verlaine, Paul (1844–1896), 134
Versailles, 8, 56, 61, 185
Vestris, Gaëtan Apolline Balthasar (1729–1808), 20–21
Victor Emmanuel II, King of Italy (1820–1878), 55
Vienna Hofoper, 180
Vienna Musikverein, 159

Vienna Philharmonic Orchestra, 17, 180, 181
"Vie Parisienne, La" (Offenbach), 23
Viotti, Jean Baptiste (1753–1824), 85
Volsungs, 112, 119

Wagner, Cosima Liszt von Bülow (1837–1930), 217–218, 220–221, 222
Wagner, Minna (1809–1866), 217, 218, 219
Wagner, Siegfried (1869–1930), 221, 222
Wagner, Wilhelm Richard (1813–1883), 3, 10, 12, 18, 19, 21, 22, 66, 89, 109–120, 121, 122, 127, 128, 138, 160, 163, 169, 182, 204, 217–223, 227, 228, 236, 237, 240, 241, 242, 244, 250, 253, 254, 269, 271, 277, 284
Faust Overture, A, 120, 121, 122
"Flying Dutchman, The," 127, 133, 217
Overture, 127, 133, 217
"Götterdämmerung, Die" ("Twilight of the Gods"), 109, 110, 114, 115, 117, 138–139, 296
Immolation Scene, 115
Siegfried's Funeral Music, 115, 296
Siegfried's Rhine Journey, 115, 117, 138
Waltraute Scene, 115
"Lohengrin," 236, 237, 239
Prelude, 236, 237, 239
"Meistersinger, Die," 3, 115, 269–271
Dance of the Apprentices, 3
Introduction to Act III, 269, 270–271
Prelude, 269–270
Prize Song, 270
"Parsifal," 66
"Rheingold, Das," 109, 110
Entrance of the Gods into Valhalla, 109

Wagner, Wilhelm Richard (*Cont'd*)
"Siegfried," 109, 110, 114, 115,
116, 221, 222, 223
Fire-Music, 115, 116
Forest Murmurs, 109, 114–115
Introduction to Act III, 115,
116
Siegfried Idyll, 204, 217, 218,
220–223
"Tannhäuser," 18, 19, 21, 22, 116,
169, 269
Bacchanale (Paris version), 18,
21, 22
Pilgrims' Chorus, 22
Overture, 18, 21, 22
Venusberg Music, 21, 22
"Tristan und Isolde," 22, 115,
217, 218, 219, 223, 225, 250,
269, 271
Love-death, 217, 220
Prelude, 22, 217, 219–220, 225
"Walküre, Die," 109, 110, 111,
113
Ride of the Valkyries, 109, 113,
116
Spring Song and Duet from Act
I, 109, 111
Wotan's Farewell and Magic
Fire Music, 109, 114
"Walküre, Die," see Wagner
Walter, 270
Walter, Bruno (1876–   ), 180, 181
Waltraute, 117
Waltraute Scene, see Wagner
"Water Music" (Handel), 142
Waterloo, Battle of, 193
Weber, Carl Maria von (1786–
1826), 11, 12, 91–92, 93, 130,
131, 169
"Freischütz, Der," 92, 93, 130,
133, 169
Overture, 130–131, 133

Weber, Carl Maria von (*Cont'd*)
Konzertstück, 91–92, 93
"Variations on a Norwegian Na-
tional Air," 93
Weber, Caroline (Brandt) von,
169
"We Must Pass Through Much
Tribulation" (Bach), 77–78
Wentzel, Herr, 78–79
Wesendonck, Mathilde (1828–1902),
217–218, 219, 221
Whistler, James Abbott McNeill
(1834–1903), 134
White Knight, the, 293–294
Whiteman, Paul (1891–   ), 302,
303
Whitewings, 299
Whitman, Walt (1819–1892), 287,
300
Wieck, Clara, see Schumann, Clara
Wieck, Friedrich (1785–1873), 210–
211
"Wiener Blut" (Strauss), 3
Windsor Castle, 49, 187
"Winter Dreams," Symphony, see
Tchaikovsky
"Woman and the World" (Dehmel),
224
"Verklärte Nacht," 223–224
World War I, 9, 24, 70, 99, 137,
181, 238, 280, 284, 285, 297
Wotan, 109, 111, 112, 113–114, 116,
119, 131
Wotan's Farewell, see Wagner
"Wozzeck" (Berg), 224

Zarathustra, 249, 250
"Zauberlehrling, Der" (Goethe),
196
Zoroaster, see Zarathustra
Zürich Theatre, 221